MONEY TREE

Gordon Ferris

author of the acclaimed
Douglas Brodie Quartet.

MONEY TREE

Gordon Ferris

Merula Books

Published in ebook and paperback in Great Britain in 2014 by Merula an imprint of Merula Books Limited.

10 9 8 7 6 5 4 3 2 1

A CIP catalogue record is available from the British Library.
Paperback ISBN: 978 0 9929281 1 7
E-book ISBN: 978 0 9929281 0 0

Merula Books Limited
Acre House
11/15 William Road
London NW1 3ER

www.gordonferris.com

Printed and bound in Great Britain by
TJ International Ltd, Padstow, Cornwall

For Sarah

"But I, being poor, have only my dreams;
I have spread my dreams under your feet;
Tread softly because you tread on my dreams."

W B Yeats – The Cloths of Heaven

ONE

The hard afternoon light forced the three travellers to pull down the wooden blinds and sit in shadow, peering at the passing world through thin slats. The baking heat, and the cradle rhythms of the wooden carriage stilled the women's anxieties. They pushed the blinds back up as night fell, but their sense of insulation was sustained by the darkness outside.

So there was no warning, no gentle transition as the train erupted into harsh light and noise. The engine shuddered and squealed to a stop at the platform. An angry mob was waiting for them, ready to drag them from the safety of their carriage. A torrent of noise poured through the glassless window as people fought to be heard in the rising excitement of arrival and departure.

Panic seized Anila's throat. She couldn't swallow. How had she let the madness bring her here, so far from home? It was one thing to walk out on a husband. It was another to abandon the security of her tiny village and plunge into this pitiless labyrinth on an implausible quest. Why wasn't she content with her small and bounded life? Why did she go looking for fights? She looked at her two travel companions sitting opposite. Eyes wide and blinking, lips parted. Chests fluttering as though they were about to run away. But it was too late for that. The trance was broken.

A loudspeaker snarled at them in rapid English, then Hindi. Anila caught the words *New Delhi*. City of thieves and rapists. It broke the paralysis. She had a responsibility to her friends. It had been her wild idea that had brought them here. She had better follow it through. At least get them off the train. She forced a smile on her broad face and tried to lift her perpetually sad eyes.

'We have done it. We are here. It will be good to move.'

She stood up stiffly and massaged her back in a pantomime to show how good it was. All around, passengers who'd shared their hard ride were stirring and bustling to get off. Pretty Leena looked up at her big friend, eyes like a terrified child's. She could never hide her emotions for long.

'Anila? I am so scared,' she whispered. 'There are so many people out there. We have heard so much about what they do to women here. Are you sure you know where we are going? And where we will sleep?'

Anila leaned closer, protectively. She touched her shoulder, felt her tremble.

'They are only people. Once we are out of the station it will be much easier, you will see. And I have the map.'

She dug into the cotton shoulder bag she'd lifted off the wooden rack and pulled out the folded sheet.

'Remember, Rajnish the teacher drew it. I have studied it and studied it. Rajnish worked in Delhi for a whole summer, so he knows all about it. I know exactly where to go.'

This with a thousand times more confidence than she felt. Their train from Bhopal in the far south had broken down and they had lost over half a day. She hadn't bargained with finding her way in the dark. As she hoped, her other companion, Divya, found her courage. She unfroze and took Leena's hand.

'Come on, Leena. We have come this far, we might as well get out and take a look.'

She stood up and pulled Leena to her feet. The three women mustered their empty plastic water bottles, their fragments of now stale bread, and the cotton shawls they'd been sitting on, and stuffed them into their shoulder bags. At the train door, Anila helped a young woman manoeuvre her old mother down the high steps. The old woman smiled and gripped her arm briefly in gratitude.

Then the three friends gathered themselves and plunged into the dense crowd that filled the platform. They clung desperately to each other, Anila their tall anchor in this human storm. The map was useless here, and Anila had no sense of the direction to take. But others seemed to. As the disembarking passengers surged forward, the three women cast themselves into the current.

They were swept along by the crowd as it poured off the platform, down onto the oily sleepers and then over the tracks. They clambered up the other side, grabbing each other's hands, pulling and pushing in turn. The human tide caught them up again, and crushed them through a narrow exit like a torrent between two rocks. They were spewed onto a concourse, stumbling over islands of squatting and lying people that the more knowledgeable crowd negotiated automatically.

They edged round touts, and peddlers of hot food. Their mouths watered at the sight and smells of the hot samosas and vegetable bhajis. But they could not afford such luxuries. Not yet. There seemed to be men everywhere, singly or in groups, prowling, assessing, measuring their chances. Eve-teasers, surely.

The three women pressed forward and broke clear and could breathe again. But walking a further few paces, they stumbled out of the cordon of light thrown round the station. In the contrast, it was as dark as a cave.

Anila told herself that she was used to darkness. Sometimes in the village, when the night sky clouded over, it would be like staring into charcoal. And there would be animals to watch out for; wild dogs or a wounded tiger. But in the village she could cling to familiar smells and sounds. Here she had no bearings. Her sight had gone and the noises and the smells were different and threatening, for they were made by men. A line of silent taxis blocked their way. Their keepers watched them with hungry eyes, weighing them as customers, targets. Men's soft voices called to them. Was this how the assaults on women started?

The crowd was thinning and dispersing, and abruptly Anila had no idea where to go next. Rudderless and reckless, she cast about. She recognised the old woman she'd helped. She was limping past a few yards away, supported by her daughter. Anila called out.

'Mother? Mother we are strangers here. Is this the right way to the Kinari Bazaar? It is near the Chandni Chowk.'

The two women stopped and the old one came close and peered at her.

'Daughter, you are a long way from your fields. What are you doing in this terrible place?'

'We have business here.'

Anila's stomach jolted. The business she spoke of was nothing less than personal survival. She went on.

'I have a cousin who lives near the Kinari Bazaar. We will stay with her this night.'

She wouldn't. There was no cousin. She didn't want to confess this to the old woman, from pride and fear of ridicule. She glanced significantly at her companions to bind them to her lie. Their plan had been to arrive in the afternoon and scout out a park to sleep in or a temple wall to lie beside. But the train delay had ruined everything. Now all they hoped was to get somewhere near to their destination and shelter in a doorway. It was high summer so the night would stay hot. The old woman reached out and took a fresh grip of Anila's arm.

'Daughter, tell me that your business is not with men. It is a terrible life. You must not go down this path.'

Leena and Divya glanced at each other, then Anila, their eyes wide. Anila put her own hand over the old woman's and leaned close so the old woman could see her smile and judge her eyes.

'It is not with men. That is not what we are here for, mother. We are coming to see a bank.'

'A bank! That is as bad as going with men!'

Then her face broke and she chuckled.

'Walk with us and we will show you the way. You are in luck. My own daughter's home lies close to your bazaar.'

Her daughter smiled in agreement. It was just over a mile,

but at the old woman's speed and having to cross two great roads with hurtling traffic, it took them over an hour. By the time they reached the street of Anila's mythical cousin the old woman had milked them dry of their story. She herself had been born in Madya Pradesh, near Jabalpur, and had recognised their accents.

They stopped to say their farewells. The three travellers stood uncertainly and unconvincingly as the old woman hobbled off on her daughter's arm. Within a few steps the old woman stopped and turned back. She curled her finger. Anila stepped towards her. Once more she took Anila's arm and peered up at her.

'Perhaps your cousin has left the city? Perhaps she has gone away and not told you?'

Anila's eyes smarted with the discovery. She lowered her gaze.

'Perhaps you are right, mother.'

'Then you had better come with me.'

Without waiting for a reply she turned and walked on, leaning hard on her daughter. The three women looked at each other briefly and followed. They were shown into the tiny front room and given hard mats to cover the concrete floor. They washed as best they could and tumbled like stones into troubled sleep.

TWO

The email hit the sidebar of his screen. Its first words blinked at him, goading him:

Are you lying or just muck-raking? The People's Bank...

Dammit, the Tribune's firewalls were supposed to protect him from whingers. Ted Saddler hit the delete key without reading further. He returned to his draft column about the infiltration of Japanese banks by gangsters, the Yakuza. He was struggling to give it urgency; in Japanese corporate life it was old news. As he nibbled at his thumbnail a second email flashed on screen. Same opening, same mention of the shady Indian bank that was spreading its tentacles worldwide. He gazed at the email, then killed it and waited. Sure enough, it popped back up. Spam or persistence?

His cell phone buzzed and shuffled on his desk, like a flat beetle on its back. Even as he flicked the screen, it buzzed again, and again. Three texts, all from a withheld number but each starting with '*Are you lying...*'

This wasn't communication, it was bombardment. Ted closed his cell without opening any of them. He studied the email again. He could simply leave it till morning. Have the IT security boys check for a virus. He was getting good at putting things off. Like letters from Mary's lawyer. On the other hand his boss had become unusually interested in these rip-off merchants. Was this some new test? Ted sucked in air and clicked. The full challenge was spelled out:

Are you lying or just muck-raking? The People's Bank deserves better. I can't believe the Tribune (of all papers!) is putting its reputation on the line like this. Not to mention your own! Do you want to hear what's *really* going on or are you only listening to one side?

– Diogenes –

Ted pursed his lips. *Diogenes* – the ancient Greek who went out in the midday sun with a lamp looking for an honest man. *Who does this guy think he is? What does that make me?!* In his 20 years in newspapers Ted had seen every variation on the crank letter, email and voice mail. More conspiracy theories than cold beers. He point blank refused to blog or tweet about his column because of the loonies it encouraged. He hadn't checked Facebook in months; just personal drivel and photos of smug couples claiming to have a good time. Fakes and flakes.

He wasn't about to let the flicker of interest this one raised turn into a flame. But it rankled strongly that he might have been suckered, or worse, that he was biased; he was still a pro, right? This was the third article he'd written about People's Bank and each time his gut indignation had grown.

He clicked on the front page of the business section again and re-read his latest copy, entitled: *'Candy from a baby; money from the poor?'* A snappy and accurate description of a bank that specialised in milking the destitute. After eight years of ripping off its customers, Ramesh Banerjee, the Chief Executive of the self styled 'bank to the poor' was finally being put on trial for corruption. The Indian government claimed he'd personally offered hush money to investigating authorities. Wasn't that how they did business over there?

Maybe the bit about 'an exclusive interview' was stretching a point. It was little more than email gossip from someone he knew on the Asia desk who'd bumped into a junior minister over cocktails. He'd found the minister desperate to inflate his self-importance by being expansive about events well outside his portfolio. Ted curbed his rising doubts and flicked to the next paragraph.

His quote from Burton Stacks, a very senior and respected

financial analyst at Global American bank, hit the mark: *"Tapping the underclass used to be the easy pickings of the money lender or shark. People's Bank seems to have found a lucrative new business, making money out of the needy."*

The World Bank would only speak off-record but they hinted at their concerns and allowed Ted to raise questions about how any third world outfit could consistently turn down a hand-out from the world's central bankers. Worried about having to open the books?

There was a video clip of one of the Tribune's glamour girls spouting a cut-down version of his article for lazy net-browsers. Ted couldn't listen. He knew her emphasis would be on all the wrong words, as if it were a foreign language. He switched to the clip with Chief Executive Ramesh Banerjee, looking and sounding more like Gandhi than a banker. There was sweat on his temple and running down the sides of his face. Ted knew how hot those camera lights got. Or maybe it was the prospect of twenty years in an Indian prison modelled on the Black Hole. The eyes were big and defenceless behind the glasses and seemed to be staring directly at Ted, daring him, as though he knew he was watching. As though he knew that Ted had substituted safe quotes and an old journalist's nose, for awkward and time-consuming investigation.

Ted clicked him off. They were always like that. All innocence until the evidence proved they were sleeping with the other man's wife, or they'd bought the election, or they'd duped their followers with guarantees of a hereafter for a hundred bucks down and lifetime instalments. That's how it was. Dirty. He wished he could be wrong. It's why he'd started in this business.

He looked north from his eyrie in the brightly lit newsroom high above Pearl Street. The Brooklyn Bridge was solid with red tail lights. A line of commuters anxious to get home to lit rooms and the hallway kiss and the day's gossip. Such domestic bliss had long since evaporated for him and Mary. But sometimes he missed the mess of cotton buds on the sink. The tissues smudged with make-up. The dent in the mattress and the smell of her pillow. Just knowing another heartbeat shared the echoing rooms. The first few nights after she'd gone, he'd slept on her side. Well, not slept so much as lay there, trying to get her perspective, to see what it had been like for her. He wondered if she was happy now, wondered what *he* was like. Now he wondered how long he had left there; it wasn't much of an apartment, but her lawyers were after a slice.

He returned to the provocative email, and his irritation bubbled up again. Irritation with himself. He had a formula that worked: Reuters' by-lines with a dash of Ted Saddler spleen. But in truth any one of the junior hacks could have done his column. Cheaper. He didn't want to go there, and thought about switching off and calling it a day. The Yakuza would keep till the morning.

He gazed out. Streets still clogged. Heat still rising from the summer-hot pavements. He'd be hanging from a subway strap all the way up to 96th. Maybe he'd go for a beer in South Street Seaport. Let rush hour subside at Jeremy's, the only real bar in the area. A dive that dispensed cold beer in 32 ounce Styrofoam cups. It was important to support the waterfront bars after their inundation by *Sandy*.

But unbidden, a bit of the old Ted, the goes-the-extra-mile Ted, burrowed up. He ran off a short response and studied it before hitting the send button. He wanted to get the tone right, maybe adding a little bit of flippancy to show he was in control, that he knew what he was doing.

If you're telling me the World Bank is behind some global conspiracy, I'm all ears. But we might have to see a little hard evidence. What you got?

Diogenes was obviously primed. The response fizzed back.

Thanks Ted. This is hard to believe, even for me. But we can't do this on email. Too risky. Too big. Can we meet tonight? I promise you it won't be wasted.–

9

He turned to his keyboard. He typed but didn't send:

how do I know you're not going to lure me to a dark alley and beat the crap out of me?

No sense being coy about the number of crazy folk out there. But if someone was crazy why would they admit it? He retyped.

I'll give you time if you can get over to the Tribune's office in the next 15 minutes.

He sent it and waited a minute, then a minute more, and was about to close down assuming he'd called the guy's bluff when a message popped up.

I don't want to meet in a press building. Too many eyes. Let's meet in Carnegie's. It's a bar on Bleeker between Thompson and Sullivan. 7pm. It has to be just the two of us or I won't show.

So Diogenes was a public figure and twitchy as a gopher. What's to lose? Unless it was a lunatic on the other end of this conversation trying to sucker him. But a bar was safe and he did need a drink, and this might, just might, have some mileage in it. He typed in the name and checked the map.

Got it. How will I know you?

I know you. Tribune web site. Sit at the counter. I'll introduce myself.

If this was a wild goose chase he could always cut the discussion short and still meet the boys at Houlihan's. It was only ten minutes ride away and it would be a conversation piece. Those young live wires were always looking for some new bone to chew on, as though they were testing him.

THREE

The cab dropped him in front of Carnegie's. He took in the façade. His misgivings fluttered to the surface. It was a bar pretending to be a night club. He went in and it was worse inside. Ice cool compared with the steamy air of a summer evening on Bleeker. Wood panels and soft upholstery. No sport screens, just dinner Jazz piping in the background like warm baby-oil for the ears. Glistening black counter staffed by a couple of young women in tasteful blouses and piled-up hair.

He sized up the sharp outfits of the clientele. He hitched up his baggy pants and did up his top shirt button. He pushed his fingers through the long strands of fair hair and settled it behind his ears. He knew it was long overdue a cut but at least it was now off his face. There was nothing he could do about making his canvas jacket look like an ivy-league sports coat, even if he cared to.

One of the first things he'd done PM – *Post Mary* – was to ransack his clothes-rail for the stuff she'd made him buy: the preppy ties, jackets and pants as if auditioning for tenure at Harvard. He took the whole pile and dumped it in the tiny spare room. He was left with his hunting outfits, she'd called them. It amounted to barely three days' change of clothes – so he paid a visit to Eddie Bauer to stock up on check shirts and baggy pants. They'd gone bust in the past. Better to have reserves.

There were a few leather high-stools round the gleaming horseshoe, most of them free. He took up position on one facing the door and placed his cell down on the counter, ready for further contact. It was just after seven. A good time in a bad bar. Before the place filled up and the noise levels rose and the booze fuzzed the head. Out of habit, regardless of where he was drinking, he ordered his usual, a large Maker's Mark on the rocks and a beer chaser.

He scanned the room. *Not* Jeremy's Ale House. More somewhere you'd meet a date, an uptown date. Couples mostly, gazing into each other's eyes or quizzing their phones. When did that happen? No sign of anyone with a lamp. A few singles. Both sexes, and probably some in between. Reading tablets or even the odd newspaper, but generally pretending they're not waiting for someone.

At least it was dark enough to hide in. It's what he loved about the big city; anonymity. Slipping through the crowds late of an evening. Or sitting in one of the concourse bars in Grand Central Station, watching the dating game unfold at the Oyster Bar, without having to give anything away. The soloist. Gathering material for the book. Ted gave a mental shrug; a lot of material. No book.

From a seat against the velour-clad wall Diogenes watched him shamble in, check the place out and climb on a stool as though it was reserved for him on a daily basis.

This was the famous Theodore Saddler? Not much like the Tribune web site, but then who used their worst photos? Twenty pounds heavier and looking like he'd just got off the Greyhound from Nowheresville by mistake. Still the swept back fair hair. Reliving his hippy youth? Wiki said he was barely fifty, but he looked ready for the retirement hammock and a non-stop supply of pretzels and beer. Big and old and slow, as though he'd never believe the story, far less do anything about it.

Do I really want to go through with this? This whole idea is stupid. A guilt trip or boardroom politics? Getting back at the boss or a dumb excuse to give up the rat race? A grand gesture. Exit stage right to applause . . . but pursued by a bear. All I have to do is get up and walk out. I've given him the tip-off, let him run with it. Maybe that was best.

Ted threw back the third and last mouthful of bourbon and

called for another. He was handing over a twenty to pay for his drinks when the transaction was interrupted.

'I'll get this. Put it on my tab.'

He swivelled to his left, struck by a woman's commanding voice wrapped in an alluring accent. Irish? Scots? He always mixed them up. This was Diogenes? Dark hair yanked back from strong features. Blue eyes holding his, unblinking, unyielding. Womanly curves wrapped in the sort of understated greys and blacks that quietly screamed designer. How had he missed her? She must have snuck up on him from a seat in the corner. Doubt struck. A high class hooker? His joker defence mechanism kicked in.

'Is this how they do happy hour here?'

'Only if your name's Ted Saddler.'

'If that's the password, I'm in.'

She slid onto the stool and ordered a spritzer. She sent it back for having too much wine. It gave Ted time to examine her sideways on. The smooth dark hair – deep brown verging on black – held firmly in place at the back of the skull by a tight clip of some sort. Light makeup; a scattering of freckles showed through. Aspen in winter, Caribbean in the summer. Late thirties, or a fancy surgeon? Who was he to judge these days? No ring on the perfectly manicured left hand. Upper East Side and big pay checks. Something familiar about her all the same.

'Cheers, Mr Saddler.'

She raised her glass to him and dropped the bantering tone. She turned full on to him. Gave him the sea-blue gaze with the power to strip a minion at twenty paces. But fronting a good brain. He had a theory that you can tell by people's eyes. He put on his listening look.

'You Scotch?'

'That's the booze. I'm Scottish.'

'I stand corrected.'

She heard the small hurt in his voice and smiled. 'Thank you for coming. I really appreciate it.'

'Your email assault didn't give me much choice.'

Her smile flickered again but there would be no contrition for the deluge. He pressed again.

'How did you get my private email and cell number?'

'Connections. The point is, you're wrong about the People's Bank. Those guys are straight.'

'How would *you* know?'

'I've spent the last couple of years analysing them and the only thing they're guilty of is altruism.'

Was that it, he thought? A bleeding heart? 'Before we go any further I need to know who I'm dealing with – Miss Diogenes.'

'How do I know I can trust you? I want this off the record.'

'Lady, I'm a priest. This is your confessional. But remember, I am a reporter. At some point I need stuff that can go on the record. Are you ready for that?'

Her eyes flicked over his double hand of drinks – professional what? She searched his face, looking for substance behind the glibness. Give him something.

'The name's Wishart, Erin Wishart. Erin will do. Global American Bank. I run the Asia Pacific region.'

Now the face came into focus. The tough Brit making it big in the biggest US bank. Her appealing brogue masking steely ambition. Mentioned in despatches as CEO material. Hence the power aura. He tried to look unimpressed.

'Okaaay. So what's that got to do with our little People's Bank?'

'Not so little. Which is the problem. They're eating our lunch.'

She made 'lunch' sound more important than any meal Ted could remember. Her voice dropped. She moved closer into him so he caught the faintest edge of her scent. It threw him off balance. He bent his head towards her, wanting more.

'And for the last year, GA has been orchestrating a dirty tricks campaign to derail them.'

Ted blinked. If this was fact, and Global American, the

biggest commercial bank in the world, was behind the current hoo-hah, the repercussions were Richter scale 10. And he'd have a front page. In fact he'd have several front pages. But why was she doing this? And could she prove it?

'How dirty? And what proof have you got?'

Proof. It was what Erin Wishart had feared. She'd tried explaining it to Sally Gunn, divorce lawyer and best friend, over dinner at the Grill. Sally was doling out her usual pragmatism…

'I always tell my clients they can't afford a conscience until they're $50 million in the clear.'

'I though it was 20?'

'Inflation, darling.'

'That's facile, Sally, not to mention immoral.'

'*Amoral*. There's a difference.' Sally nonchalantly popped a fragment of Black Cod between her tiny white teeth and waved a fork at Erin. 'It's not the man thing, is it darling?'

'God, no!' It wasn't, but Erin knew she was protesting too loudly. Sometimes she felt like her whole body had been designed as a beacon, but it always attracted the wrong ones. So she'd stopped looking and was perfectly content with her freedom and space and the occasional little fling that came her way, thank you.

Sally eyed her sceptically. 'Alright. Let's say it's not revenge; it's not early menopause or some transferred mothering instinct.' She shuddered theatrically. 'I diagnose a nasty outbreak of survivor's guilt.'

'Survivor's…? Oh, you mean the banking debacle. Maybe.'

'Perfectly understandable, my dear.' She smiled wickedly. 'You people got away with murder. But why do you have to put your pretty little neck on the block? There's other ways to get news out.'

Erin chewed for a minute. 'You mean just leak it?'

'Sure. Unleash the Fourth Estate. They love snuffling around in mud.'

Sally's eyes gleamed like she'd got her client's spouse on the ropes and was moving in for the kill. . .

Erin was thinking now that it had been good advice. But it would founder on the rocks of Ted Saddler's scepticism and inertia unless she opened up some more. She did what she always did when challenged. She sat upright on her stool and hit him with disdain, a flash of the corporate executive.

'Do you think that quote you got from the GA analyst was just a happy coincidence?'

It struck home. A tiny bit of Ted had been wondering about Burton Stacks. He worked for GA's investment banking arm, a separate division, but same parent. Stacks had made an unsolicited call. Like this lady come to that. It sometimes happened. But ten years ago Ted would have phoned three or four analysts in other banks for independent corroboration. His annoyance with himself showed.

'Proves nothing. What about the World Bank. You're not telling me they're part of some global plot?'

'You think that's a stretch? The collapse of global capitalism? The Middle East in flames? The polar ice-caps melting? The Cold War restarting? A Clinton or a Bush back in the White House? Is anything unbelievable any more?'

Ted persisted 'What have you got? And more to the point, why are you telling me this?'

'Let's grab that table.'

Erin pointed to a quiet spot outside of the bar girls' hearing. She moved, sure Ted would follow. He admired her confident stride for a second or two then slid off his stool. They blended into the tableau of couples being intimate. She took a deep breath and told him about a meeting that took place just under a year ago at Global American's head office. She was good at telling a story. He could see and hear the whole thing, as if he'd been there. But from the sound of it, he was glad he hadn't.

FOUR

The boardroom curtains slowly whirred shut, closing out the 48th floor panorama of skyscrapers, including the Freedom Tower framed by the grey-blue Hudson. Five people sat round a perfect oval of burnished American walnut studded with glowing tablets. One of the five held the seat of power at the apex facing the floor-to-ceiling windows. His dome of a forehead, his slicked back hair and the great axe of a nose came straight off a Roman coin. His left hand caressed the glowing screen in front of him.

His vassals – three men and one woman – kept a respectful distance clustered round the middle and the far end of the table. The woman's soft-cut grey jacket and slash of cream silk blouse contrasted with the men's dark suits and muted ties. Her blue eyes were glued to her tablet.

On the wall to the left of Caesar an array of flat panels displayed the upper halves of four men, like living portraits. All eyes were on the screens in front of them displaying a spread sheet entitled Global American Bank, 2nd quarter forecast outturn.

'Actuals by region, Charlie.'

It was a command, not a comment from the seat of power. In response, the man to his right flipped his finger across his controlling tablet.

'Versus budget.' Column-keeper obeyed and flipped on. There was a long pause, then.

'Forecast for Q2 and for full year.'

A graph appeared. The room froze while every person digested the meaning of the lines that projected gently upwards through the first quarter of the year, flattened in the current quarter, and fell markedly by year end. A simple, sorry story.

Eyes slowly came up and rested on the man at the centre. He was turning a sleek cell-phone over and over in his hand. He scanned each of the faces in turn before hefting the phone and sending it crashing down on the polished wood. It bounced once, broke in two and the bits sailed towards the windows. Eight faces flinched, even those hundreds of safe miles away on video link. Eagle-nose shot to his feet. His chair crashed behind him. He pointed a finger round the room and then at the four video images.

'Shit! This is fuckin' shit! The analysts will kill us. Then the board will flay us. All of you are dead meat!' He jabbed his finger at each face, as though he had a stiletto.

'You hear?! Dead meat! You think we can repay Fed hand-outs one year and go back the next for more?'

His voice turned girlish and sarcastic. 'Oh gee, sorry, we got it wrong. We're not in as good a shape as we thought. Can we borrow another $50 billion?! Again! Pretty please?' His eyes lasered everyone in his path.

'In my twenty ears with GA I've pulled this bank out of the fire half a dozen times. Do you think I should cave this time? If you do, you might as well send in your resignations right now. On the same plate as your balls. I'm not taking this shit. If you can't do better I'll get someone who can. Capice?'

Warwick Stanstead's rages had become commonplace but they'd lost none of their impact with frequency. The eyes of all the men tried to look tough, as though each had done his part, and someone else had failed to deliver. Only the woman seemed calm, though she was gripping the arms of her chair. She was studying her boss, noting the flushed cheeks and throat, the tiny beads of sweat on his domed forehead. He was thinner, his pale skin stretched over the jutting bones of his face. *You stupid sod, Warwick. All those tearful promises. . .*

She was about to speak but was beaten to it by Charlie

Easterhouse, Chief Operating Officer, keeper of the graphs and the controlling tablet. Charlie had been with the Chief for longer than anyone and had seen all his moods. Charlie began gently.

'Warwick? Maybe we should look at some of the stuff behind these figures?'

'You think they'll get better if we look harder at them?'

Warwick's soft tones made the other men wince in anticipation. Charlie held his ground.

'We need to understand where the problem is and then we can maybe focus on how to solve it. Some of these figures are good, Warwick. Great even. Considering where we've been.' He poked at the columns now appearing on all the screens. 'We're above target in two of our four regions and three out of five business lines. We can still pull it up.'

Warwick's eyes slitted and the right side of his thin mouth lifted in his famous sneer.

'Show me.'

Charlie Easterhouse enlarged the spreadsheet. He gave his colleagues a second or two to home in on the serried columns. Then he clicked on chosen lines and let them see the underlying figures.

'Europe and North America were on target for first quarter in terms of new accounts, total under deposit, and the all important Net Interest.' He paged down and highlighted some figures.

'Global M&A activity was actually 3% up on budget and 15% up on last year. Same story on our dealing operations – client and own book. We're up nearly 5% on budget for Treasuries and Triple A bonds, and almost 7% on equity market making.'

Easterhouse looked round for support, if not applause, from his colleagues. No-one responded. Charlie battled on.

'Got to admit, second quarter is forecast to be flatter, and then, sure, we tail away. But we have time. If we take the right action,' he pleaded.

The Chief Executive of Global American bank looked through slits at his Chief Operating Officer. He picked up his chair and sat back down.

'So, Charlie, you think these bums will earn their bonuses by year end? Averaging $10 million a piece? You think?'

He waited for the riposte which was never going to come. His voice strengthened.

'The recession is over. Half our competition has been wiped out. It's a fuckin' bull market out there!'

He pointed towards the massive plate glass windows of the room and the towers and drops of Wall Street beyond.

'My goddamn grandmother could make these numbers. And she's dead! What about our forecasts for Asia Pac and Latin America? What about the retail business – banking and insurance that's forecast to lose 3 points in a fuckin' quarter! What about the cost base that went up by near 10%! What the fuck is going on?!'

The men and woman now dropped their eyes. There was no hiding place.

'Ok, we go round the table. Cadenza?'

José Cadenza met his boss's eyes, swallowed and wished he was on a plane down to Rio to see his wife, kids and his deputies in the Central and Latin America region. He knew they were busting their balls off for this madman, and the plain fact was that he'd set impossible targets. He wished for the thousandth time he'd held out for realistic numbers during the budget last year. But between his boss and Charlie Easterhouse, not to mention the hefty bonus, he'd been bludgeoned into a 20% hike. Before Stanstead could begin the one-sided duel, a soft but carefully pitched Scottish voice deflected the thrust.

'Warwick?'

She was sitting back in her chair, slim fingers neatly latticed in front of her. Apart from the rising colour in her neck, and the faint quaver in her voice, she looked the least nervous round the table. It wasn't insouciance; Asia Pacific was doing worse than any other region.

'Miss Wishart. Erin. I was saving you till last.' The Chief was gentle now, caressing.

'And not because I've got the best numbers?'

Her chin lifted and her voice steadied. Erin Wishart reminded herself of the power of her accent to hold the attention of an all-American male audience. She went on without waiting for a reply.

'Asia Pac is the worst performer because that's where the problem started. Take a look.'

She began stroking the screen in front of her. The wall chart faded and came back into focus with new slides.

'These are 3D charts of each of our regions showing our results against target and against our nearest competitors in each area. See the red bumps in Asia and Latin America? And this next screen, our global business lines, it's the same story.'

She waited a beat to see faces absorb the information and got a few nods.

'Our usual competitors – the big US and European banks – are seeing the same trend line as us. One competitor is rising higher and faster than any of us. The People's Bank. It started in India, but now has a massive penetration of Australia, Indonesia, Philippines, Japan, and not least, China. Thanks to the Internet and their business model, they're coming after the rest of us. They're gobbling up our target markets and business lines like an infection.'

'But this is some nothing bank! A fucking pipe dream. It's a bank for people we don't even want as customers! They're picking up our cast-offs!'

'They were Warwick. They were. But they're getting the volumes, and now they're moving up the food chain. They're *fashionable*.'

Erin Wishart, Senior Vice President Asia Pacific, said the last word with a mixture of irony and wonder.

She went on, 'It's a post-recession reaction. We – the big Western banks – completely alienated our customers. We lost their trust. PB has an image that combines good finances with good works. No bad loans to speak of. No government hand-outs. They're untainted.'

Erin paused and watched the nods of agreement round the room and on the video screens.

'Our research shows People's Bank hoovering up everything. They've just announced they're moving into micro-insurance, so we can expect Aaron's side to be picked off next in the developed world. They have well-advanced plans for ethical investment banking and fund management.'

She couldn't hide a certain ruefulness in her voice. The Chief Executive of Global American blinked at her.

'Ethical investment banking? That's like low carb doughnuts!'

'The Fed likes that bit, even if they don't like the interest rates they charge. It's an old model retuned for the Internet. People's Bank raises money from depositors and only lends what it takes in. No big bets on the wholesale market. No fancy derivatives. No unmanageable risks.'

'And no fat bonuses!' Warwick cut her off with a slap of his hand on the desk.

He swept his malignant eyes round his underlings like a serrated knife. His voice went quiet, almost whispering, the level set so low that even with the room's magnificent sound system, they each had to lean a little forward to hear his pale words.

'Miss Wishart is right. What we have here citizens is a virus. It's a goddamn fuckin' plague. That's what this is. And we're going to eradicate it before it takes us out too. Turns us all into some castrated mutual fund. Some socialist co-op. Erin, my office, now.'

He got up and walked out, leaving the air simmering with tension and resentment.

FIVE

'I am feeling sick, Anila.'

Leena spoke into the early morning light seeping in from the window. Their body-clocks had wakened them at village time, just before daybreak. They lay still, listening to the faint stirrings in the rest of the house and watching the light grow. They were thinking about the day ahead.

'Is it proper sickness or are you just worried?'

Anila rose up on her elbow to look at her companions. Divya was listening too.

'I think it is worry, but I don't know. I just woke feeling so frightened. It seemed such a good idea back in the village but now . . .'

Even tough Divya looked troubled. Anila could understand it well enough. She had hardly slept in her anxiety. She had gone over and over why she was doing this, and though the logic worked, it was hard to convince her heart of the sense of this trip. Not in the small hours of the morning of the biggest day of her life. To reassure herself, as much as the others, Anila forced confidence into her voice.

'It is simple really, Leena, is it not? We had no choice.'

There was certainly none now. The trip itself had effectively burnt every bridge behind them. They had stolen away from the village before first light and had told only their closest friends what they were planning. But by now of course the whole village would know their business and the money lender would never lend her a paisa again. She had borrowed the last few rupees of her mother's savings for the train fare. This was her final throw.

'But what if the bank won't help us?' asked Divya for the hundredth time.

'They will. That is what they do, this bank. It is the People's Bank after all.'

'But we don't even know if they will see us!'

Leena picked up the other thread of worry hoping that Anila as usual would take it from her. This morning it was different. Anila was brisk.

'Well, we will not have long to find out, will we? Get dressed and I will see if we can use their fine lavatory and maybe get us some more water to drink and to wash in.'

They had time to wash and put on their best saris, carried so carefully, rolled up in their shoulder bags. They freshened the vermilion Sindoor on their forehead in their hair parting, and tied on their Mangalsutra necklaces. Anila felt a fraud putting on these insignia of love and marriage. She wore hers for safety and to avoid unwelcome advances on their travels. Dilip would rage and rant if he could have seen her. Even more so if he'd known what she was up to. Each wore their favourite nose studs and Leena had insisted on wearing her lucky ankle bangles as well as her bracelets. Anila and Divya stuck to bracelets. They felt better, more confident, now they were properly dressed.

They courteously declined the offer of fresh bread. Though the smell of the hot dough was overwhelming, they didn't want to stretch the family's hospitality. The old woman came to the door to see them off. She touched each of them by the arm and stroked Anila's cheek.

'Shiva go with you, daughters. If you want my advice, go back to your village. This path you take is lined with thorns. It is not for you.'

The three young women made bowing farewells to the old woman and her daughter as the door closed on them. Leena and Divya looked at their tall friend, doubt written large across their faces. The old woman had set all their fears running again. It had been done out of kindness but she made it clear that simple village women had no business with such grand ideas. But they had come this far and there was a freshness on the morning air and the light was increasing. They walked in the direction they'd been told and found themselves on the street of the Kinari Bazaar itself. They pooled their money and bought some hot chapattis and vegetable pakoras from the first street vendor they encountered. Now they could face the world.

And what a world. The bazaar was famous across India for its wedding finery. Though it was barely day, the crowds were already thickening. Shutters were being thrown back and heavy metal blinds were being pushed up. Shop after shop revealed rolls of glorious silk and fine turbans. To Divya and Leena, these were treasure houses. To Anila, the gaiety rubbed salt into her own marriage wounds. Tinsel hung in festoons from great hooks and from wires stretched across a shop front. Garlands were being splashed with water and allowed to hang dripping in the gold light that had begun to inch its way down the walls.

It took all Anila's powers to cajole her friends through the market and out onto the Chandni Chowk itself. She checked her map and saw where she was. They turned left and along another narrow alleyway and began to look for a sign. They were beginning to think they'd missed it when they saw the words on a little brass plate. It said the People's Bank and it had a tree engraved behind the words.

It was shut. They sat down on the top one of two steps and waited. A long time later it seemed, when Leena was drowsing against Divya's shoulder and Anila had worked her way through frantic to fatalistic, the man appeared in front of them. He was short and round, and dressed in a cream kurta top over black trousers. His dark hair was combed back from a moon-shaped face given character by the fine nose and the black moustache. He carried a slim leather briefcase and looked like a bumbling but amiable clerk. He spoke in English.

'Excuse me, I want to go in, please.'

He was waving a key at them and then at the door behind them. He seemed more amused than displeased. The women came to life and rose up like three startled birds from their perch. Anila was flustered and groped for the right words in English. In reflex she clasped her hands in greeting and bowed.

'Namaste. Please sir, are you working here, in the bank?'

This was the moment. The man slid his briefcase under his left arm and responded politely and in kind to Anila's greeting. He looked quizzically at them.

'Yes, yes I do. What do you want?'

He was puzzled. They didn't look like beggars and it seemed too late for night girls. Anila felt her breath leave her and her heart stop. It wasn't her voice speaking, but someone was certainly repeating the words she'd rehearsed a hundred times to herself, in Hindi and – just in case – in English.

'We are wanting a loan, for our business.'

The man looked as though he was about to drive them away, then his severe expression broke and his face settled into its normal geniality. He smiled.

'I'm afraid you have come to the wrong place. This is the head office of our bank. We don't deal with personal customers here.'

The three women looked dumbstruck, not understanding all the words but registering that their trip seemed to have been for nothing. The man saw the effect. He repeated his words in Hindi and added,

'Look here, you'd better come inside, hadn't you. My name is CJ Kapoor. I run this office.'

SIX

Ted Saddler was staring in some wonder at Erin Wishart as she came to a sudden stop.

'You've just made my boss look like Francis of Assisi. Is Stanstead always like that or was this special?'

She paused, wondering how to frame her reply.

'You need to understand him. I've worked with him and for him for almost twenty years. He's brilliant but driven. Several times over the years I thought we were going under. Warwick bailed us out through sheer force of will. Steered us through. Last time was the credit crunch in '08. It almost killed GA. We could have gone down like Lehman. Warwick rallied us. Cut deals with the Fed, took the bailout money and then paid it back. He's not about to see us fail now. This is his baby.'

'He sounds like a megalomaniac. But who'd notice on Wall Street.'

She shook her head. She'd heard all the gibes. *How much do I need to tell this reporter to get him moving? At what point does it become a betrayal? Probably the minute he walked in the door.*

'We did some fancy accounting to scrape in on target at year end, but the analysts saw through it. Our share price tanked and will again. Everyone is killing themselves to make this year's numbers.' She paused a beat. 'We won't. And that's very much off the record.'

'People's Bank continuing to eat into the cake?'

She nodded. 'And then some. But it's more than just numbers for Warwick. GA is bigger than any bank in history. Stanstead was the one who won out in the last merger between Global

Fidelity and American Mart; remember, the insurance and investments retailer?'

'Couple of years back?'

'Three. We stunned the banking world. Truly global. The first trillion dollar merger.'

Ted heard the pride in her voice and wondered why she was dishing her boss.

'There was a lot of angst and stuff about which of the CEOs would get the top job. Both tough cookies, but Bill Yeardon blinked first. It's hard to see what Stanstead's next trick will be. He's wondering that himself and doesn't much like someone else – like a jumped-up Indian bank – getting in the way of his plans for world domination.'

'OK, back to my questions: first, why are you doing this? Why don't you walk? Find someone nicer to work for? Like Vlad the Impaler?'

'Nice guys don't make Chief Exec.'

She didn't add 'stupid' but it was implied. She paused for a long moment.

'It's complicated. More than any other regional head, I know People's Bank. I'm based in Hong Kong and have offices in Mumbai and Sydney. I've been going head to head with them across Asia Pac for years. And frankly, I'm impressed.'

She bit her lip. 'This is going to sound wishy washy liberal.'

'A socialist banker? This I gotta hear. Shoot.'

'Oh, it's hard-nosed capitalism too. Do you believe in democracy?'

Ted's eyebrow went up. 'Your guy Churchill called it the worst form of government, except for all the others.'

'And your guy Lincoln kicked off a civil war in defence of government of the people, by the people, for the people.'

'Where's this getting us?'

'Full on democracy requires laws and systems that allow its citizens to own property, including bricks and mortar and the more liquid assets.'

'Like money. So they need banks. I get it. But not loans at 35%.'

Erin nodded. 'Rates are an issue. But the main point is if you can't own anything, you're a slave. The Gates Foundation estimates that more than 75% of the world's poor don't have a bank account. That's 2.5 billion potential customers! My bank won't go near them. Too risky and too costly. But People's Bank does.'

'And you want them to go on providing this rapacious service? Even if they eat into your slice of the cake? Aren't you in the wrong job, Miss Wishart? Salvation Army?'

'I've put twenty years of my life into this bank. I'm not ready to quit.'

'So what's the answer?'

'Join forces with People's Bank. Complement each other instead of competing. I could turn my region round if I could leverage off their image and customer base.'

'Let me guess; Stanstead won't wear it.'

'I've pitched this until he told me if I raised it again, he'd fire me.'

'And in the meantime, he's taking his own route to dealing with People's?'

She nodded.

'Which is?'

She took a deep breath. 'Shovelling dirt. Using his government and industry connections to spread lies and exaggerations. He's got a team round him who specialise in muck raking and generating legal claims. I'm seeing an explosion of negative press and internet articles, local court action and pundits on news shows stirring it up. It didn't take much to swing the Indian Government from support to legal attack. They don't like anyone else having power over their electorate, especially if it shows them up for failing to do anything for the poor.'

'Can we pin this on Stanstead? If we're to take this anywhere we need evidence. Hard evidence. Otherwise we won't print it, or if we did, GA would sue our ass off. And I'd be checking out Florida retirement homes. Of the trailer park variety.'

'Isn't digging your job? Now you know something funny is going on? Can't you don your fearless cub reporter gear and check things out? You've got contacts?'

She was skittish, truculent, like a horse getting its first bridle. Her accent was getting stronger. There was no doubt now about her Scottish roots. Ted placed his big hands flat on the table and leaned towards her. Then he saw his chewed nails and made fists.

'Erin, you haven't given me anything to dig into. So, he had a bad day in the office. So, he shouted at a few people and called a competitor names. But you can bet half the boardrooms in the USA are bloodbaths every quarter these days. I hear Apple's no picnic. What's different here? Show me how he got Burton Stacks to make that call to me. Show me how he suborned the World Bank. Bring me proof of how he corrupted the Indian government.'

'Look mister, I don't need this. Let's just forget the whole thing.'

She sat back against the seat and waved her slim fingers at him in dismissal. Ted put on his long suffering face, the one he reserved for his lawyer when a new demand hit the table.

'Erin, I'd love to take this and run with it. But you need to help me some more.'

She was shaking her head. 'I can't. I just can't. Look, forget we met. Forget we had this conversation. It was a crazy idea.'

She stood up, grabbed her purse, walked to the bar and asked for the check.

He thought she was going to walk out on him without even a goodnight. Ted rubbed his face. Just beautiful. He'd handled her like a complete jerk. What the hell was happening to him? This could have been a hot story, could have earned him a breathing space with his boss. He felt people at the other tables staring at him, marking him down as a loser who'd upset his date. It wouldn't be the first time lately. He opened his top button to cool down. His sightline to the bar was suddenly blocked. She was standing by his table again, a vibrating column of energy, her bag looped over her shoulder like an ammunition pouch. She took a deep breath.

'Ted, I just want to say thanks and sorry. That was rude. I wasted your time. I don't have all the answers even if I wanted to give them to you. If you won't or can't play your part then I guess it goes nowhere.'

He'd seen that look before with women. Disappointed. Mary had used it more often towards the end. Erin left him there. He looked at his watch and decided he'd earned a real drink before he headed home. In a real bar.

Erin Wishart stood in the dark in her 10th floor apartment. She gazed blindly down on 5th Avenue and the lines of cars as they crawled along, their lights blinking in and out under the black camouflage of the trees fringing Central Park. She'd come within a few indiscretions of losing all this, of screwing up her career. She could almost hear her girlfriends' incredulity: what the hell was she thinking about? What business was it of Erin Wishart? Why throw away all the hard won gains for someone else's take on morality?

And she had to ask herself just how far her public-spiritedness took her before it ran into her less scrupulous motivations like personal advancement. But there would be no advancement – no bank – if Warwick continued his downward spiral. What was his poison of choice this time? Such a waste.

There was something else she hadn't mentioned to Saddler. The conversation with José Cadenza two days ago. She'd bumped into him in a local bookshop while she was looking for good reads for her long plane ride back to Hong Kong. He invited her to have a sandwich with him in the coffee shop. She'd liked José on sight but they'd only ever met on the executive floor of the GA building and conversation had been strictly business. José had joined GA from American Mart when Warwick had taken them over. They talked books for a while, then José got serious. His dark eyes grew troubled.

'Ever meet Bill Yeardon, Erin?'

'Once or twice. While we were in the takeover negotiations.'

'My old boss. A good guy.'

'I thought so. I'm glad you joined us. You seemed to have settled in.'

'Until this People's Bank thing.'

'We'll get over it.'

'And Yeardon's wife? Meet her?'

'Veronica? A real Southern belle. Met over cocktails. I was sorry to hear about Bill. Just before last Christmas?'

José nodded. 'Heart attack. I went to the funeral. He was only 52.'

He looked as though he was going to say more, then thought better of it. Erin let the pause grow. José leaned across the table, his voice down.

'Last week I had a call from Veronica. She was pretty upset. She'd finally got around to clearing out Bill's desk at his home. She said she'd found a key to a safety deposit box at her local First County bank. Veronica didn't know Bill used First County, far less owned a safety deposit box.'

'Another woman?'

José shook his head. 'She'd thought the same. She could have coped with that. No, it was material about the merger. She said it was horrible. That it confirmed her opinion about Warwick. She couldn't speak about it on the phone. Wanted me to visit, or she'd come to New York.'

Erin swallowed. What had Warwick done?

'Why are you telling me this?'

'I don't know anyone round the table. You're all GA to the core.'

'And it's easier to talk to a woman?' she smiled.

He grinned. 'My wife's always said I prefer women's company to men.'

'Good for you. As long as its platonic?'

He laughed. 'Absolutely! Maria would kill me. And I've got two kids.'

'What do you want me to say?'

'You know Warwick. What's he capable of?'

'What's anyone capable of in our business?'

His smile was rueful. 'I'll let you know how my meeting with Veronica goes.'

José's question kept reverberating as she made her way back to the towering offices of the bank. At least until a year ago, she'd have said she knew Warwick better than most. But she'd never known quite how far he'd go to defend his beloved empire. His behaviour – with or without stimulants – was increasingly erratic, violent.

After this evening's shambles she wondered if she should have raised the issue with Ted Saddler, see if that got his old investigator's engine going. But she still hadn't heard back from José. Her mind swirled with the possibilities and she felt the warning pangs gripping her stomach like a pincer. She searched in her bag and dug out the pack containing the latest in a long line of treatments. She washed two tablets down with a swig of water. It was the usual story; no-one seemed ready to take responsibility for anything. It was always left to her. Sod Ted Saddler! She wasn't going to end on the dump over some late developing conscience.

She looked out across the park. Far to the West, and down by the Hudson, stood the hotel she'd stayed in fifteen years ago when she'd transferred from the London office. She'd vowed then to live by the park. It would be the benchmark of how far she'd travelled from the despairing towers of Drumchapel on the outer fringes of Glasgow. Even when she was appointed head of Asia Pac, it still made sense to keep a base in the West. She'd held her nerve during the housing crash and pounced on an apartment in one of the best blocks, on one of the finest streets in Manhattan. Prices had then rocketed post-crash. A smart investment and a tangible seal on the past.

So why does it seem such a bloody anti-climax? What now? What's the next target? Is it the man thing again? Who needs it – him? I'm not looking. I've got all the freedom and space I want. If I fancy a temporary wee arrangement, my pals always know someone. Fun without strings. I've got it made, everything I want. Why question its worth?

From her window she could just see the start of her jogging track when she was in town. She recalled another window in another city and a very different view. She snapped the memory shut. An early morning blast through the park would calm the stomach and clear the confusion.

SEVEN

The morning after the car crash with Erin Wishart, Ted sat gazing out his 23rd story office window at the drizzle sweeping in across the East River and drifting through the steel and glass obelisks. He was nursing a mild hangover and wondering if the Ted Saddler that used to inhabit a lesser mound of flesh would have let last night's opportunity go like that. Maybe not, but then he was smarter now. He didn't tilt windmills for a living any longer. A pity though. For a while there he was getting interested, and not just in a pair of laser blue eyes.

He checked her entry online. Older than she looked: 44 last February. But still pretty young to hit the upper echelons of a top bank. She'd had stints in other divisions, gaining plaudits every time. A top computer science degree from Edinburgh University capped with an MBA from Wharton. This girl was smart. Fizzing with energy. A result of the fitness regime? Or was that where she dumped the surplus? He patted his stomach. Maybe he should give it a try.

He was still sceptical about her reasons for approaching him; a banker with a conscience? Was she using him to get back at her boss? Some political manoeuvring to stage a coup? Maybe she was worried about the Fed finding out. Losing her banking licence for being associated with underhand activities? Nah, she could just claim innocence. This guy Stanstead seemed to keep a close lid on his shady dealings.

For the rest of the day he managed to milk something out of the looming scandal in the Japanese banking sector. Normally it wouldn't rate a mention – corruption being 'ten a yen' in his jaundiced eyes – but this one had sex and suicide to spice up the takeover of boardrooms by the Yakuza mob. He made calls, dug through badly translated web sites and hacked out a lively-enough column.

Come 6pm he had his jacket in one hand and was heading to the elevator with a growing thirst when Stan Coleman, City Editor, pitched up out of nowhere with his hands in his pockets. He was trying to look casual, so Ted knew there was a problem. Stan was short, but his fuse was shorter.

'Ted, got a minute?' He looked up at Ted, expecting a yes.

'Sure Stan. Is there a problem with the Japan story? I was just pushing off, you know?'

'Nope. Absent any real news, that is. I'm running a book on how long before the first public denials from their Ministry of Finance. I'm betting the mail box will be full by the morning.'

'No takers here.'

Stan rocked gently on his toes, inspecting Ted from under lowered brows, as if he were peering over half moon glasses. 'We need to talk.'

He took Ted's arm like a child steering a grown up, and walked him back to Ted's cubby hole. Ted dropped back into his seat and Stan took the position of power on the edge of the desk.

'So Ted, how've you been?' His legs swung nonchalantly.

'Stan, I've been fantastic. What's the problem?'

'It's this People's Bank of yours.'

'It's not my bank Stan. I only write about the damned thing. And if you'll recall, you pointed me at the story six months ago.'

'Sure, sure. I'm getting some heat from on high. This is big. The People's Bank philosophy has gone viral. They're saying could be a new model for banking in the West. Like a new diet, for chrissake. Our top guys think we've got the right angle on it. Striking the right tone with healthy scepticism. They think there's a lot more to come, and they want us to make the most of it. Fact is they think this could be a rocky few weeks for the outfit and they want the story in depth.'

'One of those 'top floor' things, huh?'

'It smells like a rerun of the Credit Crunch.'

'Fortunes being built on the back of flaky loans to folk that can't afford to repay them? Yeah, I see that.'

Stan nodded. 'The trial is going to be messy. Dirty linen washed in public. Blood on the walls. We want to be in at the kill. We're going to do a spread. You know the kind of thing; we check out its track record, interview the boss and some of the staff. Get a view from the regulators and some of the competitors. Get some unhappy customers lined up.' He tapped Ted's screen. 'It's getting a lot of attention. Emails, twitter feeds, YouTube mash-ups, etc.'

'OK Stan. So you want me to do some more digging? Call up our guys in Delhi?'

Stan looked down at Ted for a second or two longer than the question really demanded.

'Ted, you need to get really on the pulse with this one. This outfit claims it's solving world hunger and making a profit. Mutually exclusive I think we're agreed? Right? And they're making waves in the West. We want you to go out there and have a look. Get beneath the skin, soak up the local aromas. Get over to India for the build-up and the conclusion of the trial. Give it some real feel you know?'

Ted flipped his seat back so he was half reclining.

'Sorry Stan, I just thought I heard you say I should go to India. You're joking right? I mean that's why we have local correspondents right? Our man in Delhi or Karachi or Timbuktu for chrissake. It's why we invented Skype. You don't really want to send me? Think of the costs. I mean we can do the studio shots, make me look like I'm there. Right?' He was frankly incredulous.

'Ted, you're the name. Folk still recognise you.' He said it like he was amazed. 'We want the Ted Saddler by-line on this. Besides, it's been a while since you were out in the field. Blow the cobwebs away. Get out of the bars and get some sun on you.'

Ted eyed Stan carefully. It's what he wasn't saying that interested him. That, and not looking at him straight. The throwaway comment about his drinking habits had been too casual. Ted knew he hadn't been getting outstanding ratings lately, but hey, everybody goes through a patch, you know? Sometimes the stories just aren't there. You can't invent them. Well yes you can, but that way lies madness and public execution when you're found out.

Maybe he had lost some of his colour; his writing felt like he was drawing blood at times. But that had nothing to do with the booze. He made it a rule never to touch a drop before 6pm – unless it was in the line of duty or weekends. He could still punch out a column on just about anything you care to name. Twenty minutes. Word count on the button. Readable. Which is more than you could say for some of the website jockeys today. They didn't give a damn about grammar, and thought a tweet said it all.

'As a matter of fact Stan, I may have found something. Something that would make the front page. And I don't mean just the city section. This is potentially big. And it's right here in River City.' Stan looked like he'd never seen Guys and Dolls.

'Tell me about it.'

Stan's tone said he'd heard these sort of claims from every jerk with a column to fill.

'I can't say anything right now. But I've got a contact at top level that might be ready to blow up the whole thing.'

'In the People's Bank?'

'Better. Gimme a couple of days and I'll have something for you.'

Which is why Ted stayed on a little bit longer and did some fast finger work on the keyboards. The top level interest Stan mentioned wasn't too unusual but something nagged at Ted's memory. He called up the corporate web site of Global American and clicked on the list of non-executive board members. The usual assembly of the great and the good from other industries and institutes: economists and an emeritus professor from Stanford, the former chair of Pricewaterhouse Coopers and so on. But one name stood out: Martin Lanesborough, Chairman of American News Corporation, the holding company of Ted's own newspaper, the New York Tribune.

Ted thought for a moment then pulled up his email and fired off a note. Erin was a late bird. She agreed to meet at 8.00 the next night, at a cosy dive he knew, up off 82nd and Columbus. It wasn't Le Cirque or any swank restaurant that Erin Wishart might frequent. And almost certainly the wrong side of the park. But it was home turf for Ted. Gave him an edge. High intensity people like Miss Wishart had always figured prominently on his list of people never to have a drink with. He didn't need that kind of pressure. So why did this feel like he was making a date or something?

EIGHT

The three women paused at the southerly entrance to the valley, on the last little rise on the road. The village was a mile away, like a pile of shoeboxes fallen from the shelf of wooded hills rising to the east. Thin ribbons of smoke rose from the boxes as though a big fire smouldered underneath, ready to erupt and destroy everything and everyone. The hard lines of the rooftops were punctuated by the foliage of trees. A little apart from the main village sat a small clutch of huts, with walls of wood and roofs of straw cones. These belonged to the Dalits, the Untouchables.

Where the river used to run a rock-hard groove a hundred feet wide scarred the length of the valley and ran past the foot of the village. Like the cast skin of a giant python. The central planners made the river take a new course, so that higher up the valley it would cut left and join the river on the other side. They said it was to help make the dam work. And when the dam was working everyone would have electricity and fresh water, and the fields would be even better irrigated than before.

None of it happened of course. They built the dam but ran out of money for the water pipes. Great cracks opened up in the mud and will never heal. It made house building and repair much harder. They killed the land and maybe they killed the village too. No one looked that way any more.

For a moment, and without telling the others, each of the three women with her newly opened eyes, felt a pang of shame for their poverty. As they drew closer, the sweet commingled smell of animals, spices, human waste and that special tang of the dung fires wafted at them. A unique combination that separated their village from any other. They would know where they were if they'd been brought here blindfolded. It swept them up in relief and gladness to be back in familiar territory. Shame vanished and all at once they were desperate for their own tiny homes and families.

They thought it was too late to cause a great stir, that they would keep their story till the morning. But their arrival was soon spotted and news travelled like a scalded dog through the shantytown. Women dipped out of their doorways and greeted them with hands clasped together and soft calls of 'namaste'. They wanted to know how it had gone. A few men eyed them cautiously as though wondering what they'd become and how they'd changed after such a trip. They noticed the dust up to the knees, like grey socks, and the tiredness in their gait.

They knew tall Anila and were already wary of her. She was trouble. Hadn't she walked out on her husband? Why did some women mind a beating so much? They saw Divya, thin and wiry, her bare arms lean but muscled, and her fine hands clutching the fold of her sari round her oval face. But all the men's eyes began at and kept returning to the brown and cream figure of Leena. She had a temple dancer's poise and grace, and her body was slim yet rounded. But it was the bright perfection of her almond eyes and lips like a split cherry that sent their blood racing. Men made fools of themselves to see Leena smile.

Some curious children tagged along and a scrawny hound or two sniffed at their legs, turning them into a procession. Goats bleated as they were smacked out of the way and cows lay chewing in the hard shadows. Smoke from early evening cooking fires was already spilling into the street and charging the air. They walked past unmarked and barely delineated streets and alleys. No-one had addresses. Everyone knew everyone else and had a map of the village in their mind, with every hut occupied by a relative or friend or, occasionally, an enemy. The three smiled and returned the *namastes*.

'Fine. Yes, we went to Delhi. Yes, we saw the bank.'

Anila answered for them as she was escorted to her hut by her companions. In a rare moment of spite, she wished Dilip could have been here to see this. How amazed he'd have been! She would have shown him that it wasn't his grand ideas that had come to fruition, but hers. And then the anxiety settled again like a heavy shawl, and her breathing quickened. Sometimes she wondered if she were being made a plaything of Shiva; being set high, just to be cast down even harder.

'We are tired. We will talk at the pumps in the morning,' said Divya from inside her blue hood.

In fact Divya wasn't sure whether she was relieved or not to be home. She missed her two sons of course, and was desperate to see them again. But a peculiar melancholy had taken hold of her. She'd forgotten about the fearful arrival in the city the first night. All she could see was red silk trimmed with gold, and bracelets of gold and silver. The bustle and commotion, and the vitality and excitement. A taste of a life more exotic. A life she might have led but for the vagaries of the gods. The same gods who'd crippled her husband. Divya always presented herself as hard headed and sensible. Maybe that was why her husband thought her so cold. But something in her had been touched by this grand trip, something had stirred and she was afraid either to let it loose or to bury it for good.

Pretty Leena was bursting to tell to her friends. She grinned as she walked.

'You shall see. Oh, you shall see!' she called out.

She thought of her husband, Chandan, and whether he would still be angry with her for setting out on such a wild notion, even though they'd had no other choice. Not since they'd lost their field. Leena knew she could charm him round – that was her greatest strength – but she would have liked him to see her as a sensible business woman as well as his fantasy girl. She conjured images of Chandan bathing her feet and worshipping her as the saviour of the family.

Their weary legs felt the steady gradient as they pushed up

the lane towards Anila's home. They embraced outside Anila's mud-coated brick hut with its wooden door and its two square window holes either side. They helped her shake the dust from her sari and flicked at the coating on her feet and ankles. They were reluctant now to break the bonds and the spell of travelling because the next steps were so terrifying. Their voices carried. The door opened and an old woman stood outlined in the back glow of an oil lamp within. She had a hand on the shoulder of a small girl who squirmed in anxiety and delight at seeing Anila. Her thumb was full in her mouth. Anila turned from her travel companions and bent down and was almost knocked over by her daughter's lunge and tight embrace. She stood up, still holding her small smiling burden, and embraced the old woman.

'We did it Mother. We went to the city and we saw the bank and we got the money. Everything will be better now.' She said it like she believed it. She had to believe it. There was no going back.

The old woman looked at her daughter and searched her face. She had always feared for her daughter, especially since her own husband had died and there was no longer the two of them to control her. There was a spirit in her that seemed to go begging for trouble. There was a look about Anila that her mother hadn't seen for two years. Not since she'd told her she could no longer take her husband's beatings. Even if it meant giving up her reputation and living the rest of her life as poor and excluded as a Dalit. The old woman's face held a look of love and fear. Fear for what her daughter was getting into. Fear that she'd reached too far and that disappointment would follow as surely as tomorrow's sunrise.

NINE

Next day Ted made an effort. He unearthed smarter duds from the reject pile in the spare room and dropped them at the corner laundry before heading into work. He picked them up that evening and found them steamed and pressed, but there had been no time to take out the waistband. Nor had he found time or inclination for a haircut. The best he could do was shower and shave, and comb his mop to almost civilised standards. As he posed in front of the wall mirror in the sitting room, he realised how long it had been since he'd dressed for anyone. Maybe if he'd gone to the trouble more often with Mary? It prompted yet another re-run of their last evening together. . .

From deep in his favourite armchair, he'd been holding out his big arms seeking absolution, salvation. But this was no preacher in front of him.

'We can work on this.' Even he could hear the doubt in his voice.

'We've tried,' she replied.

'Not enough.'

'You can't change, Ted. It's how you are.'

'You used to *like* who I was. What's different? Come on, spit it out.'

Mary stood in the doorway, hands on bony hips, inspecting him. Behind her, bags and boxes lay piled in the hall. None of the other rows had reached this point. A TV ball game droned in the background. It was drizzling outside and growing darker, but no one reached for the light switch.

'You don't want to know.'

She pushed her chin-length black hair behind her ears. He loved her ears.

'I need to.'

It had to be said. Had to be heard. He wasn't going to let her off the hook.

She folded her arms, always a bad sign in these last destructive months.

'What's over there?'

So that's where this was going.

'It's my desk.'

'It's your obsession. What's on your desk?'

'Oh, come on. You know what's on it. Don't blame the damn book.'

'It's been there how long? Eight years? Ten? You've been writing the Great American novel. . .' She carved quote signs in the air. '. . .*forever*, Ted. And you're never going to finish it, far less get it published! You're either at the newsroom or you're at your desk. You haven't been with me in ten – Goddamn – years!'

'If that's all it takes, no problem. Look.'

Ted shot his body out of the embrace of the chair and lumbered over to his desk. He grabbed one of the piles of manuscript and took it, pages fluttering, into the kitchen. He opened the door to the garbage bin. He stuffed the pages in. Called her bluff.

'See! It's done. It's history. I'm all yours.'

He pushed his hair back off his face, and wiped his brow which was already beading with sweat – the aircon in the ancient apartment block had broken for the third time that week. He gave her his best smile, his college boy smile, the smile she'd always found cute. Mary stood looking at him, eyebrows up, hands back on hips.

'I used to be your obsession. But I know when I'm beat. We don't go out, we don't talk.' Her voice hardened. 'We don't *fuck*.' She let the word tarnish the air. 'Besides …'

45

'Besides what?'

'Nothing. Doesn't matter.' She started to put her coat on.

He strode over, put his great paws on her upper arms.

'Tell me.'

She sighed. 'You'd better know. You'll know soon enough.'

She gazed straight into the eyes that were already screwed up – a kid knowing it was about to get smacked. The truth guessed long ago.

'There's somebody waiting for me. Downstairs.'

It was almost a relief. He dropped his hands, dropped his shoulders like he was going in for one of the tackles he was famous for at high school.

'I knew it.'

'What did you expect?'

'Support? Loyalty?'

She took a long look at him.

'Ted, I used to find it attractive. What you did. Your journalism was a fine thing. But you could have been chief editor. Taken that job with CNN. Fox even. Made decent money. Moved out of this pit. But that wasn't enough. The day you won that goddamn Pulitzer, you thought you were the next Updike. Journalism wasn't enough. *I* wasn't enough.' She paused for breath. 'Well, I found someone who does think I'm enough. We have fun!'

Her voice softened. 'I haven't had fun in. . . oh shit, you know, Ted. I want a life.'

Her bullets drove home, leaving him paralysed and bleeding in his comfortable chair. Hearing her last words long after she'd gone. Long after the night fell. Long after the ball game was over. It wasn't even about losing Mary. Sitting in his dark room, lit intermittently by passing cars that swung their beams through his first floor window searching for a man of substance, and not finding one. Sitting, thinking that a man could do something about his anger or his laziness or his habit of getting drunk with the boys on a Friday night. But this wasn't fair. What could a man do about his dreams?. . .

Ted's sartorial efforts found favour with the patron of the eponymously named Giovanni's Room, a tile-floored Italian where the pasta was home-made and the Chianti came in chipped stone pitchers. Every time he'd seen the macho, happily married owner, Ted wondered if he'd ever read Baldwin's novel, far less identified with the gay barman.

Ted had arrived early and described his date to Giovanni. Maybe he overdid it. Instead of Ted's usual bare table for one, near the back, a table à *deux* was set up in the window. The rough wood top was camouflaged with fresh linen and crowned with a vase holding a single rose. Giovanni clearly hoped to draw in more customers when they saw the quality of the diners. Or at least half of them.

As the restaurant filled, Ted pretended to be engrossed in his phone, wishing he could ditch the rose and praying she wouldn't stand him up. When he saw the cab draw up he shot to his feet. Giovanni beat him to the restaurant door and glad-handed Erin Wishart into his parlour, only just refraining from kissing her hand. The awkward couple were shepherded to their table, Ted trying – and failing – to look nonchalant, as if Erin was simply one of a long line of top drawer dinner dates. In truth she was the first – of any sort – in months, and Ted could only hope this would turn out better than the night of the stalker from Accounts.

There was no doubting her presence. He was aware of other diners checking her out. The soft brogue was an aural magnet. That and the poise that comes from wearing Armani. Or just knowing you can afford Armani. Erin Wishart displayed the firm arms and shoulders of a woman who worked out but managed to keep her feminine curves. Ted appreciated that. He was old school. Another point of departure with Mary who'd fought a permanent war against anything above size zero.

'So what changed your mind?' she was asking.

Her question reminded Ted why they were here, and that his job probably depended on getting something juicy out of this.

'A little guy with a big title. It was put to me that maybe I should be looking harder at this story.'

'Sounds like we both know pressure.'

'This came from the top. Possibly from a certain Martin Lanesborough, chair of our holding company, and –'

'– one of our board directors. You noticed.'

Ted tried to ignore the irony in her voice; tongue-lashed by the Queen of Scots.

'The Tribune wants a bigger spread on this bank.' He made quote marks in the air. 'A clash of banking cultures post Crash'. Stan Coleman – my boss – even suggested I go to India. Thinks it'll give the story zing. Can you believe it?'

He waited for the shared laughter. It didn't come.

'Why don't you?'

'We don't do that sort of stuff nowadays. It's why we invented the phone and the internet. Anyway, what am I going to get out of it other than heat rash and malaria?'

'Zing? You'll survive. I do it all the time. Seen one of these?'

Erin dug into her purse and pulled out a slim black card. It said Concierge Key, American Airlines. Ted's eyes widened.

'My God. How many air miles?'

'They don't say. It's invite only. But minimum seems to be 3 million.'

'So, I'm a wuss. I'm willing to get under the skin of this story, but I need your help. I'm even ready, God help me, to go to Delhi or Kolkata or whatever they're calling them now, if that's what it takes. I need substance.'

He sat back and waited. Her face showed a dashed hope, then a kind of resignation. They broke off and made a fast pass at the menu. Ted had forgotten when he'd last seen one. His habit was a pitcher of red and the steaming pasta special.

Tonight, Ted broke with tradition, and ordered the veal and a bottle of Barolo. Giovanni smiled. Erin went for fish, broiled plain, no sauce and mineral water. During all this he could see her mind sizing things up. Then came resolution. She pushed back, clutching the table edges with both hands, about to address the board.

'OK, Ted. Look, I had a bad night and a bad day for that matter. If you hadn't called me I would have called you. I'm willing to do what I can – within reason.'

'Why? What's really behind this? I'm struggling with your democracy needs the People's Bank thesis. And you're too young to be having a midlife, Erin.'

She nodded. She knew she had to give him more. But she wasn't ready to talk about the deeper fears stirred up by her intimate knowledge of Stanstead and what José had told her. She played her first card.

'Ever been to Scotland?'

'Nope. Always meant to. Heard you've got neat golf courses. All those links.'

'None in Drumchapel, I can assure you. It's a high rise housing estate north west of Glasgow. They flattened the old central slums like the Gorbals and moved the people out to new tower blocks.'

'I've heard of the Gorbals.'

'Lovely red sandstone tenements. Once. For a population of ten per cent of the numbers in the '30's. An ant hill of refugees and unemployed. No plumbing, no care. But plenty of heart. Rather than do them up, the council tore them down and built new slums outside the city – without shops, pubs, playgrounds or soul.'

'Smart work.'

'Blame Corbusier.'

'This Drumchapel – it's where you grew up? Slum kid, eh?'

'Not exactly. More a riches to rags story. My folks had a nice wee house in a Glasgow suburb. Let's just say things went off

49

the rails. We ended up in a crumbling tower in the middle of nowhere. I was six when we moved.'

'Culture shock?'

She nodded. 'Slums, gangs, drugs, the stink of urine in the lifts – when they worked.' She shuddered. 'The whole bit. I've put as much distance between me and that life as I possibly could.'

'You're living the American Dream. So what?'

'I travel a lot in the Far East. Outside the five star hotels, down among the ordinary folk, it's just Drumchapel or Castlemilk or Easterhouse. Only warmer. You don't forget. Have you ever had to pawn something to buy food? Ever taken a pay day loan to pay the gas bill? Outfits like People's Bank are needed. Otherwise the sharks will get you.'

For the briefest of moments he caught a look on her face; yearning came closest to describing it. The first crack in the corporate veneer. He really needed to reset his compass on this lady and this situation. Bring him proof of time travel or God, and he'd believe it.

'I thought People's Bank *were* the sharks.'

'That's because you haven't done your homework.'

Ouch. 'So this is banker's guilt.'

'Sarcasm runs off me. I'm not embarrassed to have a conscience. How about you?'

The blue eyes bored into his. He emptied his glass and poured some more.

'How about your colleagues. Get 'em together and mount a boardroom coup or something.'

'We never get the chance. I'm only here for a couple of weeks during quarterly meetings. And we never have downtime. To be honest, I'm not sure I trust any of the others. One of Warwick's ways of controlling us is to keep each of us in the dark about what the others are doing. Do you have any idea what it's like to be afraid of your boss?'

Ted sucked at his teeth. 'Some idea maybe.'

'He picks us off one by one. Makes each of us think we're his right hand man and swears us to secrecy. Bribes us with promises and bonuses. Then he makes an example of one of us at meetings. An uncanny knack of picking on whoever's got something to hide. We're all spineless. I'm disgusted with myself and with my colleagues if you must know.'

Ted emptied the bottle and caught her look. Teetotallers were so prissy.

'Fine, gimme facts, evidence; documents, emails, tapes. If you're going to be a whistle blower, you need to do it properly.'

Erin snorted. 'Like Mission Impossible? Burgle Warwick's office at midnight? That kind of thing. Seriously?'

'I didn't say it was easy.'

'Our office is thick in security measures. Everything is in silos and covered in passwords and need-to-know measures.'

Ted had been thinking about this all day and weighing up the odds.

'Erin, there's a guy I know. He's got special talents around computers. He makes them talk, sing – hell, sit up and beg. He's weird and operates on a very fine line between legal and deserving of twenty years in the pen. I don't know if he's still around, nor on which side of the bars, but it's worth a call.'

'A hacker? Christ. None of the Wikileaks crew, I trust?'

He smiled and shook his head.

'No loose cannons here. I'll give him a call and then you go meet him and see what you can come up with. That is, if he'll take a call from me.' Ted looked guiltily at her. 'After our last outing, once the excitement died down, I kind of let things drift. And before you know it ten years goes by. What do you think?'

A frown was gathering across her eyes. She looked down at her barely touched fish and then straightened her shoulders.

'What would I have to do?'

'I don't know. Maybe slip him a password or something.'

'How could I trust him not to milk us?'

'Meet him and decide.'

'As an officer of the bank I could get twenty years.'

'You have to decide how much this matters to you.'

He said nothing, just waited. She nodded her head a couple of times as though she was agreeing with something inside herself.

'What skin are *you* putting into this game, Mr Saddler?'

He sighed. 'I'll see if I can find my passport and go check out People's Bank on their home turf. God help me. I'll also put out feelers to see who knows what in the market. GA can't do it all without bumping into other folks.' He paused and held her eyes.

Her voice took on her customary confidence and certainty. The thinking was done, the decision taken. Next came execution. That's how she operated.

'It's the least you should do. OK, Ted, I'll talk to your hacker friend. No promises. But you and I shouldn't meet anymore. I'll have him set up untraceable email addresses for you and me. Private cell phones. I'll text you a number. Anything he finds, I'll have him send directly to you.'

Ted agreed, perhaps a little more enthusiastically than he felt. Despite her pressure tactics, he wouldn't have minded a return match at Giovanni's Room. Especially if he could guarantee approbation from her questioning eyes. It had been a while since he cared what a woman thought of him.

TEN

As usual, in the comparative cool of early morning, the women drifted down the twisting central street and gathered round the two water pumps and the wooden trough. They stepped daintily over the nuggets of goat dung. The Dalit women hadn't swept the area yet. The five spreading neem trees ringed three sides of the small central square and formed a bank of shade for much of the day. The trees were laden with fat seeds, soon to be harvested.

The neems had stood for as long as anyone could remember. Some said they were the survivors of a forest that used to fill the valley. Younger versions of this great oak-like tree had been nurtured all over the village. Even now, in the hottest time of the year, with water so scarce that they had to crank the hand pumps for almost a minute to get the first splash of water, the trees held their leaves. They were a talisman for the survival of the village. Though the river had been taken away, so long as the neems still stood, the village would continue.

It was a full turn-out – maybe forty in all – and most got there early to grab favoured spots between the roots of the trees. Even a few of the Dalits had now shown up, but were standing well to the back of the main group so as not to offend. Everyone was trying hard to look casual, and talked of their men or their children or the new sari one had made. No-one mentioned the great journey of Divya and Leena and Anila, or discussed what they might have done and seen. They knew how to savour news.

Some passed the time usefully by taking their turn on the handles of the pumps, sending gurgling gouts of water into their friends' vessels. But when finally – at the breaking point of patience it seemed – the last of the three wanderers arrived with her plastic pail and earthen pot, pretence vanished and they quickly squatted in a tight ring around the story tellers and waited. The others deferred to Anila. It had been her idea and she had pushed the others and had dared them to do it.

'Well, we did it. After all. We went to New Delhi and we saw the bank and we got the loan.'

There was a sigh of collective disappointment. This was no way to tell a story. Too fast, and without any build up. Details were needed, to relish and discuss today and for weeks and years after. The time the three women went to the city of sin and came back unscathed with a sack of gold.

One said, 'Come now Anila, tell us about the journey. How did you get to Delhi? Was it hard and was the train very dreadful and full of eve-teasers and loose women?' A few giggled. 'And where did you sleep?' There was a chorus of approval. This was what they wanted. And if it had to be coaxed out of the three, then so be it! They would ask questions until they had got all that they wanted.

Anila saw how it would go, and smiled to herself. Divya and Leena were bursting to shower their friends with all the details. She therefore thought it better if she told the story. At least it would have a beginning, a middle and an end. Leena would have them all over the place and Divya would forget and have to be reminded. So she began. . .

'Well… there is no bank round here.' She waved her arm round the village for effect. It drew giggles. As if a bank would come here.

'We heard that the People's Bank was putting offices in all the towns and villages, but we are not yet on their plan. So we had to go to the main bank in Delhi. We met a manager of the bank, Mr Kapoor, who was very kind. Soon there will be a bank person in this area, and she – they told us they prefer to give the jobs to women, can you believe it? – she will collect the repayment of our loan every week and will find if other women want loans. As long as there are a group of at least three women who want to borrow and they have a good reason then they can

54

get the money without collateral.'

'What is collateral?' asked one.

Divya answered proudly, 'It's when you have to promise to give them something in case you can't pay the loan back. Other banks would take our donkey or our field or our house. That is collateral.'

Anila shook her head to confirm her friend's grasp of the complexity of the banking system. 'We said that the three of us had different ideas. But it was all work we were already doing.'

Divya explained, 'I told Mr Kapoor that my husband was crippled in an accident and now I had to support the family. I wanted to buy two cows and sell the milk and make cheese and sell the cheese. I told him I already worked for one of the rich men in the village and was very good at looking after cows but I only got paid in milk. So I could never save any money to buy a cow or even a goat.'

Leena blushed harder and told them, 'I said I wanted to buy the little field that my husband and I rent from Mr Patwardhan. Then we would be able to buy more seeds and plant more vegetables and maybe sell some to our neighbours or other villages.'

Now it was Anila's turn. 'I was planning to buy a mobile phone and rent it out. But as you know, the elders have banned all women from using phones.' She lowered her voice, 'in case we are talking to men.' That caused giggles and a rustle of comment through the ranks. Anila went on, 'So, you know my mother and I make stools. And every day we have to get a loan from the money lender to buy the reeds and the straight wood. You know how the money lender works: we have to buy the wood from him and sell the stools to him. And he only gives us 50 rupees for each one. It is just enough to buy food and pay off his loan every day. So we can never stop. And we can never save anything.'

She saw the head shaking all round. 'If we just had a small loan at a good rate we could buy the reeds and the wood direct from the wood gatherer. Then we could sell the stools to the agent and not have to go through the money lender. That way we would keep all the profits and save some money and get a proper roof for our house.'

The listeners were hushed by the audacity of these women. To think in such grand terms! To go all the way to Delhi and ask a bank for a loan. To have such notions! Some thought they were above their station and no good would come of it. Others put the ideas away in the back of their minds. If this bank really did send a person and if it was all as good as Anila said it would be, then maybe. . .

For over an hour the seated women held the three of them there until they had the main points of the story thoroughly understood. They milked every detail of the city crowds and the traffic. They drained from them all the smells and excitement and noise. They saw themselves sleeping on the station platform of Gwalior, huddled together, their saris swept over them like gay shrouds. They lived the journey vicariously, mile by mile, and marvelled at the brazenness and resourcefulness of the travellers.

They would now digest what they'd heard and talk about it with their closest friends and relations and then they would ask for more details. And the cycle would continue until their curiosity was sated. Soon there would be more to chew over; the women had gone all the way to Delhi and had come back with piles of money, but they still had to make the money work. And everyone knew how difficult it would be with the men. They would not like it to happen. Making money was a man's job.

As Anila finished her tale she felt the terrors return. She didn't feel brave. She knew she was standing up against tradition and power. She was now in more debt than she could ever have imagined. She owed the bank 1000 rupees, or as Mr Kapoor had described it, nearly 20 dollars in American money, which was how the bank operated internationally. She had to pay all this back within a year at 20% interest. The weekly collections of 23 Rupees including interest would begin in a few weeks and apart from the loan itself, neither she nor her mother between them had enough to buy food for more than a week. Because of the trip, she'd lost almost a full week's earnings – tiny though the amount was – but at least it had been a certainty. Moreover, the money lender would be very displeased and would refuse to lend her any more or would lend her at a rate of 50% per week!

She'd gambled everything – including her mother's savings – on the plan. What if the wood gatherer refused to sell her the reeds? What if the agent refused to buy the stools she made? What if the village men ganged up and made the elders order her not to get above herself? Like the ban on phones for women.

Anila had asked both the wood gatherer and the agent who came each week to pick up the chairs, if they were prepared to work directly with her. Both had joked about it and told her not to be so silly. Then when they saw she was serious, they laughingly agreed to deal with her direct. They were sceptical, but at the same time they were practical men, she hoped. Well, she would soon see. The agent was not due for his weekly trip for another five days. But the wood gatherer was due to arrive today and she would approach him with her offer. He came every day in a truck that blew filthy smoke everywhere and made bangs like a firecracker.

Anila stood up, and rubbed at the muscles in her stomach. Despite the crowd she felt alone. She hadn't told them she'd worn the regalia of marriage during the journey in the hopes of deflecting the eve-teasers. Nor about pausing under the skinned branches of a tree on the way back so that she could take out a cloth and wipe the Sindoor from her forehead and parting. Nor how she'd laughed, as Leena helped her to unhook her necklace, to show she was glad to have the weight off. In one sense she had felt free again without it. In another, it had been a reminder of the lost years behind her and the empty ones still to come.

She embraced Leena and Divya who seemed to be going through a similar turmoil. She saw by the length of the shadows that her first encounter would take place in an hour or so with the wood gatherer. She would go home and try to eat a little something and have a drink and then go and see if she could make the first part of her plan work. She hoped she wouldn't be sick.

She was half way back to her hut when the money lender accosted her.

ELEVEN

Mr Chowdury had been waiting for Anila behind one of the huts. With him was Mr Bhandariti, the village sarpanch, the headman. They stood in her path. The money lender had a very single-minded approach to life; money was the only thing that mattered, the more the better. Anyone who got in the way of his making more money – or much worse, losing him money – was ground underfoot. Mr Chowdury's financial antennae had been twitching for weeks ever since he'd heard the rumours of the wickedness planned by this woman. It was scarcely credible that anyone, far less a woman, should be threatening his monopoly of borrowing in Chandapur. It went against the order of things. He seethed with a sense of injustice.

Anila's breath stopped. She tried to look nonchalant. She put her water jugs down.

'Namaste, Mr Chowdury,' she said clasping hands and bowing politely to the money lender and the headman. 'And Mr Bhandariti? Did you want to talk to me? I am going home to my mother and my daughter with water.' Anila showed them her two brimming plastic jugs.

Chowdury gave her a perfunctory namaste in return, as custom demanded, but he threw his hands away from himself in annoyance. 'Yes, we wanted to talk to you. You are right we wanted to talk to you!' Mr Chowdury was quickly getting himself furious. He seemed to have been working on his anger for some time.

Mr Bhandariti was feeling more uncomfortable by the minute. He wasn't sure why he'd been dragged into this but wanted out of it as fast as possible and with minimum fuss.

'Now, now Mr Chowdury. We do not want a big scene at this time. Mrs Jhabvala, we wanted to ask a few questions that is all. Do you mind if we do that?'

Anila saw the sarpanch's discomfort and grew a little more confident.

'Why did you not come to my house then? Why are you stopping me in the lane like this? You have no right.'

'See! See I told you! She is acting up, she is above us all now! She has been off to Delhi to set up in business against me! That's what she's up to! I tell you she is trying to ruin me, this woman.'

The sarpanch's distress was growing. He and his colleagues on the village council had never recovered their authority since the disaster of the dam. They had taken a cautious line throughout the planning stage and had kept the unruly elements from mounting an unseemly protest against the State officials. Why, they even had a minister visit them. How would it have looked if they had let protesters wave banners at him and shout at him? As though suggesting that the minister was lying to them? The elders had pounded out the official line – promises of reparation and better drinking water – long after it was clear that neither was going to happen. But what else could they have done? And they had been well paid for their stance. Yet here was another issue that seemed to be unpicking the fabric of the village life. Damn the woman for not staying with her husband, and damn her for not knowing her place!

'Mr Chowdury, please! Mrs Jhabvala – Anila, is this true that you are setting up your own money lending business? And that you will be taking the clients of Mr Chowdury? The village elders cannot allow one of our esteemed villagers to be treated with disrespect and to be ill-used in this way. What do you have to say for yourself?'

Anila looked at the two men. The money lender was red in the face and clutched his long stick as though he wanted to strike her with it. He was dressed like a poor man, for all his hidden riches. The sarpanch was tall and grey haired but despite his pomp he was nervous. Anila had expected encounters like this and was steeled for them. But she had not expected such an accusation. She stood up straight and faced the men. The injustice of the lie gave her strength.

'Yes, I went to Delhi. But what you say is nonsense. I went to the People's Bank and got a loan.'

Chowdury cut in excitedly, 'You see, you see! She admits it!'

'I got a loan for my own use. I got a loan to let me buy good wood and cane from the wood gatherer. And my mother and I will make the chairs now and we will sell them to the agent. And we will do all this without going through you Mr Chowdury. That is what you really fear, isn't it? It means you won't get the fat profit from selling the chairs I make. That's what you really care about it, isn't it?'

As she said this, Anila knew that every word was a brick, and she was building a wall higher and higher between herself and any future loans from Chowdury. If she was desperate and if this bold enterprise of hers didn't work, then there would be no going back. She was amazed at her own effrontery and even more amazed at the feeling of confidence that was beginning to burn through her. However crazy this idea was, it was her idea and she was taking her own destiny in her own hands. For the first time in her life Anila tasted freedom. She found it a heady liquor.

Mr Bhandariti was torn. He could see trouble no matter which way he went. All he could do was to appear even-handed so that there would be no accusations of taking sides when this came before the council, as he was certain it would. He turned to the money lender.

'Is this true Mr Chowdury? Is this what is really behind the accusations? Anila is entitled to borrow money – I suppose – from whom she wants. It is up to her. If she does not want to borrow money from you, we cannot make her.'

'You don't understand! This is not the end of it. You will see. I know she has plans to take my business away from me. I will be ruined! Then, who will support the village with loans for a new well or seed for next year's crops? Tell me that?'

Mr Bhandariti felt the soft mud gripping his ankles again. He was speechless in indecision. Anila saw her chance.

'Can I go now please sirs? My mother and daughter are waiting for the water.'

The sarpanch stood aside with relief, the money lender with unsuppressed fury, as she gathered up her water jugs and walked past with her head up. Inside her head, a thought was stirring, put there by Chowdury himself. What if the bank did send an official here? And what if they offered more people good loans. Perhaps Mr Chowdury was right after all? Maybe he was smart enough to see what could become of him? Anila smiled to herself in a rare moment of simple and malicious joy at the amazing workings of karma.

TWELVE

Erin Wishart had never walked the streets of the Lower East Side before. Her driver had sometimes skirted the run-down tenements and the shuttered shops on the way to FDR Drive or the Queenstown Tunnel for JFK. But she'd never stopped, and certainly never gone there with a purpose.

'Ok lady. Here we are. Sure this is where you want?'

The Yellow Cab pulled up at the corner of 2nd and Delancey. Erin got out into the flattening heat of Manhattan summer. The smell of burst black bags swept over her in a sweet embrace. She'd left work early to change out of office uniform. She deliberately dressed down, but maybe not far enough. Jeans and light blouse, baseball cap and dark glasses hid her wary eyes. She paid the driver and waited till he'd driven off before reaching inside her shoulder bag. She walked down Delancey glancing at the numbers on the three and four story tenements. She crossed over. There. Number 1025, third floor. A dark blue door.

She paused uncertainly. The street smells were pricking at her nose. She remembered another door, a brown door with a broken glass panel, the cracked and blistered entrance to her new home. Staring up at the moth-eaten tower, terrified of going in, clutching her raggedy doll and her schoolbag. Wondering what she'd find behind the door. Stepping into the sordid reek of careless humanity. . .

She blinked and dismissed the past. She climbed the four steps and looked at the panel of names and buzzers. She pressed the top one, just below what looked like a fish-eye camera. There was no voice, simply a buzz of someone unlocking the door. She pushed and it opened.

She stepped into a dingy hall and pulled off the baseball cap and glasses. Light flooded the passage and the stairway ahead of her. Her feet made creaking sounds as she climbed up and round the spiral. By the third floor she was breathing hard and stopped on the landing till her chest calmed. She looked around at the three silent doors. Each bore a letter; G, H, and J. She stepped towards H and pushed the bell. She felt she was being watched. She spotted the little camera in the corner of the ceiling. Once again the door clicked and moved open. A high and amused voice came from deep inside.

'Come in, Miss Wishart. Come in.'

'Mr Feldstein? Is this you?' she called as she walked tentatively over the threshold.

'You want it should be somebody else? Come in.'

There was a short hall and then Aladdin's cave. Or perhaps a Tardis. The room was vast, more than seemed possible from the layout in her mind of the top three apartments. Light spilled in from windows in front and back. It was furnished in sumptuous and dazzling fabrics. A riot of reds and blues and rich browns. Persian carpets on dark stained wooden boards. The walls pink. A strong smell of incense tarted the air.

But in the centre of the room, drawing the eye helplessly towards it, was a pool with a central fountain. Water jetted out of the over-sized penis of a golden cherub who stood in truly gay abandon on top of his plinth. Glints of silver and black in the pool became fish. They broke the surface, gawping with their rubbery mouths. Her own mouth turned up in a grin.

She felt someone examining her. Tearing her eyes away from the centrepiece, she found him in the corner. A huge man, much bigger than the voice suggested, sat in a squashed leather swivel chair studying her. He was surrounded by banks of screens and several keyboards on top of a desk that fitted into the corner and wrapped itself part way around his bulk.

Erin fought away unfair comparisons with Jabba the Hutt. This man's eyes sparkled with human intelligence. He sported a small twist of hair under his bottom lip. His ears were studded with jewels. Small hands lay crossed on his dome-like belly as he reclined in his chair. He wore a long multi-coloured gown that shrouded his bulk from neck to feet.

'Mr Feldstein, this is quite a place you have.'

'Well I think so.' He was the only one whose views mattered. 'What do you think of Puck?'

Erin fought for a suitable response. 'He's – charming.'

She walked half way into the room towards him and stood by the tinkling pool. She gazed around, knowing he was looking for approbation. It wasn't too hard. She knew the real thing when she saw it. Though the clutter and confusion wasn't her taste, the furnishings and the art were top bracket.

'You're wondering how a place this big fits into one of these tiny apartments, mmm?'

'Well, yes. I can't reconcile. . .' She waved her hands round the room.

'There are no other apartments. The doors you saw outside are all locked up. I bought them all and knocked a few walls down.'

But if he had the money to live like this, why in god's name would he choose to live here and not up town? Though they might have something to say about a pool in the living room, she supposed. As if reading her mind:

'I like it here. The Upper East is so cut off you know? I always feel myself shrivelling when I go up there.' His big body shivered with the memory. 'Like my soul was being eaten, you know? All those tight faces and tight asses. And anyway, can you imagine me getting past one of those boards? Those priggish little creatures inspecting me to see if I came up to their standards? My dear, it's so not me.'

Erin laughed. She'd faced those tests herself and had had to bite back acid retorts to questions about her personal life. She learned later she could have told them she liked throwing sex and cocaine parties in the lobby and her accent would still have got her through.

'It's their loss, Mr Feldstein.'

'Shall we do the first name thing? I'm Oscar. You're Erin, and a long way from home. If I'd known, I'd have worn my kilt.'

A laugh broke from her. 'Glasgow, ages ago. I'm fine with Erin. Do you really have a kilt?'

'Royal Stewart. Now why did that naughty boy Theodore Saddler want you to see me?'

'I pointed him at a story. He wanted proof. He said you'd helped before. Said you were the man to turn to for – this sort of thing.' She finished lamely.

'This sort of thing?' He smiled and swivelled round, sweeping his big hand across the bank of screens behind him.

'I guess so.'

'Let's have coffee – make that tea – and you can tell me all about it, my dear. Sit here.' He pointed to a massive soft chair near his desk. He turned and touched a screen.

'Albert, can you bring us some tea please. I think,' he eyed Erin carefully, 'some Earl Grey. Thank you, Albert.'

Erin had sunk into the folds of the chair and was beginning to explain her situation when a door in the far side of the room slid back. In came a muscly young man with a tight face, and hair pulled back in a pony tail. He was carrying a tray loaded with florid china. He set it down on the low table between Oscar and Erin. He eyed her carefully, and minced out without a word.

'Thank you Albert. Such a treasure,' he said to his retreating back.

Erin sipped from her cup.

'Oscar, before we go any further, it would really help me to know a bit about you. How you and Ted worked together? Etcetera. Do you mind?'

'Etcetera indeed. Well let me say that I'm very angry with Mr Pulitzer Prize. We were so close and I gave him such fantastic stories. And then I don't hear from him for ten years. Ten years! I told him when he called. I told him, Theodore Saddler, you've got a nerve calling me up after all this time. I have a good mind not to help you. I'm trying to stay out of trouble, I said. I certainly don't need to have loud and ugly NYPD boys come knocking on my door again. All that boring interviewing and shouting. And I certainly don't want to see the inside of those grubby little cells again. I mean, I like my comfort.'

'So you won't help us?'

Relief flooded Erin. She could walk away. She'd tried.

'I need to know what you're up to and whose little secrets we're planning to reveal. My skills my dear, are all in these.' He held up his fat fingers and waggled them at her. 'The last time they had an outing with your Theodore, they dug up lots of little gems about Senator Joshua Farmer that the good senator and the good people of Idaho wished had never come to light.'

'Farmer? That was years ago wasn't it? Something about a porn ring and buying other senators? The papers were full of it.'

'Almost ten years ago. Porn, and drugs and extortion and blackmail. What makes the world go round. The good senator had a lot of interesting hobbies. I think he's still doing time. And that's what Theodore got his prize for.' Oscar mused. 'Now, what are you and Ted up to?'

Her stomach knotted again. Before she'd arrived, Erin had vowed to reveal as little as possible about herself and the bank and Warwick Stanstead. But it was like talking to an old girlfriend. She took a breath and found herself unburdening about her boss and his manic drive and massive ego.

'Is he a user?' Oscar asked, his eyes searching her face and getting his answer before she said it.

'How did you. . .? I mean. . .'

'Let's just say his behaviour is familiar. And it kind of goes with the territory. How bad?'

'I don't know. He was into coke for a while. Recreational, he said. Then he stopped.'

'Hmmm. It's hard to stay at the fun level. But tell me about this other bank. The goody two-shoes bank.'

She told him about the People's Bank and what it was doing and how she thought it was being undermined by her bank. And she told him more than she'd planned about herself and her late-flowering morality.

'My girlfriends today – those you can fit into a 24/7 life – are some help. They hear me out, dole out sympathy, then we get back to things like who's heading to the Hamptons this weekend. They're not shallow or don't care. But it's one of those problems that doesn't have an answer. Men always have to find a solution. Change your job, take up running, dye your hair, come to bed. I've heard them all. If it had been that easy I'd have come up with my own.'

'Men are such bastards, my dear,' he said complicitly.

'So, will you help?' She felt strangely liberated by her disclosures to this extraordinary stranger, as though she'd just paid for an hour's therapy.

'Oh, I think so. I think these terrible tools,' he held up his fingers in front of his face, 'need an outing. Justice to be defended, the poor to be helped, the righteous to be exalted, the wicked slapped down. Yes, I think I'll help.' He dropped his hands into his copious lap again.

'And to be clear, Oscar – all we're looking for is some evidence of the dirty tricks. Some emails or the like. You won't go into the customer files or the bank's accounting systems.'

'Cross my heart. Besides, I'm sure your office systems are completely separate from your operational.'

'Completely.'

'There you go. I'm good. But I'm not that good.'

Her face showed her relief.

'And, Erin dear, if we find anything interesting, what will you do with it?'

'Leverage? Let's see what we come up with.'

'I like the 'we' my dear. I'll need your help.'

'I thought you'd kind of do it from here. . .'

'Oh, we'll collect here. This will be our repository. But we need a teensy bit of inside help to get us going.'

'This isn't going to land me in jail, Oscar?'

'You won't feel a thing. No trace. No evidence. And in return. . .'

'What do you charge?'

'Oh you silly thing! I don't do this sort of stuff for money. This is fun! I don't need any more money. All I want is a promise.'

'What sort of promise?'

'That you'll do me a favour some day. I may never ask. But if I do, whatever it is, you'll do it. Is that fair?'

She laughed. 'That's too open-ended. I mean you could ask for something completely outrageous or illegal or impossible. Like Rumpelstiltskin.'

Oscar was amused. 'I'm glad you like *fairy* stories. Don't worry your pretty little head. You're not my type dear. And the favour won't be so awful, I assure you. Ask Ted. Do we have a deal?'

Erin was beginning to feel she was striking too many deals lately, all of them taking her further into the quicksand of deviousness and deceit.

'It's a deal. Now what?'

Oscar glanced at the Dali clock oozing down the wall. 'We're between lunch and supper. Let's do high tea. I'm sure Albert can conjure some salmon and cucumber sandwiches. And you can tell me all you know about your head office systems.'

THIRTEEN

It wasn't unusual for Erin Wishart to be working Saturday mornings. It happened most weekends. The doorman at the side doors of Global American saluted her and wished her a good day. Using her pass card, she made her way up in the lifts to the executive floor on level 48 of GA Tower. She wandered round the corridors checking she had the place to herself. All the executive offices, like hers, were locked.

She swiped her pass, typed in the code and stepped inside her office. As usual, her heart lifted and she was drawn to the window. Straight ahead, she had a clear line of sight to *Liberty* far off in the bay. The day was fine, with a heat haze already building up. The New Jersey shoreline was blurred and out of focus, as though a muslin curtain had been dragged across it. Inevitably, her gaze was drawn to the right. She wished she'd taken more notice all those years ago; she could never quite locate the exact spot where the Twin Towers had dominated the skyline. Another regret. Now the Freedom Tower cut the air and glistened provocatively; try it again if you think you're hard enough.

She turned away and walked round, touching things, and realised she might be saying goodbye. Was this how it began? The slide? She sat down at her white ash desk and wished her dad had been able to see this. Would he have been impressed or censorious? It depressed her that she didn't know the answer, not for sure. But she had a sneaking feeling that some of his drunken sermonising had stuck after all. Or why else was she doing this?

She touched the edge of her desk and her computer screen slid up into view. A panel opened and her keyboard lifted up. The screen swirled and settled.

'Password please.'

The voice was female and friendly. Sexy even. Why did Scarlet Johansson need the money? Erin typed in *lochlomond* with zeroes for the Os. The picture cleared and brought up her preferred icons and layout. Erin fumbled in her purse and pulled out a memory stick. She put it on the desk, played with it for a bit, then got up and paced back and forth. Why was she really doing all this? Was it really worth the risk?

Oscar had explained that the first task his software performed was to create a safe area, shielded from all firewalls and bug detection code, for his code to operate in. It would be like an invisible cloak thrown over a corner of her drive, or like the camouflage on a stealth bomber. She perfectly understood the approach. But her computer science degree had taught her scepticism. What if the whole bloody system crashed and they traced it to her? What if it triggered a complete shut down and she got locked in until the cops led her off in cuffs?

She sat down, took a huge breath and slid the stick into the USB slot.

'Please wait.' An icon appeared on the screen showing speed of loading.

'Software accepted and loaded. Activate?'

She swallowed. 'Activate.'

A trumpet volley blared. She jumped and jabbed the sound key to lower the volume. When her heart slowed down she smiled. It was the William Tell overture. The screen cleared and a figure galloped towards her on a huge white horse. They crashed to a halt in a swirl of dust and the camera zoomed in on the head sporting a white cowboy hat and a black mask.

'Tonto! My trusty friend! You summoned me?'

The voice was high-pitched and camp. Oscar's. A grin spread across Erin's face. It would turn into hysteria if she didn't control it. Her dad would have loved this. He'd made her sit through some early Lone Ranger reruns. She knew the response.

'Yes, Kemosabe.'

She knew the software was doing a voice recognition check based on the words she'd recorded at Oscar's.

'Tonto, have you scouted ahead?'

'Yes, Kemosabe. The way is clear.'

'Mount up Tonto. It's time to ride! Hi-Yo Silver. Away!'

The face moved away and became a full shot of the rider dressed in white and wearing an old-style six-gun on his hip. He caught up the reins of the majestic white horse and made it rear on its hind legs. He waved his hat in the air and the horse landed and galloped off into the distance to the strains of the overture.

Erin sat back and waited. Her stomach was playing up again. The ache and the rumblings were sawing for attention. She'd forgotten her pills, so she took some water from her fridge and sat sipping it and gazing sightlessly out of her window. A few minutes later her screen flickered and she turned in time to see the horseman galloping up in his dust cloud. He leapt down and strode towards her. Oscar's masked face filled the screen.

'Mission accomplished, Tonto. But I'm out of silver bullets.' He brandished a six gun. 'The place was full of bushwhackers and bandits. Tell Sheriff Oscar that he won't have any more trouble round these parts.'

'I will, Kemosabe.'

'Time we were out of here, Tonto. Let's ride!'

This time the screen dissolved without anyone riding into the sunset. Erin removed the memory stick and closed down her computer. She took a last lingering look around her office, locked it and left the building.

She hoped to God, Oscar Feldstein was as good as Ted thought he was. And that Oscar was as disinterested in money as he said he was. If neither was true, alarm bells were already going off, telling the world – including Warwick Stanstead – that Erin Wishart, Senior Vice President, Asia Pacific region, had just sabotaged the entire head office computer network.

Or worse. She knew the admin systems were physically separate from the operational and in theory the layers of firewalls protecting customer accounts, treasury systems, the dealing rooms and the bank accounting systems were impenetrable. But if Oscar Feldstein was really at the top of his game, she might just have handed a hacker the keys to riches beyond avarice.

FOURTEEN

Ted Saddler was clamped in his seat on a 747 coming in to land at Kolkata airport. He was dehydrated from the in-flight bar. His head hurt and his body was imploding. As the big jet bounced down the runway and jammed on the air brakes, death seemed a good option. It made Ted doubly determined that this would be the fastest report in journalistic history. In and out before his lungs had fully emptied of fresh Manhattan air. That was the plan.

He picked up his old Samsonite and wandered out of Kolkata's international airport terminal to be slammed by heat and light. The gleaming new concourse was littered with people sitting or lying in sprawled groups. He stood, surrounded by bodies; Wyatt Earp after the OK Corral. Only the flies were stirring. Like a plague ward. He was spotted. Some figures jumped up and made towards him with intent.

He fought his way through the ambush to the first taxi. He stared at it. It was an evolutionary branch-line of the motor car. A black bodied, canary-topped relic of the British Raj. The Brits also left the gift of irony; the cabs were called Ambassadors. He was certain that it would have all the mechanical artistry of a broken pen-knife.

He squeezed into the back seat, his knees pushing into the driver's back. Then they were off into lunatic traffic. It took so long to work up speed through the clunking gears that the driver was loath to lose it. So he tackled roundabouts left elbow on the horn, right arm out the window – holding the roof on maybe – with a fine disregard for the grandma on her bike, and the family of 7 piled on the two-seater trike.

The roads were a bedlam of bicycles, scooters, stumbling

rickshaws, gas-spewing three-wheelers with 5-up plus the driver, dented trucks and black and yellow taxis like his. Everybody hell bent on keeping the middle of the road. He guessed it was their Mogul blood. They wouldn't retreat or take avoidance action unless and until mayhem was imminent. Roundabouts were the only medium for converting certain death at a crossroads into an even chance.

They passed miles of corrugated-iron shacks where the sidewalk should have been. Each was a good bit smaller than Stan Coleman's office and without the amenities. People's lives were on show like a thousand TV sets jammed side by side, all showing personal disasters. Closer to the city, old colonial buildings mouldered in the heat and sagged into the street. They'd given up the fight long ago when the Brits left. Maybe it was to teach the West a lesson about trying to change things; trying to implement Anglo-Saxon discipline in equatorial torpor.

Ted felt overwhelmed with the sheer foreignness of it all. He wanted to turn the taxi round and get the next flight home. Then, soaring out of the gloom, was a white castle. His castle apparently. The Oberoi Grand. They pulled into the sanctuary of the white courtyard. He trundled his sweat-encased body into an oasis of greenery and wood panelling away from the eyes of the poor and thirsty. Ted checked in, shivering in the air-conditioning, and when he got to his room, tried to dispel his anxiety with two stiff Jack Daniels – ice-free for fear of bugs.

Ted sat on his bed and fought the urge to phone Mary. He'd always phoned her first thing on arrival if he was travelling on business round the States. He'd never worked out whether it was to share the moment or to provide a comfort blanket. Her brisk voice would chop the distance and make him brave. Now, though the need was stronger, he had to face his middle-aged fears alone. He'd get even less sympathy from the hardnosed Miss Erin Wishart.

He had the afternoon off to recover from the flight. So he showered, raided the mini-bar again, lay on his bed, switched on CNN and fell deeply asleep. He woke much later, feeling worse than before, stunned and disoriented. It was dark outside. To prove something to himself he showered, put on clean shirt and pants and stepped out into the fetid night. In seconds the clammy air plastered his clothes to his body. Within ten yards, the lights went out. His safe white towers were blotted out as he stepped through this looking glass into the underworld.

An urchin tagged him and softly jabbered at his big white bulk. Maybe he was importuning. Maybe he was cursing him gently for having so much. Ted shook him off with difficulty. The boy was tough and well filled out. His conscience let him off the hook for this one. He passed a slim woman in an electric blue sari rooting in a heap of garbage by the roadside. She was intent on her plunder, driven by a need stretching back to a family somewhere.

He stepped over sleeping figures, their arms twisted for a pillow, dirty cloths round their thin hips. Their skins glistened as if they'd been dipped in oil. Other figures moved in the shadows, creeping to their beds or to assignations beyond his imagination. He tried not to see people, or watch them or catch their eyes just in case. But there was no smell of danger among all the other stinks of urine and stale food. You wouldn't feel so relaxed on Brooklyn's meaner streets.

Then he saw her. Framed in an open ground-floor window. On a pile of mats surrounded by tumbling boxes whose guts spilled into the street. A man by her side. Father? Pimp? Please, not that. She was ram-rod straight, in a red sari, poised like a princess with calm sovereignty over her midden. He looked at her once and shied away and then again. Into her eyes. Large and dark in a face of perfect symmetry. She was all of 12, with a life that should have been special going forward. But how could it. How could it?

Kolkata's heat and humidity grew too much. He left it behind for his cool hotel. Result, he found himself fighting a chill – but not the onset of malaria he initially imagined. He slept fitfully and woke at 3 and 5 and finally at 7 am.

The image of last night stayed with Ted as he headed off into the frantic morning for his interview. He felt stupid at coming over maudlin and sentimental. Who was he to judge what was going on around here? Maybe this was what they chose? How they wanted to live? If he'd learned nothing in his twenty five years of reporting, he'd at least understood you couldn't apply Western rules and standards to the outback.

But whatever the reason – needing a drink, jet lag or still smarting at having to make this trip at all – Ted was angry. It made him mad to think of some bastards cleaning up from high interest loans to these poor suckers. He'd seen it before in the burst housing bubble across America. Ghost towns created by banks foreclosing on homes they valued less than their mortgages. Millions of poor bastards suckered onto a housing ladder with low starter rates that flipped to high regular rates beyond their income levels. Now the same wolves were marketing the foreclosed houses – people's homes – as great investments. Bankers always win and always find another variation on the sucker loan.

By the time he arrived at the head office of the Peoples' Bank, Ted Saddler was spoiling for a fight. The taxi shuddered to a stop and several pairs of hands dragged at his cab's door handle. All these scruffy gents pretending to be doormen at the Waldorf. He eased out, and took his bearings. They were well off anything that could be called a main street. Yet the small brass plaque on the wall confirmed it was the People's Bank head office. It said so, beneath a stylised engraving of a tree. The bank was housed in a block that would have been condemned and knocked down in Harlem in the '70s. Its façade was distressed concrete and smeared glass.

He forced his way past the human barrier and into an echoing hall of concrete slabs and doorways. It was about 20 degrees cooler – making 90 seem bracing – and a fan chugged round

77

overhead, spilling the humid air at him. A young woman in a cream sari sat behind a counter at a window on the right. He went over to her.

'I have an appointment with Mr Ramesh Banerjee. The name's Saddler.'

She consulted a screen in front of her. It shouldn't have taken long. No-one else was waiting.

'We are all very pleased to welcome you, Mr Saddler. May I offer you a nice cup of tea?'

While smiling at the quaint offer, he thought of the billion bugs he could get from the water, far less the milk, and politely declined. He took a seat on the other side of the small lobby from her window and went over his interview questions one last time. Then he got back up and began to pace up and down, relieved that despite his fears some of the old excitement was working its way through. The hunter's instinct not yet dead.

All the time he paced he felt her proprietorial eye on him. She half-bowed at him every time he looked her way. He guessed he'd been prowling for five maybe ten minutes when a door opened in the centre of the lobby facing the exit. A little man came through. He looked like any one of the threadbare characters Ted had seen around the hotel and streets this morning. Maybe a porter or clerk or something. He came over. He was wearing glasses and looked maybe mid-forties. He was thin and short. His black hair smudged with grey around the ears. He smiled. Ted smiled back, wondering what he wanted.

'Mr Saddler?'

'That's me.' He stood, assuming the man had been sent to get him. The man reached out a hand and they shook. Then the face became familiar from the news clip.

'My name is Ramesh Banerjee. Please call me Ramesh.'

FIFTEEN

Ted Saddler had met many top men in his time. Ramesh Banerjee fitted none of the profiles. His unheralded and low-key arrival almost punctured Ted's annoyance. But of course it was all for show, all planned. Ted easily regained his sense of anger and injustice on behalf of the poor people of India.

He followed Ramesh through the swing doors and into a shabby corridor. They pushed through another set of doors into a large room. It was full of desks, computer screens, people and mounds of papers. They wove their way through the crowded units, with Ted trying desperately to avoid knocking down the paper towers with his bulk. The clerks smiled and wished the CEO and Ted a good morning as they passed.

They stopped in front of a desk no bigger than any others but considerably less cluttered. Behind it, on the wall, was a giant version of the bank's logo. The bank's title was in gold across the spreading branches. This time the tree was coloured green and the branches were studded with fruit. Its roots were as long and powerful as its surface limbs.

'This is your office?'

'I only need a desk and a phone you see. It helps to be with my colleagues. In the West you call it open plan.'

Ted thought that there was open plan and then there was ostentatious humility; something for visitors to see, especially reporters.

'How do you motivate people if you can't give them something to aim for?'

'A big office is important in the West, not here. Every one of us – me included – will spend time working in the branches, setting up credit and collecting loans. Everyone is important. Everyone is equal.'

Ted was hearing sanctimonious bullshit, but he smiled and said, 'In that case, call me Ted.'

Ramesh smiled back, then the civilities were over.

'Why do you hate me, Ted?'

He asked it like he was asking if Ted took milk in his coffee. Ted blanked his face. He wasn't the one who had to explain himself.

'I don't hate you. I hate what you're doing. Your bank has a clever marketing angle to make money out of the poor. Your own government, the World Bank – just about any bank of repute in the world – they all think you're pulling the wool over the eyes of people that can't fend for themselves. My job is to expose you.'

Ted's voice took on the ringing tones of the righteous, the temple clearer. At that moment, he believed it. Ramesh looked at Ted quietly for a minute or so, until the silence had dragged itself out too long.

'Sometimes even the most honest men reach views using incorrect information. That is why I am glad you have come. Unlike those who criticise from afar. My books are open to you. As am I,' he added as an afterthought.

Ted had the grace to look slightly abashed at the noble motivation credited to him. A rivulet of sweat ran down his spine reminding him of his plans to get back to civilisation as fast as a 747 could carry him.

'Good. Do you mind?'

Ted brandished a small tape recorder at Ramesh. At his shake of the head, Ted set it between them and turned it on.

'Mr Banerjee, why did you set up this bank?'

'When I came back from the USA, I set up the investment bank operation for Kolkata Regional bank. We began to make good money from local businesses and from Western businesses coming into the city.'

Ted wondered why he omitted his stellar background; a first degree at Kolkata, then a post graduate course at Cambridge, England and an MBA at Harvard. Four years in New York with JP Morgan Chase. Why would anyone would want to come back to some crummy bank job in India at a twentieth of the salary?

'But every day, when I came to work and when I went home in the evening, I saw what you saw, Ted, unless you were asleep in your taxi. I kept telling myself that I was helping to cure this, but that it took time. If I helped top businesses make money it would trickle down to the poor. Eventually. The Western model worked and it would work here.'

He took off his glasses and Ted could see the tiredness under his eyes. He could also see the intensity.

'For five years I fooled myself. I made a great deal of money for the bank. But out there – on the streets and in the villages – nothing changed.'

'Are you saying capitalism doesn't work here?'

'That is a very interesting question. Capitalism requires all the ingredients to be in place before everyone begins to benefit, and not just the top layer. Here in India there is a big missing piece. It is mass ownership.

'That sounds pretty Marxist.' Or Erin Wishart, he thought.

'Is that what you will write about me now?' He smiled.

'Well, are you?'

Ramesh sighed. 'There are many truths in Das Kapital, but I am not an advocate for communism, just for working capitalism. Capitalism is about trade. Trading your right to work for a wage, trading your future earnings for a house, your crops for money, your credit-worthiness for a loan. If you have nothing, if you own nothing – no land, no money, no roof over your head – if you don't even own the right to work – then you cannot trade, and you cannot trade up. More than half my people don't own a thing, and work exists only in the form of slave labour. So they cannot participate in the merry-go-round of capitalism.'

'And the answer is. . .?'

'Banking services to the poorest people. It buys them a ticket on the merry-go-round.'

'Why set up a new bank? Why not within your Kolkata Regional Bank?'

He nodded. 'I took my ideas to the board. But they could not comprehend my proposal. They were not bad people. They honestly believed in the theory of trickle down of wealth. They saw the millions I was earning for them from investment banking and wanted me to stick to that, not go into some poor people's retail banking that would lose money. And certainly not loans to women or Untouchables. It was unthinkable. It would upset the whole caste system that is no longer supposed to matter here. I could not convince them. So I left and set up the People's Bank.'

'Just like that?'

Ramesh smiled at some memory. 'No. By no means. I had to beg for funding from one or two philanthropic foundations. I had to bring in people to help me without any salary at first. I sold or mortgaged everything I owned.'

He looked down. 'And my wife left me. I don't blame her. This wasn't what she'd signed up for when she married a successful investment banker. The first three years were touch and go. But I was right. And now, thanks to the internet, we are building a global service.'

'So now you're a *global* money lender.'

'It's not just loans. We insist on saving.'

'But your savers earn a pittance; half a per cent? While interest on loans hits 35% and above, for god's sake. We call that sharking.'

'We are like the old mutual societies in England. Presently we only lend what we can afford from the deposits and the loan repayments. Which is why we were unaffected by the madness of sub-prime lending, Collaterised Debt Obligations, Credit Default Swaps and all the rest of the gimmicks that brought down the mighty Western banks. We lend tiny sums to very many people. The cost of setting up and administering these loans is very high. But each year we improve our systems, and we are bringing these rates down.'

'So, you admit it.'

'Our loans are very short term, usually to a small group of people – women mainly – and over 98% repay their loans on time. We lend to tiny businesses, not to people who want to buy flat screen TVs. That is key. The interest payments are affordable.'

Ramesh turned and pointed behind him at the stylised tree with its deep and spreading roots, and its flowering and seeding branches.

'This is our logo. The neem tree. It is a remarkable tree, indigenous to India but now growing in many parts of the world in some of the poorest and hottest conditions imaginable. It stays green throughout the year on very tiny amounts of water. Its roots go deep, you see. Its seeds and leaves and bark have a multitude of uses. We have cultivated this tree for thousands of years – it is known in Sanskrit medical literature. It is called the village pharmacy. Interestingly, one of your western drugs companies has managed to take out patents on some of the tree's properties. A fine example of western capitalism, don't you agree?'

Ted was thinking that this guy was just too good to be true. He couldn't see his angle yet, but there had to be one. Maybe it was a power thing? Some people just got carried away with an idea and needed to prove it. Ted stayed on the offensive.

'So how is it that a bank with such scruples and integrity ends up in a court case accused of corruption and profiteering? Smoke without fire?'

Behind his glasses Ramesh blinked. 'Shall we have some tea? This is thirsty work, Ted. Let me show you our canteen.'

Ted picked up his recorder and set off after him. He wondered how fast those little bugs in the tea would take effect and whether this was how Banerjee got rid of unwanted guests.

SIXTEEN

Anila was squatting in her hut trying to appear nonchalant to her mother and daughter. She had not told her mother about the confrontation with the money lender and the sarpanch. It would have worried her even more. As she prepared the water to soak the rice, she was listening hard. Time stretched out. Perhaps he would not come today? Perhaps his ancient truck had finally died under him? Perhaps. . .

Far off came a growling which died away and rose again. Then it came closer and the growling stayed more or less constant. There was no mistaking the grinding noise of the gears and the bucking and clattering axles bouncing over the ground. The engine always sounded in pain. She was told that it was because he mixed too much kerosene with diesel to make it go further. Though she knew nothing about mechanics or driving a car, Anila could tell that the wood gatherer was a terrible driver. It was a miracle that the engine didn't explode with the strain he put it under.

By the noise, she could tell exactly where the truck was in relation to the village. When it was drawing towards the little square in the centre of the village, she got up, went to the side wall and lifted off the small carving of Krishna hanging at eye height. It revealed a hole that she had painstakingly carved out of the hard mud and straw. The hole went four inches deep into the nine inch thickness. She took out the precious little parcel with its cord strap. She put it round her neck and under her sari and walked out of the hut.

Anila strode down her lane with an air of greater confidence than she felt. There was no reason why the wood gatherer would not sell her what she wanted. Was there? Did he care where his money came from? But this was her first transaction in her own right. And once she'd bought the wood she was stuck with it. She would then have to make the little stools every day and sell them to the agent every week, to have a hope of making enough money to live on. Until that first step was taken, until that first little amount of money was handed over, she could still back out. She could keep the money from the bank and give it back to them. Maybe they would not ask for interest if she paid it back quickly?

Her heart was beating like a goat's before the knife, as she came into the open area of the village centre. The truck was there and its sickly engine had just coughed and died. A noxious cloud of smoke was drifting away through the neem trees. The driver was getting out and already several people had gathered: some women who had come to see Anila make this first step, and a group of men including the money lender.

By the time she got to the truck there was a small line. A few men were buying wood for roofs, or fencing, or a lean-to. She waited patiently until no-one else stood before her.

'Namaste, Mr Roy.'

The wood gatherer looked up at her and away from her. 'Namaste, Anila Jhabvala. What do you want?'

'I would like to buy a bundle of cane and two lots of good flat wood, please.'

The wood gather looked down and away from her. His eyes kept flicking over to the money lender whom Anila had seen standing a little way off near the back of the truck.

'I am sorry Anila. All the wood is sold. I cannot sell you cane or wood.' He turned as if to make off.

'That is impossible, Mr Roy. You always have wood. And I can see your lorry is half full.' There was a growing panic in Anila's voice. Her worst fears seeped into her bones like mountain mist.

'No, no. You are wrong, Anila. It has all been sold.'

Anger was beginning to take over. 'Who has bought all the wood Mr Roy?'

The wood gatherer was dancing in front of her in his anxiety to be away from her. 'Mr Chowdury has bought it all.'

Anila looked over at the money lender. He was standing smirking at her while one of his men off-loaded the canes and raffia that she wanted.

'Now I have to go, Anila.'

She was desperate. 'Wait Mr Roy. Are you coming back tomorrow? I want to buy wood tomorrow.'

'Yes I will be back. But Anila, it is still no use. All my wood is already promised to Mr Chowdury. He has guaranteed me payment for tomorrow and the days after.'

Anila could feel the tears well in her eyes. She was nearly paralysed with anger at the unfairness of it. 'How many lots of wood has Mr Chowdury bought Mr Roy?'

The wood gatherer shook his head. He was in torment standing in front of her. 'Anila, I am sorry. Don't you see that I cannot sell you the wood. Mr Chowdury is my best customer and he has told me not to sell you the wood. If I do he will not buy any of my wood in future. There is nothing I can do.'

'That is not fair Mr Roy. You know that is not fair! I told you before that I wanted to make my own business and you said you would sell me the wood. Did you not?' Anila felt her face burning with her hot tears. She would not wipe them away. She would not give him the satisfaction. Or the grinning Chowdury in the background.

Knowing he was in the wrong, Mr Roy turned to anger himself. 'I did not promise you. I am a business man, don't you know?! How can I sell one little lot of wood to a woman who will not last five minutes in business?! Why should I put my whole business at risk? I have a family you know. Your requirements are piddling compared to Mr Chowdury's. Don't you see that! You are only a woman!'

Some of the Mr Roy's words triggered off a fearful idea in Anila. 'What does Mr Chowdury want the wood for?'

The wood gatherer calmed down to reply. 'You know what he does with it. He sells it to women like you. He has many women who buy the wood from him. He lends them the money.'

'How much does he pay you for the wood?' A terrifying impulse was growing in Anila's stomach. It seemed like it would eat her insides and burst out of her.

Mr Roy wondered where this was going. He didn't want to give out this sort of information, yet he recognised an opening. His brows furrowed and his voice quietened. 'He gives me 500 rupees for my load. Every day.'

'What if I gave you 600 rupees for your load?' Anila scarcely knew her voice. A demon was driving her forward. She could hear someone talking and asking wild questions but her head was on fire and she felt the demon controlling her.

The wood gatherer looked at her differently. 100 rupees extra every day would make a big difference to his profits. If only he could believe in this woman. She had shown she could find the money for her own plans but where would she get so much?

'You do not have such money. How would you get it? That's what I want to know. And how do I know that you would be able to get so much money every day? I cannot afford to lose a good customer like Mr Chowdury. He might never buy wood from me again.' The wood gatherer had moved closer to Anila and was speaking quieter to her so he could not be overheard. In the background, the money lender had stopped smiling and was peering at them, wondering what was being said.

'I have enough money for five days on my person, you know. And I will get money from all the women who borrow from Mr Chowdury. We have a –' Anila searched for the word, '– a cooperative.'

Mr Roy stood weighing up the arguments and the risks. Anila felt the demon rise in her again and it took over her voice. 'Mr Roy, we know that you get your wood from Udaipura.' She pointed. 'I have a cousin there and we stopped with her last week when we were travelling from Delhi. I know the place you get your wood. If I can't buy my wood from you then I will walk into Udaipura and make arrangements for another lorry to deliver wood to the village. And I will get all the other women to buy their wood from the other lorry.'

Mr Roy looked as though he'd been struck on the head by one of his biggest planks. He was not a weighty businessman. He was good at one thing and had been doing this one thing for thirty years. His mind could not accept the possibility that there would be competition for his business. It was impossible!

He thought of his wife waiting for him at home. He thought her wrath would be without bounds if he told her he'd let another lorry take away his business. He thought too of the extra 100 rupees every day. 700 rupees extra every week! Why, his wife would be amazed and delighted. She would stop her scolding. For a while. If he told her. He looked at Anila and searched her face. This sort of woman never gave up. He did not think she was bluffing about going to Udaipura and arranging for another lorry to deliver. She'd gone to Delhi! And the same determination might just make this proposal of hers work.

'Are you sure you can get the other women to cooperate with you?'

'I am sure.' She was not, but one battle at a time.

'Then I will do it. I will come tomorrow and you will pay me 600 rupees and I will give you my load. And we will do this every day?'

The deal was struck and Anila stood rooted with terror at what she'd just agreed to. She watched as Mr Roy got into his now empty truck and cranked the ancient engine into life. She watched as he crashed the gears and bumped his way out of the village. And she watched as Chowdury gazed thoughtfully at her before shouting at his assistants to prepare the piles of wood for the women who would shortly be coming to pick up their small stocks and commit to the daily embrace of his usury.

Anila drew back and found a seat in the shade by the pumps to wait for the women. She knew most of them already of course, but now she needed to choose her allies. She also needed some time to think quietly about what she would say to them. It would have to be such a wonderful opportunity that they would not be able to resist. If she failed to get them on her side, then she might have to throw herself down the old well. It was the first place people looked if someone had gone missing.

SEVENTEEN

Ramesh Banerjee led the way, conscious of the big white man bearing down on him like a threatening devil. They pushed through some doors and into the canteen. It was a bare hall with plastic tables and chairs, all looking second hand or rescued from the dump. Against one wall was a trestle table with a steaming urn, cups, saucers and milk and lemon. They helped themselves. Maybe a third of the tables had people at them. Nobody got up or batted an eye at their Chief Executive in their midst making his own tea.

Ramesh was pleased at this. It was how he wanted it. He knew how it would come across to this reporter so conditioned to the trappings of rank and power in the west. They found a quiet table. Ted looked gingerly at his plastic cup. Ramesh read the signs.

'It's perfectly all right. The water has been boiled and the milk is pasteurised. But I will tell you something.' His voice dropped conspiratorially. 'If there is one thing I miss from New York, it's Starbucks.'

Ted whispered back, 'I know exactly what you mean. Now, can we talk about these charges against you and the bank?' He took out his tape recorder.

'It will not surprise you to hear me say that the charges are trumped up.'

'Now why would anyone want to do that? If your bank is such a success at alleviating poverty?'

'It is a sad reflection on this world of ours that there is quite a list. Let us start with the Government of India. Ten years ago I applied for a banking licence and got it. At the time I had good contacts in the Finance Ministry and also in the Banking

Supervisory Board. Now, not only have all my old contacts gone, but we are on. . .' he counted on his fingers. 'the sixth change of Government since then. Unfortunately the bank does not get on with this one.' He considered for a moment. 'Or indeed the previous three.'

'But I still don't see why they would want to close your bank. If I'm to believe you, it's taking one of their problems off their plate?'

Ramesh sighed. 'Many honestly believe that microfinance will simply lead poor people into deeper debt they cannot repay. South Africa is just such an example.'

'How?'

'Micro loans were handed out willy nilly to the poor in the townships. No saving accounts, just loans which they spent on consumer goods. Sky Sports to watch Manchester United and Real Madrid in a tin shack. They had no way of paying back the debt. It was not invested, just spent.'

'But you can point to a different model?'

'Yes, but some in the Indian establishment think it disturbs the natural order of things. They preach democracy but really prefer to act like the Raj. We are making a difference to millions of people across the country, and they have nothing to do with it. We show them in a bad light. They want to control us and put their people on our board and run the bank as a state bank so that they can get the kudos.' He hesitated for a moment. 'And big salaries.'

'I can see how that might be. Why don't you give them a slice of the action? Take the heat off?'

Ramesh slammed the table with his open hand.

'Because they would kill us! With bureaucracy, hierarchies, conditions, rules, restrictions, delays, and the usual layers of bribery. I would rather they closed the bank!'

Ted was taken aback. Silence fell briefly at the other tables, then the chattering took up again.

'What about at the grass roots? Don't you have a big following there? Wouldn't they stand up for you?'

Ramesh took a deep breath and clasped his fingers together.

'Our account holders are poor, they have no voice, no power. Between them and the ruling classes sit a very large number of people who don't want to see their own position eroded. Money lenders or local politicians who don't want their system of corruption bypassed.'

'Anybody else?'

Ramesh smiled grimly. 'All the people with caste, who lord it over those without. Over 150 million people in India have no caste. The euphemism is they belong to the 'unscheduled' caste. But they are still the old Untouchables, the Dalits. They sit at the bottom of every heap. They do the most menial jobs – like carrying away the shit of the higher castes. We lend money to anyone – especially to the Dalits – so the upper castes are faced with the possibility of having to clear up their own shit.'

He saw the reporter wince. It was funny that Westerners used the word so often but only in the abstract. When confronted with its real meaning they were disgusted. A useful weapon.

'I can see how that would make you unpopular.'

'Yet there is another even bigger group who are not happy.'

'Who?'

'Men. Over 97% of our loans are to women. It frees them. It gives them power over their own destinies. Men don't like that.'

'Why don't you lend to men?'

'Women have more to lose. Women pay us back.' He leaned closer. 'It is their *life* we are giving them.'

Despite himself, Ted was finding it hard to stay cynical, far less angry at this quiet little man. He mustered another argument

'Why are you a pariah with organisations like the World Bank? They keep offering you cheap money. Surely you have common goals?'

'They too want me in their pocket. They want to list me in their annual report. To launder their conscience. While I keep them at bay, they are embarrassed by me. Ted, may I go off the record for a moment?' Ted pressed pause on his recorder.

'A few years ago – before the Credit Crunch – I gave a speech at a conference in New York. Alec D. Paterson, the President of the World Bank was in the front row. But I did not pull any punches. After my speech – which was well received – he came up to me and shook my hand. Very deliberately and publicly. In front of the press, all the important people and a five hundred strong audience. All I could do was smile back. He said. . .'

'Ramesh. Loved your little talk. Goes right to the heart. But I think you have us wrong you know, and I'd like to straighten the record. Why don't you and me get together and sort out how we can help? I've made plenty of offers, but you keep turning me down.' Paterson kept smiling as he talked.

Ramesh smiled back. 'Thank you, but perhaps you missed the middle part of my talk? Where I set out why organisations like yours have never helped the poor and never could. By their very nature.'

To the rest of the audience they were key figures on the world financial stage, talking like colleagues, sharing ideas and intents.

'I heard it. And I wanted to get my side over to you. I told you, I think you've got us wrong. You're going to need us, you know.'

'Thank you. But you have nothing we need.'

'Everybody needs money. Especially charities.'

'We are not a charity. We are a bank. We make our own money. We have 250 million customers who borrow from us and – unusually it seems – repay us.'

Paterson took his arm. 'Ramesh, you're a smart guy. You've been on Wall Street. Don't you want to play at the big table again? Where it matters? I could get you on to the right boards, get you the right – shall we say recognition? Including financial recognition?'

Ramesh looked down at the white hand gripping his arm.

'My present recognition as you put it, is adequate for my needs.'

Paterson smiled and put his mouth close to Ramesh's ear.

'Then fuck you, Mr Banerjee. Fuck you.'

The President of the World Bank pinched his arm and walked off.

Ted asked, 'Are you sure you want this off the record?'

'My word against the Chairman of the World Bank? His army of lawyers?'

'But they do some good. With all that money?' Ted persisted.

Ramesh smiled grimly. 'The way to get on in the World Bank is to have the biggest investment budgets to spend on the highest profile projects. If someone can find a way of spending $500 million on a project to build a dam in Africa then he gets noticed and gets promoted.'

'But these projects are useful surely? Maybe the motivation is wrong, but the results are worth having?'

'Are they? Who gets the money? Not the poorest. Not the locals even. The money goes into the pockets of the international companies with the tools and the expertise to build big dams, or roads or airports. It goes to the consultants and the money men who fly in and out first class, and stay at the nearest Oberoi.' Ted wondered if he was being watched. 'And most of all, it goes to the middlemen, the government backers and intermediaries. We might as well send it straight to their numbered accounts in Switzerland.'

Ted switched his recorder back on.

'What have they got on you? Or are they making it up?'

For the first time Ramesh's trained ear heard no cynicism in the last question. Maybe he was getting through to the big man.

'They are bribing influential people and planting evidence which is then leaked to the press.' He looked meaningfully at Ted. 'Including the foreign press.''

'What else?'

'For some months now we have been hit by a series of technical problems. It is a moot point whether we will be shut down by the Supreme Court or sabotage.'

'Who do you blame?'

Ted saw the pieces beginning to form an uncomfortable picture, part of which showed a spineless reporter being guided like a dumb steer.

'I fear we have little proof at this stage. And I don't want a libel suit on top of the present problems.'

'Maybe I can do a little fishing in my column?'

'I will be most interested to see how you portray our little chat, Ted. One never knows with the press, does one?' His tone left no doubt about how low he set his expectations.

'But I almost forgot. I have a small present for you.' Ramesh pulled open his desk drawer. 'Unless you have already read it?' He placed a pristine paperback of E M Forster's 'A Passage to India' on the table.

Ted smiled to hide his surprise. 'Am I being bribed?'

'Enlightened perhaps?'

Ted took the offering and stood up, towering over the little man. 'Thanks Ramesh. Make sure you check tomorrow's Tribune.'

EIGHTEEN

Anila spoke to first one then the other. It was easy to get their attention. Everyone knew that Anila was trying to break away from the money lender and do her own business. What they had not expected was her call to revolution!

'We would form an agreement to buy the wood direct from Mr Roy. We would not borrow the money from Mr Chowdury.'

'But Anila Jhabvala, where would we get the money from? We have no money.'

'I have enough to get us started. I could afford to buy five days of Mr Roy's entire wood if we had to. But we would not even need five days. The agent comes every week, so it would only be another four days before you sold your work. Then you would pay me back and pay back Mr Chowdury for the loan for the last three days. And then we could afford to buy the next week's wood for us all.'

'But how is that better Anila? It sounds like you have become Mr Chowdury! What is the difference between one money lender and another we want to know?! Except you are inexperienced and maybe you will run out of money and we will all have to beg Chowdury to help us and he will probably put up his rates.'

'It is much better, because I don't want to make a profit from you. All I want is to be able to buy my own wood. But Mr Roy is committed to selling it all to Chowdury because Chowdury puts pressure on him. If I cannot buy the whole pile of wood at a better price, then Mr Roy will not sell it to me.'

'You really mean we could buy the wood cheaper from you and you would not want any profit?'

'That is right. On my word. In the name of Laxmi, goddess of wealth, this is what the arrangement would be.'

'And we would then sell the stuff we make directly to the agent? And we would keep the profit?'

'Now you see.' Anila hoped they did. They broke into voice.

'It is too good to be true...

'I will have to ask my husband...

'I will have to think about it...

'I will only join the cooperative if everyone else does...

'I will wait and see how it goes for a while and then maybe...'

And so on and so on. The excuses for not joining in with Anila's proposal piled up. But she knew if she could persuade more than half, the others would fall in. She now had the entire group of women round her – twelve in all – and she let them argue and debate the issues for a long time. This needed time. She could not push them. She let them gnaw the idea to shreds. Then as the debate was going round the same point for the third or maybe fourth time, she reached inside her sari and pulled out the small leather bag that hung by a cord round her neck.

She quietly tugged at its top and pulled the neck apart. She reached inside knowing she'd caught the attention of several of the sitting women. They in turn nudged their neighbour as Anila brought out a thick wad of Rupees. She began to count it slowly in front of them. She laid one bill on top of another and counted out loud until she'd reached 3,000 rupees. It was the total amount given to the three of them by the bank. It was more than most of them had seen in one pile in their lives. Anila was breathing hard as she finished. Only 1000 belonged to her, and neither Leena nor Divya were here to defend their share. She had no right to be flaunting the others' money, but she knew it would give her more credibility. They all looked at her and then at the pile.

'Here is our start. Tomorrow when Mr Roy comes back with his truck I will give him 600 rupees on behalf of this cooperative. Then you will each take the wood you need and make your chair or your basket or your mats. Then four days after, you will sell your chair and give me the cost of the wood. You will keep the profit and make your husbands very happy!' Anila braved their looks.

One of them, a big woman called Sandip, cursed with four daughters, broke the spell. 'It sounds like a good deal to me. I will join your cooperative Anila. Think what I can buy with the extra money? Why, I could get a whole chicken every week for the profit I would make! Instead of always eating rice!'

It was the breaking of the dam. The others began to do quick sums, scratching in the dust with fingers and twigs. The numbers made sense. In a state of excitement and anxiety, the entire group of women rose up like a startled cloud of birds-of-paradise. They clasped hands and swore to work as a cooperative. They vowed to meet at the same time tomorrow and support Anila in transacting their first deal.

As Anila watched them go, chattering in little groups, she hoped their enthusiasm would last the night. Anila turned and headed home. She had planned not to tell her mother what had happened until everything was in place and working, but a village gossip mill pours out its news at the speed of a monsoon river. By the time she got home her mother was waiting for her in tears.

'You have gone too far, Anila! This is the end of you and your daughter and your mother! Don't tell me, I know! You are trying to become a big trader and a money lender. I hear it all round about. And the Panchayat will meet and throw us out of the village and we will be destitute and die in the hills! Or we will have to go to the city and beg or become prostitutes. I am too old to do this and I will just kill myself rather than face such a life. How can you do this?!'

Her mother was wailing and weeping now. She knelt and pulled her shawl over her grey head and smote her head on the ground. Anila quickly knelt alongside her and pulled her up into her arms.

'Mother, mother, you have it all wrong. It is not like this at all. Mr Roy is going to sell me all his wood every day and we will work with the other women as a cooperative. In four days' time when the agent comes, we will sell all our work and the women will give me back the money for the wood.'

Her mother wailed harder. 'How can you buy so much wood every day!? You will use up all your money and we will starve. This is madness, daughter. Stop it before we are all lost!'

'Listen to me. There are twelve women now who are working together. Like the cooperatives that have been set up in other places. I am only helping with the first few days of funding. Then once we are going, the other women will pay me back. You will see.'

In her heart, Anila was terrified of tomorrow. Then she would know if the women would stand by her. Overnight, people have a chance to cool down. They might not think it such a good idea in the morning. Husbands have ways of applying pressure. But she smiled and looked confident in front of her mother.

Her mother's tears were drying. They were face to face in the dust in front of the hut. Behind them Anila could see her daughter clinging to the door post, her thumb in her mouth, and looking scared.

'Are you sure, daughter of mine? This is so big! No-one in this village has ever done anything so big. What if it doesn't work out?' Her mother's eyes searched hers.

'It will, mother. It will. Now get up and come inside. Everyone is looking at us.' She lifted her mother up and shook the dust from both their saris before gathering her own daughter under her arm and walking them both inside to wait for the morning.

NINETEEN

In Warwick Stanstead's mind was a familiar image. It was a runner. Thin and wiry, breathing hard and forcing the pace. Behind was the pack. The runner occasionally looked behind him but mainly faced forward, into the distance. He waved to the viewer – a shadow figure on one side of the rugged cross country track – as he scythed past, arms pumping and legs flailing and feet thumping on the frozen ground. The runner smiled and kept going. It was a winter scene with the trees frosted and rimed, and the sun hung without warmth on the horizon. But its light was strong, and sometimes when the runner erupted from the cold dark places where the tall fir trees kept the sun out, he had to fling his arm up to see where he was going.

The runner always shouted something to the viewer as he went past. But Warwick could never catch it. Nor could he hear the words flung back by the viewer as the runner receded quickly into the shadows ahead. He knew it was a warning, but it was always tantalisingly indistinct. He was never sure if the runner or the viewer was him.

Warwick tumbled forward, feeling he'd fallen a great distance. But it was only a fraction of an inch. Enough to wake him with a start. He'd been nodding on and off for some time without becoming fully conscious. He checked his watch. He'd been 'out' for half an hour following the first glorious warm rush, the delicious weighting of his limbs, until he was swept into unconsciousness. Into the dream. He could never quite recall it. The shreds clung to his waking mind for a moment but not long enough to remember details.

He stumbled to his washroom. He tidied away his kit, throwing the used syringe in the metal bin. Duschene would empty it later and leave a clean needle. He needed to clear his head. He threw water on his face and took a cold drink from his fridge. He took out his silver tin and the polished steel plate. From the tin he took out the solid silver tube and blade, and tipped a small heap of white powder onto the plate. He drew three 'rails' with the blade. He pressed the cold tube into his nostril and hoovered the plate clean. He wet his finger and cleaned off all trace of white. He rubbed his finger on his gum and towelled his nose. Light flooded his head. Confidence and well-being poured through his body. Better. Much better.

He went back into his office, unlocked his door, and returned to his soft leather seat. He called up the discreet bank of video screens that folded seamlessly into the polished surface of his desk. He began playing his keyboard, opening up a different picture on each screen. They showed scenes inside offices. Seven of the ten were occupied. A steady murmur washed over him as the occupants talked on the phone, dictated or spoke to other people in the office. Now and again the volume on one screen rose above the others until Warwick leaned over and quietened it with a touch.

He was pleased with the system installed by Joey Kutzov and his team. A hidden camera and microphone sat in each of his subordinate's offices continually monitoring their every word and deed. He could input key words at any time. Triggers. Whenever any of his first line reports uttered them, the volume rose to an audible level. Warwick was currently running with a list of forty words including his own name and a set of swear words that indicated high emotion.

There wasn't an idea floated, or a problem bubbling that he didn't know about before the executive belatedly brought it to Warwick's table. He was always one jump ahead. As though he could tap into their thoughts. Warning him of any sign of revolt. Telling him of any whispered negative word or doubt about the bank's direction. Flagging up any weakening of faith in his own infallibility. Enabling him to snuff out the faltering sparks before they caught light.

Kutzov had persuaded him to install the system – or a rudimentary form of it – after one of the several upheavals that had threatened to tear the bank apart. It had proved its worth many times over. Each time, he knew how to smooth the waters, who to back, who to cut, and which strings to pull. The great conciliator.

Lately, running the bank had seemed to require harder skills. People were becoming more difficult, less tractable. Like Doubleday about a year ago. Stirring up his fellow executives to form a cabal to confront him with demands – demands! – for an easing of the spending restrictions. Well, he was history now. And not just with Global American. Warwick had made sure there wasn't a bank in the country – maybe the western world – that would take him on as anything higher than a messenger. Kutzov's boys, with their special bent in negative PR had seen to that. Doubleday had the problem of disproving it. In this community, you didn't need to have evidence of doing something wrong. Shit sticks.

But now there was a problem of a different order. José Cadenza, regional head of Central and Latin America – had begun asking questions about his old boss, Bill Yeardon. Cadenza was one of the old American Mart guys, and Warwick had assumed that like all Latinos, Cadenza would be even more susceptible to being bought off. He was also a born leader, and his numbers were some of the best around. It was such a pity he'd begun digging up old bones.

He'd almost missed it. It had been so long since anyone had mentioned him. But the word Yeardon was still there in the system from the early days when Warwick needed to be vigilant for disaffection after the merger. So the incoming call to Cadenza from Yeardon's wife, or more accurately, his widow, had surprised Warwick. When Yeardon dropped dead six months back, it seemed like that was end of story. Loose ends all tied up.

Warwick remembered meeting Veronica Yeardon three years back when they were all trying to put on an amicable front for the shareholders. She was a stuck-up Southern Belle. A drawling, charming blonde who hid a tough streak behind lace and breeding. So when the volume on Cadenza's screen went up, Warwick found himself listening to some very bad news indeed.

Veronica was bitter and distraught. She'd finally got around to clearing out his desk and found a key to a safety deposit box at her local bank. Inside was material about the merger. What the hell was it?

Cadenza was a smart guy. Warwick was sure none of his directors knew about the surveillance – otherwise there would be hell to pay – but some of them were naturally more cautious than others. He cut her off and arranged to call her later and meet up with her.

Kutzov had tailed them and tapped Cadenza's cell phone. They'd met on Saturday at a discreet Village restaurant. A directional mike got the details. The safety deposit held political dynamite. Maybe enough to blow up Warwick Stanstead, Global American and a number of senior officials in the banking business.

TWENTY

Erin Wishart – not knowing her boss was watching – was also staring at her office screen, stomach knotted, silently cursing Ted Saddler. She was calling up various old emails and spreadsheets to see if she could see anything amiss. Oscar had assured her the Lone Ranger programme was undetectable and would self-destruct leaving no trace if anyone started poking about. Erin wasn't so sure. She reached for the pill pack and washed two down with a swig of cold tea.

She just prayed that Warwick wouldn't summon her today. She couldn't stand even the mildest questioning. She knew nothing stood in Warwick's way when he wanted something or someone, so Erin had Madge Peters, her PA, fix a slew of meetings with her team leads. Back-to-back, no lunch and no interruptions unless it was life or death.

At 3pm Erin was interrupted by death.

Madge called her to the outer office where there was already pandemonium. José Cadenza hadn't made it in today. After checking all known locations, Viv Stanley, the head office assistant for the regional bosses when they were in town, had called his apartment block. The concierge was persuaded to ring the door of his apartment, then when there was no reply, to use his pass key to enter.

José's body was found draped in black PVC and dangling from a hook in the ceiling. Around his head was a plastic bag. The TV was in a loop advertising a hard core streaming service. The last movie played was about large men having sex with small children. Forensics had found that the time of download tied in roughly with the time of death. The police's initial diagnosis was an auto-asphyxiation that had gone wrong.

Further evidence of sexual perversion was found in a library of videos and magazines in a locked cupboard. His home computer was full of similarly harrowing download material. It looked like a tragic accident to a closet paedophile.

No-one could believe it. He had kids of his own. It just was too out of character. Warwick Stanstead volubly and publicly refused to accept that José was capable of such a double and distorted life. He immediately sent his head of HR in his personal jet down to Rio to inform José's wife and family face to face. Mrs Cadenza was to be offered the services of Warwick's jet and private staff to fly up to New York or whatever she wanted to do. Money was no object. Warwick took personal control of the press release and went to some considerable trouble with the NYPD and press corps to quell any mention of José's quirky death.

Erin's mind shut down. It was unthinkable either that José had hidden a vile streak or that Warwick had instigated his death. All she could do was watch Warwick in action. It veered from masterful to bizarre. There was no knowing which character would emerge from his office. His eagle head, with its slick blue-black hair, bobbed in and out throughout the afternoon and early evening, controlling and ordering, making sure nothing was left to chance then throwing everything up in the air in a tantrum over delays to his orders being executed. In his saner moments, the very epitome of the caring leader, dealing sympathetically and equably with secretary and executive alike. Exuding calm and deep concern. Then Mr Hyde emerged, an emotional wreck with no safety valve for his anger or torment. Even Madge was moved to comment:

'Mr Stanstead's really upset, isn't he?'

'Isn't he though,' Erin managed.

At his most perverse he summoned the corporate psychiatrist and demanded to know how someone this perverted could be working for him. She'd heard some of Warwick's thoughts on gays, so this was no surprising divergence. Throughout the performance Erin tried desperately to stop her brain straying into the dark paths of conspiracy and murder. It couldn't be countenanced. It was insane. Just coincidence. Bosses fired troublesome subordinates. They didn't have them executed. Finally, Erin fled the building and sent herself early to bed with a very strong vodka tonic and a double dose of Melatonin, her jet lag pill.

Next day she stumbled into work, hung over and drained. Throughout the day the coincidences mounted, became farce, became nightmare. It was only a line or two on the daily web clippings, but the name caught Erin's eye. Veronica Yeardon the widow of the former CEO of American Mart, had gone missing. Her daughter was anxious as her mother had been depressed for months following the sudden death of her husband. There was speculation she may have taken herself off for a few days to New York to be on her own, or had broken down completely and wandered away. But her daughter insisted that this wasn't how her mother behaved.

Erin concurred. Veronica was sweet and feminine in the way of Southern women of good stock. Beneath the unblemished white skin was a steel core. When it came to managing husbands or family estates, those girls were made of stern stuff. Erin recalled a ten minute conversation that started innocently enough with Paris couture and switched rapidly to capital punishment as an example of New World decadence. It was easy to draw the opinion that Veronica Yeardon would have been one of the last people to vanish without cause. Just before she met José Cadenza and revealed some dreadful news about Warwick Stanstead.

Erin nursed her feelings of dread to herself until she got to Oscar's apartment that evening. She'd arranged the meeting to check out the success or otherwise of the Lone Ranger bugging. It was also an opportunity to put a call in to Ted Saddler in Kolkata to share news with him. Oscar had advised – strongly

– that she make no calls or emails from her office. Or indeed from her apartment. Before Monday Erin would have rubbished such fancies, until Oscar had shown her how easy it was to turn her phone and every other internet-enabled device in her apartment into listening and recording facilities. Erin had begun to be afraid of the dark. She told him about José

'. . . but what's worse is that I chatted with José just last week.'

She told Oscar about Veronica's call to José just a few days before.

'This is beginning to sound a little more severe than spreading nasty stories, my dear.'

'Don't say it! I can't – *won't* believe my boss is a . . .'

'Murderer? If you say so, my dear.' Oscar drawled. 'We won't jump to any naughty conclusions now, will we? We'll take it at face value. I mean some of my best friends – how shall we put it? – have some very interesting ways of getting their rocks off, my dear. Pal José is not alone, let me tell you. But it is a teensy bit coincidental to have two misfortunes in two days. Not that Mrs Yeardon's headless body has been found yet.'

His enlarged eyes opened wider in lurid speculation. Erin jammed fingers in her ears and closed her eyes. Then she took her hands down and looked at Oscar.

'So what do we do?'

'Why, nothing. Nothing except listen and watch. Come sit by me, my dear.'

Oscar pulled out a stool on wheels from under the bench that held part of the array of computer boxes and screens. He patted it. Erin got up out of her deep armchair and gingerly sat alongside Oscar. She could smell a faint but not unpleasant aroma of lavender.

'Shall we see how clever you were? And how clever my little Trojan horse is? Don't you love it? The Lone Ranger on his Trojan horse? It's the laughs that keep us going, don't you think?'

Erin smiled dutifully and admired Oscar's command of the keyboards. He had not been exaggerating about his magic fingers. He was working two keyboards at once, like a piano virtuoso. In front of him was a large split screen with rapidly changing menus, and instructions being submitted and processed. At last he slowed down and both hands came to rest on one set of keys. A now familiar figure appeared on screen.

'How well acquainted are you with our hero?' he asked, without turning his head.

'Johnny Depp made a very bad movie of him based on a silly kids' programme from the 50s.'

'Not kids! It was too good for kids,' said Oscar, fast forwarding the compliant cowboy through a series of actions till he again paused. 'And don't diss Johnny in front of Albert,' he whispered.

He turned to her and pointed at his screens.

'You've done good, girl. Welcome to the dark side. Your office has desktops and tablets and cell phones linked by Wi-Fi and sharing central applications running on your company cloud. Each machine has a few client apps running locally including your individual voice-response systems. So does everybody else.'

He went on. 'My gizmo gets past the firewalls into the servers. It turns every workstation, every phone and tablet into a listening and viewing post. I can read your email, Word docs and Excel sheets. I can call up your family albums, and even watch your screen while you use it. Lovely. . . And what's specially nice, is what I've done to the voice app. It still works for you and your pals, but it also works for me now! The mikes have been 'turned'. We can tune into anyone's computer and hear conversations or phone calls or people talking to themselves – I hope you don't have any funny little habits when you're alone, Erin?'

'Certainly not.' She sat up straight, knowing her cheeks were calling out her lie. Twice – just twice in three years – out of nowhere, a simple need burst into her head, an itch that wouldn't stop. It took over her body, like an alien. If a man had touched her then she'd have consumed him. Behind her big official desk and with the rest of the executive team and her PA just a wall's breadth away, she slid a hand down her skirt and brought blessed relief. But not a sound passed her clamped lips. Only her voice, after, might have given her away.

'Just checking. It's surprising what we all do when we think we're alone. Shall we see?' There was more than a hint of malicious glee in his face and voice.

'You mean you've recorded all that's been going on in all the exec offices since the weekend?'

'See that little rack over there?' He pointed to a tall framework of metal uprights and crossbars in which a large number of bare computer innards were displayed. 'It can hold a thousand years' recordings for the dozen or so folk we're dealing with here.'

'Could we listen to yesterday afternoon? In Warwick's office?'

'Oh yes. Oh my word, yes.' Oscar brought his fingers across the keys once, twice and then sat back with Erin to listen.

Warwick's voice filled the room and Erin covered her mouth, her eyes wide.

'Sorry! Too loud.'

He turned Warwick's voice down to its normal threatening level. They listened as he held intercom discussions with Pat Duschene, his executive assistant. Pat had been with Warwick for longer than any of his three wives. He made calls to other banks and businesses. He had one outburst with the head of the Forex desk in New York after summoning him from the floor. The Euro had taken off and GA hadn't hedged it enough. Erin shuddered. There were also long silences punctuated by occasional bursts of voice from one of Erin's colleagues.

Just then she heard her own distinctive tones. She rose out of her chair and stood in terror gazing at the screen.

'What the hell's going on, Oscar? What are we listening to?'

She listened to herself talking to Madge. She remembered the moment, just after two o'clock. She had a short gap in her meeting schedule and queried if Warwick had tried to get hold of her at any stage. They talked for a couple of minutes with Erin making less than polite comments about how nice it would be to pass a whole day without hearing from her boss.

'What are you doing in my office?!'

Oscar paused the recording. He turned to her with pressed lips.

'I'm not in yours. Warwick is. He's bugged all your rooms. Probably video and voice. Like us. My guess is that it's a clever little app to pick up particular key words. So maybe if I were a paranoiac, control freak of a chief executive I'd set it up to let me know whenever my name was used. Just in case anyone was saying anything disloyal, you know?'

'Oh my god. I'm dead. I've called him terrible things over the last year. God knows what I've said!'

'Relax, my dear. He may be paranoiac but he's not stupid. He's smart enough to know that when the troops are saying nothing about the general then he's really got problems.'

Erin sat down. 'Right. Yes.' There was no conviction in her voice. 'So we're sitting here, tapping him, tapping me? How on earth am I supposed to act normal from now on? I mean for God's sake it'll feel like I'm on stage. He'll know I'm acting!'

'Well he'd just better not, is my advice.' Oscar peered hard at her. 'Shall we continue?'

They listened as the crisis over José Cadenza emerged. Oscar skipped through passages that were uninteresting. Throughout, Stanstead flitted from being the caricature of Mr Angry to being the very model of an efficient and caring manager. The time marched on and it was late evening. The screen clock showed it was 9.30 pm and it seemed Warwick was on the point of leaving. But one last call was made.

'Joey?' Oscar asked, pausing the recording.

'Joey Kutzov. Warwick's Mr Fixit,' Erin wondered why she was whispering. 'A very smooth operator. No-one ever quite knows what Joey actually does. Been with Warwick for years.'

Oscar released the pause. A new voice cut in.

'Mr Stanstead. How are things?'

'Pretty good, Joey. We had a lot of excitement around here this afternoon.'

'Absolutely Mr Stanstead. Any problems, or did it go as we thought?'

'Exactly as planned. Tears and incredulity. They'll do a check on his office here and in Rio of course.'

'That's all taken care of. It all fits.'

'Have you found the Yeardon documents?'

'She's not being helpful.'

'She never was. Keep me posted if things change.'

The conversation stopped. They looked at each other, Oscar with a sardonic, what-do-you-expect expression, Erin with a white face, frozen between terror and disbelief. The façade crumbled. Erin Wishart gulped until she found her voice.

'Let's call Ted, shall we?'

TWENTY ONE

'Why didn't you tell me about your meeting with Cadenza?' Ted was pacing his room in the Oberoi with a Skyped cell phone in one hand and a whiskey in the other. As agreed with Erin, he'd bought a new cell at Kolkata airport and a handful of pay-as-you-go SIM cards. The line to Erin and Oscar in New York was now clear after a couple of tries. Unfortunately. He didn't want to believe what she was telling him. He shivered. The air conditioning seemed set at Arctic levels compared with the tropical heat at Ramesh's bank.

'Don't tell me off, Mister! I was waiting till he'd met Mrs Yeardon. Waiting till there was something to tell you.'

'Oh pardon me, I thought this was just a regular story of banking chicanery. Not murder.'

'We don't know that for sure.'

Even from 5000 miles away her voice sounded less than convincing.

'Really? We've got a taped phone call – thanks to Oscar's box of tricks – that shows Stanstead and Joey Kutzov knew about José before it happened. And they could be involved in Mrs Yeardon's disappearance. There's no other way of reading it.'

'It's not 100%. Wait. Oscar is sending it now. Check your email.'

Ted put the phone on speaker and turned to his laptop. He found the emailed clip and played the conversation between Stanstead and his fixer. He aimed at the cell phone.

'It might not convince a Grand Jury, but it's good enough for me. Is there any way Stanstead would know you bumped into Cadenza?'

'A week ago I would have said impossible. Now. . .'

'Can you take some vacation time, Erin?'

'Are you seriously suggesting I should go on the run? Why not send this to the police?'

Oscar's dulcet tones joined in. 'Illegal phone tapping? They'd love that. I agree with Ted. I think you should disappear, Erin. Soon. Of your own accord.'

Ted chimed in. 'If you're worried, Oscar, then we should all worry. Any suggestions?'

'Before we get to that – Erin, dear, there's nothing to trace anything to me, is there? I mean you have been careful in coming here, haven't you? Lots of diversions and changes of cabs and such like?' There was a pause.

'Seems like we're going to have to teach you a few tricks before we send you off into the woods. And I'd better check my ass! Meantime, let's spirit this young lady away. Maybe back to one of her cosy bases in Asia Pacific. Sydney's nice this time of year. Then we continue with our surveillance.'

Erin's voice cut in. 'If you boys are quite finished deciding what's best for me? I'm already booked to fly back to Hong Kong tomorrow. It's my regional HQ. I'll stick with that – officially – but hop on the next flight out of there.'

'Where to, Erin?' asked Ted.

'Kolkata of course. Direct flight from HK. Four and half hours.'

'You mean, here?!'

The last thing Ted needed was a high-powered, organising broad on his case and running his life. He knew exactly how she'd operate; interfering, pushing, arguing, making him feel slow and old. Digs about his drinking.

'It's no picnic, Erin. This is the hottest time of the year . . .'

He trailed away, glad he hadn't set up the pc cam to show just how tough he was finding it, glass in hand.

'. . . but then you know that.'

'They have aircon last I looked.'

He tried again. 'Well, it's going to be pretty boring. I've done the main interview, and now all that's left is sitting through the first couple of weeks of a trial. You can imagine the pace of an Indian court.'

'You do the court stuff. I'll talk to Ramesh Banerjee. Banker to banker. There's more to find out. And I'll be a long way from Joey Kutzov and his gang. I'll be with you in, say, 36 hours. Stay where you are.'

Was she confining him to his room?

'Let me know your flight. I'll book a room for you. In the meantime, Oscar?'

'Yes, Ted?'

'Can you hook me up with what else is coming through from GA?'

'Already done. I've set up a secure web site. I'll filter out the garbage and dump all the goodies – documents and audio – on to the site. I'll text you an encrypted password. Then you should swap SIMs. How's that?'

'Agreed. So, Erin, keep your head down and get the hell out of town as fast as you can. Right? Good luck people. And Oscar. . . thanks. I'm sorry it's been so long. . .' Ted stuttered to an embarrassing halt.

'That's alright Mr Pulitzer. Just don't let it happen again. And you still owe me dinner at a restaurant of my choice. I'm told the Jules Verne has wonderful views of Paris. Have fun out there. Ciao.'

They disconnected, and a middle-aged, over-weight man, who'd seen too much and felt too little, sat back on the bed thinking about blue eyes and gym membership.

TWENTY TWO

It was a long night for Anila, full of terrible dreams. She was exhausted but couldn't sleep. When the first light brushed the hut and softened the darkness of her room, she lay quiet, thinking about her life. She looked over at her daughter Aastha, soundless on her cot. Only a small billowing of her chest confirmed she was alive. Aastha was more precious to Anila than her own life. She wanted something better for her. A husband who would be kind to her, not like the man forced on her.

Dilip had his mother's looks and her conceits. They shared the same puffy face and sallow skin. Their small hands – which were frequently entwined – were cut from the same roll of dough. Their eyebrows were continuations of each other's. His mother was forever touching him and stroking him, and placing sweets in his mouth.

Her wedding night had been worse than she'd feared. Dilip had been a grunting thoughtless fish on top of her, his skin sweaty and yielding. Mercifully it had been as short as it was brutal. It had set the pattern for a nightly agony that left her nauseous and unfulfilled. Despite the perfunctory process, she'd found herself pregnant within three months.

Her mother-in-law made no allowances. They were living in her spare room in a village where Anila was a stranger. The household chores led straight onto work in the small field they rented. Anila was more servant than daughter-in-law. Especially when the dowry money stopped flowing after her father's death. Dilip took to beating Anila. Sometimes she was so sore that she could not go to work in the field. Then Dilip's mother beat her again and called her lazy.

Anila endured the beatings as her daughter grew from baby to schoolgirl. What choice did she have? Until one day a year ago. . .

At first light Anila stole out of the hut to fetch the water and prepare the fire to make the morning bread – everything with the gentlest touch to avoid making a noise. Dilip had not come home till late and she knew he liked a long sleep to recover. Especially if he'd lost more money at the dice game; the pattern these days. She knew that her mother-in-law would also expect to catch up on sleep. She'd waited up for her son, soothing him and tucking him in.

Anila carried her sleeping daughter outside and tenderly washed her face and hands as the child blinked awake in the warming sun. She left Aastha outside to study her school book and scrawl her letters in the dirt for practice.

But coming in from the bright light into the darkened room Anila didn't see Dilip's discarded sandal. She stumbled and fell all her length into the rickety cooking range; a small fire with a frame holding a pot of steaming rice. She managed to stifle her own cries of pain and shock as her hands scrabbled among the hot coals, but the clatter of the pots and pans, and the hissing of steam and the singed smell of burning rice filled the hut.

A mound of bedding flew up and an angry bellow reverberated round the single room. The curtain was torn back, and Dilip's mother shrieked and flung the first stone at Anila from the ever handy pile by her mattress. Anila scrambled to her feet.

'So sorry, so sorry! I will fix everything!'

But apologies were never going to be enough. Her husband and her mother-in-law would want retribution. Wanted scolded ears, thrashed flesh and piteous appeals for mercy from this ungrateful, useless, penniless creature that they'd given house to. All their generosity at taking such a troublesome wastrel into their bosom had been flung back in their faces. Why, she wasn't even of their caste! The dowry hardly made up for the shame of diluting the family bloodline. Anyway, the money was all spent.

Anila's husband was the first to find his whippy bamboo stick. Anila backed into the corner and crouched there, arms covering her head, presenting a smaller target for them to get a good swing. Suddenly a small figure burst into the hut and hurled herself on top of her mother to shield her.

'Don't hit her! Don't hit!'

Anila smothered her daughter in her arms and turned her into the corner so that her own back would take the flailing canes. In that moment, Anila made a silent vow. She could take the beatings – it was only pain – but she would never allow Aastha to grow into a cowering, damaged young woman. Broken before she'd ever known life or love.

Dilip and his mother paused for a moment, astonished at the child's intrusion. The girl was just as bad as her useless mother. See how she shamed her father and her grandmother. Such ingratitude would not go unpunished.

One night shortly after, when the snores of her husband and her mother-in-law chorused in their sleep, Anila gathered up her daughter and slipped out the hut, taking only the clothes they stood up in, and some dried bread and vegetables secreted from their meagre rations. They simply walked away. Over three days they trudged home to Chandapur and Anila's mother. In the weeks to come, Dilip came and raged at her door. His mother joined him, shrieking like a harridan, demanding Anila's return or payment of more money to let her go. There was still an outstanding amount on the dowry and they wanted every paisa of it.

But eventually son and mother grew bored. There was nothing left to milk from Anila and her mother, except fear and despair. Even that lost its edge and became tedious. Dilip announced he was divorcing her and left her to the life of a permanent social outcast. At least they hadn't marked her; one woman in her village had had her face burned off in a kitchen 'accident'. Another had been blinded by acid so she would never set eye on another man.

Now, a year on, Anila was taking another gamble with her life. This time there was no fall-back position. This time she could not walk away. She lay on her back clutching her small purse to her chest, and tried not to let the silent tears that were running down her cheeks and past her ears erupt into a flood. Today was no time to be weak. Today she would need all her dead father's strength and her mother's wits if they were to avoid destitution. She rolled over and touched her sleeping daughter – lightly, so as not to wake her – and drew strength and purpose from the contact. Then she rose and began to prepare herself.

But before Anila could go down to the village centre and begin her wait for the wood gatherer she heard her name being called. It was Leena and Divya. They were squatting on the ground in front of her hut. Leena's bright smile was hidden. She was looking down and frowning, and drawing circles in the dirt with her finger. Divya's thin arms were gripping her knees tight as though she was afraid they'd start knocking if she let go.

Anila squatted in front of them and faced them. 'I know why you have come. It is about the money, isn't it?'

The two women looked at each other, then Leena, who was always the first to let go, burst out with, 'Please say you have not given all our money away Anila! Please tell us it is not true!'

Divya chimed in, 'After all our troubles and adventures and going all the way to Delhi, how could you betray us?' She said it quietly and it hurt more.

'I have not given your money away. See, here it is!' Anila tugged at her neck purse and pulled out the fat wad. 'See it is all there.'

Relief spread across both her friends' faces. 'Then we are sorry, Anila. The other women have been telling terrible stories of you and how you had used up our 3000 Rupees. And we knew that you did not have 3000 Rupees. Only 1000 is yours. So we are very relieved that our money is still safe. We gave it to you on the journey because you were the biggest and strongest. We let you keep it here as we did not want our useless husbands getting their hands on it too soon.' Divya smiled at Leena.

'But now we would like to take care of our own money, if you please Anila,' said Leena feeling brave and anxious all at once. The money sat where Anila had put it, in her lap. All Anila had to do was count out two piles of 1000 Rupees and hand them over. But that would kill everything.

'Listen to me, Divya and Leena. Do you trust me? Have we not been successful so far? Was it not my idea to go to the bank? And was it not me who arranged everything and got us the money and brought it all back safe and sound?'

'Yes it was you. All those things. But what are you getting at Anila?' There was a strain in little Leena's face and voice again.

'Let me tell you what happened yesterday.' She explained about the money lender and how he was trying to stop her buying the wood. She told them of the deal which she'd struck to buy all the wood today and how she had organised a cooperative of 12 women who would pay her back once they sold their work to the agent. How it was the only way of making the great plan work. And most of all, how she needed to be able to pay for the next four days of wood.

'But why did you not tell us of all this yesterday? And why did you not ask us about using our money in this way?' Divya was rightly cross with her, Anila could see.

'Things happened too fast. I did not know what to do. But it seemed to me that if I had not acted then, all my plans would have been thrown away, and my mother and my daughter would lose everything.' The tears were running freely down her broad face, making her tired eyes seem sadder than a widow's. Soft Leena was crying now too.

'But we are your friends,' Leena wailed. 'Why could you not trust us?'

'I do trust you, and now I am asking for your help. I may not need any of your money but if the other women don't pay me fast enough, I need to be able to pay Mr Roy every day so that he trusts me as a business woman. I must pay him 600 Rupees today which would leave me only 400 for tomorrow, if I only used my money. So I need your money too to tide me over. All I need is 2400 Rupees. So it is not all of our money.'

'Almost all. It might as well be all,' said Leena accusingly.

'But I am sure I will get the money from the other women in four days time when the agent comes.'

'But what if you don't?' Leena was sniffing now. 'What if they can't pay you back or their husbands won't let them. Or the money lender gets up to his tricks again, you know what he's like.'

'That is why I need your money. Just for a few days. Look, I will even pay you interest if you like.'

Divya shook her head. 'No. We don't want to make money from you Anila. All we want is our money back within the four days. Is that not right Leena?' Leena nodded dumbly. 'But if you lose all the money then it must be your responsibility. You will have to pay it all back. Is that fair?'

'That is very fair. I will take the risk.' Anila had reached the point where she would have agreed to anything. She would have walked through hot coals if that had been required of her. She was beyond concern now. The thought of prison for herself, and the streets for her mother and daughter no longer seemed to matter. In ten years she would be dead. And maybe next time she would come back to a better life. 'Most beautiful Saraswati, goddess of purification,' she prayed silently, 'into your hands I place my life this day.'

To show their trust and to give their friend support, the two smaller women took up their now familiar stations either side of Anila and walked with her towards the sound of the straining truck engine.

TWENTY THREE

After three taxi detours and the purchase of a headscarf and dark glasses on her way home from Oscar's, Erin Wishart snuck into her apartment building like someone who hadn't paid her rent. She instructed the concierge to tell anyone who called that she'd gone away. Then she fled up the stairs avoiding the possibility of being trapped in the lift.

She shoved open her door, hit all the lights and shouted 'Come on in, darling. Let me show you around' for the benefit of the hidden assassins. The silence echoed back at her. She dimmed the lights, packed a case and took one last look out at the park. She slipped down the stairs and back out the building and let four yellow cabs go by before hailing the fifth from the kerb. She made two more changes before a final trip out to Newark.

She checked into the Marriott and sat for a long while in her darkened room staring at the glittering lights from the freeway. *Is this real? I could get killed. But I've done nothing. Not yet. Apart from the Lone Ranger bug, of course. Have they found it? Did Kutzov's snooping software betray me? Surely Warwick still has some feelings for me? But why hope for rational behaviour from a bloody coke-head?*

Later, she lay back on her bed and gazed at the ceiling wondering how this craziness had started and how fast it had spiralled out of control. As her imagination drew lurid scenarios, she found herself shaking and panting. She took two of her 2 mg Melatonin pills and curled up under the duvet until warmth and fatigue enveloped her.

Next morning she showered away the grogginess under a torrent of hot water. She packed and then sat on the bed. She checked her watch. *I've got loads of time. I could head into the office as though nothing was wrong and stick my head round his door. But that would mean taking the long march down the blue carpet. Duschene was always there, desk square-on to visitors, jacket buttoned right up, guarding Warwick's office. All he lacked were sandbags and a machine-gun. I can see his dirty wee eyes weighing me up, assessing my current position in Warwick's hierarchy of favourites. Maybe Duschene sees me as competition?*

She hefted her cell phone, then put it down and picked up the room phone. Do I even need to call? Why not just get on the plane? Because they'd know I knew something. . .

She hit the pad and put on her smile. Smile and dial, the first rule of trading on the Fixed Interest desk. Grudgingly Pat put her through. She forced lightness into her voice.

'Just wanted to say I'm off, Warwick. . . time to get back before they forget me. I'll catch you at the next quarterly. Unless you're doing one of your globals? Passing through Hong Kong?'

'I'm tied up here for a few weeks. Preparing for our monthly call with the press analysts. Needing Charlie to be inventive, given our figures. Then I need to get down to Rio to meet José's wife and chose his successor. For the job not the husband,' he laughed.

She swallowed, thinking of the unctuous insincerity that he'd ooze over poor José's wife.

'Look, Warwick, about José, it's still hard to take in. I'm due some downtime. I'm going to set my out-of-office for a week. Book into the Peninsula Spa in HK. My number two can handle things, but my PA will haul me out of the steam room if you need me. OK?'

'Sure. Recharge. You sound tired. We all need to shake this stuff out of our heads. You fly safe and keep those reds out of your bed.'

She wished he'd stop using that stupid quip, and hung up before she screamed at him.

Warwick too, cut off the speaker connection and pulled over the photo. Kutzov had left it on his desk and had marked the time, date and place. It was taken inside the café of the local bookshop. It showed José Cadenza and Erin Wishart in earnest conversation. Warwick's face flooded with blood, his jaw muscles contorted and he felt the room closing in on him. Slowly, he ripped the photo into tiny pieces before heading for his washroom.

A day later in travel time and two days by calendar, Erin Wishart was wheeling her trolley towards the exit signs in Kolkata airport. It was nearly midnight local time. No matter how many miles she clocked up, it didn't get easier. In her weariness she wondered again why she'd been so impulsive, other than being annoyed at Ted Saddler's attempts to thwart her. There were a thousand better boltholes than this. Like the Peninsula Spa in Hong Kong. And the thought of having to whip some life into a reluctant reporter with a pickled liver held little attraction. But as usual, if she wanted anything done well, she had to take charge.

Her trolley had a faulty wheel and she had to wrestle it round the cluttered arrival hall. It wasn't like the last time she'd come to India – barely a year ago – when she'd descended from on high as GA's top executive in the region, outranking the area manager. Back then, before landing, she'd changed into the power suit in the toilet and donned the boss make-up and heels. The metaphorical red carpet and the very real limo were waiting, along with a small group of flunkies to cosset her and make her feel important. She'd swept in, cell phone ringing and urgent messages piling up, to lord it over her fiefdom.

This time, her phone was silent. In the private lounge for Concierge Key holders at Newark she'd called her regional assistant to tell her she was taking time out for a week and didn't need collecting at Hong Kong. Then she'd personally fixed the second leg of her journey to Kolkata. At Hong Kong she'd showered in the VIP lounge and had a manicurist remove her nail varnish, knowing it would chip to pieces within a day.

This time, coming into land at Kolkata airport she put a brush through her hair and pulled it back in a single ponytail. Her eyes were gritty from the recycled cabin air so she kept on her specs. Trainers dropped her height. The low key grooming left her feeling inconspicuous, as planned, but also curiously naked. The pampering rituals of New York had seemed outrageous vanity on first arrival but it hadn't taken long to get used to the weekly blow dries and manicures.

Now, instead of a bunch of nervous little men waiting for her, dressed to the nines in suit, collar and tie, there was one shambling big guy. She saw Ted and realised he didn't recognise her. He looked anxious. She hoped he hadn't been drinking. She steered towards him and slapped on a smile.

Ted was calling himself stupid, crazy. She was bossy and full of Scottish rectitude, and in any other circumstances, wouldn't have wasted a glance on him, maybe not even in his heyday, whenever that was. She was only coming to make his life more difficult. He kept finding his finger nails in his mouth and pulling them back in annoyance.

For the first time in – well, who knows how long? – he had the glimmer of a sense of purpose, as though something had been switched on inside of him. It left him schizophrenic; half irritated and half expectant. Half ready to bolt, half up for it, whatever 'it' was. He analysed the expectant emotion: he was waiting for a girl at an airport, and no matter how he weighed up the case against Theodore Saddler ever getting past first base with this girl, it still felt good. As the notion crystallised, he chided himself. She was just the source and symbol of meaningful activity. That was the sensation he'd not felt in a while.

Her flight was late and he wandered over to the newspaper shop and bought a New York Tribune, printed in New Delhi and circulated across India. He flicked through to the business section and scanned the headlines till he found his piece. The copy he'd filed was more even-handed than Stan had wanted; than Ted had expected. Guilt was a powerful driver. Glancing through the article, his own phrases jumped out at him:

> …hard to visualise this decrepit office block as a breeding ground for corruption. Flies maybe…
>
> …micro-finance if applied right, can work…it's how Bank of America started a century ago in Manhattan's Lower East Side among Italian immigrants.
>
> This story might indeed be about corruption. The question is whose and where? Mr Banerjee talks … about underhand tactics by a major competitor. A Western competitor. . .

He'd left plenty of room for rowing back in the light of new facts but it was still a tonal shift. It had been a wrestling match to begin with; Stan sceptical of the softer line and muttering how hard this would play on the top floor. But say what you like about Stan, he was an old-style newspaper man and he didn't like being dictated to from on high. He always backed his boys down on the street, especially unfriendly foreign streets.

Ted began his prowling again, wondering if Erin would appreciate his new angle, or even detect it. He pulled out of his waistband the light-weight sports shirt he'd unearthed from his discard pile in the spare room. Better – cooler and less constricting. He kept casting around. There was a fresh eddy of arriving passengers chugging behind their piled trolleys. He almost missed her.

Then he caught the smile and the eyes behind the glasses. She looked like her younger, smaller, less threatening sister. She was in sneakers, and like him, shirt loose outside blue jeans. As she closed in on him he saw the gaze of the tough executive he'd met in New York. For a second, all his doubts flooded back, and he wondered what the hell this stranger had got him into.

So he was glad of the smile. It might have been all that was on offer, but it was at least a recognition that they were in this together. He didn't know whether to shake hands, embrace her, or do air-kisses like they were in a Chi-Chi Manhattan restaurant. In the paralysis of their forced relationship they mustered a couple of self conscious waves from way too close.

'Hi, Ted! My god, that's a long haul.'

'Thought you were used to it? Can I push that?'

He took over the recalcitrant trolley holding her one case and smart leather backpack. They pushed through the doors into the steam-bath outside. He fended off the touts and beggars – feeling positively like a local – and waved to the car he'd hired from the hotel. It was a small Merc with a bright young man driving. He was out the door and hauling her case into the car before they knew it. They fell into the air-conditioned luxury of the back seat and Erin was immediately on the attack.

'So what have you been up to? When can I see Banerjee?'

'It's midnight. Don't you ever sleep?

'I like to plan the day ahead.'

'Fixed for tomorrow morning. Do you get sick in cars if you read?'

'Nope. Travelling is catch-up time between meetings.'

'Try this.' He handed her the Tribune, folded at the place.

She read it once, then again. She smiled, genuinely this time.

'Not quite on the side of the angels yet. But progress. What was he like?'

'Ramesh? A combination of prophet and financial whiz. Is he really that good? Is anyone?'

'We'll see tomorrow. But my research says so.'

He heard the challenge. 'Let's keep the notion open. But I still need hard evidence, so maybe I'm more Thomas than Paul.'

'Why's it so hard?' She wasn't asking it of Ted in particular.

He thought for minute.

'Altruism embarrasses us. Too unsophisticated, too heart-on-your-sleeve. Too naïve for us Western sophisticates?'

She was silent for a while, looking out the window. They both gripped the door handles tightly as the car braked and dived through the traffic, still manic at midnight.

'So why are we here?' she asked turning back to him and inspecting him.

'I'm just trying to keep my job.'

'One of us should. I'm hoping that it doesn't matter how it started out. That what counts is how we take it from here and what we make of it.'

Ted didn't like the way the conversation was going. It sounded too much like a quest for his liking, and he'd given up all that tilting at windmills stuff.

They dropped the philosophical discussions and pointed out the poorly lit streets to each other as they drove to the Oberoi Grand. It was like passing an endless series of Caravaggio tableaus; lives lit by cooking fires, neon tubes and cigarette glows. She mentioned how nice it was to be travelling on the correct side of the road for a change. He pointed out the irrelevance of that remark given the chaos outside.

By the time they got to the hotel her face was showing the strain of the last 24 hours flying and the last few days of playing spies. There were red spots on her pale cheeks, and behind her glasses her eyes were dark ringed. They agreed to meet at breakfast prior to seeing Ramesh together in a small conference room at the hotel. Ted had convinced Ramesh it would be good to get some real privacy. But he was also thinking of air conditioning and imported coffee.

In the meantime there was his bed, CNN, and a restocked minibar.

TWENTY FOUR

Carly Sofersen got her first real job just three months after graduation. Her heart had been set on becoming a news reader – she had the right voice and looks, all her friends had told her. It was there in her year book Carly Sofersen, the next star of stage and screen! And Carly, CNN's anchor! So it would be true.

Her father had pulled a few strings with some old marketing buddies who in turn had mentioned it to a news executive. Carly had taken the train into New York, all the way from her home in Albany, to be interviewed for and offered the job of trainee journalist at the New York Tribune. Carly's initial sense of awe at living and working in Manhattan, and being on the first rung of the ladder to news reader was beginning to wear off. Sure, she'd now seen plenty of her heroines in the flesh. And sure there was a buzz about the place. But essentially her job was a glorified office junior.

It had been particularly humiliating to be told by two of the older journalists and one sub editor that she couldn't write. What that had to do with news reading was beyond her. All she wanted was the chance to get in front of those cameras and she'd show them. So she wore smart two-piece suits, bought for her by Mommy after a huge expedition to Madison Avenue, and she kept a clip-board under her arm at all times and made sure she was often in the sightlines of the top executives. It was only a matter of time.

Meanwhile, she fielded odd jobs for some of the senior journalists, like Ted Saddler. She liked Ted, even though he scared her at times. But he was friendly without wanting to get too close, like some of the other men. Ted always seemed more interested in her; his eyes didn't automatically go to her legs or her chest. He looked her straight in the face. Like her father. He kept telling her she'd make it; it just took time. Occasionally he would let her work on a piece so that she could get the 'feel' of the words, he said. In return, Carly did helpful things like check his mail or get him a sandwich if she was heading to the canteen too.

So when she noticed the flat, book-sized package on his desk, she picked it up and looked at the labels. It was from Florida and it was marked Urgent, Private and Personal, Theodore Saddler. She knew he was over in India doing something big about a bank, so she let it sit for a day or two. Then, as no-one else seemed to care about it one way or the other, she decided to show some initiative; which would please Ted, she was certain. She put the package inside a FedEx envelope and, after checking with Travel, addressed the package to Ted's hotel in Kolkata. Before she closed the envelope, she stuck a post-it note in the shape of a heart on the original and wrote in a big round hand, Thought this was important, love, Carly.

She called FedEx and left the package at the reception desk downstairs. Feeling pleased with herself, she went back up to check her make-up and hair in the women's restroom, the one that Sandi Carmichael herself sometimes used just before going on air.

TWENTY FIVE

'OK, what are we trying to get out of this meeting, Ted?'

Erin looked much sharper when she joined him in the meeting room. Sleep or make-up had erased the dark from under eyes. Her skin looked clearer, tighter. She was back in contact lenses, work blouse, skirt and jacket. The switch threw Ted. Here we go – back in the board room.

'Ramesh talked generally about the bank being under attack – from the press, the government, the competition and the like. I need more details. Specifics. This is your area. See if any of this stacks up with your insider views of Stanstead's methods.'

She nodded. 'He also mentioned technology attacks. That's a different ball game.'

'Absolutely. Over to you. I don't have a sense of what it means.'

'Does Ramesh know who I am?'

'I had to tell him something.'

'Like what?'

'I didn't give a name. Just said you're a senior exec in one of the lead Western banks – I didn't say which – and that you're struggling with your conscience.'

He waited for her reaction.

'With regard to the senior exec – we might already be talking past tense. But I have no trouble with my conscience, not now.'

There was a knock on the door. It opened and a young man in immaculate whites entered. 'Mr Banerjee, madam, sir.'

He stood aside and Ramesh walked in, beaming from behind his big glasses. They all shook hands.

'Well, Ted, it is a start. We will convert you yet.' He waved a copy of the Tribune.

'Don't get carried away Ramesh. You'll note I hedged my bets. I'm the original sceptic. I need more evidence, which is partly why Miss Erin Wishart is here.'

Ramesh stood back and inspected Erin. Just as frankly, she stared back, getting the measure of this man.

'I've heard of you, Miss Erin Wishart. Global American is it not?'

She didn't hesitate. 'Yes. Though it's moot whether I still work for them. Things have been moving fast lately.'

She was confident and open, as though she'd stepped over a line. Ramesh sucked in his breath.

'And what would the regional head of GA want with a humble bank manager like me?'

'Why don't we sit down and I'll tell you all about it, Mr Banerjee?'

Erin led them over to the small table with four chairs. She then took Ramesh through her story in a lucid and utterly candid exposition that left nothing unsaid – except the stuff about José Cadenza and Mrs Yeardon. Ted was impressed. There was none of the patronising, talking-down style that he expected. She was formidable without being hectoring.

Ramesh interrupted only once or twice to check points or get elaboration. At the end, he sat back and looked at them both. He took off his glasses and made himself defenceless for a moment while he cleaned them with a fresh piece of linen taken from inside his tunic.

'First, Miss Wishart, I want to thank you for being so open with me. You have put yourself in a very difficult position. The question is, what do we do about it now? I am sitting on top of a bank that is about to be closed. I myself am about to stand up in court and face a trial whose outcome has probably already been decided by my government. And your bank might be responsible. What was it a French general said? Hard pressed on my right. Centre is yielding. Impossible to manœuvre. Situation excellent. Attack!'

'I bet it wasn't a woman general. We like better odds. Can you give me a run-down of the main ways you're being pressured?'

'Pressured? How very British. A fine euphemism for fraud, sabotage, attempted murder, slander and libel!'

'Attempted murder! Anything missing from that list, Ramesh?' she asked wryly.

'It will do.' His grin showed his sense of humour had survived. 'There are three ways in which we are under attack. The first – and this is in no special order you understand – is obviously the trial.'

'I thought you said that was just the Government with a particular grudge against you?' asked Ted.

'Yes, but someone is working on them behind the scenes – an agent provocateur if you will. Perhaps Mr Stanstead's doing? Otherwise I would have been able to head off the Government opposition. I still have friends there, and it is not as if we are child molesters or some such. I know the men in charge. In fact if I hadn't known them they would have issued a non-bailable warrant for my arrest and those of my officers. I would have been in prison now till the trial. As it is, they don't answer my phone calls, they avoid me at top level receptions or I simply don't get invited. You have to be born here to detect it, that little shift in expression, that cast of the eyes, that change in tack. They have been bribed. And they know that I know! But they also know I can prove nothing.'

Erin butted in. 'If money changed hands, then there should be a trace. There's always a record somewhere.'

'That may be true, Miss Wishart, but how would I find it?'

'Let's assume that we're talking about serious sums of money,' she said. Ramesh nodded. 'And that it's probably a reserve currency – forgive me, no disrespect to the Rupee.' Ramesh smiled and shook his head. 'Dollars or Euros. Then somewhere there will be a record of cash leaving a bank and

132

going into accounts somewhere else, right? My bet is that if we could do a pass on Global American's transactions we could spot some interesting movements to named accounts.'

'But that's a needle in the mother of all haystacks, Erin! Not with all the transactions that your bank sees daily.' Ted was incredulous.

'GA has spent hundreds of millions on the most sophisticated data warehouse systems in the world. We have a daily volume of around 100 million transactions peaking at 250 million some days. But we have computer power that can sift the whole customer database over the past year and pick out a single transaction. If need be, we can go into the historical details up to three years back, but that takes longer.'

She looked down for a minute with a puzzled frown. 'The only problem is getting access. Even I had only limited powers – general searches, spotting trends, and so on. This would need a dedicated slice of our computing resources for – oh I guess – two, three hours.'

Ted thought she was going to say days or weeks. 'That doesn't sound too bad. Can you call someone?'

She shook her head. 'That amount of high-priced computing power needs Warwick's personal authority. And I guess he's not going to play ball.'

'What about Oscar? Could he hack in?'

She looked hard at him. 'You really think this guy is pretty special don't you.' He could see her brain sifting the problem. 'It's possible I guess. If the Lone Ranger software we 'installed' at GA could be used, then maybe. . .'

'Lone Ranger?' asked Ramesh with a raised eyebrow.

Ted waved a hand. 'Don't ask. Why don't we call Oscar and see what he can come up with?' Erin agreed and she turned back to Ramesh.

'Ok Ramesh, what's the next offence against you?'

'Despite our third world image, the People's Bank is one of the most technologically advanced in the business. We are number one for the ratio of branches to Internet accounts accessed by mobile phones. It's why we have been so successful in the developing and the developed world. We offer superb technical facilities to our clients along with the chance to salve their consciences.' He smiled.

'And the problem is….?' Ted asked.

'Our computer systems – our lifeblood and backbone – are under attack. We have the best firewalls in the business, and fall-back capacity that would be the envy of our armed forces – if they knew we had it. But over the last six or so months we have come under a series of bombardments aimed at crippling us. My technical chaps can explain it better. So far we have managed to deflect them, but they tell me it is only a matter of time, Miss Wishart.' He looked meaningfully at her.

'GA's work?' Ted asked Erin.

'Could be. I'm sorry, Ramesh, and please call me Erin.'

'It is not your fault – Erin.'

'Let's put this on Oscar's list as well.' Ted said. 'What's the third problem Ramesh? You mentioned attempted murder?'

'They are inciting the villages. They say we are worse than the money lenders. That we will call our loans in and steal their land, and the dispossessed will have to go and beg in the cities. Gangs of thugs are stirring up fears and targeting workers from this bank. Some are still in hospital.'

'Can't you get the local police to help?' Ted asked, with a sinking feeling about the answer.

Ramesh smiled sadly at them and shrugged his thin shoulders. 'We think that in many cases, it is being coordinated by the local police.'

Erin broke in, 'Where's your tech centre? Could we visit it?'

Ted's stomach flipped. More gadding about in this mosquito zone.

'Certainly. In Delhi, they can tell you better about what the cyber attacks. It might make it easier for your colleague – Oscar? – to get a proper understanding. New Delhi is also where the trial starts in a week. I am meeting with my defence team there on Monday. We are going through the process of discovery of evidence.'

'That would work, Ted.' Erin seemed childishly excited. 'We could talk to the techies. And maybe some customers. We'd be back in time for the trial.'

Ted noticed the 'we' commitments, but decided to save his arguments for later, when they were alone. He felt cornered. Just as he'd expected, things were beginning to run away from him. He wasn't quite sure who was in control of this operation, but it sure as hell wasn't Ted Saddler.

Erin and Ramesh spent a further while talking banking – most of it over Ted's head – while he wondered if he'd had enough shots before he'd left New York to deal with whatever was out there waiting to bite him. Then his heightened instincts for self preservation strayed to thinking about the death arranged for José Cadenza and whether there were any vaccinations against a bullet.

TWENTY SIX

'I feel like a voyeur.'

Erin was walking beside him, her arms clasped around her, hugging herself. She'd felt jet lag clawing at her mind again, and needed out of the hotel to stretch her legs before dinner. He advised against it, but at her insistence, took her round the block, just like his first night. It didn't get any better, but the big-eyed kid wasn't there when they passed the spot. He told Erin about her.

'You're a funny man, Ted Saddler.'

'How so, Miss Wishart?' They were re-entering the world of privilege and air conditioning as he asked this.

'I'm sorry, I've no right to make any comment about you. I hardly know you. But we can put that right. You can tell me about the real Ted Saddler over dinner.'

She'd better get to know something about this man if they were forced to spend the next few days together. She was aware of his resentment at being pushed around. She knew the signs. Men found her hard to be around, threatening, especially those that worked for her. And for now, that included Ted Saddler. So be it. He was going to help this bank, whether he liked it or not. She knew it would oil the process a little if she showed some interest in him.

Ted ducked her questions right through until his second double bourbon had chinked its way down and they'd ordered food. She pushed him again as he pulled on a large glass of wine. Tackled him while he was still more or less sober.

'You go first,' he countered.

'Typical.'

'Just being a gent.'

'Just being a man. Never give anything away.'

'Self preservation. The more you explain, the more women want.'

'Hey, I'm not your therapist. What are you hiding?' she asked.

'What do you think?'

'Your light?'

'Do these qualify as bushels?' Ted flicked the nearby potted palm. 'Ok, ok. I'll keep it simple. I'm 51, born and brought up in Denver, Colorado. Came to New York – a long time ago. Been a hack ever since I can remember. Started with the college journal, then three years in the Army Press Corps – embedded with the Marines. Even had to do the training and carry a gun. Just in time for the Iraq War. Gave me plenty to write about but I struggled with the house style. Not to mention the house message. With the Tribune ever since.'

Erin noticed he didn't mention the Pulitzer or his wife.

'For a journalist, you're short on words.'

He shrugged, and refilled his glass. Her eyes followed the movement.

'Drinking to forget?'

He lowered the glass slowly and put it down carefully. His eyes narrowed.

'Anti-malarial. Do you always mind this much?'

'I don't care what you do.'

Their eyes locked in challenge, then broke at the same moment. She'd better rein back. She'd spent so long avoiding over-indulgence of any sort – booze especially – that she knew she came over priggish. God help him if he smoked, too. She examined him more closely, looking for any sign of the Marine-trained athlete. Maybe it was still there, if he lost a couple of stone. And gave his liver a holiday. She waved away the wine waiter before he topped up his glasses.

'Folks?' she changed tack.

He stretched for the bottle, and with deliberation, poured his own. The departing waiter looked hurt.

'Mom and Pop still in Denver. Retired now. And a kid brother. Mom was a teacher and my old man used to work in the marshalling yards. I grew up surrounded by trains and cattle. Pop would take me out with him in the summer to the signalling box and we'd watch trains coming through with miles of wagons, two engines pulling and one pushing. Sometimes they'd take forty minutes to pass us by.' His face took on some light.

'Your brother?'

'David works up at Vail. Got a ski shop in winter and rents mountain bikes and stuff in the summer. Wife and a couple of kids. Has it made.'

'I love Vail! It's my favourite.'

'I took you for Aspen.'

'Ski bunnies.'

Food came and they started in on their meal. Erin sipped water.

'Do you go home much?' she asked.

'It's been a while. Maybe after this, I'll take a trip out there. Head up to Vail in the summer. Get Dave to teach me how to ride those bikes of his. I haven't skied in years. Probably forgotten how.'

'You won't. Go do it.'

She touched his arm in her enthusiasm and wrenched it back as if she'd hit a live wire. Quickly she changed topic.

'Did you always want to be a journalist?'

'Just wanted to write. My folks always told me I should. Teachers and other kids, too. Line of least resistance.'

'Lights and bushels, again. Just reporting? What about other stuff? Scripts, novels?'

She was surprised at the flush that suffused his face.

'I stick to what I'm good at.'

She picked at the spot. 'We've all got a book in us. Where's yours?'

He chewed at a nail, inspected the damage, and put his hands in his lap.

'I guess I've spread mine across a thousand columns.'

He shrugged. This was as far as he would go.

'You were married?'

'Uh huh. I've been going through a messy divorce, like forever.'

Erin had heard a dozen stories like it. Next it would be his wife didn't understand him. She wondered if he'd make a pass at her? The way he sometimes looked at her.

'And in the same spirit, what about you, Erin? Marriage, kids? What brought you to New York? It's a long way from Bonnie Scotland.'

'It's not all bonnie, trust me.'

'Well, is there some sort of master plan?'

'Good grief no. There was a direction once. But sort of vague. Just a determination to get out of a crummy flat in a crummy estate.'

'You sure managed that.'

'But now I'm stuck. Scared to go forward and no idea how to go back.'

'No guy in your life?' he asked softly.

'Hah. Assuming you find the right man – and it gets harder with every year and every promotion let me tell you – it means giving up your own time and space.'

'Always a trade-off.'

She nodded. 'I'm not explaining this very well, am I? Look, my Dad died when I was in my teens. Mum lived for him. No matter what he did. There was nothing else. I mean nothing. I came a distant second, and when Dad died, so did Mum. Once I started earning I got her out of the crummy tower block and installed her in a smart wee flat in the West End of Glasgow. She's just sitting there now, waiting her turn. Is that what it's about? Because if it is, I'll stay single thanks and make the best of the chances that come my way. On the other hand, if somebody waved a wand and made me seventeen again, with the same choices, would I take it? Would you? Wouldn't you like to take another run at it?'

'Acne again and going back to high school?' His big hand made balancing motions above his plate. 'I don't think so.'

'Or breaking your heart over a new girl? Skiing first powder in Vail's back bowls?'

That made him laugh. She saw her chance.

'There! Don't you see? That's what this is all about? This isn't just another story, it's a second chance. Another Pulitzer Prize. A fresh start!'

Ted wondered who'd mentioned the Prize, and thought he could guess. He studied her excited face. When she let go she was really quite cute. A little of her fire lit a spark. Why not? He straightened his shoulders and his eyes gained focus. As though he was seeing her and the problem properly for the first time.

'Ok. Here's the deal. I'll give this my best shot if you stop organising my life for me.' His chin jutted forward.

'I'm not!'

'Well I sure hadn't planned to interview the rest of the bank in Delhi. And I'm no teetotaller, is that understood?'

He'd been saving this. His face was red. She denied nothing, but inspected him challengingly.

'Only if you're ready to drop all this – this – world weariness. Why don't we both put our scepticism on ice, open ourselves up to whatever comes our way? Try leading with our hearts instead of our heads for a change. What do you say?'

She wondered where this juvenile bravado was coming from. He eyed her critically, and she thought she'd gone too far. Then he lifted his glass and let out a grudging smile.

'I say, here's to being seventeen again! Cheers!'

They clinked glasses and she wondered just what sort of genie she'd released.

TWENTY SEVEN

By reputation, Air India was the least likely of the local outfits to fall out of the sky, but Ted Saddler was still clutching hard at the armrests as they took off from Kolkata next morning. The lack of booze on board was probably a good thing for his liver, but less good for his peace of mind. While the sun chased them across the northern plains he thought about last night's dinner and how Erin had manipulated him into taking up a lance. It wasn't his style. She hadn't mentioned it this morning. But it was always hard to tell what Miss Cool was thinking.

They bounced to a halt on an empty runway while the tannoy played Ciao Ciao Bambino without visible embarrassment to the Indian crew. They rescued their cases and walked through the new concourse towards the exit and the now familiar crowds of well-wishers with hands out. They were back in the steam bath.

It was clear that taxis in Delhi were no different in style, dents, and age to Kolkata. Same for the driving. But somehow it was better with her beside him. It turned a survival test into an adventure, and they pointed like kids as they wove past elephants and a troop of the scruffiest camels he'd ever seen. Not that he was a connoisseur of the beast, but somehow he could imagine there might be better models around.

They showered and changed at the Hyatt and met in the lobby. Erin switched from jeans into a linen blouse and white skirt. She left her hair in a pony-tail but was back in glasses to rest her eyes. A high-school teacher from the fifties. Ted didn't trust the transformation; it was just another front by a trained manipulator. Ted himself mustered an off-cream, plantation owner suit that Mary had made him buy years ago. Another item from the discard pile. He'd had it laundered for the trip but it already looked slept in. India was turning out to be a place for second chances all round. It was 4 pm and they had an interview at five with a Mr CJ Kapoor, the local regional head of the People's Bank in Delhi.

It was New Delhi rush hour. They had to go clear across town, which meant they saw more than their fair share of British architectural relics. Erin pointed out mischievously that America had also left its mark: Big Mac and Coke signs were everywhere. Even Starbucks had penetrated Delhi, and were heading to Kolkata. Soon they entered the chaos of the Chandni Chowk across a throbbing flow of battered traffic hurtling in all directions. Hanging from dented rear bumpers were mocking 'Green Delhi' signs coated in their own noxious deposits.

Their driver pulled down a ludicrously jammed side street and gave up. An ox cart was demanding right of way over a truck, and a good sized crowd had collected to watch the fun and rate the quality of the insults.

'Come on, let's walk,' she commanded, opening her door.

She left him no choice. He hated being ordered around, but in the funniest of ways, and not that he'd admit it, he was excited. The din and the heat were twin hammers, the ant-heap in perpetual jostling motion. They stuck out, milky pale, and tall. Even Erin in her trainers had the advantage over these nimble people. Against the onslaught of begging Ted learned fast, persisting with three 'no thanks' until a conscious stop and stare into their eyes and a final slow but smiling 'no thank you' deflected them. Was it the eye contact? Did they need to be recognised? Or just four times telling?

Erin grabbed his arm and stuck close, which made him feel strong. Which was partly what she intended. The bank was supposed to be on the left, behind a wall. They almost missed it until she yanked him back and pointed out the small but clear plaque in English and Sanskrit. It was timely. They were unpicking beggars' hands as fast they could without causing offence. Erin was getting most of the attention.

'That man groped me! He bloody well groped me!'

Erin whirled round, outraged, and pointed at a smirking face as it melted in the crowd. She was ready to chase when Ted took her by the elbow, with maybe a little more firmness than was absolutely necessary.

'C'mon. Let's get out of this!'

He pulled her back by his side and ushered her up the steps. He pressed hard on the bell for entrance. The door eased and sanctuary beckoned. They flung themselves inside, into a cool reception area where they were obviously expected. A woman came forward, magnificent in a green sari. She established who they were, and escorted them through to a courtyard a thousand miles from the street. It was hushed and cool under a great Pepul tree. A small lily pond lay at its centre and the four walls of the surrounding buildings were softened by creeping vines. A small round man with glasses was standing by a table with four chairs.

'I thought it would be nice to have tea out here.'

His voice was clear and friendly. He wore a brown kurta and white trousers, and his round features were dominated by a fine nose and a carefully cut moustache. He beckoned them over and they sat down with expressions of pleasure at the tranquillity and coolness. Erin's face was beginning to lose its heat. She was rubbing her elbow.

'This is a great pleasure. Ramesh has told me all about you both. It is quite an unusual meeting, don't you think?'

'It certainly is, Mr Kapoor. But then, there's been a slightly surreal quality about everything recently,' Ted said.

'Please, call me CJ. Ramesh said you wanted to have proof of the attacks on their bank?'

The lady in green brought tea as he asked this. The ceremony of setting out the fine white china and the serving of the lemons and finally the pouring of the 'chai' itself took several minutes. Finally they were left to themselves and they got down to it.

'CJ, we want to help.' Ted and Erin's voices collided with each other. CJ looked amused. Erin deferred.

'Both of us,' said Ted. 'But just so it's clear; I report the news. I don't make it. I can get your story some international exposure, but I have to be certain about what I'm writing.'

'It is refreshing to find a reporter who only deals in the facts, Ted.'

CJ said it with an absolutely straight face. Ted didn't look at Erin.

'Whereas, I *can* act CJ,' she said. 'As Ramesh will have told you, there is a possibility that my bank is involved. Though I'm not sure I can refer to it as *my* bank any more. There seem to be a number of burnt bridges immediately to my rear.'

'I would not worry if I were you. If this is what your heart is telling you, then it is the right path, this time. Each time we return to earth we learn if our past life has been spiritually profitable and try to make the next one richer for others.'

'I prefer the carpe diem philosophy myself,' she said.

'That too has its place. Shall we meet some of my people?'

He led them from the cool sanctuary into a huge noisy hall that looked like it had once been three separate rooms. It was an incongruous blend of oak panelling and racks of modern technology, crammed with people. Enough computer screens to fight Star Wars. Ranks of air con units pounding away in a losing battle against the sauna temperatures.

They threaded their way to the epicentre of the maze, tripping over cables as they went. They found themselves at a small round table that seemed to be used for ad hoc meetings. Around it, with their backs to them and their fingers clacking over keyboards, was a circle of young men and women. Most wore headsets and were talking as they typed. The hubbub was immense.

CJ raised his voice. 'This is the heart of the bank. Around you is the core technology that handles all our customer accounts, and networks together the call centres we've set up in other cities. Over there is our Internet banking team. And over there is the control centre of our branch banking network. This circle of people,' he indicated the group ringed about them and the table, 'are the lead technicians for each of the sections.

'They all look about sixteen.' Ted cupped a comment to Erin.

'Young and quick. Lovely.' She was chirpy. This was her element.

CJ was tapping shoulders and signalling. About half the young people in the ring turned round and rolled over to the centre table on their wheeled chairs. They gazed curiously at the Westerners.

'Ok, Action Woman, this one's yours,' Ted said gallantly.

Erin pulled up a spare chair and sat down at the table. Ted joined her. CJ made the introductions. A young man touchingly raised his hand.

'Please, shall I go first, CJ?'

'Why not? This is Vikram Vajpayee. He is the team leader of our branch banking division. Tell them what has been going on Vikram.'

Ted didn't understand all of it, but Erin clearly did, from the way she kept asking questions and the way the conversation got increasingly heated as Vikram showed her examples on his main screens and on his tablet.

The bank was broken down into districts and branches. The branches operated autonomously day to day, apart from central direction about bank rates. As often as not, the branches were little more than a secure van equipped with a computer and satellite phone. The branch 'manager' – usually a woman, drove round her district, setting up mobile phone accounts, and then organising savings and loans and collecting repayments. Vikram called up a Google map of India on his tablet, zeroed in on some areas to show how huge a slab of territory could be covered by one branch.

They appointed local representatives in selected villages and gave them laptops with solar power units and satellite internet links with the rest of the bank network. Each day they'd do their entries and email the information to the branch officer and then to head office here in this room in Delhi. Every few days the branch manager would make for a district office and deposit the cash. For security they were never allowed to hold more than the Rupee equivalent of $500 in their van.

Vikram got onto the dirty tricks. It varied between jamming transmissions so that half the branches were unable to report, or sending waves of dummy transactions to flood the servers at head office. Sometimes the floods went the other way, as if from the Delhi centre, and knocked out the district computer and the van laptop when they logged in.

Vikram and his team were working round the clock – he meant it literally – to rebuild firewalls and create new security codes that would counter the attacks. There would be a few days' grace then another onslaught would begin, using different techniques and volumes. The story was similar from Shivani Jaffrey, a young woman who ran the Internet team. There was no hint of surrender about her. A clear light of battle was in her big dark eyes.

'We have over 250 million Internet accounts now. More than most banks have customers. Over 70% are from outside India. We give them the same range of account facilities as our branch customers. But because we can manage so many people over the Internet, we can keep the costs very low and give very good deposit rates and interest on current accounts.' Erin looked impressed and Shivani looked proud to bursting.

'Like Vikram's branches, we are being hit by waves of dummy transactions. The first couple of times it happened we lost our servers for two days! The next time, we were better prepared but they still went down for a few hours. We have added lots more servers and rebuilt our own firewall software to sift and kill the ones that are wrecking us. Only the good ones can get through from our real customers.'

Shivani went on, 'But they have got hold of some of our

customer identities and also set up dummy accounts with us. They use those as Trojan horses to get in through the firewalls and release some nasty viruses that attack our customer account files. Fortunately our virus detector software is very strong. We have so far managed to kill every one! But we are worried,' she became solemn, 'the next one may get through. So we are having to build redundancy into all our records. We keep complete back-up files for months in separate systems. Separate buildings even.'

Erin was nodding all the while. 'We have a very clever friend who's one of the best –' she groped for a polite way of describing Oscar '– software specialists in the business. And we would like to get him to look at what's happening here. He may have some ideas. He's very experienced in dealing with hacking and counter hacking.'

'What is he called?' asked Vikram with a little hint of knowing something about the opaque world Oscar operated in. 'Is he a hacker?'

'His real name is Oscar, but he uses a different handle. He's called 'The Lone Ranger' . . . on the dark net'. Erin tried not to sound silly.

There was a flurry of smiles and chatter among the kids round the table. Then Vikram turned to Erin.

'We know this man. He is one of the best. Or the worst. Are you sure he is on your side? How do we contact him?'

'Give me your email address now and I'll text him. I'll call him this evening to make sure he's opened up secure channels with you.'

They left them to their battle. Ted wondered what these young people and one gay hacker could really do against a western bank with thousands of top technologists and the best computer systems dollars could buy. He still hadn't entirely squared away the notion that they were making money out of the neediest, but none of the bank employees seemed in the slightest doubt about the morality of their work. That was convincing enough for his next column, but apparently not for Erin. He listened with a sense of stunned outrage and impending doom as she set him up for a further test of stamina.

'CJ, all Ted needs now is to meet some of your clients and maybe spend some time at one of your branches.' She turned to Ted. 'You can pop out and visit a village while I sort out the links with Oscar.'

Ted's mouth opened like a fish and closed without sound. CJ beamed at him.

'I think I have the perfect example for you, Ted. It will involve some travel, but you will see first hand how we start up an operation in the villages. Do you mind taking a longish trip? It might not be very comfortable.'

Ted wanted to say that of course he minded, especially if a local was suggesting that accommodation on the trip might fall some way short of five stars. Ted's imagination filled with large bugs, rivers of sweat, zero sanitation and rare bowel disorders. It was likely to be as close to purgatory as made no difference. He was glad he'd secreted a couple of bottles of Old Tennessee in his bag for just such an emergency. One bit of luck was that Erin wouldn't be joining him; it meant he could suffer out loud and have a drink without the air frosting around him.

'No problem, CJ.'

'Good. Good! Then I will make the preparations. Tomorrow I will send one of my new district managers with you. She is opening up a new district for us. She is specifically following up a small loan we made just a few weeks ago. The loan was to three women who made their way here to Delhi from their village in Madya Pradesh. A five day round trip to open a bank account. Remarkable really. It shows they are the right sort of customer, don't you think? And now we need to give them local support. So early tomorrow we will send you off to Chandapur.'

TWENTY EIGHT

Anila found herself shouting at Mr Chowdury in front of a large crowd. They were standing next to Mr Roy's truck. The money lender was dressed in his usual humble garb like the toilers in the field: a simple tunic top, a loin cloth, bare feet and a turban. He clung to a tall pole with both hands, one leg curled round it. From time to time he unwrapped himself and brandished the pole to underline his gestures or to threaten this upstart woman who was holding forth.

'This is your own fault Mr Chowdury! You have brought this on your own head! All I wanted was to buy my wood direct from Mr Roy and you would not let me. You wanted to hold onto the market did you not? That is why I have had to make a cooperative with my friends. That is why we have bought all the wood.'

'You are killing my business! You are killing me! My family will starve and it will be because of you and your fancy ways. This is no work for a woman. A cooperative! What is that, I wonder?! I will tell you what it is. It is a silly notion by silly women who know nothing about business and you will all rue this day!'

The money lender was stamping on the ground and shaking his fist at Anila. His face was contorted with anger and frustration. How dare these women! Mr Roy was standing well clear. He had the 600 Rupees from Anila and wished the whole messy business would go away. Life was fine until yesterday. He didn't care who won as long as he kept getting a good price for his wood. He was keen to off-load his present bundle and be on his way, but a couple of Mr Chowdury's men were standing looking menacingly at him from a position in front of his truck. He didn't have a reverse gear.

The crowd was enjoying this, and in its way its sympathies lay with Anila. Most of the women she'd co-opted yesterday were there but not saying much, waiting for Anila to win or lose. A few called out support, including Sandip, who'd tipped the balance of the argument yesterday.

'She is right Mr Chowdury. This is all your own fault. Now we are all right behind Mrs Jhabvala here. Leave her alone and let us all get on with our business!'

Leena could not contain herself either. 'You have robbed us with your high interest for years Mr Chowdury. Now is your comeuppance!'

This stunned the crowd and the two protagonists at the centre. Leena wished her tongue back in her mouth and felt her face go hot.

Mr Chowdury drew himself erect on his pole.

'So that is the way of it, is it?' He filled with righteous wrath. 'For years I have helped you all. I have beggared myself and my family to lend you money. When your crops failed, Mrs Arundati, whom did you turn to? And when your husband died and you needed a loan to pay for the funeral, Mrs Lal, where did you come to? What will you do now? Where will you go if you drive me out of business? I ask you this? Because if this – this cooperative – starts up, then I am finished with you.'

He stood looking round the circle seeing the doubts in faces, feeling the mood changing his way. Anila sensed it too, felt her arguments fading, saw her little business idea evaporating like a puddle in the dust. The demon stirred in her again.

'If that is how it must be, then it must be Mr Chowdury. We will just have to go to the bank instead.'

He whipped round to her. 'What bank?! What nonsense are you talking? There is no bank here.' He was dismissive, derisive. 'What bank would lend to people like you?'

'The People's Bank. That is who. You will see. They will come here and offer us loans at good rates. They will not make our lives impossible.'

As she said this, Anila kept her mind on CJ Kapoor. She trusted the man who'd let her and her friends into the head office of the bank in New Delhi and arranged the loan. He would not, must not let her down.

'Hah, the People's Bank! I have heard of them. They are snaring gullible people like you with cheap loans and then waiting to catch you. When you cannot go anywhere else then they put their rates up and up. And they make people sell their homes and their animals and their children to pay off the debts!' He pointed tellingly at the children hanging from their mothers in the front row. They pulled back behind their mothers' saris, terrified at this prophecy. 'They are grabbing land and taking over the country, that is your People's Bank!'

He strutted up and down now using his pole like a marching stick. His chest was puffed out and his gnarled legs stamped the ground like mistimed pistons. 'And where are they? Where are these bank managers who work in the fields? When will we see them?'

'Soon. You will see them soon. And then we will all see, won't we?' Anila challenged him.

He stopped and turned to her. A look of calculation seized his face. 'If this is how it is to go, I want my money now. I am owed three days' money from the members of your wonderful cooperative. If you are breaking your deal, then I want it paid back now. With all due interest. I am within my rights.'

Anila felt her legs shake. 'How much are you owed?'

He worked his fingers. 'Six hundred Rupees,' he announced triumphantly, sure that this would kill the wretched business.

Anila was making also calculations in her head. If she paid him 600 now, she would have just enough to keep the payments going to the wood gatherer until the agent arrived. But if he didn't come? Sometimes he was a day late. Or if he came and refused to buy the goods from the women. . .?

She reached into her sari and pulled out her purse. She looked over at her friends Leena and Divya. They looked at each other and nodded to her. She pulled out the diminishing pile of money – 600 had already been paid to Mr Roy – and counted out a further 600 Rupees. She held it out to the money lender.

'This is from the cooperative. Now we have no more debts.'

The money lender grabbed the wad like it was a snake. He looked round. He had lost his hold, temporarily. There were no other ways he could think of scoring against his enemy, which she now was. It was time to leave with dignity. He flicked his head and his two men broke their stance and walked over. The three men turned and marched away together, the money lender hobbling in the middle.

Anila felt her shoulders sag. Around her, women were coming over and touching her and saying how strong she was and how they would back her. Others were already picking at the piles of wood coming off the back of the truck. The rusty body swung and creaked on its hinges as Mr Roy stood on its back and began unloading.

Anila selected her own materials and bundled them together within a long rag. She pulled the ends of the rag together and made a pack. With help from her friends she hefted the ungainly bundle onto her head and set off home to make her stools. She had a lot of hard work to do before the agent came. And she badly needed something physical to do to take her raging mind off the all-or-nothing situation she'd contrived for herself.

TWENTY NINE

Ted was tight-lipped as he and Erin stepped out of the bank and back into bedlam. It was a shock after the serenity of the inner courtyard and the ordered bustle of the bank's operations room. It was eight pm and still broad daylight, yet the narrowness of the street and the three storey buildings in drab cement conveyed twilight.

They were accosted instantly – like flies round a tasty turd – by salesmen asking them to buy their hunger and gain absolution for their Western sin of plenty. A tiny hand touched Ted's arm like a warm feather. A girl-child stood with a thin quiet baby in her other scrawny arm. She wanted money, simply and clearly. Probably love too, but that was too nebulous.

He spared her neither from his tourist fortress; straight-jacketed by the warnings about giving to one, drawing the rest like magnets. The guilt would go with him, and always would, so much so that within five paces he was considering seriously going back to find her and press his guilt away with an Olympian donation. Instead he diverted his annoyance to Erin. He stopped in the road and grabbed her shoulder to halt her and turn her to face him.

'Listen lady, I'm fed up with you fixing my life for me. I told you before. I'm the reporter around here and I decide what I need to support my story. Am I making myself clear?!'

He had to shout above the din. They glared at each other. He dropped his arm at her withering look. She was unabashed and shouted back at him.

'But you have to go see a village bank, Ted. How else are you going to find the truth?'

'Look, just butt out, will you? I've got enough material to file my report without acquiring a dose of malaria. I managed to avoid it in Baghdad. I don't need to put my body on the line for a goddamn bit of local colour.'

'If you didn't have someone push you now and then, Ted Saddler, you wouldn't even get up in the morning.'

'I was right! You're a control freak. You can't help acting the big executive, can you? I'm not one of your boys, you know. And the one reason I didn't object to a little trip to the back of beyond is that I'll get some peace for a couple of days. By comparison, mosquito bites are going to feel like love pecks.'

'Only if you have the skin of a rhino!'

'What would you know about sensitivity?!'

Both their faces were red, and they realised they were gathering a small crowd. His exasperation subsided.

'This is stupid. C'mon. Let's move,' he said. 'CJ said we'd get a taxi at the end of the road. Are you up for this?'

'I can take anything you can. Come on, tough guy, lead the way. I'm hanging on.'

She took a grip of his upper arm with both hands, and he was forced to laugh and shake his head. He wished he'd kept up the press-ups. He would join the gym when he got back. Give up the doughnuts. Maybe even the beer. Stick to whiskey. Gingerly they began to pick their way down the narrow street. They passed a deal being struck over a gutted electric motor, its copper innards being drawn out, weighed and exchanged for limp Rupees, pulled – soiled and damp like salad leaves – from some secret hiding place on the dealer's body.

Ted made the connection. This was New York's Lower East Side, a hundred years ago, awash with 40 degrees heat, and 100% humidity. Endless noise, perpetual bustle, honing the new factories and salesmen who could beat the West, given the freedom from the choking embrace of corruption and poverty. He wondered if he could use the image in the book? His lofty thoughts crashed to earth.

'Shit! 'Scuse my French.'

Ted gazed at his foot and wiped off what he could of the sacred cow dung on the broken kerb. Erin kept the smirk off her face. The dark faces round him grinned broadly.

They twisted past street traders and stepped over beggars. They declined offers of help and cries for rupees. They took to the road to get past the odd cow chewing at a lump of spicy cardboard. The intimacy of the shared and outlandish obstacles forced them to swap their sullen faces for wry glances and even the odd grin. Ahead was daylight and the main Chandni Road. They were almost there when a man stepped in front of them.

'Taxi, Sir, Lady?' he bowed and swept a hand towards a two-tone cab sitting by the roadside with a driver behind the wheel.

There were no others in sight. Ted felt like showing who was boss.

'Great. Let's grab it.'

He helped her into the back of the hot cab. They settled on the springy seat with its off-white cotton cover and Ted told the driver to take them back to their hotel.

They drove for a while, neither ready to make the first peace overture. They edged through the crammed streets, jolting and swaying. Ted was conscious of the smell from his shoe, and thrust it as far under the seat in front as possible. Abruptly their driver found a way through. They took off down a side street and began to make zigzags, sometimes running foul of jams in narrow streets but more often seeming to make real progress.

Ted had begun by thinking that they'd got lucky and found a driver who really knew the best way through the city. But as they travelled he began to worry that they were being ripped off. It was an odd faculty of his. At any time, anywhere, Ted knew where he was facing, and where his start point was in relation to his present position. It worked in forests and in deserts and in cities. He'd established a reputation for it in his army days. It had been a sense that really came into its own on liberty nights in a strange city. Ted was unerringly able to get his cronies back to their unit no matter how blitzed. He was increasingly convinced they were heading in the wrong direction. They were heading north and away from their hotel.

'Driver. Say, driver! We're going the wrong way. We want the Hyatt Regency. It's on the Ring Road.'

The driver's dark eyes flicked back at him from the mirror. 'Yes, sir. I know, sir. This is quicker way. First we have to go round.'

Ted sat back reluctantly. 'I'm not sure about this.'

'How can you tell Ted? I'm totally lost.'

'Just something I'm good at.'

They went on for a minute or so until Ted's patience began to run out. He saw the driver's face in the mirror. It was looking back at him with increasing nervousness. The roads grew quieter, and if anything, narrower. They seemed to be edging further away from the great hulking buildings of the Raj. The houses were getting more run down. Ted leaned forward and put his big hand on the shoulder of the driver.

'Ok buddy, that's enough. I want you to turn round. Do you hear me?!' The man shifted forward away from him.

'Everything is ok, sir. Just a little further, you will see.'

Ted was sweating now. This was a tough call in a strange city, but he knew he was right.

'Stop the car. Now! We want this car turned round. We're going back into the city, do you hear!'

'Ted? Are you sure about this?'

Erin was getting agitated. What was he trying to prove to her? How could he possibly know better than a local taxi driver? The driver was in a state now and began to speed up, crashing into top gear and careering through crossroads with total abandon.

'Stop the car, you idiot!'

Ted reached forward and with hands pulled on the shoulders of the driver and shook him. It didn't work.

'Ok buddy, enough is enough!'

He put one arm round the man's neck and squeezed.

'Ted! My god what are you doing, you lunatic! We'll crash!'

The driver, gasping and gagging, made one last wrench of his wheel, The car swung down a narrow street, demolishing a pile of refuse in a cloud of rotting green and cardboard. As the screen cleared of debris, the taxi broke out into a small bare patch of ground, a maidan formed by squat grey houses on four sides. It was perhaps half the size of a football pitch. There was no exit ahead.

With Ted's arm tight round his neck, the driver came to a jerking stop half way across the dusty square. The engine stalled. Ted let go. The driver took his chance, shoved open the door and started to run back the way they'd come.

Ted's eyes followed him just in time to see a car draw up, plugging the way in. It held a driver, and two men in the back. They were all hanging out the open windows. The car reversed a couple of feet to make sure it was blocking as much of the exit as possible. Ted's driver reached the new arrivals and started shouting and pointing furiously back at Ted and Erin. The two men in the back piled out and began to run towards them. Knives glinted in the sun.

THIRTY

'It's a set-up! It's a goddamn set-up!'

Ted pounds the back of the driver's seat. Erin is going *oh god, oh god*. Ted launches his great bulk out through door.

'Where are you going!' she wails.

He dives in through the open driver's door and jams himself behind the wheel. Fumbles for the key left in the ignition. The engine splutters, the car jumps forward and dies. In gear. Hasn't used a stick shift since his army days. He wrenches it back and forward and finds neutral. Tries the ignition again, floors the accelerator at the same time. It splutters but still doesn't catch. Flooded.

'Hurry! Hurry!' she's shouting.

He leans back, breathes, takes right foot off the accelerator, checks mirror. Men charging, light flickering on knives. Gently, gently, turns the key. Feels the rumble. Touches accelerator. Senses revs dropping again, about to stall! Lifts foot from pedal. Hears engine stutter, gasp, roar into life. Got it! Flings the gear-stick into first, releases the hand brake. Flattens the pedal and kangaroos off.

First man hurls himself onto the bonnet, face contorted in anger, scrabbling at the windscreen. Second man gains purchase through the open window of the rear passenger door. Begins climbing in.

Ted wrenches the wheel back and forward. The engine races as the revs mount. Slams into second gear and spins the wheel hard to the left. Man on bonnet sails off. Man two now half way through Erin's window, slashing at her. Pinning her in the far corner.

Ted flails with his big fist. Gets lucky and catches the man full on the side of the head. Man lurches back, dazed but not out, and still clinging to the door pillar. Erin delves into her small shoulder bag, pulls out a small canister. Rams it into the face of the attacker and presses. Jet of pepper spray floods his face. Howls and drops his knife and falls backwards out the window. Ted helps him on his way with a final swerve to the right.

Running out of square now. Slams gearstick into reverse, kicks up a dust cloud making it impossible to spy the way out. Wrenches at the handbrake and spins the steering wheel, all the time foot hard to the floor in second gear. Engine shrieks and car judders round on the dirt and gravel. First man comes at them again. Ted doesn't hesitate. Slips off the brake and shoots forward. The man crunches into the bonnet and smashes the windscreen as he bounces and caterwauls up and over the roof.

Ted punches out the shattered glass. As the dust clears he makes out the car parked across the entrance. Takes aim, revs the engine, holding the car rocking on the handbrake. Wheels spin as the engine howls up and up. Ted lets go.

'Hold on, Erin!'

'Go! Go! Go!' she pounds his shoulder.

Ted guns the car straight down the narrow exit. Sees gaps either side of the blockading car, but not nearly wide enough for the black and yellow. Blasts down the alley until he can see the driver's face, sees the scar running from the bridge of the nose down across the right cheek. Sees a mix of fear and rage distort the already splintered features.

Ted too, consumed with anger. Thinking only of ramming, of crushing scarface. Making the killer tackle. Twenty yards out. No seatbelts, car a tin can on wheels. Reason cuts in. He swings to the left, aiming for the rear. Assuming engine and the greatest mass are at the front. Maybe. A gust of smoke erupts from the exhaust of the marauders' car. Driver chicken? Trying to move before getting hit? Too late.

Ted's hefty old Ambassador cannons into the rear wheel and wing in a grinding shockwave of tortured metal. Impact tosses the stationary car round 90 degrees, enough to clear the way. Tears his own wing off, exposing the whirling tyre, but momentum ploughs them through. Wrenches at the wheel, hopes the front axle still answers. Taxi lurches, bounces off a low kerb and keeps going.

Sees and feels the front wheel out of kilter. Grapples with the unbalanced machine. Wrestling it round a corner, grazing the side of a building. He plunges the car ever northwards, turning and twisting but always knowing his direction. Makes a final left, drives as far as he can, then left again. Stumbles onto the ring road and turns south again, heading back to he Hyatt, back to sanctuary. Rumbling and bumping and swaying along at low speed, wind blasting through the broken screen.

Ted sucks at his torn knuckles as the adrenalin starts washing through, leaving him trembling and chilled. Continually checking the mirror. Erin sitting twisted round in the back seat scouring the traffic for pursuit. Dabbing her streaming eyes.

'You OK?' he shouts over the wind noise.

'Gassed!'

Their faces were sandblasted and raw by the time they took the hotel slip road and pulled to a halt in front of the main entrance. Ted slowly relaxed his bloody hands on the wheel. His arms were trembling with the effort of keeping the car running true. They sat in stunned silence wiping the dust and the perspiration from their faces, and breathing deeply.

Suddenly a turbaned head with a magnificent moustache thrust itself through the smashed screen. A massive doorman dressed in the uniform of the Bengal Lancers registering astonishment at finding a white man furled over the steering wheel. He stood back, inspected the damaged wing then came round and opened the doors for Ted and Erin. The pair stumbled out and embraced each other.

Ted turned to the wide-eyed doorman.

'We were attacked. Can you call the police please?'

The giant saluted him. 'Certainly, sir. What name is it please?'

'Saddler. And hold onto this taxi. It's evidence.'

'There's a knife in the back as well,' Erin said.

'Do you need a doctor, sir and madam?'

Ted looked at Erin. She shook her head and wiped away the last pepper spray tears.

'No. No, we're fine. Just a drink.'

They found the bar and flopped into two easy chairs. They sat staring at each other not knowing what to say. Their drinks came – double brandy for him, soda for her. Erin took a gulp and called back the waiter. She pointed at Ted's glass.

'Another one of those, please.'

When it arrived, Erin drank greedily. She spluttered and coughed, and wiped her eyes.

'I thought you'd gone mad…'

'I thought the car wasn't gonna start…'

'That guy who bounced off the bonnet…'

'The way you blasted him with the spray…'

'New York training…'

'Remind me to buy you a refill…'

'Where did you learn to drive getaway cars?'

A smile cracked his face and was reflected on hers. They began to guffaw and finally they were laughing until the tears reappeared on her face and she wept uncontrollably. He got up and went over and sat on the arm of her chair and put his arm round her. Any man's arm might have done just then. But there weren't that many who could have pulled off such a stunt. She patted his hand. He got the message and took his arm away. She took a deep breath and stilled the shuddering.

'I'm ok now. Those bastards. That wasn't a random mugging, was it?'

'It was planned.'

'Terrorist kidnapping?'

They exchanged looks, each hoping for some comforting explanation from the other.

'Maybe. But why pick on us? We just got here. The city's full of foreigners.'

'And they didn't want hostages. They were out to kill us.' Erin's eyes filled.

'Maybe their plan went wrong. They panicked.'

'You panicked them, Ted. You were great. Look I'm sorry about railroading you back at the bank. And for shouting at you.'

'Forget it. I'm sorry I blew up.'

He went back to his seat and dragged it closer. She smudged at her eyes. and tried a smile.

'It was Warwick, wasn't it,' she said.

'Nah. Local gang.'

They didn't want to think it. Too farfetched. Too scary. She shook her head.

'He's found us. If he's tapping phones at head office, he'll know I'm not having a facial and a back rub at the HK Peninsula.'

'Did you book your flights to Kolkata and Delhi with your GA card?'

Her face crumpled. 'Oh, God, Ted. They were after me. Both of us, now. After your last column. What have I got you into?'

'We don't know for sure it was him. Anyway I'm paid to write a column.'

But not enough. And not from here. The job is sitting at a nice safe desk in Manhattan filing a column like any sane journalist. So what the hell am I doing here, fending off knife attacks in the middle of a twenty mile slum? This woman on a mission was going to get him killed. Stan wanted him to get some 'colour' into his column. It could be red.

Erin doubled over, clutching her stomach, her face etched with pain.

'Are you ok?' he asked.

'It's a stomach thing. I get it sometimes. I'm out of practice.'

'So what do we do now?'

'We file a report with the police and then get the hell out of here. Back to the US of A. I'll call Ramesh and CJ and tell them it's off. This is too dangerous.'

'We can't do that! We have to see this through. Especially now. Sure, let's get the police. And then let's get out of here. But we'll go to wherever it was that CJ mentioned. We tell no one where we're going. It's a big country.'

He heard the 'we' word. That convinced him. Not only would he continue to be exposed to local assassins, but she'd make his life misery right up until his final moments.

'You are completely crazy. You know that? You come within a blade's width of getting killed and you want to carry on? No way.'

She looked stricken. 'But we have to, Ted. If we walk away now, we might as well give up the whole bloody thing. Remember what we said? What we agreed? Lead with our hearts and not with our heads? Give it our best shot?'

'But not get shot.'

The silence grew between them. They held each other's stares trying to read what was there. He broke first.

'Ok, ok. Fine. No-one's gonna miss my hide. And look, when the police come, I think it best we make no mention of the bigger picture, ok? Either these guys won't believe us or they'll have us spend a week filling out forms in some downtown hell hole. Keep it simple. We're tourists. This was a mugging. And we'd probably best not say we're checking out in the morning. Speak of the devil.'

Ted got up to greet the two policemen in khaki who were being pointed towards them by the doorman.

'This is going to take a little explaining.'

THIRTY ONE

Oscar was exuberant. This was turning out the best fun since his coming out party at 16.

'Albert! Come quick. We have work to do.'

Albert walked sulkily out from the kitchen and stood in exaggerated enquiry with his muscled arms folded across his tight vest.

'Oh put that look away, darling. I promised you we'd have a ball. Well it's getting better all the time.'

'You've been talking to that snooty bitch haven't you?'

'Albert, she's a perfectly nice lady – as ladies go. And she's not snooty, as snooty goes. That's just her accent. Now stop being a moody boy and help me gather up a few of our friends.'

'A party?' Albert dropped his arms and his eyes widened in enthusiasm.

'Sort of. It's time for the Lone Ranger and Tonto, his trusty sidekick, to ride. And we're going to need some help this time. All hands to the keyboard. Now what is it?'

Albert was pouting. 'Can we do it properly then?'

'You silly thing! Of course we'll do it properly.'

Oscar climbed off his seat and tripped across the room followed by a happier Albert. Some time later, following giggles from the bedroom, the pair returned. Oscar was wearing a skin-tight pale grey shirt and matching trousers. Round his Michelin middle was a black leather belt studded with silver stars. From it, hung a brace of glittering Colt revolvers. On his feet were black cowboy boots with silver snakes and silver spurs. On his head was an immaculate white ten gallon hat. Across his bulging eyes was a black mask.

Albert was bare to the waist except for a glittering chest-guard of strung beads hanging from a cord round his neck. Two red stripes ran either side of his nose. A leather strap ran round his head, a single feather jutted up from the back. A copper band gripped his muscled upper arm. He wore soft leather chaps with tassels running from hip to ankle down each side join. His feet were clad in moccasins. He twirled in mock war-dance round the fountain, showing off the string of the thong disappearing between his bare cheeks.

The Lone Ranger and Tonto took up seats alongside each other facing a bank of screens. Lone Ranger took off his hat and carefully placed it on top of his screen. He raised his arms like a grand pianist above his keyboard.

'Are we ready, Tonto?'

Albert smiled. 'Yes, Kemosabe.'

'Then Hi-Yo Silver! Away!' Their hands plunged on to the keyboards and began to raise images.

'OK, Tonto, let's get in touch with this other tribe of Indians!' He cut and pasted Erin's email giving the contact details of the team leaders in Delhi. Albert watched the action on his second screen.

I've been given your names by a mutual friend. Please confirm id.

Lone Ranger–

Almost instantly a message came back.

we are so happy to connect Lone Ranger!! Please tell us what to do!

Vikram Vajpayee and Shivani Jaffrey–

show me whats been attacking you and what responses you've made.   –LR–

we will need a few minutes to package it up please. We will send you copies of the main viruses and attack programs. You will need a quarantine area. Please stand by.

–VV– SJ

'Ok, Tonto. Set up a corral for incoming wild mustangs. These guys are so the business!'

Some twenty minutes later Oscar and Albert were fielding huge downloads and penning them in an area on a separate drive ring-fenced with firewalls of Oscar's own design. They split the work between them and began to manipulate the virulent material like surgeons going after cancer cells.

'I know this stuff. I've seen this guy's handiwork before,' said Oscar after half an hour of picking away.

Tonto nodded. 'It's Viper isn't it?'

'Absolutely. When did he get sprung? And what's he doing working for a bank like Global American? That was rhetorical. I wonder how much they're paying him? And if I'm not mistaken he's got his team together again. I recognise some of his old hacker stuff here. God, doesn't he ever move on?! So crude. So, not stylish!'

'Fine by me, Lone Ranger. Makes our job easier.'

'But not much of a challenge, darling, is it? Oh well. Let's see what our Indian friends have been doing to stop Viper and the other snakes in the grass.'

Again they massaged their keyboards and dipped into and out of the programs that the team at the People's Bank had used and patched together to combat the assaults.

'Now these are what I call coders! Very clever! What do you think of this routine? And this one?' Finally they sat back.

'I've got just the silver bullets our friends need. Don't you think? I'll put them up on our web site and send our friends the links to strengthen their firewall. That should block the next 50 moves of Viper and his gang. Unless they do something different for a change. But why would they show any originality at this stage of their unremarkable careers? And then… then my gorgeous little redskin, we'll plan the counter-attack.'

They worked through the day and long into the night on the virus control software. The Lone Ranger recording software chugged away in background, amassing phone calls and emails at GA's head office. Crucially and almost fatally, it meant that Oscar and Albert didn't catch the initial coded instructions to the team in New Delhi to waylay Erin Wishart and her companion. It was only in the early hours, when they'd paused for cake and coffee and checked status that they found out about the unsuccessful attempt.

Oscar's panic calls to Ted and Erin reached them at four am in the hotel. Erin and Ted convened in her room and huddled together in dressing gowns on her couch. In front of them on the coffee table they had her cell phone on speaker and her laptop open and receiving.

'Really, we're fine, Oscar,' Ted was saying. 'A bit shook up, but fine.'

Erin concurred. 'It's not your fault, Oscar. For god's sake, who would have thought it?'

'If they'd succeeded. . . I'd never have forgiven myself. Look, here's the clip. Listen for yourselves.'

Erin reached forward and clicked on the attachment. Through the speaker, came the snarling voice of Warwick Stanstead:

'I don't want fucking excuses! I want results!'

'Boss. If the dame had been alone, it would have worked fine. She had a pal. A big guy. We've tracked him down. We know who he is.'

'Who?'

'A reporter. The guy who's been writing about the bank in the Tribune, you know? The one we got Stacks to call. Saddler, Ted Saddler. Seems he pulled a gun on our team and hijacked a fast car. Our guys only had knives, you know? Otherwise it wouldn't have looked right. And the local cops would have pulled up the drains if there had been a big shoot-out.'

'Yeah, yeah. I guess. But what's she doing with this Sir fucking Galahad? What's his angle? What's going down, Joey?'

'We traced things back, boss. Saddler's over there covering the trial and he's been talking to the top guy at People's. We think Miss Blabbermouth has been spilling to him. If you take a look at the Tribune's web page you'll see he's stopped picking holes in People's and started a love-fest. Coincidentally with miss blabbermouth's arrival.'

Pause. . .

'It's going to be hard for another 'accident' to be arranged, Joey. They'll be warned. Assuming they link it with us. But they can't prove a damn thing.'

'Not a thing, boss. We're clean. Trust me.'

'We can't chance this. Joey, get yourself over there. Take charge of the local team. Finish it. And don't fuck up this time. There won't be a next. For any of us.'

A phone slammed into its cradle.

Silence.

Erin was hunched on the couch, her face held in her hands. Ted was chewing his knuckle.

'He's aff his heid.'

'What?'

'Off his head. He's a dope head. Psychotic. Unbelievable.'

'Better believe it. I think it's time we disappeared, Erin. Don't you?'

She hauled herself forward and spoke at her phone.

'We've got the bastard, right, Oscar? This is proof.'

'Leaving aside all minor stuff about legality of our taps, sure. All safely tucked away on our web site. Are you guys heading home?'

Ted said, 'No. But we're not leaving a forwarding address.'

They disconnected and stared at each other.

'Madhya Pradesh?' he asked. 'Wherever that is.'

'The train leaves at six. See you in the lobby.'

THIRTY TWO

Anila brushed the floor twice and shook the rugs three times. She ground enough maize for several meals, all the time waiting for the sound of the agent's lorry. Other women from her syndicate kept dropping by – casually, just passing, no reason – but really to share their misgivings and add to the suspense. By mid afternoon Anila had convinced herself she would not see the agent that day. Maybe he wouldn't come back? Maybe Chowdury had already got to him and warned him off? That was it! He'd sent one of his men to intercept the agent and tell him they had nothing to sell him this time, or maybe next time, or the next. She was going mad.

Then through the sounds of the children calling and the animals bleating and the villagers chattering to each other, she heard it. Different to Mr Roy's straining engine and clashing gears. A smoother, more powerful motor driven by someone who knew how. She tried not to run. With nerves breaking she walked inside and gathered up her few flimsy offerings. Now they seemed tawdry and ill-made. How could anyone want to buy these? Nevertheless she lashed the four small stools together and hoisted them on a sling round her shoulder and over her back and walked towards the meeting point.

Others were already gathered by the well surrounded by their handicraft. They aimed to meet the agent before Mr Chowdury could get to him and infect his mind. When the remainder joined her, looking excited and worried in turn, Anila led her little band of women to where the land opened out at the edge of the village. The ground was beaten flat and soiled with oil stains from other lorries that, like the agent's, were too big to drive into the centre. A solitary neem tree softened the picture and offered some shade. They arrived at much the same time, the lorry and the women. They set out their work alongside the lorry while Anila explained the new situation.

She tried as hard as she could to show confidence. She knew that fear on her face would at best get her a bad deal, at worst make him refuse to treat with her.

'Good afternoon Mr Bedi. We were expecting you today.'

'I can see that,' he swept a hand round, indicating the line-up of women and their wares. 'But where is Mr Chowdury? I do not see him. I want to finish my business quickly today and get back to Udaipura.'

'There has been a change Mr Bedi. Mr Chowdury is not coming today. Do you remember I asked you and Mr Roy the wood gatherer, if you would deal with me directly?' He looked quizzically at her. 'Well, that is now the situation here. This is the Chandapur Women's Cooperative. All these women here are members and we have come to sell you our work.'

'I see. I see. Well this is a big surprise. I am not sure I want to deal with a cooperative.' He made it sound like a dirty word. Anila's heart fluttered but she held on to her calm face.

'But it is just the same Mr Bedi. It is the same work by the same women. All that has changed is that there is no longer a man in the middle.'

She took the risk, even though it gave away some of her negotiating position.

'This means we can do a better deal for you.'

The fact was that none of the women knew what the old miser had been getting for their work and how much profit he'd been making from them over the years. Anila would have to prod carefully. The agent's eyes took on a gleam.

'Well, that may be true but I have to tell you the price Mr Chowdury got was very fair, you know. It would be difficult to better it. And I also need to be sure about the quality. How am I to know that the goods will be of the same quality as before? I have very demanding customers. Very demanding.'

He began to walk slowly down the line of hunkered women, picking up a table here, a chair there, fingering a basket and testing a fly swat. He made humming noises and sucking noises but no words. If anything of course, the little offerings were even more carefully made than ever. They were on show, direct to the agent. They had to be good.

The agent had quickly acclimatised to the new state of affairs but made a long pretence of incomprehension just to see these women plead with him some more, and make a fuss of him. The idea of a cooperative was not new to him. He could see he had several advantages dealing direct with the workers. There was definitely a better bargain in it for him. But he mustn't show his enthusiasm.

'So who am I dealing with? I cannot deal with every single person individually, you know. I am a busy man. Are you their representative?' he confronted Anila. She looked round at her colleagues. They looked back and nodded at her.

'Good. Then here is what I will do. I will give you a good price for each of the articles and you must tell me how many you are selling and then we will agree on the price for each set. Do you understand? My price is very fair but you must remember that I am taking a big risk dealing with you. I do not know if this cooperative thing will work and if it doesn't then what? What am I left with? So I must build that into the price, you see?'

Anila did see. She saw exactly his game, but had to play along with it. But she was determined not to let her desperate financial position make a fool of her. Unless they started on the right foot with the agent, they would never catch up.

They squatted in the dust a little way from the line of women using the long shadow of the lorry for shade in the late afternoon sun. They called each woman over in turn and she brought a sample of her wares. The agent set a ludicrously low price and Anila came back at him. The battle raged as the shadows lengthened. The agent found this woman with the sad eyes a tough bargainer. She argued their case well and didn't cave in to his early ranging offers. Item by item, they wrangled a deal which seemed to satisfy both sides. He negotiated a nice cushion for future haggling – better than old Chowdury's – and the women seemed grudgingly happy. Maybe he should have pressed harder? But it was the first time. Anything could happen from now on.

They helped to pile their goods on to his lorry and watched it trundle out of sight before they surrounded Anila and embraced her and praised themselves for being such fine businesswomen. Anila was reeling with relief. She had died a thousand times as the agent had pressed her. She would have taken his first offers if necessary. Even that would have just about covered their costs and she could have paid her two friends back. But she had drawn on an inner toughness to go for a better deal and it had worked. She could have held out for a little more, but she was sure her heart would not have stood it. Next time.

The women sat about under the solitary neem tree and worked out their individual profits and costs. It was noisy, uncontrolled and occasionally heated. Anila could see they would have to manage things better in future. They needed to write things down in a ledger, not make scratches in the dust with sticks. This was no way for a professional cooperative to work. She had been taught to write and do sums at the little village school and she was sure she could learn how to keep accounts. Her mother could help her. She wondered where she could get a book or at least some sheets of paper to write the transactions down. Next time she would have her ledger ready for Mr Bedi. The thought made her heart pound.

By the end of the reckoning, everyone was satisfied and agreed that Anila, as their representative, should be given the money to buy next day's materials. Anila stumbled back to her hut, her legs rubbery and her eyes wide with exhaustion. The bag round her neck was filled with the repaid loan to her fellow workers. Not only did she now have enough to pay back Leena and Divya but she had made a little profit on her own investment, enough to please even her mother. That, plus the money for tomorrow's wood gave her over 4000 Rupees to mind. She put the money in the pot and placed the pot in the hole in the mud wall of her hut and covered the hole with the small carving of Krishna to protect it. She made a simple prayer of thanks to the god and bowed to the carving.

Her daughter found her lying on her mat, her limbs tossed around like an accident victim. Aastha pulled the cotton sheet over her sleeping mother and watched her for a long time before lying down beside her, carefully and quietly, like a smaller spoon. Anila's arm came over and pulled her daughter to her without breaking the rhythm of her deep sleep.

THIRTY THREE

The hotel lobby was empty at five in the morning, except for CJ Kapoor and a vexed young woman who was haranguing him with hands on hips.

'Why is my father so keen to weigh me down with this reporter? Americans are for shopping malls. Out here they are whales in the desert. I will have to nanny him everywhere, like a baby! Most of them don't even have a passport, though they can afford to go anywhere in the world. They have no idea of real life. Shanty towns. Starving kids. AIDS epidemics. Bribes for everything.'

'I know, I know, Meera,' he pleaded. 'But your father thinks this will help him. Please understand. Look, they are coming. Smile!'

Ted and Erin were walking towards them, talking. Ted was pushing a trolley with two glaringly new and bulging backpacks on it.

'You OK?' Ted was asking her dark-ringed eyes.

'I will be. Once we're out of here.'

He squeezed her arm in sympathy. She didn't pull away, but there was no give either. Maybe he'd over-estimated the intimacy created by their shared trauma of this morning's news from Oscar. But Ted was aware from her manner that yesterday's events had shifted the balance in some subtle way. Some of her burden had slipped onto his shoulders. He tested the weight and found it bearable, even welcome.

CJ introduced the young woman as Meera Banerjee. She carried an old leather briefcase and a Nike sports bag. Her hair was cut in a short layer all round her finely shaped skull. Her eyes were large and questioning.

'No relation to the boss?' asked Ted automatically, reflecting that it was probably as common a name in India as Jones.

CJ had been desperate to reveal it. 'As a matter of fact, yes. This is Ramesh's daughter. She has a degree in business law from Kolkata University and like her father she has also graduated from Harvard with an MBA.' He was as proud as if she were his daughter.

Meera shrugged away the praise. The resemblance across the eyes was now apparent. 'It is a pleasure to meet you both. This is a very exciting day for me.' It was said a little mechanically, but then it was an unearthly hour.

'We are putting her in charge of the Sagar district which includes the village you are going to visit, Ted.'

'Both of us, CJ. We've been forced into a slight change of plan.'

Ted gave an abbreviated version of the events of the day before, omitting for the moment, GA's hand in the hijack.

'. . . and so we think it's best if Erin comes with me just in case she was the target.'

Meera's eyes widened and she kept staring from Ted to Erin. She turned to CJ and said something forceful in Hindi. CJ found a suitable translation.

'Meera is telling me off. I am so sorry. This is my fault. I should have arranged a car. I did not think. And you were almost killed! How can I ever make it up?'

'CJ, it's fine. Look, it wasn't your fault. How could it be? But it's time we got out of here. We're leaving no forwarding address and would ask you to be discreet. Tell no one.'

'Of course, of course. Meera will enjoy having Erin too.'

Meera found a weak smile and her English.

'I will phone now and get another seat on the Bhopal train. Once there we will pick up one of our jeeps which is being driven up from Bangalore. We will then drive over to Chandapur and set things up.'

She looked a little amused. 'I am afraid the accommodation will not be so grand.'

Her expressive eyes took in the waterfall and marble of the lobby. Erin caught the edge.

'As long as we have a roof over our heads, Meera.'

Meera looked at CJ for confirmation. He gave a loose smile that stood for a shrug.

'Of course, we will provide proper accommodation. Normally we stay with one of the senior villagers or one of our local representatives. Do not worry Miss Wishart, we will look after you.'

CJ hated to disappoint a guest and would rather bend the truth than cause any discomfort between them and him. As it was, he was relying on the warmth of the welcome to provide shelter.

The hotel car pulled away in the pre-dawn coolness. Inside, Erin and Ted seemed chastened by the thought of the trip ahead of them. The morning was still, the air soft. Only birds and an old beggar were stirring in the bushes all along the driveway of the hotel.

As they left through the exit, a van pulled up at the back of the hotel. The driver brought his mail sack in through the tradesman's entrance. The boys who reported to the concierge took delivery and soon sifted and sorted the correspondence. Among the packages was one forwarded from Kolkata, from the Oberoi Grand. It was addressed to Mr Theodore Saddler.

Having established that Mr Saddler was no longer a guest and that he had in fact departed only five minutes before, the under-manager put it on the pending shelf in the cloakroom. He had no forwarding address for Mr Saddler, though he knew that a hotel car had taken him and another guest to the railway station. There seemed no urgency. It could wait for a few days. Maybe a week. If Mr Saddler came back they would give it to him. If he did not, there was a return address on the package and they could send it back to New York. Or if it had anything of value inside, maybe it could simply get 'misplaced'.

The hotel car broke onto the ring road and merged with the morning traffic. Within ten minutes they were being bludgeoned by the noise of car horns, scooters revving, street hawkers and the jabber of hundreds of people jamming the entrance to New Delhi railway station. Its importance as a gateway, a jump-off point, sucked in an entire industry of fruit sellers, tea makers, cafe owners, tour guides and watchers, always the watchers, eyeing other people's lives. People with nowhere else to go, nothing else to do but steal a little of the shine of those who could and did travel.

The driver edged his car into the mass but finally ground to a halt, afraid of having his splendid bodywork scratched against the inertia of the crowd. They struggled out of the car, opening the doors with difficulty. With even more difficulty they ploughed their way through the deafening bustle and the grabbing hands towards the station. Ted used his weight and size to clear a path and fend off the beggars, all the time trying not to step on families who seemed to have set up home in the station forecourt. They had been promised an air-conditioned luxury train and were puzzled at Meera tugging them towards a battered looking blue train with old-style computer printouts hanging from scotch tape on the side of the coaches.

'The Bhopal Shatabdi. We are in coach G,' shouted Meera leading them down the platform. They came to the relevant coach. 'Look for your names.' She pointed at the printouts. Each had a long column of names. Ted began at the top, Erin at the bottom.

'Here we are,' said Erin with triumph. She was pointing at the typed names of Meera and Ted and the hand-written insertion of her own name. Erin asked if the sheets were removed before departure or left to flutter like banners as the train thundered through the morning. Meera pretended she hadn't heard. They scrambled on board and clambered their way to their seats over mounds of luggage, apologising as they went.

Inside, the decor was branch-line British Rail, circa 1960. Walls and ceilings that were once a shade of blue were now decomposing back to the original steel. There were nameless smears on floors, seat backs and walls. Nameless, till breakfast was served, Ted remarked. A dull metal tray was placed in front of every passenger. It contained two pieces of white bread whose like he'd last encountered in giant catering packs in army canteens. A hot tin-foil covered an egg dish supported on a bed of tepid chipped potatoes. And tea bags. Two. Later to be converted to tea by the application of hot water from the giant urn wheeled through the carriage by the chai wallah.

They set off exactly on time. Arctic blasts of air conditioning competed with Indian taped music to see which would be first to drive the passengers insane. The flat brown countryside ran by like old news-reels through windows yellowed by sun-filters and dirt. Trees flicked past. And people, bent over and pecking at the iron ground, or scything dead grass before the sun took full charge of the day.

Agra station arrived, but it felt like they'd been conned, as though the train had looped back to New Delhi. The same bodies stretched on the platform. Same dark faces inspecting the new arrivals for signs of hand-outs. Ted watched in admiration as two Kiwi girls with packs as big as sheep on their back and small ones on the front for balance, cut their brown-limbed way through the ruck and headed out into the sunshine of the station yard. For one piercing moment of regret, Ted Saddler wished he were going with them. Wished he had the time again.

The train jolted into life and the process repeated itself six more times, though the stations were visibly more decrepit and the crowds thinner. The journey was passed in long silences. Meera seemed to have an unending amount of laptop work to do, and Erin finally gave up trying to make conversation. Once when Meera had gone to the toilet, Erin turned to Ted.

'I don't think she likes us here.'

'Would you? This is your first big job and you get stuck with a pair of middle-aged – sorry! – whities. We're an encumbrance. I don't blame her.'

Erin dozed off and on, and noticed Ted left his seat a few times. When he came back the second time, she was certain. There was the whiff of alcohol.

'Is there a bar on this train?'

'It's a do-it-yourself arrangement.'

'You're not getting canned are you?'

'What else is there to do on this converted refrigeration unit?'

It was true, she thought. There was nothing romantic about this trip; it was freezing in the carriage, noisy, smelly and dirty. For a moment she pined for the soft carpets, the sumptuous leather and the monastery quiet luxury of the First Class compartment of the airlines she normally travelled in. Used to travel in, she reminded herself. Her anxiety grew about the toilet arrangements up ahead.

Ted Saddler sat fuming. He was prepared to admit that he woke every morning – had done for as long as he could recall – with his end of day drink as his first thought. So what? It was the solitary high spot of the day. The hours between waking and that first sip were only there to postpone and enhance the pleasure. Like delaying orgasm, if he recalled rightly. The really annoying thing was that he'd eased up a fraction since Erin had arrived, but obviously not enough for her highness. He was still getting grief. No good telling her it was medicinal; that during yesterday's brush with the muggers a big muscle in his left arm had been pulled. The booze soothed, as did the memory of the satisfying impact of his fist on the attacker's head.

The physical pain had been a wake-up call. It wasn't anything as simple as a near-death experience provoking a stack of fine new resolutions. It was more the realisation that there was still something there, some ability to perform, to take risks and make things happen. In his head he'd written himself off a while ago. Now he thought of Erin and the agreement, the vow, over the table the other night. To be 17 again. That would never happen, but he didn't have to be 70 either. Not sure exactly what he was going to do about it, he let the scorched continent seep into his eyes as the train rocked through the day.

THIRTY FOUR

The challenge was to get the mix just right. That perfect combination of depressant and stimulant; smack and snow, the legendary, the high of highs, the speedball. He trusted Joey to get the best stuff, no adulterated shit laced with rat poison. But then you didn't want it too pure. The ideal was heroin and cocaine cut to about 50% using some soluble but inactive substance. Not, absolutely not, Fentanyl, for example. Twenty deaths in the past month. Maybe the dealer thought he was being nice, offering something special. Fentanyl was surely special, an anaesthetic and painkiller about a hundred times more powerful than plain old smack. Must have been a wild way to go. That was part of it wasn't it? Walking the cliff edge. Skis running too fast to even think about turning. Working the Porsche round the mountain tracks at the limit, feeling the tail go.

His washroom was big enough to have a walk-in shower, Jacuzzi tub, toilet, sink and leather lounger. He set out his equipment on a pristine white towel by the sink. A syringe, two silver pots, a Velcro strap, a sachet of Vitamin C, a pack of alcohol wipes and a little burner with a receptacle sitting above the wick. Carefully he spooned a small measure of coke into the pan and added a mound of Vitamin C. He added a dash of water – enough to let the mix dissolve and fizz. He lit the wick below the small bowl. As the solution began to bubble, he spooned in a larger amount of brown smack, a little more water, and carefully mixed it till all the lumpiness had gone. The sharp vinegary smell filled the small room and made his eyes smart. He flicked the extractor fan to high. Ready. . .

Bare the left arm. Check the soft skin on the inside of the elbow. Old puncture marks studding the lines of the veins. The only downside; playing tennis in long sleeves. Maybe try the ankle next time. Wind the Velcro strap round the bicep. Flex the arm and ping the skin until the vein stands prominent. Turn off the flame in the cooker and let the mix cool. Swab the elbow area with an alcohol wipe. Stay clean, stay safe. Poke the needle into the melt. Pull the plunger and see the warm brown fluid rise inside the tube. Tap and check for air bubbles. Breathe. Smile for the mirror. Now the skill. Point of needle against the vein and gently, sweetly, break the surface and slide it in. Test the aim. Pull the plunger back. A tiny red line appears. Got it first time. Smile, release the strap and push the plunger.

Watch the level drop steadily in the glass chamber. Long before empty, feel the first rush. Mirror. Face and upper body flushing red. Eyes widening. Jaw slackening. Deep breath, sigh, shift weight and ease onto the lounger, still clutching the needle. Peer at the glass chamber. A last drop left. A final push.

Rocketing bliss in head and body. Fingers numb. Needle falling clattering on the wood floor. Head orgasms. God's presence.

The slow fall from the coke high into the longer, laid-back bliss of the heroin. All pressure gone, all tensions dissolved. Rolling happiness. Body heavy and slow and hot. . .

Warwick Stanstead began drifting to the surface. He dragged himself upright and stood swaying. He dropped his clothes and stepped into the shower. He sat beneath its tropical rainfall until some of the euphoric lethargy lifted. He dried off, donned his clothes and checked the time. Two hours gone. He cleared the kit away except for a sachet of white, his silver tray, tube and blade. He emerged in his office and sat at his desk. He drew three lines on his silver plaque and snorted them clean. He slid the equipment into a drawer. New energy coursed through him. Well-being, confidence and super clarity. He buzzed his secretary.

'Show in the first one.'

After yesterday's debacle in Delhi and this morning's washroom session Warwick was just in the right mood for the one-to-ones with a chosen few of his executive team. On a rotating basis, without fail, regardless where anyone was on the planet, Warwick Stanstead lined them up for 'coaching sessions', in the flesh or by video link. Death or incarceration were the only excuses for opt-out. That they were less about coaching and more about roasting, was simply a question of style. His view was that men worked better if they were frightened or bribed. Fear and greed were much more reliable drivers than self-actualisation or any of that caring management bullshit.

His take on human nature meant he was never surprised how many of the sessions seemed to be carried out by video-link. Even if the office had been swarming the day before and the day after, it was astonishing how many of his first reports had to be away from their desks the day of the one-to-one.

First up was Marcus Nightingale, Senior Vice President for Global Retail Banking. As luck would have it, Marcus had had to fly to the West Coast two days before. It seemed he'd rather connect by video at 3 am San Francisco time than face to face. Warwick studied the man for a minute or two before switching on his side of the link. Marcus was in his usual state when facing his boss. Fat and flustered. Flapping around making sure his tie was straight and all his papers were set exactly where they needed to be to answer any of Warwick's penetrating questions. He was having a last minute confab with two of his minions who'd no doubt spent the last two days briefing and rehearsing Marcus for his inquisition.

'Ready, Marcus?' Warwick's voice cut into the room in San Francisco without warning. Marcus's face went stiff and he shooed his colleagues out of the room. He clutched at his papers for support.

'Good morning Warwick. I can't see you yet.' His deep voice rumbled back at Warwick with hardly a quiver. 'Ah that's better.' Warwick chose to switch on his camera so that he could be seen as well as heard. He gave him no time for pleasantries.

'How are those ATM costs, Marcus?'

'All the upgrades are done and we've pushed the costs out beyond Q3.'

'The analysts will be pleased. When will they show up, and how much?'

Marcus Nightingale's eyes flicked to the tablet in front of him.

'Q4 this year and Q1 next. We've also gone back to the suppliers and told them we're taking out a writ against them for failing to supply us with fully Internet compatible kit in the first place. Told them we're not paying any bills till we get a settlement. They're pretty upset but we've got them over a barrel. Either they play ball or we go elsewhere for the next tranche.' Marcus looked smug.

'A bit dirty Marcus? A bit underhand? You're learning.' He watched the smugness grow, then, 'So that's all the costs out on the table. No more to come?'

Marcus was confident, over-confident. 'That's it. Should be no more hiccups this year.'

'So Project Hannibal is complete too. On time and budget?'

A tick began under Marcus's left eye. He began flicking at his keyboard.

'Last lap, Warwick.'

'So all customer accounts transferred to the single customer file by … when exactly?'

'Year end. No later.'

'Sure? No cost over-runs? I mean this $350 million project isn't going to cost me – let's think of a number – $500?'

Marcus's face crumpled and he began opening new tabs and scrolling.

'There might be some tidying up. Some loose ends. I'm looking for the figures. . .'

Warwick's voice shifted from cream to razor-wire.

'Save your time. You won't find them there. But I know it's going to cost me 500. I know it's going to be delayed till March next year. The question is why the fuck don't you?!'

Marcus was lost. His wits were scattered with his screen full of opened tabs. Warwick hit the zoom button to see the sweat breaking out on his florid face. He was probably wetting himself under the table.

Warwick let rip. 'You fucking disgust me! You know that? You're supposed to be on top of your fucking department, and you're nowhere near! You get your ass over to your project team and find out what the fuck is happening. And then you tell me. Right?! And that means face to face, you fucking cream puff!'

Warwick cut off the stammering reply. He got up from his desk and walked out onto the balcony. His blood was zinging with the confrontation. He was fever-high on righteous anger. He broke out a cigarette and inhaled deeply as he looked out across Manhattan, king of this castle. This was what he was good at. This was how to keep GA on top. He threw the butt over the side and watched it spiralling away into the cavern below. He wondered whom it would hit. He walked back to his desk and flicked the intercom.

'Who's next, Pat? On screen or in the flesh? Anyone with the balls to actually show up?'

'Europe, Middle East and Africa in person. Mr Abraham Kubala. Here in the flesh.'

'Send him in!'

The tall African-American walked in. He was a similar height and build to Warwick and carried his head high. He showed dignity and control. Warwick didn't like that. Not from someone that would never be allowed into his country club. Abraham stalked in and laid his folder carefully down on the table in front of him. He made no move to open it. He sat back, hands clasped casually in his lap, waiting for Warwick to begin. Warwick decided he was being patronised. He'd break his cool soon enough.

'At our last exec meeting you said you'd fix things in Q3. Did you?'

'Yes, sir. Europe is on plan, providing our Corporate Finance boys bring in the big Russian telecoms deal. But you know the Russians. At worst it could slip into Q4. That would dent our top line by $50 million in Q3 but I have some cost items to play with to minimise the hit. We'll know Friday.' Abraham's voice was mellow and slow paced, as though he was always in control of events. It infuriated Warwick.

They went through the region country by country, business line by business line with Abraham Kubala showing complete mastery of his turf. Several times Warwick thought he'd found a weak spot, but each time Abraham was equal to it. He knew to the last penny what was going on and had put in place workable plans to keep the business on track in a region which ran from London to Moscow, across the Middle East and on down to Cape Town. Warwick was grudgingly impressed that at least one of his men was on top of his job. But Warwick had kept one throw for last.

'You personally meet clients?'

'It's essential.'

'No problems? They're welcoming?'

Abraham looked at Warwick with one eyebrow raised.

'It's fine. We meet and establish working relations.'

'Take your wife with you much, Abe?'

Abraham tensed. He didn't like the Abe much. 'Not often. But, yes, sometimes she comes with me. I travel so much it makes sense for her to join me on some of the trips.'

'And that causes no problems either? You and her.' Warwick was slouched back in his seat, hands above his head, clasping the back of the chair.

'Why should it?' Now Abraham was seriously on edge. He smelled where this was going and yet couldn't, wouldn't believe it.

'It must turn a few heads. Especially in Dubai or the old white colonies down in Africa. A big black guy like you and a pretty white lady like your wife. She's blond too, right?'

'So what? And why is this of concern to you, Mr Stanstead?'

Warwick couldn't seem to get his tongue working. At last he managed to swallow. His words were slurred.

'No need to get upset, Abe. It's perfectly understandable that my boys acquire the best things in life. Shows they've made it. I mean old Marcus is into Porsches. Charlie likes property. Erin's into pictures. I can't blame your taste. Man to man, it's what I would have done in your shoes. I guess it's the dream of all you boys.'

Abraham Kubala's face turned purple under his smooth black skin. He shot to his feet.

'I think this session is over don't you, Stanstead?'

Warwick was still laughing as he flicked on the intercom.

'Pat, you've probably been passed by a seriously pissed Kubala. Make sure he doesn't do anything stupid – like resign. If need be, get Joey to have a word with him. Give me five, then send in the next clown.'

Stanstead pulled open his drawer and reached for his silver box.

THIRTY FIVE

Oscar was in full gallop after a snatched sleep. Between answering queries from Delhi and plundering the emails, data files and voice recordings of Global American, he and Albert were working eighteen hour days. They were in their element. Oscar loved the accolades and recognition he got from his new friends in the People's Bank. As keyboard wizards themselves they were well aware of the top dogs in the hacking echelons. The Lone Ranger handle got him immediate admiration, making him throw his best efforts into everything he did for them. Oscar intended to dazzle.

He was also impressed at the quality of the work coming back to him. The counter-measure programs wrapped round his own code were elegant and tightly woven, with little redundancy, even when written under massive pressure. The resulting routines were like something produced by Benny Goodman and his Orchestra; a complex and harmonious blend of free-wheeling improvisations on a majestic structure.

After the near miss of the attack on Erin and Ted, Oscar and Albert were working in parallel on virus combat and GA eavesdropping. Albert was taking the heavy end of the GA analysis. It was exhausting and boring. It required him to page through email after email, and open up all the copies they'd made of the folders using the Lone Ranger spy programs. The sheer quantity meant that he could do little more than sift the material into two piles: 'killers' and 'krap'. The first pile was pumped down to the web site Oscar had set up. This was to be accessed by Ted and Erin to do the second level of sifting. The criterion was simple: whether it would help to hang Warwick Stanstead. It was a thin file, but growing.

In the background, just audible, Albert played the recordings from Stanstead's office. Oscar and Albert relied on their ears switching on to something unusual in the conversations. Any phone call or face-to-face with Joey Kutzov was listened to avidly and usually compressed as an MP3 file and uploaded to the web site for retention. Much of the stuff was dross; mundane operational discussions, or more usually, instructions going out from Stanstead to his hapless lieutenants. It was frustrating at times, amusing at others. Amusing if you weren't on the receiving end of the sarcasm and venom. Stanstead was out of his office frequently, and key meetings took place or decisions were made which were then referred to back in his office. This took some disentangling and interpretation.

Both their ears pricked up when Stanstead made a call that was answered personally by the President of the World Bank. It was obvious by the ease of access to Alexander D. Paterson and by the subsequent tone of conversation, that these two top executives were on very friendly terms.

'I see the court date's set, Alec.'

The answering voice was in a deep Boston drawl, the tones of a senior statesman, sure of his breeding and position. 'For once they seem to have gotten their act together. But it's taken some persuasion, I can tell you.'

'I bet. How's the case looking? I mean do we need to do anything more? Will it stick?'

'As much as anything seems to stick in the third world, Warwick. Of course they could throw the whole game away by calling an election between now and then. It's been at least 18 months since they last changed governments. I forget who's turn it is this time, but I'm hopeful that all parties will take the same line on our little problem. After all, we bailed them out. Mmmm?'

'I hope you're right, Alec. Banerjee is slippery as a greased pig – maybe I shouldn't use that allusion with these guys?' There was laughter. 'But as far as I'm concerned he's not down till he's behind bars and their whole set-up is dismantled.'

The languid voice took on an edge. 'We need to talk about

that. The aftermath. We don't want any panic. No runs. No mess. God knows we've had enough of that these past couple of years. We want the bank transferred intact to the control of the Indian Government. We need to show the international community working together, dealing fairly and equitably with all account holders. And saying we mustn't let this sort of shady business happen again. Back to basics. Back to the old order, because it works and can be relied on.'

'Well, GA is standing by of course, but just so's you know Alec, I don't want to take any of the small accounts on my books. That's pissing money away. I reckon we should just call in the loans for anyone with less than a three star credit scoring, and write off the rest.'

'That would eliminate most of their accounts, I imagine. There's a better way. We'll need to walk carefully. Moral outrage and all that.'

'I thought that's where you came in, Alex?'

'Most certainly. We'll move quickly to offer new loans to India and any of the other ASEAN countries with high levels of small debtors, so they can cushion the effect locally. We don't want civil unrest do we? Or the markets disturbed. We'll probably cordon off the small debtors in one area of the bank under our control – I've got some bright young things standing by eager to show off. Then we'll just let the debts run off. Most seem to get paid back, amazingly. Might as well maximise the returns. We can then put the profits down to our prudent governance, can't we.'

The conversation ended in discussion of families and holiday plans. Alexander D. Paterson was looking forward to giving Warwick's new yacht a 'spin round the bay' as he called the two week trip in the Caribbean. There was the sound of Stanstead hanging up.

Albert twirled on his chair. 'Holy shit, Batman!'

'Let's not confuse ourselves, Tonto. But yes, indeed, holy shit. I think Theodore Saddler may have found himself another Pulitzer Prize story – should he live long enough to write it.'

THIRTY SIX

Anila had heard nothing in the night, sleeping solidly for the first time in days. It wasn't until she became aware of a little more light in the room than normal that she focussed on the carving of Krishna that hung on the wall. The carving that now had an aura behind it. The carving that covered the hole that was only supposed to go part-way into the wall. The hole where she kept her 4000 Rupees safe. This was no godly visitation. Unless it was Kali.

Her heart flipped and she gently disentangled herself from her daughter, easing the sheet back over her sleeping form. Anila rose and moved in slow motion towards the crude wall-safe already fearing what had happened. She hoped she was having a very bad dream and that she'd wake shortly. She touched Krishna and lifted the god from his hook. Light hurt her eyes. There was now a hole all the way through to the outside, letting in the day. It wasn't a dream. The money had gone.

She searched futilely and frantically through her hut and outside, knowing she hadn't put it anywhere else, but needing to believe anyway. Before she went mad. This wasn't possible, not after her success yesterday. Not after things had begun to go right for her. Not after consigning her money to Krishna for protection! Her noise woke her daughter and her mother. All three stripped the hut again, but their eyes told each other the truth.

Krishna had decided to punish her. For her hubris, no doubt! For the first time in months she had slept a dreamless sleep. She had woken refreshed and eager to get about her new business. Which is exactly when the gods punish pride. From the outside it was clear how it had been done. Very carefully the robbers had soaked the wall, patiently eating away at the hard-dried mud until they'd broken through to the brick. Then they'd eased two bricks out from the crumbling mortar. The wonder was that they'd known exactly where to attack.

Anila was in tears of anger and terror. She knew they were wasting their time rooting through all the pots and her few clothes in case she'd put the money elsewhere. She knew she hadn't, knew it was pointless, but she kept trying, to divert herself from the grief that was banking up. But finally she threw herself down on her bed and wept in despair and self-pity. Her mother and daughter sat by her, helpless and with stricken faces. And that was how Divya and Leena found them.

'There is only one person who could have done this!' Leena was puffed up and furious as they gazed at the outside wall and its hole all the way through.

'But we do not have proof. How can we confront him?' asked Anila.

'We do not need proof! We know it was Chowdury and his thugs! Who else could it be?!'

'First we must report this to the council and see if we can get the police to come to the village.'

'What good would the police do?' asked Divya. 'They are never on our side. They are only on the side of the rich. You know that.'

By mid morning, the hut was surrounded by a small crowd, mainly of the members of Anila's cooperative. They were aghast at the crime and panicking over their stolen money. They began to think that they'd been stupid setting up this cooperative and letting Anila Jhabvala turn their heads. Things were fine before. This was a disaster caused by greed. That was how the gods worked. The village hardly knew what crime was. Everyone left their doors open. No-one – except one notable person – had enough money or possessions to worry about theft.

The anger grew, and despite the pleas of the sarpanch the little army began to march on the money lender's house. It stood on the edge of the village with its own land. It was two storeys tall and had – as much as anyone could conjecture – 6 rooms. Though what on earth one old man and his childless wife needed six rooms for, had long been a source of scandal. As was the dark curve of a satellite dish which stood arrogantly on the lip of the rooftop balustrade.

Only two other houses in the village owned a television set: a wealthy farmer and a trader. At times of great national events – an international cricket match or a specially-loved film – the villagers were allowed to crowd round these two TVs, peering through glassless windows and the front door. But not so with the money lender. He kept what belonged to him tight to his miserly chest. Often, from his open windows, the sound of laughter and clapping could be heard across that corner of the village. There was no point having wealth if it could not be flaunted.

Anila was carried along reluctantly in the angry mob, and stood back as they pounded on his front door. A face appeared at one of the small upper floor windows. It was Mrs Chowdury. She looked more annoyed than fearful.

'What do you want, hammering on my door like that!?'

The big woman with the four daughters called up, 'We want your thief of a husband! And we want our money back. The money he stole from the house of Mrs Jhabvala.' This was greeted by noisy support from her colleagues.

'How dare you! My husband is no thief! We do not need your money. We have plenty already.'

'Where is your husband, then. That we may ask him?'

'He is not here. He went to Sagar on business two days ago. Then he was going on to Jabalpur. He will not be back for two or three days, maybe longer. You see, he could not have stolen your stinking money. Could he! So now, go away.'

The crowd was stymied. Even if the money lender had got his minions to steal the money, they could not accuse him till he showed up. All they could do was get the police to come from

Sagar, and that would take two days at least. If they could be bothered to come at all. In the meantime, they had lost the money to pay for the wood today and Anila had lost everything. They could manage to scrape enough together for today's purchase and maybe tomorrow, but further ahead looked desperate.

Anila walked back up the hill to her hut, her bare feet scuffing the ground, her sari pulled up over her face.

THIRTY SEVEN

Eight hours after leaving Delhi, they fell out of the ice-cold train into the Tropic of Cancer. The noise and heat at Bhopal station concussed them. Erin was stiff and sore, and desperate to get back to her tree-lined running track or air-conditioned gym. She stumbled after the fluid young limbs of Meera Banerjee, Outside in the hard light, a long wheel-base Land Rover sat cooking in the forecourt. Its driver sprawled in the shade by the entrance. Meera strode over. The young man jumped guiltily to his feet.

'This is it,' Meera called to the travellers proudly. She patted the scalding metal gingerly but with affection. Close up it showed the scrapes and dents of countless miles on India's roads. 'We are buying second hand LRs and refurbishing them. These machines go on for ever.'

'Of course. They're British.'

Erin tried to put some irony in her comment to cover an unexpected surge of pride. They opened all the doors to let the heat out and gazed inside. Even with the young man taking the train back to his base in the south, there was little enough room for three people and their luggage. The back of the jeep was already packed with equipment and boxes.

'We have everything we need. We can operate as a remote branch of the bank for up to three months,' said Meera.

They were glad to be out off the train and glad – however briefly – to be on the main road heading east to Udaipura. They travelled barely 10 miles before pulling into a grubby car park at the back of the extravagantly named Hotel Splendid. It was a four storey concrete building, painted pink some time ago. The colour had faded unevenly, so that it looked like badly blemished skin. The acne-like effect was exaggerated by eruptions and flaking where the paint and the top layer of the concrete had reacted with each other. Ted and Erin entered the hotel warily and were pleasantly surprised to find the interior in better health.

'This is wonderful, Meera.'

Erin scooped her chapatti through the remnants of her vegetable curry and rice. She prayed she wouldn't pay for it later and had taken precautionary pills. Ted grinned over his beer. There was nothing to do except talk after dinner and wait for the food to digest before bed. He turned to Meera.

'If you hadn't been stuck with us, you would just have gone off by yourself to set up the district?'

'Why not? I am trained. Many have gone out before me. And the people need us.'

'But aren't you a little bit scared?'

'What should I be scared about?'

'It's such a huge country and you're miles – thousands of miles – from your family and your friends and colleagues.' Ted knew he was viewing Meera's challenge through his own fears at that age; uprooting and coming to New York.

Meera looked at him curiously. 'It is my country. Wherever I go, I make new friends and new family. The women look after me. Is there anything better to do with my time? It is maybe a small thing we do. Not on the scale of America.' Ted picked up a little vinegar in the comment. 'But when you add up all the small things they come to a big number. I am just one small person but there are thousands like me.'

Ted leaned over, notebook in hand. 'Meera, I'm still struggling with the profit side of your business. Do you mind if I ask this? If this was all about helping the poor, why don't you simply take the money the West offers and give it them? Your bank is charging average interest of around 25% on loans. But in other countries it can be as much as a third of the capital. How can you justify that? It's maybe a lot less than the money lenders, but it's still a heck of a price to pay on a $50 loan.'

Meera was nodding. 'I used to think the same. I was always arguing with my father. Partly it is about the cost of transactions but it is also about how people behave. If we gave hand-outs, the people would simply expect more. They would take the money – especially the men – and spend it. If the money is free or cheap there is no respect for it. Or for the giver. That is one of the reasons everyone hates the World Bank except the politicians with their hands out. There is a saying: a hundred Rupees in Delhi is worth two in a villager's pocket. There are so many layers. And every layer wants a little slice.'

'I'm sorry. I didn't mean to upset you.'

'We go directly to the people who need it. To the women, who will use it best and who truly value the money. It will make the difference between feeding their family or letting the weakest ones die. And we know that they will repay it. With the surplus – it's not a profit – we give more loans to more people. Don't you see? This is a great network of self help!'

Meera was leaning forward, her hands underlining her message, her eyes brimming with certainty. Ted disliked sentimental speeches; they always came over false. But there was substance to this kid. Maybe he was getting old and emotional.

Erin was watching him and thought she saw something new in him. It had taken a murder attempt to get Ted going, but there was no doubting he was now more absorbed. And as far as she could judge, it wasn't all Dutch courage. Ted Saddler seemed finally to be getting off his knees. Was there a change in her too? That despite yesterday's traumas, and today's Spartan amenities, she could detect some lightness? Of being more at peace with herself than she'd felt in years? Maybe. Either that or she was coming down with something.

In the morning, after a restless night fighting mosquitoes and heat, they bounced back on to the road. Meera took the wheel, and they drove for three hours through increasingly hilly and forested countryside to Udaipura. Once there they forked left and began the bumping ten mile ride to Chandapur.

Within a hundred yards Erin was clutching her stomach, wishing she were dead. Sweat broke out on her brow and her face was blotched. She fought it off as long as she could but was forced to call a halt twice. She was beyond embarrassment. The yawing and pitching of the Land Rover's hull over its much abused suspension had felt like all her worst school jaunts rolled into one.

As they jolted down into the hollow of the valley they could see the same blasted scenery that Anila and her companions had crossed on foot just two weeks before. If anything, it was worse. The fields had been harvested. They stood bone dry and stubbled as though devoured and salted by a retreating army. The last tufts of green on the low shrubs and thickets had given up the fight and had turned the same dull ochre as everything else. The cancer spread from the valley floor up the hillsides where some last green tinges at the rim suggested what the valley had once been like when the river had run through it. Meera was shouting above the grind of the engine and the crunching of the jeep's body on its springs.

'This was all green once. Just a few years ago.'

'What happened?' called Erin, grasping at the chance to take her mind off the nausea.

'Our government has big ideas. One administration starts off a grand project, they get voted out, and the next one cancels it, or they run out of money, or it all gets too hard. Usually it's twenty layers of officials who all have to be bought. Maybe that works the first time. But a big project means doing it in phases, and every new phase requires more paperwork and more bribes.'

'And this is what happened here?'

'The Indian Government is very proud that we have built over 5,000 dams. Regardless of the Adivasi.'

'The Adivasi?'

'The original people. The ones who have always lived here.'

'What happened?'

'We don't know. Isn't that funny? No-one knows. We have mislaid 50 million people. Like losing all the people in Britain. The government says they were displaced and compensated.' Meera underlined the words with heavy irony.

'They weren't?'

'They paid huge sums – bribes – to local officials and landowners who then drove the Adivasi off the land. Fifty million people were swept like dirt under our national carpet. To end up begging in the cities. The women becoming prostitutes, the men just dying of drink and shame. And the children. Oh, the children. India has nearly 60 million child labourers – slaves in all but name. In just one sector – cottonseed production – 400,000 children, aged between 7 and 14 are working 16 hour days. Mainly girls of course, because their parents can't afford dowries.'

The jeep was quiet for a time as the facts tore home. Erin's nausea shifted from the physical to the mental.

'But. . .' Erin pointed out the window. 'The dams – did they at least improve the water situation? Drinking, crop irrigation?'

Meera had been waiting for this. 'When we meddle with nature, we get it completely wrong. The earth has always depended on the monsoon. It happens once a year and gives the land time to recover. The dams make it worse. No-one thought to look out the window and ask if the earth could take a continual deluge from irrigation. We are drowning the land. All the water is forcing the salt that lies deep down in the earth to come to the top. Then it kills the land. Only a madman would have dreamed of such an idea.'

'Is this throughout India, or just around here?' Erin asked desperately.

'India has 55 billionaires, the nuclear bomb and sends rockets into space. But around 150 million people – twelve per cent of our country – still have no access to clean drinking water. UNICEF says more than 500 children die every day in India from diarrhoea – that's like a full jumbo-jet crashing to the ground. Each day.'

Erin winced. 'Why won't the government stop? They must know what's going on?'

'And admit they were wrong? Would yours? Loans are a drug, don't you see? We have become dependent on loans from the West, from your World Bank. We just took another $360 million loan for more waterworks in Uttar Pradesh. How much of that will end up in the pockets of the politicians? They are wined and dined and taken on foreign trips and they use the loans to keep them in power. It is the most vicious of vicious circles.'

Erin looked at Ted and shared the shame. They were relieved as their vehicle trundled into the outskirts of the village of Chandapur. They drove past a lone tree that looked like an oak but wasn't, in some indefinable way. Then Ted noticed the olive-like fruits hanging in the branches. He placed it. It was the bank's logo. A neem tree.

The Land Rover jolted in and out of the ruts scored in the bare earth by trucks and carts. Curious faces came to the doors of dilapidated huts and scrutinised the travellers unashamedly. To the Western eyes the villagers seemed poorer even than the poorest they'd seen in Delhi. Their skins were darker and their features coarser. Two dogs chased them all the way in to the centre, marked by the round wall of a well. The jeep drew up under the spreading shade of five neem trees, and quickly gathered a crowd.

They stepped out of the Land Rover into a minefield.

THIRTY EIGHT

Ramesh Banerjee was staring ruin in the face and trying not to let it show in front of his two colleagues. He was sitting in the courtyard of the office in Delhi reviewing the trial papers. His lawyer, Medha Sardar, had just taken him though the written evidence to be presented by the prosecution team. There were depositions from twenty six key witnesses that were particularly damning. Ramesh stabbed the document.

'I've never even met these men!'

'I know, Ramesh. I know. It is all innuendo and exaggeration. But the difficulty is disproving it.'

'Why? These are lies! There is not one iota of truth in any of this. And that is your job, is it not? To expose the lies.'

'Of course. And we will attack them good and hard. But these men,' he swept his hand contemptuously over the pile of typed pages, 'have been well paid I think. And maybe they are terrified too.'

'Tell me again why we can't have a jury trial? I wanted this to come in front of the people. They would have defended me.'

Medha Sardar shifted his broad bottom on his seat and tugged at his tunic, smoothing the front down over his prosperous belly.

'You have answered your own question. That is exactly why the Government has set it up this way. The last thing they want is a populist movement starting in their courtroom. Their excuse is that the case is too complex for a lay jury, and that the three trial judges will be able to make better sense of the arguments and deliver a safer verdict.' He shrugged.

CJ Kapoor, who made up the third member of the little group sitting in the early morning light, leaned forward.

'What do we know about the three judges? Are they fair men? Will we get a good hearing?'

Sardar shifted uncomfortably in his seat. 'It is hard to say. But I do not think we could say any one of them sits in the liberal camp. The senior judicial magistrate – Justice Nayak – is a pompous man. He is very full of himself and lectures his courts to show his great learning. He is more likely to side with the government, just because he is an establishment figure. He will not go against the mood of the ruling class. He would find it too difficult at cocktail parties and receptions.'

Ramesh and CJ looked at each other with resignation. 'What about the other two?' asked Ramesh.

'Judicial Magistrate Jhaveri is known to take bribes. All the judges take bribes of course, but Jhaveri is especially susceptible. And yet at the same time he is very hot on offenders. It is how he allays his conscience.'

'It sounds like his pocket wins out over his scruples. What about the last man? Is there any hope there?'

'Judicial Magistrate Sharma is something of an unknown quantity. A dark horse. He is new to the bench this year and we know little about him. But all we can say is that he is the most junior, and will tend – if precedents are anything to go by – to follow the line taken by the senior justice. We do not think he will step out of line. And remember, he was appointed by this government and will not want to bite the hand that is feeding him.'

'So we should give up now and admit our guilt, and beg for a lenient sentence? Is that your recommendation?' Ramesh looked crushed. His eyes were tired and unseeing.

'No, no, Ramesh. There is still hope. We have good witnesses of our own who will testify to your honesty and probity. And we will go all out to pick holes in the prosecution witnesses. Some of these testimonies are so patently contrived that even the trial judges will have difficulty not being embarrassed by them.' He lifted a pile. 'Look, even the words are the same in each of the testimonies. I am sure they were all concocted by the same hand.'

'But can we prove it?' asked CJ.

'We can draw the court's attention to it. And then we will question the witnesses to shake them. We will also take each instance of supposed bribery and ask you and your officers what they were doing at the time. If we can find alibis for every occasion when some supposed bribe was offered or money was passed to make something happen, then it is just their word against ours.'

'That sounds flimsy. What else?'

Sardar looked hard at Ramesh.

'The hardest charge to beat will be the political one. That you have worked to undermine the freely elected government of India. That through an insidious process of gaining control over the lives and minds of the poor you have incited them to rise up against the State. I am only quoting, you know!' He saw how angrily Ramesh was reacting.

'This is monstrous, you know! It is unbelievable! What possible proof have they?'

The lawyer flicked through a second pile of papers.

'They are citing five separate riots across the country by Dalits and Adivasi.

'Riots! There were no riots! There were marches and demonstrations!'

Sardar smiled over his glasses at him. 'Do you think the Government sees any difference? These riots took place this year and the rioters were waving banners demanding positive discrimination for the Dalits, an end to dam building and a return to traditional irrigation techniques... and so on and so on.'

'But why would they blame us for that? It is common sense.'

'It is not State policy. Therefore it cannot be common sense. And they blame you – or your bank – as you are on the record for espousing this cause. They say that many of the rioters were account holders in the People's Bank and that you coerced them to their riotous acts through threatening to increase the loan rates.'

Ramesh and CJ were speechless with indignation and incredulity.

'Moreover,' went on Sardar, 'they have photographs of crowds waving banners calling for foreign consultants to keep out and to get rid of the World Bank. Some banners read…' he checked his notes, '… follow the way of the People's Bank' and 'Small loans to the poor = democracy'. They are saying in their prosecution case that you are aiming to overthrow the government by 'fomenting sedition and insurrection'.

'But what is a few photographs?' CJ tried to be dismissive.

'They have so-called witnesses again. People who will swear that they were forced by the Bank to march against the Government. That they were threatened with ruin and told to break the law and to move against the State. It will be a hard one to fight against, I'm afraid, Ramesh.'

'It seems we have no friends,' said CJ.

'Only our customers. It is a pity we cannot get them into the witness box.'

THIRTY NINE

Anila sat in the dark of her hut, her legs folded under her, rocking gently as if in a trance. She was exhausted. The fight was lost. The dark rings round her big eyes testified to a night without sleep. Her mother had been gentle with her instead of railing at her. Which was of course worse. Her mother had taken Aastha to visit a cousin on the other side of the village to give Anila some quiet time on her own.

She'd spent it obsessively rehearsing the options, such as they were. She could wait for the police to arrive and hope they would find the thief. But she knew – as everyone did – that the police were at best useless, at worst as corrupt as the criminals themselves. She could bring the cooperative together again and see what money they could find between them. But she knew they had so little, and they would not trust her again. It was impossible. Divya and Leena especially could never forgive her. Why should they? She had lost all honour among her friends.

She was left with two choices. She could take her own life, but that would leave her daughter defenceless and destitute. Or she could flee with her daughter to Bhopal and join the beggars on the street. But it would be fierce competition among the blinded and the maimed survivors and deformed children of the Union Carbide disaster.

Maybe her mother could find sanctuary with one of her cousins or more distant relatives. Maybe she could take her daughter with her. Anila could then vanish into the city and no longer be a burden on anyone. Yes, that was the way. She wasn't sure how to kill herself anyway, not now the river had gone. She shuddered at the thought of throwing herself down the old well. Maybe she could lower herself down on a rope and just starve to death?

Anila was hardly aware of the rumble of noise of a small crowd coming her way. It wasn't until the noise was right outside her door that she became fully conscious of it. There were familiar voices and one she hadn't heard before. She guessed they were coming to get her and take her before the council. They would drag her out and then beat her for all the fuss she caused. Maybe they would throw her on a fire. She deserved it. Then she heard Leena calling her name. Surprisingly the tone wasn't stern or murderous. The next moment, her door was pushed open and light flooded the room.

'Anila? Look whom we have we brought to see you.'

How could Leena sound so happy? How could she even talk to her, after what she'd done to her? Leena was standing in the doorway, her head bent under the low frame. A strange young woman stooped and entered. Anila could not make her out against the white light from outside, but her head was bare and her hair was short as a boy's. Then another woman was coming in behind her, a white woman, wearing jeans, she could see that much! Anila felt her small hut become too crowded all of a sudden. Were these people here to take her away for losing all the money?! She jumped to her feet. She backed away, fearful in her own house.

'Leena, what is going on? Who are these people? Have they come for me?'

'They are from the bank, Anila. They are from our bank!' She sounded excited and worried at the same time.

The Indian woman spoke. 'Mrs Jhabvala, I am most sorry to arrive unannounced. My name is Meera Banerjee. I am from the People's Bank. I am your regional manager.'

Anila struggled to take the words in. They had come for her! This woman was the regional manager? How could she be? She was only a girl, surely younger than herself. And looking like she was going to one of those clubs, with her short hair and her trousers and blouse. She must be here to punish her. To demand her collateral! And why did she bring this white woman? Anila felt her heart loosen and everything poured out of her at once. Her guilt, her fears, her dashed hopes.

'Namaste, Miss Banerjee. I throw myself at your feet. I have lost all the money your bank gave me. I let it be stolen. I will work for nothing to pay it off but I do not think I will ever manage to pay you back.'

Meera reached out and touched Anila.

'May I sit with you and talk about this? I am sure it is not so very bad. But first, do you mind if this Scottish woman sits with us? She does not understand Hindi so I may have to explain to her in English from time to time.'

Anila was almost beyond surprise or shock. But why had a woman come all the way from Scotland to see her? She nodded dumbly and motioned to the three women to sit. She moved quickly to retrieve the little stools that her mother and daughter sat on and gave them to the strangers. She and Leena knelt on mats on the bare ground and began automatically to prepare tea. While she was doing this the bank woman was explaining a little of what was going on to the white woman in English – what did Scottish sound like? Anila understood some of the words. But they were speaking so fast. Her father had tried to pass on some of his own education, but there were too many strange words. She became conscious of the buzz outside. Leena saw her ears prick up and explained.

'Anila, half the village has come to see the bank lady and the Scottish lady. And there is an American man – a great big one! – sitting outside. They came in a very powerful car.'

Leena giggled and Anila could not suppress the smile that came to her lips. Meera too was smiling and explaining to the woman who also smiled. Anila kept staring at her. Anila whispered to Leena in Hindi.

'The Scottish woman is so beautiful. Such white skin.'

'It is their weather, surely. They have no sun, I hear.'

'Her figure is perfect, so shapely in those blue jeans. The men in the village will go mad for her!'

Ted Saddler sat outside, surrounded by a grinning mass of people. They jammed the narrow alleyway on either side, with a bunch directly in front of him. They were inspecting him hard, and discussing him freely. A stool had been brought so he could be exhibited properly. Meera had told him he wasn't allowed into the hut under the rules of Purdah. He took off the hat he'd donned when they got out of the jeep. It was already sweat-stained. He used it to fan himself.

Ted gazed back. He'd got used to close scrutiny by villagers during his Iraq tour. But he felt even more incongruous surrounded by these skinny people with scraps of cloth round them. A lot of bad teeth. Mainly old women and children. He assumed the young men and women were out in the fields. Though god knows what they grew in this heat. He felt the sweat coursing down his back and his sides. The underside of his trousers was damp. He would have given anything for a cool bath and a tall glass of beer with condensation running down the side. A scrawny boy approached, about ten years old and with big white teeth and a crooked arm.

'Please sir? What are you doing here? Are you come to take Mrs Jhabvala away?' He wore a knotted cloth round his thin hips and a grubby T shirt advertising Singa Beer. His feet were bare, his English laboured but understandable.

Ted grinned back. 'No, we're not taking Mrs Jhabvala away. We are here to help her.' He went beyond his remit. 'We are here to help the village.'

The boy translated and raised excitement through the crowd. He was encouraged to ask more questions.

'Excuse me, what is your mother country, sir?'

'America.' It brought a sigh from the crowd as though they had expected it from his size and colour. 'A place called New York.'

The sigh grew louder and became an Ahhh. 'New York!' interpreted the boy, 'that is a wonderful city. We have seen it on television.' He looked troubled. '9/11, yes?' His hand did an aircraft dive. Then the smile came back. He pointed at the hut where Erin had gone.

'Is she your woman?'

The boy was completely without caution now and brimming with curiosity. Ted toyed with the notion of Erin as his woman. He wished Miss Cool had been around. How would she have answered? Fat chance. Without skipping a beat.

'She is a friend. We are working together. We are working with the People's Bank.'

'Will you give money to everyone?'

A woman had whispered the question into the boy's ear then told her friends. They went quiet waiting for his answer.

'It is not for me to talk about money. It is for Miss Banerjee, the woman who came with me. She is the bank's representative here. You must ask her.'

The crowd digested this and there was a general movement closer. Many of the women began to settle down on their hunkers. Ted realised his interrogation could go on for a while. He reached into his chest pocket and pulled out a damp fold of dollars.

'Is there anywhere I can get a beer here, kid?'

FORTY

'She thinks we have come here to take her away. All her money has been stolen. The other women believe it was the money lender. This is not surprising. Often these men lose their power when the bank comes in and offers fairer loans. The problem is being able to prove this.'

'How big was the loan?' asked Erin.

'4000 Rupees. Around 65 of your dollars. We gave them 3000. It was meant for use by three women. These two and a friend. I'm not sure how it got to 4000 rupees.'

Meera turned and asked some more questions. There was rapid fire exchange with the two local women. She turned back to Erin.

'They had to set up a women's cooperative so that they could get proper attention from the traders here. Some of the other women's money was stolen as well. Now she is completely lost and thinks her family – her mother and daughter – will starve and she will have to go and beg in the city. Or kill herself. It is a question of honour.'

'No, no, tell her she won't!'

Erin was appalled. For the sake of sixty bucks – or eighty, whatever – this woman's world would end. She tipped her doorman more than that at Christmas.

'Tell her I'll give her the money. Tell her not to worry.'

Anila was looking at the white woman with astonishment. She could understand enough. Meera sighed inwardly. Westerners always thought money was the answer.

'Do you think we would let one of our customers down so easily? It is a setback, but it is not unusual. Tell me, Erin, if this happened in England, what would the customer do?'

'Well, for a start they'd be complaining their heads off. In America their lawyers would be sniffing for a law suit. If the money was really stolen, they'd probably be covered by insurance. The bank would look again at the case and maybe work something out with the insurer.'

'Exactly. When a person takes out a loan from us, there is a tiny amount of the interest for insurance. Tragedies happen all the time and it is as well to anticipate them. I have the authority to lend her more money until we have cleared matters with the insurance company. Of course we have to be careful. We do not advertise this service much. As you can understand, it is open to abuse. So I will get a few more facts from these women and also speak to the cooperative. We prefer cooperatives. It shows great courage and initiative, and coops work better.'

Anila was calmer but still apprehensive. She'd thought she'd misheard the English woman's offer. She certainly didn't believe it. No-one did such a thing for a stranger. She sat with her back straight trying to answer all the questions put to her by this Meera Banerjee who still seemed too young, but was so clever and strong. Anila wondered what it was like to have all her hair cut off and to wear men's clothes. She must have been wonderfully educated. Anila wondered what that would have been like instead of getting married to Dilip.

She wondered if Meera believed her about the theft. She got up and pulled back the little carving to let the daylight come though the ragged hole. A beaming villager's face filled the gap.

'See, there is the hole where I kept the money. You can see it has been attacked from the outside.'

'It is alright, Anila. I believe you. Are the police coming? Has anyone called them?'

Leena answered, seeing her friend at a loss. 'One of the women is going in to Udaipura today to see her son. She said she would report the theft.'

'And I suppose the police will take a month to send a jeep to find out what has happened. If they come at all?'

The two local women shook their heads in unison.

'I will call them myself later this day and ask them to come.'

'But we do not have telephones in the village. Will you drive back to the town?'

'I have a telephone that works here.'

'Ah. A satellite phone.' Anila said it in English to make Erin's ears prick up.

'Exactly. Now Anila, I would like to talk to some of your friends in the cooperative please. Is that possible?'

Leena leapt to her feet. 'I am one. I will get the others. They are already outside. How many do you want to speak to?'

Meera looked round the small hut. 'I think two more will do.'

Leena came back with two nervous looking women, one of them Sandip. Meera put them at their ease even though there were many sidelong glances of curiosity at the white woman.

The big woman, supported by her friend and by Leena, gave her account of the brief life of the cooperative. She praised Anila for taking the lead and being so brave in front of the whole village. She told her of the hard negotiations with the agent and what a good deal Anila had struck on all their behalves. She explained how strongly she felt about the viability of the idea and what it could mean to her and her friends. Throughout it all Anila sat with an embarrassed look as her praises were sang. To Anila it all sounded like madness now. Or something done by someone else. How could she have dared do so much!

Finally Meera had answers to all her questions, and realising they had been seated for almost two hours, she suggested they take a break for lunch. Meera politely but firmly declined Anila's offer of food. She knew Anila would hardly have enough to stave off her own hunger, far less feed two guests – three, she thought, remembering with a guilty pang, the American outside.

They emerged blinking into the afternoon sunshine to find Ted had assumed the role of story teller to what seemed half the village. The narrow lane was completely blocked for yards in either direction. Ted was surrounded by a ring of children who'd crept within three feet of him. By his foot lay two empty beer bottles. Beyond the children were their parents and old people who'd come to listen and wonder at the halting translations coming from the boy who now stood authoritatively by Ted's side. Some of them could understand Ted's English, but it did no harm to hear it twice. More time to savour it.

Ted looked broiled but happy enough. He was in mid flow, left hand gripping beer bottle, right waving excitedly, explaining baseball to them. Erin stood stretching, listening to Ted's account with amusement. She found many eyes on her, and a number of women pointing at her jean-clad legs and talking to each other. She and Meera rescued Ted, and followed by a gaggle of jabbering kids, they inched through the crowd and back down to the centre and their vehicle.

'You've got a fan club,' said Erin.

'I thought you'd never come get me. I was beginning to think there was a back way out of the hut.'

Great quarter moons of sweat soaked his back and sides, a dark ring stained his hat.

'I see you found the bar.'

'It's just a beer for chrissake. Warm, at that.'

As if warm beer didn't count. He didn't raise his voice, just kept smiling, and turned to Meera.

'How was it?'

'I think Anila Jhabvala is – how do you say it? – the right stuff?'

FORTY ONE

'I have your wife on the line Mr Stanstead. Do you want to take it or are you in conference?'

'Where's she phoning from Pat? Somewhere on Madison I'd guess.'

'My dial says she's at home sir.'

'I'll take it.' There was a pause and a click. 'Hi honey, what's up?'

'I've just had your mother on the phone. She was reminding me it's her birthday. She wants us over to celebrate. You know what that means.'

'Charmaine, there's no way I can find the time to flip up to the Vineyard to eat birthday cake. What's the boyfriend sitch? Is it still Big Benny or was that last month?'

'That's why she's so keen for us to come over. She's temporarily out of men. No-one to get laid with, no-one to get canned with.' The voice dripped distaste.

'And how would either of us fill those roles? You want I should pimp for her? Look, talk to Pat and arrange a big party for her. Get her lush friends along. Spend some money on something glittery. She'll never know we weren't there. You know the score.'

'I know the score, baby.' The voice softened, became wheedling. 'And this is going to cost you, my precious. This isn't what you pay me for you know.'

'Some day we need to talk about what exactly I do pay you for, my angel. What'll it take?'

'There's a new line of Manolos coming out next week. I so need new shoes.'

'What happened to the other three hundred? Ok, ok, just do it. Anything else, honey child?'

The sarcasm bled down the line. When the call was over Warwick sat back thinking about wives and mothers. He could – and did – change the former, but he was stuck with the latter. He wondered if Charmaine was getting over greedy and whether he was getting as much out of the deal as she was. She still turned heads, and she *gave* great head whenever he called for it, but there were definite lines round the mouth and eyes and there just seemed less enthusiasm than he really should expect. Like it was a duty or something. She joined in the powder parties with him at weekends but was squeamish about mainlining. Her loss.

On the other hand she did take care of his mother and she didn't try to change him. A big plus. Not like wife number one. Donna had had everything going for her: figure, face, family, and money of her own. It had been the society wedding of the year. But turned out she was cuckoo. She thought she could improve him. That he needed help. Her own therapy bills were sky high and she wanted to justify them by getting him to admit something wasn't working in his head either.

He'd played along for a while to keep her quiet. It had amused him at first to wind up this jerk with an alphabet of letters after his name. Then it began to irk him – partly the time, partly the price. But mainly the way he was digging into his head.

'I don't want to talk about my father. It's such a fucking cliché, Doc.'

'That in itself suggests we should, don't you think?'

They sat facing each other in big soft chairs that swivelled – deliberately low key, informal – the ambience had to be right of course for 'relating'. Dr Young – 'call me James, please' – was mid forties, dressed in dark slacks and black crew-necked top. He was clever with his silences. Though Warwick considered him a quack, he wanted value for his money, so felt obliged to fill the conversational gaps.

'What do you want to know?'

'What do you want to tell me?'

'For Christ's sake, Doc!' Warwick knew the title annoyed him. 'I don't have time for these games! Where are we trying to get to with this?'

'Nowhere. We're not trying to get anywhere. We're here. We're just talking. I'm interested. That's all. Interested and just happy to listen.'

James Young eased back in his chair, hands loose on the arms and his glasses slipping casually down his nose. Warwick thought of the fee clock ticking away.

'He was like most dads. Never around much. You know how it is if you're a big name in business. Running a global corporation and travelling a lot. Preferred to keep the family home in Maine instead of moving to New York. So he didn't get back much. . .'

Warwick let the soft afternoon light seduce him into talking about his father and how he loved to see him and how he looked for him – or a sign of him – on the special days. Sometimes Dad made it, though it happened on even fewer occasions when Warwick was at boarding school. But he always sent a real expensive present; like a BMW 3 series on his 17th birthday. The other guys were so green at that! He remembered the big cigars and the sharp suits and the way other men stood around him; like he was the epicentre of their world.

'Did you talk?'

'Sure. About lots of stuff. He taught me everything I know about business. We weren't into all that hugging and bonding stuff; didn't need to; we knew where we stood with each other. All that ostentatious declarative shit wasn't our style. In fact I guess that summed up my old man: style.'

What he didn't say, what was none of a quack psychiatrist's business to know, was that because of the rules between them he'd never told his father about his mother. How can you say,

216

'Oh by the way pop, I caught mommy getting screwed by the pool cleaner last week,' or 'Your old pal Prizio, the one you set up in business? Yeah, good old Prizio was round again for cocktails and blowjobs with your wife.' And that he'd first caught his beautiful, golden, whore of a mother at it when he was twelve.

He'd been dropped home early from a friend's party and had wandered round the house looking for her and had found her – heard her first – heard the gasping and the rhythmic smack of wood against wood – in the changing room down by the pool. He'd found the crack in the wall that he'd made before to spy on others changing. Through it, he could make out the bench and the shunting body of his naked mother being pounded by 'Uncle' Andy, another good friend. They were in vivid profile to him barely six feet away. He could see his fat arse pumping between the scissoring legs of his mother and the look of pain on Andy's face and the lost look on hers, like she was dreaming with her eyes open. . .

'Do you miss him?'

'What kind of dumb fucking question is that? Course I miss him. He was my father, wasn't he?'

'Why? Can you say why you miss him?'

His voice was so soft it was almost like Warwick was hearing it inside his head. Warwick thought it was a good question, one that went on echoing, and which he couldn't answer then or now. All he remembered of that last session was the sun sifting through the blinds, the leather under his palms growing warm and sweaty, the smell of tall white lilies and the wetness running down his cheeks.

He blamed the quack for the dreams starting up. Or for making him notice them. For a while, he'd thought about suing him. But how can you sue for opening up your own memory?

FORTY TWO

They ate by the jeep under a tarpaulin stretched from the roof. Erin and Ted slapped on factor 50 an hour too late. Erin's face, devoid of make-up, was already taking on a glow and more freckles were appearing. Meera reviewed with Ted what she'd learned from Anila.

'My god, Meera, this is some story. Can I talk to her my self? See if I can use it?'

'I will ask her. But remember, this woman has lost everything. You must be mindful.'

They cleared up and Meera drove back through the village to park outside Anila's hut. They ignored the crowds as best they could and set up the tarpaulin to span the roofs of the jeep and the hut. She then snaked a cable from under the jeep's bonnet through the hole in the wall made by the thief. She and Erin hauled equipment and luggage inside.

Ted set himself up on the LR's footplate under the shady awning. He was left to cool his heels for half an hour until finally Meera brought out Anila's mother. The tiny woman squinted up at his towering bulk. Formal introductions were made, enough to satisfy the conditions of Purdah. The old lady went back inside and held the door open to let Ted duck in. Once inside, the old woman returned to her place by the fireside where she had been beating dough on a metal cooking plate. Ted looked around and found some very serious business already underway. A little girl was seated at a table made from two boxes from the jeep. In front of her, a computer screen glowed with colour. Behind her were Anila and Erin.

Erin looked up and came over. She looked much better, as though she'd had a transfusion. She whispered. 'We're up. I tell you, it makes the whole thing seem like magic when you look through someone else's eyes. But the kid took to it like she's grown up in front of a computer screen.'

'What's her name?' Ted had just got a flicker of a smile from the little girl, and a longer one from Anila.

It was Anila who answered, in careful English. 'She is named Aastha. It means hope.'

'It is a beautiful name. And I can see she is an expert already.'

Anila smiled, catching most of what he said. Meera translated fully and she smiled again. Ted continued now he had her attention.

'Anila? May I call you that? Can I talk to you for a little while please? I want to hear how you got involved with the bank. Is that possible?'

Anila grasped most of it but turned to Meera to check if she should speak to this man. Meera gave her blessing and Anila came and kneeled in one fluid motion in front of Ted inviting him to sit opposite. Ted struggled down to the ground and hauled his legs under him to sit cross-legged. He pulled out his little notepad and pencil for old times' sake – the electronic version had been discarded at the bottom of his pack – and began his interview. It progressed in a halting, smiling way for some time. Ted listened rapt, as she told him why she needed to get the loan in the first place. It got through to him that this young woman had been prepared to risk her very life on this venture.

'You mean you went all the way to Delhi, you and your two friends, and you weren't even sure the bank was real or that they would see you? Far less help you?' Meera had to translate this for her.

'I had no choice. Sometimes that is better, is it not?'

Her big sad eyes left him stripped bare. Ted continued with his questions, but he had already heard all he needed. After a time they were finished, and he eased himself upright feeling his knees creak and grind.

'Thank you Anila. I think you are a remarkable lady.' He turned to the others at the table. 'When you guys are finished, I'd like to get online and check what's happening with Oscar. I also need to file a report.' Ted waved his notebook.

'We will be done soon,' replied Meera. 'I just wanted to show Anila how easy it is. Aastha is already an expert. I think Anila will have no problems.'

Ted wondered what she meant, but then he took in Erin's face.

'You look better. Did you catch some sleep or something?'

Erin grinned. 'Anila noticed I was a bit low. The stomach pains were still pretty bad.' She pursed her mouth. 'Look, I have IBS – Irritable Bowel Syndrome. So – I kid you not – she gave me some tea made from the leaves of this neem tree of theirs. Like the big trees down by the well. It tasted simply awful – really bitter, despite the three spoons of sugar – like a good medicine should. A local concoction by their medicine woman. Meera says it's ok. It's standard prescription round here. But if I die, save the air fare and bury me out here, will you?'

'You mean you took the stuff?!'

'Have you checked out the restrooms? Actually it seems to have done something. My stomach's gone quiet. Before the storm maybe. But frankly, I was ready to perform a colectomy on myself if I thought it would've helped.'

Five minutes later Meera had gently pulled Aastha back from the screen. The child still held some of the light in her eyes, and shyly wrapped herself back round her mother. Ted took over the keyboard. He opened out his notepad on the box. It was covered in scribbles. Only occasionally did he have to turn to it as he typed in his despatch to Stan:

Customer Care

If you want to find out how a bank works, ask the customer. That's what your reporter has been doing in an effort to get to the reality behind the myths about the People's Bank. Here in a village in the heart of India, in a dust bowl that used to be a fertile valley, we see first hand how this bank's customers are being served.

The People's Bank truly seems to go the extra mile, or maybe 1000 miles. From New Delhi, the Tribune travelled out with a newly appointed district manager of the bank to set up a branch in the middle of nowhere special. But that's the sort of service you expect if your customers are prepared to travel the same distance to open a new account…

Erin read the text over Ted's shoulder as he recounted Anila's story and Meera's response. Ted was conscious of the heat and scent of her body.

'Have I missed anything?'

'Only the bit about the big tough New York reporter shooting the breeze with village kids.'

'So who'd be interested in that sort of stuff?'

He was glad she couldn't see his face properly in the poor light.

'You'd be surprised,' she said.

She let him finish, re-read and do some tidying up of the text and then hit the send key.

'That's official business out of the way. Let's take a look at Oscar's web site and see what we've got. Anila, is it all right to keep working here? Your mother does not mind?'

Anila smiled and turned to her mother and posed the question. The old woman shook her head and smiled back.

'Please, my mother says, her home is yours.'

Erin thanked her and turned to her keyboard. The blast of music that filled the small hut brought Aastha and her mother back to the screen. The galloping figure in white raised grins all round. Then it was down to business. The material was set out in two broad categories and they began to plough through them, sifting and discarding the irrelevant.

They began with the audio. Erin explained to Meera, who explained to Anila and Aastha that they were listening to recorded exchanges between her former boss and a variety of people that he phoned or talked to face to face in his office. They had to apologise several times for the language used. They got to the conversation between Stanstead and the President of the World Bank. They had to play it twice to be sure of what they were hearing.

'Dear God,' said Erin. 'What are we into?'

'And how do we use this stuff? I mean do you realise what we've got here?'

'Of course I do. But is it legal? Would it stand up in court?'

'I don't know. Let's see what else we've got.'

They listened to three more, then had to sit back to get away from the screaming voice of Warwick Stanstead. It was the piece Oscar had sent them in the hotel. Castigating Joey for the blundered attack in Delhi. And sending him to take personal charge of doing the job properly. It wasn't news but it reinforced the danger. Somewhere, out there, Joey was looking for them.

'This is a small village in a big country, right?'

Ted forced a bright voice and nodded at the walls of the tiny room as if to point up the absurdity of Joey making his way to Chandapur.

'It's not as if we left a forwarding address,' said Erin.

'Let's take a peek at the written stuff.'

Ted thought action would take their minds off the image of a mad gunman heading their way. Page after page of emails appeared. They flicked through them one by one. Occasionally they paused and re-read something to check they'd understood, or went back to tie one email or attachment to an earlier. Over half of the emails required password access to open them. Oscar had thoughtfully provided them with the keys.

They grew aware of a frequently referenced word. Several emails between Stanstead and Nick Trevino, his technology director, mentioned Project Monsoon. The references were oblique and all were guarded by password protection – or so the originators had thought. They'd never met Oscar. Erin took charge of the keyboard.

'This is the project that's been tying up a third of our IT resources, Ted.' She turned to Meera. 'We're looking at the evidence of Warwick's assaults on your bank. And it's obvious they're not going to give up. Looks like they're planning another one in –' she checked her watch, '– three days. Better warn your father and CJ, Meera. This looks like it's going to be a big one. Let's hope Oscar and CJ's techies are building some pretty high flood walls.'

'Or an Ark,' he said.

Erin and Ted worked quietly away at their task, talking over their findings and categorising them. They shared a lot of common ground and skills. Both noticed a growing ease between them, but said nothing in case it evaporated. When they were finished, they emailed Oscar to tell him what a brilliant job he and Albert were doing, and pointing out what they'd done with the web site. Mostly they left the emails but they set up a document list itemising all the opened attachments. The web site now showed a clear chronology of the crimes of Warwick Stanstead.

Throughout the concentrated collation task Meera had been a close observer. Finally she spoke into the quiet.

'You are risking everything, aren't you?'

For the first time her voice and expression took on a note of approval.

Ted and Erin could only shrug.

'No more than Anila, here,' said Erin.

FORTY THREE

The corruption was stifling. Ted and Erin needed air. They went outside and sat side by side on the rear running board of the jeep. The village was in darkness except for the little glows of oil lamps from some of the roofs and windows. They faced down the ragged lane and out across the valley. The crowd had long since dispersed. Finding themselves alone, Ted and Erin became shy with each other. They slumped forward, head in hand, and back bowed, quiet for a while with their own thoughts. Ted was wondering what he'd done to deserve this woman and her mad crusade, and half wishing he'd simply deleted the email from a certain Diogenes. Erin was more than ever convinced of the morality of her cause, but frightened of the consequences.

Warm air settled on their limbs. Unfamiliar smells gathered on the new breeze. Smells of animals and cooking and burning wood. Smells of the lost river and dried grass, and of the earth, giving up the heat of the day. A dog barked for a while, then was quiet. It drew their attention to the million insects sawing away among the nearby fields.

'I'd forgotten stars could look like this,' she said.

He looked up. 'It's the same from the hills above Denver. Last time I looked.'

Erin gazed until she felt a need to throw herself on the ground and hold on or she'd be catapulted into space.

'It's great, but I could still make an argument for New York.'

He snorted. 'You'd argue with me if I said the sea was salty.'

'Am I such a bitch?'

The opening he'd been waiting for. His words grew a little hotter.

'You don't know when to stop.'

'And you don't know when to start!'

'What's that supposed to mean?'

He lurched to his feet and stood in front of her, looking big and menacing against the night sky. She stood up and squared up to him.

'Let's face it, I had to jump-start your conscience.'

'Are we sure it's my conscience that's fuelling this crazy trip?'

'Look, I got you wrong, all right? You were incredible the other day with the muggers. There's a lot more to you than –'

'Meets the eye? So now I'm an iceberg?'

'But melting fast.'

She tried a smile in her voice to defuse him. He wouldn't be softened. This had been brewing.

'So why are you always needling me?'

'Because you drink too much and you might, just might, be worth salvaging, you big dummy.'

'You condescending English –'

'– Scottish. Bitch?'

'Whatever!'

'You're better, angry.'

'What are you trying to do to me?!'

'Get a reaction?'

'Like this?'

He took one step closer, took her by the shoulders and pulled her to him. She kept her eyes wide open in challenge right up to the moment he kissed her full on the mouth. She broke first.

'Whoa boy. Stop.'

He was breathing fast, and still had his hands on her.

'I knew you'd be a teaser.'

'It's just not the time. Or place.'

She tried to get him to see that somewhere, sometime there might be a place. He dropped his hands.

'Then – don't – lead – me – on. Goodnight, Miss Wishart.'

He grabbed his gear from the jeep and blundered off into the night. Erin watched a small shadow race after him. She shivered and touched her mouth with her fingers.

Ted found himself taken by the hand and led off proudly by the young boy who'd been his interpreter. Now Ted stood outside the boy's own hut with his rucksack and a small brown paper bag, like a giant waif. The boy emerged highly excited, followed by a young man and woman. They bowed slightly and the man held out his hand and touched Ted's tentatively, then shook it hard. The woman stayed in the background smiling nervously.

'My father, Rajnish, is teacher. So he speaks English by me. That is how I understand.'

'Speaks English to me, Ranil,' he gently chided the boy. 'Please sir, welcome sir. I would be most honoured if you spend this night with me and my family in our home. It is not a big apartment like New York I believe. However it offers you a room to yourself. Please enter.'

'I am the one who is honoured, sir. May I ask your name? I am Ted Saddler. Please call me Ted.'

The man beamed. 'I am called Rajnish Tadvi, and this is my wife Hema. Will you please to call me Rajnish? And will you come into my house and take food with us?'

Ted followed them in to the hut. It was twice the size of Anila's but still little more than four brick walls coated with a dried mud and straw mix. It was dark, but cooler than he'd expected. The earth floor was well covered by woven mats of bright colours. A wood table and four chairs stood against the wall. On one wall was a shelf bearing a small, but clearly treasured set of books. Ted found he was trying not to breathe.

There was a smell of worn clothes and unwashed humanity mixed in with farmyard and kitchen smells. He chided himself for his prissiness and sucked in the air. He'd survived sharing a tent with six marines in a Middle East war zone.

He could choose to sleep here with the family or on the roof where it would be cooler. They took him out the through the back of the hut to the little yard. Two goats were tethered and fought with some chickens over scraps of vegetables and bread. A little stairway without handrails led to the roof enclosed by a low balustrade. Ted liked the idea of sleeping outside. Liked it a lot. The boy made up his bed for him in one corner, a straw mattress covered in rugs. His sleeping bag was carefully unrolled on top of it.

Back inside Ted handed over the paper bag and was pleased with the response to the three cans of food and the last of the fresh vegetables they'd managed to buy at the store. It seemed a tiny offering but was clearly appreciated.

Once more Ted was pumped, this time a little more grammatically but with no less interest. They served him some tea. It was like nothing he'd seen before. This was a rich creamy concoction. He'd watched it being poured and noticed its thick viscosity. All the ingredients had been boiled together for some time. He sipped a few drops and felt his teeth melt. The taste of sugar and hard tannin and rich milk would never leave his mouth. He grinned and applauded it as best he could. He had a sudden yearning for New York tap water. Or whiskey.

Finally, still hungry but deeply concerned about eating them out of house and home, Ted took his leave, climbed up the steps in the back yard to the rooftop. He could see other roofs with bodies stretched out on them, like mortuary slabs.

He rummaged inside his pack. He found the two bottles and drew them out. One full, the other three-quarters. He replaced the full one and took the other over to the low wall that ran round the roof. He sat down, feet dangling over the edge. He uncorked the bottle, took a pull and enjoyed the hit in his stomach. What with the pungent currents of evening air wafting around him, Ted found himself thinking about letting go of several things in his life that no longer seemed quite so important. Like his moribund career and the sorry state of his pension portfolio. Maybe it was time to ditch the book too; he'd been fooling himself for too long. But then what?

Had he really just grabbed a kiss? He couldn't remember when he'd last made a dive at a woman. Sixth grade? It constituted date rape these days didn't it? Damn the woman. Plays it tough and cool for days then throws him a line. Just to see him fall on his face. That was how kids behaved: challenge, flirt, taunt and then the big let-down. He wasn't up to these sort of games any more, or maybe he'd never learnt the rules.

He shook his head in bafflement. He took one more good pull, coughed as it stung its way down, and recapped the bottle. He got to his feet and tucked the bottle away. He flicked some leaves out of his bedding, stripped to his underwear and tried a press-up on his sleeping bag. He managed eight before his arms quivered and gave way. That would have to change when – if – he got back. He got inside the bag but kept the zip down while the perspiration from his mild exertion dried in the warm night. He gazed up, and for the first time in way too long, felt engaged with life, with people. It scared and excited him all at once.

He woke the next morning disorientated, and as stiff as after a first day's skiing. He had to lie and stretch his back and his side before he could sit up. His face felt swollen. He found mosquito bites all over his head and hands. The sun wasn't over the horizon yet but a pale glow seeped across the landscape. Other rooftop dwellers were struggling awake and standing and stretching. Some were greeting the day in prayer, raising their hands with small vessels in them and pouring water as an offering to their gods. Ted thought he understood how that worked and tried to give himself a moment's contemplation. But his bites itched and his arm muscles ached, and he was thinking about what a fool he'd made of himself last night. That and the trial, and pal Joey, crowded in on his morning.

His hosts were up and Hema was cooking a flat lump of bread on a griddle over the open fire glowing under the chimney in one wall. It smelled great. Before he ate he ran his little travel razor over the stubble, and managed to brush his teeth using water from the bottle Meera had supplied. They gave him a bowl of opaque water to bathe in, and he began to feel human again. A clean but creased shirt helped.

He asked about the toilet. Ranil led him to the backyard and gave him a battered shovel with a broken handle. Ted caught the drift and went back for his pack and took out the roll of toilet paper he'd borrowed from the hotel in Delhi. Ranil walked him out of the village to a field behind a few scrubby bushes and two trees. Other men were already there. Ranil indicated the process. Ted dug a small hole, grimacing and thinking of his army training. This wasn't so hard, he kept telling himself.

'What happens when the field is used up?'

'The Dalits come and plough up the earth and we move to another place.'

'The women?' He meant Erin.

'Over there.' Ranil indicated an area just to their left delineated by a pair of bushes.

They went back to the hut and Ted washed as best he could. They had breakfast, Ted noticing that his gift of tinned fruit was being presented back to him. They saw his bites and were anxious. Hema fussed round him.

'Did the leaves not work? We are very sorry. They always work for us.'

'You mean the leaves in my bedding? The ones I threw away?'

She put her hand to her mouth to hide the laugh. 'They are from one of our trees. They keep insects away.'

'This wouldn't be a tree called the neem would it?'

Hema shook her head in smiling agreement with him. She went to one of her shelves and produced a small tub of grease.

'What's this?'

Rajnish answered. 'It is also from the neem. It is very good for insect bites. But it is best if you put it on before you get bitten.' They all laughed with him.

'This tree gets itself around,' he answered as Hema indicated he should dip a finger into the pot.

She couldn't touch him of course. He took a dollop. It smelled of sulphur but he gently dabbed the cream on the bites and rubbed it in. It had an immediate soothing effect. He was glad there was no mirror.

He thought he could find Erin's hut again without help, and set off, causing chatter and diffident smiles wherever he went. He was amused to see the boy Ranil following him at a distance and hiding behind buildings as he twisted and turned through the alleys. As he got closer he found himself trying to shake off the sense that he was going into school the day after the Prom. Facing the girl – in a cordon of her giggling friends – after a fruitless fumbling behind the track-stand. Would she be mad or amused at him? Just spare me contempt, he silently pleaded. He found his feet dragging, and he slowed to make sure his hair was patted down and not sticking up like a clown's. There was nothing he could do about the spots – acne as well, he thought. It figures.

He arrived at the hut with an gaggle of kids wondering what new stories they'd get from him today. The scene that greeted him wasn't so far from his remembered youth. Meera, Erin and little Aastha were sitting outside on wooden stools. Anila stood behind Erin brushing Erin's hair. It was the first time he'd seen it down. It seemed thicker and wavier somehow. She looked better than she had in days. Erin coloured as he approached, but at least she smiled.

'This wasn't my idea. Anila wanted to do it. Honest.'

'Girls are the same everywhere.'

He raised his eyebrows at Anila who smiled nervously back. Anila too looked different this morning. Still dark wedges under her eyes, but the tension had dropped from her frame. She'd switched from half empty to half full.

'How's the. . .?' he rubbed his stomach at Erin.

'Much easier. I may be onto something. But just don't ask about the restrooms, ok?'

'Fine by me.'

'What happened to your face?'

He touched the bites. They already felt less sore.

'It seems at least the bugs are attracted.' Then he wished he hadn't said that. Like a rejected teen. 'So, what's the plan?' he asked Erin and Meera.

Meera seemed more welcoming than usual.

'Last night I called the police in Sagar to tell them about the theft. And then I called my father and asked him to put some pressure on them too. He said he would speak to the Inspector-General of Police for Madhya Pradesh. My father went to university with him. My father said the police would come today. We shall see.'

'If they do, Meera, could we get a lift back to Bhopal first thing tomorrow morning? The world is catching up with us. We can get the train back to Delhi by ourselves. Ok with you, Erin?'

'Fine by me. I was thinking about sanctuary at the British consulate or taking the first flight back to the States or running for cover in Europe. Italy's nice this time of year. Venice. Any better ideas?'

She was blustering and knew it. He was thinking about gondolas and her.

'What we need is time and evidence. The problem with the stuff that Oscar got hold of, is that he did it illegally. Stanstead's lawyers would have a field day with us. We'd probably end up doing ten for wire tapping and hacking.'

Erin dropped the cooperative façade. 'Then what was the point of getting Oscar to do all this?!'

'Well for one thing it probably saved your skin. For another? Well, I'm still thinking through the other. But I'm going to let Stan Coleman have a look at what we've got and ask the Trib's legal beagles to sniff around and see if there's anything we can use.'

'Sounds good to me. So, we go on the run until something turns up? Is that about it?' The irony was softened by her eyes.

'Not quite. I want you to make a personal call to Mr Stanstead when we get back to civilisation.'

FORTY FOUR

Oscar and Albert had been working flat out for the best part of three days, subsisting on a diet of cola, pizza and 1000mg of brain-enhancing, sleep-denying Modanifil per day.

As well as his trusty side-kick, Oscar had rounded up a team of five others. He had never met any of them except in cyberspace. Never spoken to them. Even after he'd swapped the black hat for a white, Oscar had distanced himself from DefCon, the annual hackers convention in Las Vegas. There was something sullying about net warriors meeting in the flesh. Made them mortal. And sillier. The only contact he'd had over the last fifteen years, had been through carefully chosen direct channels on darknets.

Darknets, or the Deep Web, was where all the main search engines couldn't or wouldn't operate. Oscar's start point was to create a virtual pc within his hardware array and drop into Onionland within the TOR anonymity-protecting network. Sure, it was peopled by gun runners, drug cartels, sexual deviants, Islamist terrorists, scammers and organised crime using encryption software and constantly changing URLs. But it was also the communication method of choice for Wikileaks, freedom fighters in China, Russia, the entire Middle East and North Korea. Hell, even the establishment magazine The New Yorker had set up a Tor based Strongbox to receive secure and anonymous leaks from whistle-blowers.

He shot his first question out to Mighty Thor, whom Oscar suspected was a girl. There was just a certain way Thor went about constructing his/her web site for heavy metal fans. But, hey, Oscar was the last boy on the street to care about such things. Thor's sexual proclivities didn't stop her/him from cutting some mean code. And her/his access to an impossible number of interesting web sites on a web-master basis was a valuable addition to Oscar's team.

Mighty Thor, we have need of your thunderbolt. The forces of darkness are riding again. I need a team of heroes to defend the little people against a global menace. Fancy some fun? – Lone Ranger–

The reply was instant. Thor was 24/7. Oscar also wondered if Thor was a gang.

hammer ready and at your disposal. Say who when how
– Mighty Thor–

Oscar rounded up the other four over the next 24 hours. There was Slick Willy, an old cracker like himself, who'd switched sides after the turmoil of the late 90's when hacking had gone from a demonstration of teenage rebellion and power, to criminal acts. Slick Willy was out of Mexico and once took over the entire cable network of CNN via their own web sites to advertise the plight of the 'wetback' hackers. Kids who'd been imprisoned both sides of the border for repeated crashing of the surveillance systems.

There was Switchblade. Now retired from hacking at the age of 22 and working as a 'fireman' for the Seventh Day Adventists out of Utah. Switchblade was using his remarkable gift for slicing through the best software defences in corporate America to maintain and protect the computer systems of his church. Oscar appealed to Switchblade's new found saintliness by offering him a crusade.

Then came an enthusiastic confirmation from Magus, a new script-kid Oscar had seen in action recently. Magus had splashed on the scene with some of the most vibrant new music delivered over the net. He'd composited tracks from some of the finest musicians in the last fifty years – anyone from Buddy

Holly through to Hard Wired Brush. But instead of producing a simple mish-mash of sliced up tracks, Magus had created something entirely new. It was as though he'd stripped the music right back to the base notes and then built it up again into haunting and compulsive sounds. It was the music of the Internet itself. The big music companies had posted offers of mega-millions on the net to buy Magus's stuff. But he wasn't for sale. He did it for the sheer spiritual beauty of it. He gave the same reason for throwing in his lot with Oscar.

Oscar had one last handle to secure to make up the seven. It had to be seven because that's how Karma worked. And it had to be Worm though there was a high chance he was in jail somewhere. It was a risk. Worm wore a black hat and a white one when it suited him. He was just as likely to be breaking into NASA as helping track down the clowns who'd knocked over half the ISP's in the Southern Hemisphere with a killer virus. The job needed to interest him and to suit his very finely nuanced moral code.

Worm. We've got an A team up to do something mighty. Its small people war against big biz. Better than dragons or kill-zone. This is Thermopylae! Interested?   – Lone Ranger–

is there money?   – Worm–

only glory–

how do you spend glory?–

you trade it. This will shake the net. Legends will be made –

I'm already a name –

that's why we need you. You're the best. This is the A+ team. This is Gunfight at the OK Corral, the Alamo, Butch and Sundance, Apocalypse Now! –

whos the team? –

Mighty Thor, Slick Willy, Switchblade, Magus, Tonto, me –

a harsh crew! But it's not enough –

How clean is your line? Just you and me…

A while later Oscar set up a web conference with the whole team in a particularly dark and secure corner of the TOR network. He described the work of the People's Bank and told them about the trial and what could happen if the bank was closed. Then he told them of the dark dealings of Global American and the mass attacks on the Delhi hub. He set up a private chat room to bring his team together with Vikram Vajpayee and Shivani Jaffrey. He let them fire questions at each other until one by one he was receiving private emails from each of his band offering total commitment to the cause.

Oscar wound up the discussions,

I have it on best that another attack is due in 48 hours. this is the biggie, the full rush. timed with the start of the trial on Monday. Global America's going for broke to bring down the house. Here's the plan…–

FORTY FIVE

Joey Kutzov hated the heat. He hated being out of New York. He hated flying. He hated Warwick Stanstead for sending him to this hellhole. But most of all he hated Erin Wishart and Ted Saddler for being the cause of his misery and discomfort. They would surely pay.

Joey was getting the treatment. No-one had told him about taxis that didn't have air con. Or suspension. No-one had thought to mention that the place stank and there were goddamn fucking elephants and camels in the fucking main street! This place was a 3-ring circus! His perfect English-cut suit – 5,000 bucks, hand tailored by Quinn's of New York – was a wringing mess of limp cloth and sweat. He cut no chic figure now.

His sweat-darkened shirt gaped at the neck and the tie weighed him down like a noose. His chubby, child-like body felt inflated like a Michelin man. He had hardly been able to get his $800 shoes on when they landed, and now, as the taxi bucked and jerked its way into New Delhi, they pinched and rubbed on his sweat-encased feet.

By the time he arrived at the Hilton and checked in, his fine blond hair was plastered to his reddened scalp, and his blood pressure was off the dial. He shook off the attention of the bell hop who pleaded to carry his case up to his room. He didn't need help and sure as hell didn't intend to pay for it. When he took the wrong turning and missed the elevator bank, Joey could be seen on the hotel security screens – had anyone been watching – kicking plant pots and screaming. He stormed back to the lobby and demanded directions before finally shouldering his way through his bedroom door.

Joey peeled off his ruined suit, showered, and made a large dent in the minibar collection before he was ready to make the first call. A couple of lines of coke and he'd bounced back. His call resulted, half an hour later, in a knock on his door. Joey answered it wearing a white Hilton towelling robe and bathroom slippers. His manic eyes still registered persecution. Two young Indian men in smart dark suits stood nervously on the threshold. One had a scar from nose to right cheek. The other carried a briefcase. They introduced themselves as Akash and Pratik. Joey made them sit so he wasn't shorter than them.

'So what the fuck happened? Tell me in your own words. From the time you picked them up.'

'You mean the Americans?' gulped Akash, unsure of this milk-white man with the baby face and the unkind eyes. Akash was a hard man, out of the back streets of Old Delhi, and he had used a knife and a gun on more than one occasion. But he was rocked by the mad fury and impatience of this little man. He fingered his scar nervously.

'What the fuck else do you think I'm talking about? Don't you guys speak English for chrissake?!' Joey's temper hadn't cooled. It was just capped.

The two men looked at each other. Pratik took over. 'Everything was perfect. It was all beautiful, sir. We were waiting and ready. But the taxi driver did not do his job. He says the big American had a gun and was going to shoot him unless he stopped. So he stopped too soon.'

'A gun? Are you sure? For chrissake what's a fucking reporter doing with a gun? Are you sure?!'

Pratik knew there was no gun, but somehow it seemed better if there had been one. Indeed there might have been one, which was just as good. The event had already happened. Nothing could be done about it now except explain it in a way that made the white man less unhappy and less angry.

'Absolutely, sir. In fact he shot at one of our men. That was when they got away. You see we did not think there would be a

237

gun. Just like you. So we did not bring any ourselves. Guns are so noisy, you see. So when we threw ourselves on the taxi and tried to stop it we were most surprised.'

Joey squinted at them. 'So the big guy starts popping away and then drives off in the fucking taxi, calm as you like? That's what you're telling me? This guy is some kind of special fucking agent or something? Special forces. Like the guys who got Bin Laden?'

'That may be right, sir.' Akash thought that this would be a helpful thing to say as well. The more impossible the odds, the better and braver they sounded. 'Indeed it may well be that this American is not a reporter but is from the FBI or CIA.' This was good. This was making the story much better. Akash began to believe this version.

Joey got up and began to pace. The white robe was too big for him and he looked like a pampered toddler. With a similar tendency to tantrums. The two men watched him, fascinated by the virginal white of his legs.

'Maybe you're right. It kinda figures. What kind of gun?'

Akash had the quicker imagination. 'It was an automatic. Big calibre. You could tell by the noise and by the hole in the glass of the taxi. A big gun.' Pratik nodded gravely in confirmation.

'Shit. Shit! Ok, let's do some planning. Do we know where they've gone?'

'No, sir. They checked out and went to the train station. That is all we know. I have a sister who works at the Hyatt Regency and this is all she could find out. She is very friendly with the doorman. They gave the doorman a big tip and told him to tell the driver to take them to the station.'

'Just the two of them?'

'Oh no, sir.' Akash was proud of this information. 'They went with an Indian woman. And an Indian man was with them but he stayed behind, then got another taxi.'

'Where did he go?'

'Back to the People's Bank. In the old city. We know his name.' Akash paraded his detective work. 'He is the manager of the bank here. He is Mr CJ Kapoor. And we think the woman who went with the white people was the daughter of the chief of the bank.'

'His daughter? Ramesh Banerjee's daughter?! Where were they going with his daughter for chrissake?'

'They took the train. A Shatabdi Express.'

'Great! Where does that go?'

The two men looked at each other unwilling to disappoint the very white man now, but unable to come up with a suitable answer. Then Akash made an effort. 'There are many such trains. But this one stops at Agra.' Pratik brightened at this. 'Ah yes, Agra,' he said meaningfully.

'What the fuck's at Agra?!'

'It is the Taj Mahal, sir.'

'You're telling me they went fucking sight-seeing?'

Akash was offended that his imagination was being challenged. 'It is very normal is it not? All visitors want to see the Taj Mahal. Especially men and women. It is very romantic.'

Joey looked at his colleagues as though they'd just grown another head each. Was this likely, he asked himself? What the hell would this pair be going sight-seeing for? Or having some sort of fucking rom-com excursion? They get attacked by a bunch of idiots with knives one day and the next they go and play at tourists. Oh yeah!

'How many men have we got?'

'Many, many. How many do you want sir?'

'We need to cover every train station, every airport – local and international – and every five star hotel in Delhi. Got it? I want the alarm bells to be ringing the moment this pair is sighted. Got it? But nobody goes near, you hear? You just get on the phone to me and don't lose them this time! Got it?! And I need a gun. Did you bring it like you were told?'

Pratik proudly unclipped his cheap, pseudo-leather briefcase and took out a bulky object wrapped in cloth. He undid the cloth and held out a dull grey handgun. Joey took it and hefted it and checked it was the Browning M1935 Hi-Power that he'd specified. It looked too big in his hands, but he'd always been lucky with this model. He pulled out the clip and checked it had its full fourteen rounds of 9 mm shells. Satisfied, he slammed it back into place and sat back with the gun in his lap.

'Ok, now beat it till you've got something to tell me.' He waved the gun at them and motioned them to leave. 'The money'll go into your account.'

They left the very white man sitting in his bathrobe, sliding the clip in and out with a loud click, and aiming at the mirror.

FORTY SIX

The police truck rolled up to the village square trailing a dust cloud that had heralded its approach for three miles. The sandy particles shimmered listlessly in the intense afternoon light. Two police constables in creased khaki leapt out of the canvas-covered back and a lanky sub-inspector and his driver stepped down from the front cab. The sub-inspector smoothed his thin hair back and placed his black cap squarely on his head. He hitched up his gun-belt on his scrawny hips, and tucked a swagger-stick under his arm. His face lost some of its frown. He walked round to the side of his truck and inspected a large dent. They had collided with the wall of a house on the way in through the narrow street. This would need a report. The thought irritated him, like the whole wretched business of being here.

Though it was the time for sitting indoors out of the sun, the village elders were summoned and a noisy crowd quickly enveloped the small group of police. Emotions were running high over the robbery. Nothing as exciting had happened in the village since the officials had come to tell them about the dam and why their river would have to be moved.

The sub inspector faced them, thwacking his stick into his left hand for emphasis. He bawled at them, his voice surprisingly deep for his thin chest.

'How can I learn what is happening if there is so much shouting going on?! I must have a sufficiency of quiet!'

He was shouting in English. He couldn't or wouldn't speak the local dialect of these rustics. English was still the language of the governors, no matter their colour. He was sweating under the brim of his polished peaked hat. He was wondering why the commissioner had taken him off the lucrative drugs busting unit and sent him out into the countryside among these barbarians. One constable on a motor bike would have done.

Quiet fell across the crowd as Anila and Meera moved through and stepped up to the front row. Meera faced the policeman.

'My name is Meera Banerjee. I am the area manager for the People's Bank.'

The sub-inspector recognised the woman's name. She was the trouble-maker who had made the complaint. If he had his way he would start with her, given her a roughing up to check her story and to repay her for the long, hot ride he'd endured. But he could not touch her. She had top contacts. This had been part of his briefing. The woman was talking again. As if she was an equal. The nerve of her.

'And this is my client, Anila Jhabvala who was robbed. All the money of the People's Bank in this village has been stolen and we want a suspect arrested.'

The sub-inspector sweated harder. His annoyance grew. This had gone from a reported theft of a few rupees, to being a bank robbery! He wasn't sure how that had come about but he knew what to do about it. There was a routine that could be applied to any situation. It would be an uncomfortable visit for someone, but it would get results.

'First, you must furnish the details to me. We must complete an Accusation form. We will sit here and we will write down all the details. You will tell me when the money was stolen, and whom you suspect of perpetrating this criminal deed.'

He signalled furiously at his three men and out of the back of the truck, they dragged a small trestle table and two folding chairs. They set them up carefully in the shade of a neem, shoving aside the people who had already claimed that vantage point. The sub-inspector, importantly, eased himself behind his desk, his long legs forcing his knees against the underside. He laid his baton with precision on the table, so that it sat as a symbol and barrier between himself and the complainants. A constable sat at the edge, on the second seat and took out a notebook and a set of crumpled forms from a battered briefcase.

'Find another chair. Find two.' He called out impatiently. Two stools were passed through the crowd and Meera and Anila sat down. 'And push that crowd back!'

His two remaining constables drew their long clubs and began to flail the people with a practised brutality that pleased the sub inspector. The crowd eddied back several feet, and like a tide exposing a rock, left two shining white faces stranded in front of the sub inspector. A chill ran down the inspector's spine. The white people were gazing at him fearlessly and with frank curiosity. This unnerved him. What were they doing here and who were they? He hadn't been briefed about them. White people tended to have authority and were important. He couldn't imagine any tourist coming to this god-forsaken hole. He reached for his stick. He aimed it.

'Who are you, please?'

Ted and Erin moved forward, Ted towering over the tableau.

'Good afternoon, officer. My name is Ted Saddler. I'm a reporter from the New York Tribune. This is Miss Erin Wishart. She is a representative of an international bank that is working with Miss Banerjee's bank.'

Ted smiled and waited for the sub-inspector. The sub-inspector was beginning to think that the police commissioner had a grudge against him. First this stupid little village has a bank robbery, next, they send a reporter from an international newspaper to cover it! And this very pretty white woman with impossible eyes was an important banker! Disquiet was added to annoyance and turning him angry.

'This is not for reporting you understand! I cannot allow notes being taken. It is all sub judice you understand.'

'No problem, officer. I'm not taking notes. We're just here visiting.'

Ted raised his arms to prove he had neither tape recorder nor notepad. The sub-inspector was scarcely mollified. Why would anyone visit this backwater without a reason?

'Then stand back. Go on. Get back please.' He turned back to the two women. 'Now you will tell me what is happening here. My constable will write everything down on the Accusation form.'

Meera made a conciliatory smile. 'It is very simple, inspector.' He liked being called inspector by this intelligent young woman. Though her hair was much too short.

'My bank has been robbed and all the money taken.'

There was a long pause while the constable laboriously scratched out this information on the form. The sub-inspector looked over his shoulder till he had finished the sentence.

'How much money was taken please?'

'4000 Rupees. It was the first deposit for our new branch in the village. And I am now fixing for much larger sums to be left here. I want to make sure my bank is properly protected and that the money is safe. I will soon install a metal safe but I want you to take responsibility for ensuring that the bank is not robbed again.'

She smiled. The sub-inspector ran his finger round his collar. Words like 'take responsibility' made it tighter.

To his scribe, 'Don't write that down, idiot! Just the amount that was uplifted unlawfully.' To Meera, 'It is very good that a proper safe will be installed here. Very good. But I cannot send any men to look after it. It is impossible out here.'

'I understand. All that we are looking for is two things. First that you arrest the man everyone thinks robbed the bank. And second that we have a direct telephone line to you for emergencies.'

'You have a telephone?' the sub-inspector looked round. It seemed unlikely.

'It is a solar powered, satellite telephone.'

The sub-inspector was impressed. But he was quite certain that he would not be giving his own telephone number to this woman. He wanted nothing to do with this obviously career limiting set-up in the future.

'Good. That is very good. Write that down! Now what is the name of the suspect? Who is this villainous party?'

The sub-inspector thought that sounded properly formal and dramatic. He said 'Ahah!' when they denounced the money lender, as though it was something he'd already concluded from his analysis of the evidence. More notes were taken from Anila, provoking the sub-inspector to unwind from his desk and make an official visit to the crime scene. The hut was inspected and a constable with a camera-phone photographed the hole in the wall.

After a sufficient amount of strutting to and fro and smacking of stick into hand, the sub-inspector signalled to his men. The whole circus moved towards the home of the money lender, even though it was generally known that the prime suspect, as the sub-inspector had it, was not in residence. They moved through the village in a babbling flow, like a festival.

They found the suspect standing on the roof of his house, clutching at the balcony. He had crept back in the night and had had men running backwards and forwards for the past hour with news from the police investigation.

'Mr Chowdury?' the sub-inspector called up to him.

'That is me, and you have got the whole situation all wrong, you know!'

The money lender was already shouting, his nerves were stretched to the limit. No policeman had ever come out to the village, not since the outcry over the dam.

'I must interview with you formally about an incident involving the suspected robbery of the bank. Get down immediately so that we can apprehend your whereabouts.'

The words bank robbery seemed to have a bowel-loosening effect on the money lender. He fell to his knees on his balcony and clutched at the low railing as though trying out a life behind bars.

'I cannot come down!' He was weeping now. 'You will beat me and arrest me and take me to the vile jail in the city, and I will never see my beloved wife again. I am too old. I will die very easily in prison.'

At this, his wife appeared beside him on the balcony and fell on her knees alongside. The sub inspector looked disgusted. He turned to his men.

'Get him out.'

The two constables needed little urging. They heaved their way through the wooden door and were gone from sight for a minute. They reappeared on the terrace and began clubbing the money lender with quiet diligence. They stopped after a little while and dragged the now whimpering victim off the roof and out of sight. His wife was left wailing behind the parapet.

Erin was shocked to her core. 'Dear god, they've killed him!'

She made to go forward and Ted held her back. 'This isn't the Upper East. There's not a thing we can do here.'

The two constables appeared with the accused hanging between them. He was stumbling, and red ran down his head and into his eyes. They pitched him at the feet of the sub inspector. Behind them the money lender's shrieking wife appeared in the doorway and fell to her knees alongside him begging for mercy. The sub-inspector was satisfied with this display of his authority. Now they were getting somewhere.

'Bring my table!'

Two constables scurried off for the table and chairs. On their return, they recreated the outdoor interrogation room. The sub-inspector sat down with great solemnity. The accused was lifted up and placed in the chair opposite, where he sat swaying and bloodied. The sub-inspector raised his stick and pointed at the keening wife.

'You will be quiet,' he ordered. Her lamentations fell away to intermittent sobbing. He turned to the prisoner. 'Now, I am taking notes of your situation and what is known about the robbery.'

The money lender tried to speak but nothing came out. The sub-inspector signalled and the constables demanded water. A bowl was found and flung in the money lender's face. Then he sipped a little and spat out some blood. It vanished into the dust. He tried again to speak and this time managed to mumble.

'It was not a robbery.'

The crowd buzzed at this unlikely statement but admired it as a fine opening gambit.

'What do you mean? This woman had money in her wall. Now it is gone. Stolen. That is robbery. Explain yourself.'

The prisoner took another sip and his voice strengthened a little. A cunning edge reappeared.

'Perhaps it was not stolen? Perhaps it was simply taken for safe-keeping?'

The sub-inspector reflected on this doubtful circumstance.

'How is that different from robbery, if the person who owned the money was not told about its removal?'

The crowd were filled with admiration for this shrewd policeman. With a sharp mind like his, he would make inspector-general one day, mark this moment! Seeing he had the advantage, the officer pressed it home.

'Did you unlawfully take this woman's money for so-called safe keeping?'

The wailing began again from his wife until a club quietened her. The money lender looked round and saw his wife nursing her back and fighting back the sobs.

'I did it to help Mrs Jhabvala. I took it to keep it safe. It was not safe in the wall and I was worried for Mrs Jhabvala and the People's Bank and the women's cooperative.'

There was a collective ahhh from the crowd. This was deft. Preposterous but deft. It encouraged the money lender. He spat out another mouthful of blood.

'I knew Mrs Jhabvala would not trust me if I said I would look after it. I have a big safe you know. It is the only proper place to keep money in the village. So I told my men to take it into safe-keeping so that the women would not lose their money if a criminal person was in the area.'

Anila could stand it no longer. She stepped forward from the edge of the crowd. The beating she'd witnessed had terrified her and made her regret deeply what she'd brought down on the money lender's head. But hearing his words, she stopped feeling sorry for him.

'That is a terrible lie! You are a thief and a liar, Mr Chowdury! You and that wife of yours, who is also a thief, should be locked away! You took my money and now you say you were only keeping it safe for me?! What a lie! Do you think this police officer is stupid?'

There was a babble of agreement from the villagers. The sub-inspector stiffened, wondering if he was being insulted and if so, how, and by whom. Then a thought came to him.

'Silence! Do you still have the money in your safe?'

'Yes sir'

'Then you will take me inside and show it to me. Then we will decide what to do with you.'

In the mind of the sub-inspector, there were two possible outcomes. One involved the completion of lengthy Accusation forms, interview notes, arrest notes, taking a man into custody, beating a full confession out of him and his ugly wife, more paperwork and probably having to come back to this hell-hole several times.

The second option resulted in the money being given back, the case being dropped, the bank officials being happy and the sub-inspector never having to come this way again. Moreover, a money lender had money, did he not? The sub-inspector was sure the money lender would be properly grateful if the sub-inspector appeared to believe his story. He'd show them who was stupid.

Half an hour later the police truck was trundling out of the village and everyone in sight – Anila, Meera, the policemen, the villagers – was smiling. The money lender and his wife chose to stay indoors. As the crowd dispersed, the wailing began from within the two storey house, as though a child had died.

Meera handed Anila the 4000 rupees retrieved by the sub-inspector, together with a further 500 rupees 'fine' by which the money lender had avoided arrest and a further beating. The two women walked back up the hill to the hut, Anila near tears at the upturn in her fortunes.

As the crowd thinned it exposed two people watching events with greedy eyes: a woman with her sari pulled over her head and a fat young man tugging at his sparse moustache. Their small hands were intertwined.

FORTY SEVEN

Ted and Erin took their last evening meal in the village at the house of Anila. They were still shaken by the official brutality they'd witnessed, but they tried to convince themselves that the end result was what mattered. Meera and Anila seemed less affected. They had enough experience of such goings-on to appreciate rough justice. Erin came to the door of the hut to see him walk off down the lane. She let him go a few steps, then called after him.

'Ted?'

He slowed and turned.

'Ted, I'm sorry about last night.'

She was hugging herself and twisting her shoulders nervously. He looked hard at her. Her hair was down again and the light from the hut was catching it from behind turning it dark auburn. He walked back and examined her face.

'So am I, Erin. I was a dork. Taking the 17-again thing too literally.'

Their smiles were rueful. They had so much else to say that they said nothing. Just nodded at each other.

Ted turned and walked back to Ranil's house with a sense of lost opportunity. He climbed up to the roof of his hut and decided to sit and watch a few shooting stars for a time. He reached for his pack and dug out his bottles. He left the unopened one by the side of his rucksack and walked over to the parapet with the other. He sat, gazing at the night, bottle cradled in his hands, but not yet drinking.

He touched his mouth to see if he could rediscover the sensation of her lips from the night before. She hadn't rejected his kiss; her mouth hadn't been unyielding. And this morning she was definitely making an effort, maybe too hard. But why was she sorry for last night? Sorry he made a grab? Sorry she upset him in the first place? Sorry she pushed him away? What was happening here? What was happening to him?

After so long drifting downwards, he'd stopped fighting gravity. There'd been a certain comfort in letting go. But if he was reading all the signs, he could, if he chose, come out of the dive. He was certainly going to need to be at the top of his game over the coming days. It would be hard and he could stall and fall all the harder. As for her – he might be acting like a big fool. Why would this high-stepping woman be interested in an old wreck like him? He squinted at the label on the bottle. For some reason she hated this stuff. Which was crazy. He didn't need it. He knew the difference between a boozer and an alcoholic, didn't he?

He uncorked the bottle, sniffed, hefted it, then, in silent libation, leaned sideways to the drain hole on the roof and emptied the drink away. He shook his head at the arch symbolism. The perfume of the bourbon filled the air in a sweet choking cloud.

Erin Wishart decided this was the silliest thing she'd done in years. But then there was a lot of that lately. Her standard – and so far successful – response to awkward situations was to act. And act now, otherwise she wouldn't sleep. It was the same attitude that had shattered her subordinates' nights with phone calls as she travelled across time zones.

She lay for a while tossing over the thought in her head and then rose and went to the door of Anila's hut. Anila heard her rise and got up to be with her. Erin explained. Anila smiled in the dark and moved fast and quietly to waken her daughter and explain to her what was required. Erin was embarrassed at the fuss but the little girl was bright-eyed and beaming, willing to guide her through the quiet village. She gripped Aastha's warm little hand as she was led through the alleys.

Erin stood outside Ted's hut, in sudden and uncharacteristic indecision. Under her arm she carried her sleeping bag. It seemed the sensible thing to do; in case they talked for a while and it got cool. And it might be nice mightn't it, to lie side by side and watch the stars thunder overhead. Aastha tugged at her hand and drew her round the side of the hut to the back yard. She could see the steps leading up to the roof. Aastha squeezed her hand and then was gone into the night.

Erin stood irresolute at the bottom of the stairs. She knew enough about men to tell when there was an interest. The problem was distinguishing between lust and anything else. She wasn't sure where Ted was coming from. She didn't want to be caught in the rebound from his wife. And for herself, the whole romantic thing of being stuck in the back of beyond with starry skies and a common enemy was almost too trite for words. Wasn't this how she'd gone wrong before, letting her heart rule? But sometimes you had to take risks. Sometimes you had to let the kid inside have her day, or what was the point? It wasn't that she was going to fling herself on him; just sit and talk, try to make sense of last night and not let the door close.

He was a man who'd let his talents atrophy but his performance the past few days suggested he was retrievable. The drinking had worried her at first, but it didn't seem as though he did it to excess. And wasn't it time she let go of the past? She couldn't go on seeing every bloke who liked a glass now and then as a potential drunk and woman beater.

Erin began the little climb, her heart racing in excess of the gentle exertion. She got to the top and peered round. She felt a jolt. He was sitting facing away from her on the parapet. His big dark bulk stood out clear against the sky. She padded softly towards him then began to worry in case she surprised him and he fell off.

Then she caught the smell. At first she refused to identify it. It was some sort of spice mix, or it was coming from somewhere else. Surely? Then it became unmistakeable, overpowering. By his side on the ledge was an empty bottle. There, by his pack, was a full one. She froze. Past terrors rose and mixed with these new images, and engulfed her. Her heart burst with disappointment. She wasn't going into that again. She hugged her sleeping bag to her chest and said sod, sod, sod under her breath. She turned and began to creep away, towards the stairs, tears blinding her.

'Erin? Where are you going?'

'Never mind. Just never mind.'

'Wait. I was thinking – about you – about us.'

She spun round, her pain turned to anger.

'So you were thinking about 'us' were you? But you couldn't think about us sober, could you?'

'What are you talking about? That's not how it was. But what if I took a drink? What the hell's wrong with that?!'

He swivelled fully round on the parapet and faced her now. She came back across the roof towards him, still clutching her sleeping-bag to her chest. Her childhood accent broke surface.

'Not a thing – in moderation! But from the moment I met you it's being going doon your neck like you were being hanged in the morning.'

There was something particularly chastising about a Scottish accent to an American ear. Echoes of Presbyterian probity from high-minded preachers, marshalling their flocks as they pushed back the frontiers of the new world.

'Trying to save me again, huh? Trying to run my life for me?'

'Well, look at you! One bottle finished, and another waiting.'

She dropped her bag and reached down and picked up his full one.

'You don't know how wrong you are, lady. But then I guess you'd never admit you were wrong. Now put that down.'

'I'll put it down all right.'

She yanked at the foil round the neck, and then pulled the cork with a pop. He saw what she was about to do and got to his feet, angered beyond words at her arrogance.

'Give me that!'

'This is for your own good! Don't you see? Can't you get

along without this even for a day?'

Her voice was breaking, somewhere between desperation and fear. They were crouched, facing each other, like wrestlers looking for a hold. Erin kept his rucksack and bedding between them.

'Put the bottle down, you stupid broad!'

'It's going down.'

She took two quick steps back to the ledge and upended the bottle. His cry of anger was too late to stop the whiskey glugging into the night. He got to her and grabbed her body with his right arm while stretching out to wrench the bottle from her hand. He won it, but it was Pyrrhic. The bottle was empty except for a last inch. He stood back from her, inspected the bottle, then carefully emptied the rest over the side. They stood facing each other, glaring, chests heaving with the tussle.

'You stupid, stupid, interfering…'

'Broad. I ken.'

She'd swung from reckless anger to fear. He didn't seem drunk, just thoroughly pissed off. He walked away from her as though he might throw her off if he stood any closer. He took up his seat again on the ledge by his bed.

'Why, Erin? Why? What's going on here? Why did you come up here? Why that?' He pointed at her sleeping bag.

'I … I just wanted to talk. Thought I'd be cold. I didn't like how we left it last night.'

'Then you go and do something like that.'

'You don't understand. I didn't want to talk to you when you were fu' – when you'd been drinking.'

'What makes you think I'd been drinking?'

'Well of course you were. The place is littered with bottles. It smells like a distillery. What else…' She began to run out of words.

He got up and came towards her so that he was again within touching distance. She inched back, cowering, scared he would hit her. Not again. Ted saw the fear in her eyes and was wounded by it, grieved by it. He bent a little at the knees to put him level with her. He smiled as if at a panicked child and whispered.

'I'm not going to hurt you. See.'

He lifted his big hands. She flinched but held her ground. He extended them and put them gently on her shoulders. He took one last step and kissed her lightly on her lips. So lightly she felt denied.

'Taste anything?'

'No. I mean… You mean…'

'I haven't had a drop. I poured away the first bottle. I was planning the same with the one you took. We've got work to do.'

'Oh, bugger.'

Her face collapsed and her shoulders fell, her sandcastle wiped out by a wave. Ted took her hand and pulled her over to the corner of the palisade. He took one side of the angle and she took the other. Their knees touched.

'Tell me,' he said.

She shook her head. 'It's such a bloody cliché.'

'It's the human condition.'

She sat still for a while. He waited. She let her chest rise and fall, drawing in the night smells, sucking at the stars. Then it trickled out of her.

'My father was a teacher. We had a nice life, a nice wee house, I went to a nice school in Pollokshaws. South West of Glasgow. But Dad was never happy. Just seemed bitter about everything. I think – I'm sure – there was someone else. He should have left us. Instead, he started to drink. See what I mean? Total cliché.'

'Not to you. It was unique to you.'

She held his eyes for a long second then she told him of the bad years, of the shouting and the violence and the growing debts. The dread each morning as another brown envelope landed on the mat. Her mother bearing the brunt, sheltering her daughter.

'She just took it all, you know, like it was her cross to bear. Sometimes they'd make up, and everything seemed all right for a while, then Dad went off the rails again. He lost his job, the bailiffs moved in and took everything we had. I was sleeping on the floor for a bit. Until we lost the house.'

Erin was silent for long moment, reliving the final wrench. Ted leaned over and touched the back of her hand. She jerked it clear, but then brought it back and touched his briefly.

'We applied to the council. All they could offer us was Drumchapel. A tiny wee flat on the 18th floor in the middle of nowhere. Away from everyone we knew. All ma pals. Living on benefits until Dad died of liver disease and we were free. Or rather *I* was freed. Ma Mum never got over it. Never shook off his grip.'

The tears started. They ran down her face and dripped at her nose and made her sniff. He dug in his pocket and passed her a tissue. He listened quietly, and at some point took her hand again. She squeezed it.

'I know it's stupid, an over-reaction, and just because you have a drink doesn't bring out the latent woman beater in all men.'

She grimaced and borrowed her hand back to wipe both cheeks with her knuckles, like a child. She swallowed and choked through her tears.

'And normally I don't care what a man does to his body. Do you see?'

'Yeah, I see. You ok?'

'I'm fine, now. Really. Fine. I'm sorry about your bottle, and I'm sorry. . .'

'Doesn't matter. It really doesn't matter.'

'Look, thanks for listening. I'm going to go now. Best get some sleep.'

She stood up with some resolution. He rose beside her. They dropped hands, all at once aware of what they were doing.

'You don't have to go, you know.'

'It's best. Till all this is over, and I know where ma head is.'

He nodded. She leaned in and kissed him on the cheek.

'Thanks, Ted Saddler. You're a good man. Goodnight.'

FORTY EIGHT

They were quiet with each other in the morning, the quiet of people who'd revealed too much, and not enough. Neither knew how to ask what came next. Erin felt foolish and chastened. Ted was in turmoil. Had they overshot, taken the friendship fork rather than the lover? Was there a way back? He couldn't read her silence or the sad smile.

There was also the unspoken fear of what lay ahead. The village had taken on a friendlier, more attractive hue, and they were reluctant to leave its simple sanctuary. From the roof of Ted's hut they could see the whole length of the valley. Could spot any unusual dust cloud and have 30 minutes to get to the hills. But they'd made their commitments. Meera had phoned Bhopal railway station and had managed to wait-list them on the early morning train to Delhi.

She dropped them at the station, dazed from their early start and the bucking ride. The absence of a guaranteed return ticket forced Ted to join a scrum at the opaque windows of the booking office. No patient queuing here. No legacy of the Raj. Every man for himself. Brown arms snaked past his reticent white ones, beating him to the attention of the man with the power over life, death or getting back to Delhi's sanctuary that evening. Abandoning his civilized restraints Ted used his bulk and barged to the front, blocking out all other would-be travellers.

Peering through the smeared glass, Ted could now see the source of the print-outs taped to the side of the carriages. Ancient dot-matrix printers dashed out their decisions. Clerks crouched in front of battered black and white screens with green columns chugging up and down, telling a man's destiny. Telling him his wait was over, his wait-list confirmed – possibly

– for how could he tell for certain what the Sanskrit on the proffered ticket meant?

But it worked. They embraced Meera and said their goodbyes to her with new fondness. They settled in for the long cold ride, sitting side by side, but alone with their tangled thoughts. Sometimes he dared a touch on her arm to see how she was. It provoked a strained smile and a 'fine'. He remembered Ramesh's gift and tried to immerse himself in Passage to India to see if he recognised the world. What was Ramesh's point? That Ted was misreading India – and therefore Ramesh himself – just like all white Westerners? Was Ramesh the vilified Dr Aziz? Then who was Ted?

Mostly though, Ted fidgeted, looking for hit men. Every time a passenger came through the connecting door of the rocking train his eyes ran down the man's body to check for a knife or a gun. He swivelled if someone was coming from behind and he searched faces for signs of deadly intent.

He didn't tell Erin. She was already badly rattled and didn't need any more anxiety piled on her. As if a death threat from her boss wasn't enough. Ted tried to keep his mind off the possibility of a knife in his back or a bullet in the head by running over his plan, such as it was, for countering the bad guys. He wished now that they'd made the phone call to Warwick Stanstead the night before, but somehow it had seemed too big an intrusion from that other world.

They stumbled into the hotel lobby, weary to the bone, and desperate to collapse on a soft bed. A carpeted floor would do. But the ever efficient Meera Banerjee had phoned ahead and had adjoining rooms waiting for them. It felt like coming home. It was 10 pm and all Erin wanted to do after removing the layers of grime from four days travel, two nights in a village hut, and two thousand miles of Indian railways, was sleep, but Ted urged her on.

'We have to make that call. Meet me in my room as soon as you've dropped everything.'

Erin squared up to him. She didn't mind him taking charge, sometimes. But there were limits.

'I am carrying the Gobi Desert in my hair. I absolutely, must have, will have, at any price, a shower first. Then I'll come by.'

Twenty minutes later she was sitting on the couch in Ted's room, swaddled in a white robe, her face scrubbed and glowing, her hair still damp

'Going native?' had been Ted's smiling comment at the towel turban. 'I've ordered coffee and a sandwich. Stiffen the sinews. Shall we?'

He picked up the hotel phone, ready to dial New York. She leaned over and gently but firmly took it from him. She clutched it to her chest.

'Wait. We need a moment. The other night. I told you stuff that I haven't told anyone.'

'It's fine, Erin. I understand. No wonder you were –'

'Po-faced? I was. Am. But, look, can you take some more?'

Her jaw muscles were working overtime. He looked her over.

'Sure. If it would help.'

He sat down next to her on the couch. She pulled herself back, tucking her legs under her. She searched his face, wondering how he would react.

'Before we phone Warwick, there's something you should know about him. It doesn't change where I am on all this. Where we are. What we're doing. OK? Trust me?'

She was pleading.

'Okaaay. Shoot.'

'Remember that night in Carnegie's? Our blind date?'

'A million years back? Sure.'

'I told you about the exec meeting a year ago? At the end Warwick called me into his office. . .

Erin Wishart waited a respectful minute or two before entering her boss's chamber via the connecting corridor from the conference room. The door to his washroom was ajar and she could see his shadow moving. Oh, God, what's he up to? Rather than take a seat and wait for who knew what to emerge – Jekyll or Hyde? – Erin strolled over to the floor-to-ceiling window that opened onto the balcony hanging high over the narrow wynds of downtown Manhattan. The morning sun flooded the outside space. Flower tubs and shrubs marked the periphery of the patch of real lawn, mowed and manicured like a pool table. She stood at the open door and sucked in the warm air. In the background – so faint that it might have been from another room – the usual Chopin played.

The door clicked behind her and she turned. Warwick was standing watching her, his face flushed, eyes bright. His hand went up to his nose and wiped it, once, twice. He sniffed. At a sign from him she walked back to the centre of the room and took one of the four plush armchairs. They were clustered round a low coffee table of Hazelwood, its whorls and grains glowing with the patina of age and gentle hand polishing. She sank into the deep cool leather and crossed her legs. Warwick took up her vacated position at the open balcony door. The light now came over his shoulder, shrouding his pale eyes in the peaks and troughs of his angular face.

From his vantage point, he studied her. She looked smaller and more vulnerable against the slab of brown leather. But he knew there was nothing vulnerable about Miss Erin Wishart. He wanted to hear her talk. There was always something about those dependable Celtic cadences that he ached to disrupt. He began pacing. He prowled round the room until he was standing behind her. Her shoulders tensed. He leaned over and said quietly,

'So, Erin, you think we're sending out the wrong message?'

She shook her head.

'This isn't about PR, Warwick. We've spent the last 10 years through four acquisitions, a merger, and a bailout building an image and offering a service that we can't change overnight. Our culture is at odds with our customers.'

'Be specific.'

She was acutely conscious of his hands gripping the headrest. She kept gazing straight ahead, afraid of looking up. Afraid of what she'd read on his face. She fingered her blouse buttons, checking they were closed. She felt her cheeks warming, her stomach tightening. She cleared her throat.

'We never recovered from the bad press we got over our 500% hike in bank charges for our least profitable customers. It got rid of most of them and did wonders for our bottom line. But it left a picture in the public's mind. We're elitist and uncaring. Cold and hard.'

The leather creaked again.

'Cold and hard, Erin? You know I'm not cold, don't you? Whereas. . .'

She tensed, knowing what was coming. Her toes curled in her shoes. His hands slid down to her shoulders and began to massage them gently. His fingers shifted to her neck and fondled her bare ears. They found the hair clips. They clattered to the wood floor and her hair tumbled about her face. He leaned forward, lifted bunches in both hands and buried his head in them. He breathed deeply and massaged her scalp at the same time.

His smell was rich in her nostrils, the familiar shower gel mixed with maleness. His smell. She uncrossed her legs and pushed her head back into the chair. Her fingers clawed into the chair arms. The sound of the piano seemed louder now. Maybe it was her senses sharpening. She recognised the tune from her lessons as a child a million years ago; Barcarolle in F. The intent was so crass and contrived. Yet. . .

'. . . I am hard, Erin.'

The blunt crudity broke the hold. She swung forward and up on to her feet, clutching at her hair and dragging it behind her ears. She staggered a fraction, dazed from the rapid rise. She was panting but found her voice.

'I can't do this any more, Warwick. We agreed this was crazy.'

Anger twisted his face. The veins stood out on his forehead. Then he smiled and shrugged. She scuttled past him, wanting to smack the smug grin off his face. Wanting to pin him to the floor and make him beg. She shoved at the heavy door and was gone.

FORTY NINE

Ted stared at her as she drifted to a halt. Her face was tight and her neck scarlet. He took a long time finding his voice. When he did, it was low, and controlled. Barely.

'It was never about the poor and democracy and all that bullshit. Was it? Your were dumped. By a cokehead!'

She shut her face with her hands, tore them away, displayed hot tears.

'I knew you'd think that! It's why I never said. It wasn't like that.'

He was on his feet.

'Oh really? What was it like then? How long had it been going on?'

'A couple of years or so. What does it matter how long?'

'So, more than a quickie behind the filing cabinets. Or on top of the mahogany board room table?'

'Stop! Stop! It wasn't – like – that.'

'Yeah?'

Her voice fell to a whisper. She was talking into her bath robe, clutching her knees to her chest.

'I don't fall easily. You don't know him, what he's like. I thought we were equals. Coming together. It took a while to see I was wrong. That he was using me.'

'Whereas it's only taken me a couple of weeks.'

She tugged off her damp turban and threw it at him.

'That's a cheap shot!'

'You played me. Wound me up with talk of saving the world. But all the time you just wanted back at him.'

'I wasn't dumped. I dropped him.'

'But he wouldn't take no for an answer. So you thought you

needed to teach him a lesson!'

She pounded the cushions. 'No! No! Do you really think I've done all this – got nearly killed – given up everything – for a bloody psychopath who's out to murder me?!'

They were both panting, mouths twisted, eyes blazing. Ted's shoulders dropped.

'It's ok. I'm used to it. Nothing new here.'

'Don't talk like a bloody loser, Ted Saddler! Look what you've achieved here.'

He shook his head. 'But not with you. For a while there. . .'

She sprang up and marched over to him and threw her arms round him.

'You great oaf. Are you blind?'

He looked down at her, searching her face. She went up on her toes and pressed her mouth to his. It was brief but it left its mark. She gave a small smile.

'Let's call Warwick. I'll show you how it is.'

She pushed back, still holding his arms, gave him a shake or two to try to drag a grin out of him. He wasn't playing.

'Anything else I need to know first?'

'Only that you're about to witness my formal resignation.'

She dropped her grip and found the phone. They sat down, Erin on the couch, Ted in the armchair, the phone perched between them on the table. She glanced at her watch.

'Perfect. It's ten to one in the afternoon in New York. Stanstead is at his desk, with a salad brought in by his PA. This will go through to Pat Duschene. Let's hope Oscar is getting all this. Ready?'

Ted nodded. She stabbed the pad with complete familiarity and put the phone on speaker. Despite preparing themselves, both jumped when the voice cut through loud and clear.

'Mr Stanstead's office. How can I help?'

Erin put on her smiley voice.

'Hi Pat. It's Erin Wishart. How are you?'

There was the faintest of pauses. It wasn't the time-lag on

the line.

'Just fine, Miss Wishart. And you? How's your vacation? Where are we today?'

'Well Pat, I guess you're in your office and we're out of town.' Nerves and anger were making her flippant.

'Put me through to Warwick, please. It's urgent.'

'I'll just see if he's in his office.'

She could picture his little face puckering up with ill-intent. The line flipped to that day's holding music, Tchaikovsky's Romeo and Juliet. She almost smiled. It gave her time to examine the man sitting opposite her. He still seemed to be in shock, but Ted Saddler didn't give much away. Could this still go somewhere? Probably not. Men hated hearing about other men. But he looked a great deal better than she felt. How had his eyes avoided the black rings and the red rims? Even the bones on his face stood out more clearly, his hooked nose looking like it belonged to him again.

The music stopped and Stanstead's refined and relaxed tones fell clearly from the speaker phone. A hand grenade in the room would have had less effect.

'Well this is a pleasant surprise. How are you, Erin?'

She couldn't hold back.

'You mean it's a surprise to find me still alive, Warwick?'

'What? This is a bad line. How is Hong Kong? I hear typhoons are on their way. Keep your head down, Erin.'

'Warwick, can we cut the bullshit? You know where I am. And you know its not Hong Kong. And before we go any further, and for the record – are you getting this, Pat? – this is my resignation, effective immediately.'

'Wait, Erin. Don't. . .'

'Shut up, Warwick. I'm resigning because you tried to have me killed the other day. By any standards that constitutes breach of contract on your part. Don't you think?'

'Erin. How can you say this? You know how I feel about you.'

'A convenient lay? But who cares. The other reason I'm calling is to tell you that I know you murdered José Cadenza. We have proof.'

'Erin, I'm horrified at these accusations!' His voice had just the right note of astonishment and hurt. 'What poor José did has really upset you. It sounds like post traumatic stress, frankly. Now, we can help, Erin. . .'

'Don't be so bloody patronising!

Ted's eyes widened. He made a two-thumbs up sign.

She went on. 'I want you to take a peek at a web site that's been set up. I think you'll find it interesting. In fact you'll be knocked out by it.'

Stanstead's voice lost its flippancy. 'I don't like games. What's this about Erin. You need help, you know.'

'You're blown, Warwick. Just take a look at *sevensilverbullets. com*. Let me spell that.'

She did and they heard him say and spell it out loud to his desk computer.

'I'll give you one minute to browse through it. That's all you'll need. Then we talk.'

Ted's doorbell rang. He signed to her to indicate he would get the coffee and food he'd ordered. He got up and walked into the small lobby leading to the bedroom door. He peered through the peephole, saw a waiter with a tray, and pulled the door open.

The first punch took him in the stomach. The second smashed into his face and knocked him over. Before he could get up, two Indians in the white uniforms of hotel servants were pinning his arms and jamming a gun against his temple. Another smaller figure joined them, a white man.

'Mr Saddler, I presume?' asked Joey Kutzov stepping over Ted's legs and kicking the door closed behind him.

FIFTY

Joey pressed his gun against Ted's head and marched him into the sitting room. Erin stood up in terror. Joey's eyes lit up.

'This is cosy. Saves me a visit. Hope I wasn't disturbing anything?'

Joey signalled to his companions. They dragged Ted upright and hauled him over to stand alongside Erin. They frisked him professionally and signalled he was weaponless.

'Where's the gun, big boy?'

'What gun?' Ted got out, dabbing his jaw.

'I think we'd better take care of you first, Saddler, just in case you pull another stunt like last week. No chance for heroics this time.'

Joey lifted his arm out straight and walked towards the couple. Erin grabbed Ted round the middle. He swung his arms round her and pulled her into his chest, turning his back on Joey.

'Now ain't that touching!'

Ted closed his eyes. Erin went rigid. She could see the silencer attached and wondered how loud it would be and if it would hurt. She regretted never having held him properly until now. Her timing was always rubbish. Then her brain started up again.

'Warwick! Call off your dog!'

She leaned towards the coffee table and shouted at the phone.

'Warwick! Stop Kutzov!'

'Joey?! Joey, is that you!?' came the voice from the phone.

Joey's gun arm swung down in surprise.

'Mr Stanstead! That you?' He glared at the speaker-unit in disbelief.

'Yes, it's me you fool. Don't shoot them. Not yet!

Erin unfroze and grabbed the phone. She shouted at it.

'Tell him to get out of here. Right now, you bastard! I mean right now!'

She shoved the phone into Joey's face.

'Joey, back off. Leave them and call me later. We need to talk.'

Joey lowered his gun reluctantly.

'You two,' to the two puzzled Indians. 'Out! Let's move it.'

He eyed Ted and Erin up and down. 'We'll be in touch,' he sneered.

When the door had closed behind them, Erin stumbled over to the couch and collapsed on it, still clutching the phone. Ted stumbled over and landed beside her. Blood ran down his face. He took the phone.

'I guess you found the web site interesting, Stanstead?'

'What do you want? This is shit and you know it. I don't know how you got all this shit but I do know none of it's useable. Wiretapping is illegal.'

The voice was high and threatening, the words spilling from him. Erin had seen the rages and knew he was sitting like a pressure cooker about to blow.

'If you're that sure, Stanstead, why'd you call off your thugs? As for legalities? I'm a reporter. I can bring this to the public's attention. Allegations. Which is all it will take to destroy you.'

The line went quiet. Ted and Erin looked at each other.

'What do you want?' from the speaker.

'First, call off your hound permanently. Second, stop your attacks on the People's Bank. Third, announce your resignation as CEO of GA. Fourth, no, make this number one: if Veronica Yeardon is still alive I want her released safe. Now! Have you got that?'

'I think you've both been out in the sun too long. I don't know what you're talking about, mister.'

268

'You've got till 10 am tomorrow morning, New York time. And Stanstead, there – is – no – choice.'

'Oh, there's always a choice.'

The line went dead. Erin needed to do something. She went into the bathroom and came back with a white towel soaked in cold water. She began bathing his cut and generally fussing over him. He was conscious of her hip touching his shoulder and of the clean smell of her. He wondered if she'd object if he put his arm round her waist. A hug with a gun pointed at your head was no test, and it wasn't the time or place for open heart discussions. But they were back to the stage of joshing with each other again; could even laugh at coming through another near-death experience together.

'Miss Wishart, the last person that kept trying to get me killed was my platoon sergeant. You don't believe in rein-carnation do you?'

He fingered the large plaster over his forehead.

'Mr Saddler, if I'd come back to haunt you, you can be sure I'd have done the job right. Admit it, you're enjoying this. You haven't felt this alive in years.'

The doorbell rang again. She grabbed him.

'Oh my god, they're back!'

'They wouldn't knock.'

Ted reluctantly disengaged from her. Clutching his bloody towel to his head, he sidled up to the door. He opened the eye hole, and finally let the waiter in. The waiter placed the tray of coffee and sandwiches on the room table and had Ted sign for them.

'Sir? There is also this parcel for you. We have been keeping it for you in the hotel.'

He pointed at the tired looking white plastic package on the tray. Ted dropped his towel and picked it up gingerly. A present from Joey?

'Sir, are you wanting me to get a doctor?' He pointed at the revealed wound

'What? No. No, I'm fine thanks.'

Ted dug into his pocket and gave the man a preposterous tip. He closed and locked the door behind the waiter and returned to examine the parcel. It was well travelled and covered in scrawled redirections. Post-marked two weeks ago in Louisiana, it had been to New York, then Kolkata and finally here. He hefted it. It bent in the middle like papers do. An unlikely bomb. He grinned when he saw the return address on it: c/o Carly Soferson. He took the letter opener from the bureau and sliced into it, ripping open the FedEx packaging.

Between the plastic and the brown paper he found Carly's note in her big childish hand. He smiled before tugging out the documents and a bubble-wrapped memory stick. He glanced quickly at the papers and looked up at Erin with triumph.

'If we've been building a scaffold for Stanstead, Mrs Yeardon just sent us the rope. I don't know if she's still alive – god help her – but before she got taken, Veronica Yeardon did a great big public service. C'mon, we've got work to do. We need to speak to Oscar right away. You can bet your life – mine too – Stanstead's already on the move.'

Stanstead was pacing his balcony, smoking. His cell phone rang.

'Boss, Boss what's going on? I had them dead to rights. All I had to do was squeeze and they were gone, you know? What's happening?'

'You think I had a goddamn choice! What took you so long?! You should have got rid them days ago.' He paused and gathered himself. 'OK, let's chill. This is just a little hiatus while we sort out a couple of things. Be ready to finish your business when I give the word.'

'So how long do I have to stay in this shit-hole, boss? The temperature's topping 100 every day.'

'You stay as long as I fucking want you to! That's how long! By the way, don't call my office number again. Ever. We're being bugged.'

'Impossible! I check the systems myself.'

'And you've been screwing up!'

'Sorry boss, sorry.'

'We'll get back to that later. What about the Yeardon woman. How is she?'

'Alive, just. But that was a couple a' days ago according to my boys. She still hasn't said where the papers are, but she sure ain't standing up to the heat so well, boss. Does it matter?'

'No. Not really. Not now. Joey? Joey, get ready to go. Tomorrow!'

Warwick cut the call and hit Pat's button again.

'Get me Trevino.'

'Certainly, Mr Stanstead.' There was a click and a pause.

'Sir? It's Nick Trevino.'

'Project Monsoon. I want the deluge. Now! Do you understand? I want you to throw everything you have at them. And Trevino, before you do, I have a web site I want taken out.'

'Give me the name, sir.'

Stanstead spelled it out. 'I want it bombed, destroyed, obliterated! And I want to know who did it and how to find them. And I want this by yesterday. Understood?'

'Yessir, Mr Stanstead!'

FIFTY ONE

Anila was in her little backyard, breaking up a dried cowpat for fuel for the cooking fire. She shivered in the early morning air. But it wasn't because she was cold. It was simply too much to take in, too good. How could such a thing last? She'd got her money back and the cooperative was now besieged by new candidates. Well of course it wouldn't last. Not if she'd understood about the trial. It was to start next week and Meera's father would go to prison and the bank would be closed and all the dreams that Meera had set running in Anila's head would be ripped apart. But there was nothing she could do, nothing that an ignorant villager could fix that would help Meera's father.

She'd been explaining this to the white woman while she combed her wonderful hair. In her halting English Anila had said that if she lived in Delhi she would have gone to the court on Monday and stood outside and shouted support for Mr Banerjee. She knew all the people who'd been helped by the bank would have done the same. Maybe if they'd all shouted loud enough they would have listened inside the court and maybe seen that all the crazy charges against the bank were untrue. Erin had asked her simply why didn't she? And why didn't she send an email to all the other customers?

Anila couldn't think about it then, not with all that was happening to her. But she was thinking about it now. She felt her heart pounding. The demon was loose again. But she held herself in check until she and Meera were alone before broaching the subject, tentatively at first then with more excitement as she saw Meera's face light up.

'Miss Erin said we could talk to all the people in the bank

from this computer. Is this true? Could we ask everyone to go the trial and show their support? If we got a fifty people to go, or a hundred even, then it would show we were happy with the bank.'

'Yes, but it is not so easy. We have a website and we have been telling the customers what is happening about the trial. But the customers only see the messages if they read the website.'

'Can we not *send* messages to everyone?'

'The team in Delhi can. They are the administrators in the centre. So they could send a message to every account.' Meera was beginning to share Anila's excitement. 'But we cannot incite people, Anila. Do you understand? We cannot be seen, as a bank, as a company, to be inciting people – our customers – to make an assembly against the government. This is just the sort of thing that the bank is charged with, you see. That we are encouraging people to fight the government.'

'Erin said that too. But she said it might be different if the message comes from us – the customers. She said there was something called Twitter?'

Meera's face fell.

Anila gulped. 'Have I said something wrong? I am so sorry, Meera. . .'

'No, no, Anila! It's me who is sorry. I have been very stupid and slow. As an officer of the bank I don't tweet. But I have an account and I follow some important people's tweets.'

'Like who?'

Meera's face darkened with embarrassment.

'Oh, some silly film stars, that is all. But come, we will set you up with your own Twitter account. Then we will need a memorable hashtag to attract attention.' She thought for a second or two. 'How about #*savethepeoples bank*? Now you and I will start tweeting to newspapers, politicians, film stars, everybody!'

Anila clapped her hands. 'That is perfect!'

'Even if you don't get many followers, we might get a few

friends to support my father when he arrives at court on Monday. Today is Saturday, which gives us two days to stir things up.'

'Should *we* go?'

Meera looked at this ingénue with frank admiration. How far could she go with proper training and education? But before she could answer, a burst of hammering shook the front door, as though there had been a terrible accident in the fields. A woman's voice was calling out. A woman's voice that Anila knew in the darkest, most scarred piece of her heart. She shot to her feet, her hands over her ears. But the voice cut through.

'Come out, Anila Jhabvala! We know you are in there! Come out and pay your debts to your husband. We know you have money now.'

'Who is it?!' asked Meera, rising to her feet, shocked at the terror in Anila's face.

Anila couldn't get the words out. Her mouth moved and gulped as she gasped for breath. Another voice cut in, a man's voice, softer, wheedling,

'Open up, wife of mine. We saw everything yesterday. I have come for my due. That is all. Open up and I won't beat you, precious jewel.'

Anila's body twisted as though she had been stabbed in the stomach. Finally, she got it out.

'It is my husband and my mother-in-law. They have come back. I knew this would happen. That it would all go wrong.'

FIFTY TWO

Erin returned to Ted's room fully dressed, her face make-up free, scrubbed and glowing. She'd pinned her hair loosely held behind her ears with a big clip. Ted gave her hair a second glance. It looked different. More volume. And along the central parting was a line of lighter colour. Sunburned scalp? She saw what he was seeing and touched the seam. Her jaw clenched.

'The last guilty secret. Go on. Take a look.'

He stepped closer. She didn't retreat. She bowed her head. He studied it in disbelief.

'It's red. You've got red hair.'

She raised her head and stared defiantly at him.

'Ted, I've got *curly*, red hair.'

He grinned. 'And freckles.'

'Goes with the territory.' Her chin jutted out.

'But why? Some women spend a fortune to become a red head.'

She shrugged. 'Camouflage. Even in Scotland – red hair central – I got called ginger. When I was job hunting in London after university I thought it would make me look more serious, more business-like. Especially when I landed my first job. There are enough wolves in a dealing room without dangling red meat – so to speak – in front of them. It just got to be a habit. Now, shall we get down to business?'

Ted had already set out the package content on the coffee table: two distinct sheaves of papers and one small memory stick. They each took a sheaf and began to read. Within moments, Erin looked up.

'We need all this up on the web site. Use your phone, Ted, and I'll upload.'

He hefted his cell. 'I've never actually used the camera bit.'

'Call yourself a reporter?'

Erin took the phone and set the camera zoom to take a full page in its view finder. She tried out one of the Yeardon papers on the pale carpet. The matte cream colour was perfect background for the documents. The words would stand out clearly on the faxes, contracts, private letters, and the single sheet that explained everything. They fired up Ted's laptop and connected the phone camera to it by USB cable.

They began to sift properly through the documents. They sat quietly, Ted on a chair, Erin on the two-seater couch sipping coffee and orange juice, and passing each other page after page of devastatingly incriminating material. Erin took photos of each of the key documents then uploaded them to the computer. They made few comments, just the occasional 'this one' or 'take a look at para 3 and 4'. What they had was a chronology of the deal between Stanstead's old bank Global Fidelity, and the insurance giant American Mart.

But it wasn't the official story, and the papers they were examining had never seen the light of day. The press at the time had seen only the surface: a hostile take-over bid by a power-hungry bank, astonishing at the time, but heralding a wave of consolidation among retail players, be they banks, supermarkets, insurers, clothing manufacturers, or automobile manufacturers. In the public version of the battle of wills, the American Mart boss, Bill Yeardon, had blinked first.

Behind this smokescreen, the real story had been a lot dirtier and a lot more personal. Bill Yeardon might not have been a saint, but nor was he the embezzling, bribing, backstabbing corporate criminal made out in the second set of documents. This was a bound dossier cataloguing the 'findings' of a team of Warwick Stanstead's researchers – muckrakers and forgers, more like – into Yeardon's business and personal life over the previous three decades. Much of it was hearsay and unproven. A large chunk was almost certainly made up, but with a grain of truth in it that would have made the lies seem plausible if they'd gone public.

There were the purported close links with Senators and at least one President, at auspicious moments in the growth of Yeardon's company. There were the interesting bank account details showing – apparently – personal transactions at key times between Yeardon and the heads of companies he'd taken over or presidents or top officials of countries that he'd moved into. The coincidence of these bank account details, which went back ten or twenty years, being made available by the very bank that was mounting the take-over would have been glossed over in a public exposé. Erin explained to Ted how the counterfeit records could be created. As they stood, the faked-up dossier would do little more than blacken Yeardon's name.

But the memory stick changed the game. Ted slotted it into a spare USB port on the laptop. A number of voice and video files popped up. Ted began clicking on them, each clearly labelled and dated. He started with a video clip. It was poor quality, taken by laptop camera in a hotel room. A man was staring into the lens. He was grey-haired and haggard. But his voice was strong and filled the room.

'My name is Bill Yeardon. I'm Chief Executive Officer of American Mart. I'm sitting in room 942, the Four Seasons Hotel, New York. I'm wearing a wire and waiting for Warwick Stanstead, CEO of Global Fidelity. The conversation you will hear after this is between him and me. It concerns Global Fidelity's hostile take-over of my company and the dirty tricks' campaign against me and my company.'

Ted closed the video and clicked on the audio file. It was silent for a few seconds then restarted. Now there were two voices. They listened to the familiar voice of Warwick Stanstead and the new voice of Bill Yeardon as they slugged it out. There was incredulity and outrage at first from Yeardon concerning the receipt of the first pieces of the damaging dossier. Stanstead was flippant, cocky and contemptuous. They talked back and forward over the details in the dossier, with Stanstead readily admitting to – no, gloating about the quality of the forgeries and the exaggerations.

The second recording began the same way, but a week later and in a different hotel. This time Yeardon was losing control and making accusations of blackmail and threats of going public and calling in the police. Stanstead was turning the screws, becoming more venomous, saying there was worse to come unless Yeardon caved in.

The final recording, just three days later was about defeat:

'What sort of animal are you?' Yeardon's voice was leaden. The anger had been replaced by a dull, aching monotone.

'It's a jungle, call me a lion.'

'I'd call you a roach but it's an insult to the roach.'

'Does this mean you concede?'

'Concede? No. This means I'm walking away from the vilest, foulest piece of work I've ever seen in my business life. I've met a lot of tough guys in this business world Stanstead. Guys a lot tougher than you. But I've never met anyone who'd stoop so low as to falsify records, produce fake photos – of that poor, poor mite! – and threaten my wife and family.'

'Come, come, Bill. Don't tell me you didn't get a little horny when you saw the pictures? Don't tell me that you didn't wonder in your heart of hearts what it would really have been like?'

'You shit! You total shit!'

'Ok Bill, enough. Can we cut to the chase. Are you out or not?'

There was a long silence. Then a voice came over like he was speaking from under water. 'I'm out. My lawyers will be in touch. What about the photos and papers?'

'So glad you've seen sense. We'll be generous in the pay-off.'

'What about the photos?!'

'Oh, well I guess I'll hang on to them for a little while. You never know, do you, when they might come in handy?'

'No way! The deal's off! Unless I get every scrap of filth and all the copies, I'm signing nothing. You hear?!'

'Sure Bill. Sure. We can do that.'

The recording stopped. Ted and Erin looked at each other.

'Photos?' she asked. Ted opened a zip file and found a batch of JPEGs. But heading the list was another video clip. It was Bill Yeardon again. Looking demented, looking suicidal. He had a drink in his hand. He knocked it back and stared straight into camera:

'Hi Vee… darlin',

if you've ever loved me as much as I've loved you then you'll know that the attached photos are false. Photoshopped or something. On the life of our children, these are lies! They are so sick that they are beyond my comprehension. This is all part of the filthy tricks and blackmail by Stanstead and his black crew. But they've done their work. I can't go on with this business if there are people out there prepared to go to these lengths. I'm sick to my stomach and they can have the company if they want it this bad. I'm just terrified that they won't stop until they get what they want. They'll do anything and they've already made threats about you and the kids.

If you're watching this it's because I'm not around to protect you any more. They've got copies of everything in this folder except maybe the voice records, and they're just as likely to use the stuff or it could come out by accident or something. So I thought you should be prepared.

Believe me. *This isn't me*. These photos are lies. I love you more than life itself and you have to trust me at the last.

God look after you, Vee. I love you.'

Erin was wiping at her eyes as Ted clicked open the first photo. She took a quick glance at the screen and put her hands to her mouth.

'I don't think I'm ready for this. I'll never be ready for this.'

Ted steadily clicked through the folder of colour photos. They showed what looked like Bill Yeardon in a series of loving and intimate situations with children. The top ones showed 'him' with a boy of no more than 7 or 8. They were in a hotel room. Both were clothed and 'Bill' was holding the worried looking child close to him and looking into the camera. They moved on quickly to naked bedroom scenes in which 'Bill Yeardon' was skewering the beautiful boy in a number of different poses. The child was weeping and distraught. Ted flicked to the end and sat back in his chair.

'The bastard. The bastard.' He said it softly and carefully like a benediction. 'None of this goes up on the web.'

Erin wiped her eyes, blew her nose and got back to work.

'Let's keep it simple. We'll send the whole lot, garbage and all, to a lawyer I know in London. So nothing gets lost no matter what happens to us. For the website, let's put up all the key papers we sifted, including the faked-up dossier. Also the voice recordings that refer to them. We can embed them in the documents at the right places.'

'Do we have to put the bad stuff out?'

'I thought you were a newspaperman? Never underestimate people's powers to see through lies.'

'You're right, but it needs some perspective. I'll knock up an intro to the material putting it in context. A document and a video clip. That'll do the trick.' He looked at his watch. 'It's ten pm. Let's get this done and aim to sync up with Oscar at midnight our time.'

Erin took over Ted's pc and handed her own laptop to Ted. While she formatted the digital records of the papers and the audios, Ted hammered away at his keys shaping an article that explained the background to everything going out. He felt the adrenalin flow like he was 20 again and had a deadline to meet and the presses were waiting. During the next hour they smiled at each other a lot in recognition of their respective contributions. Ted emailed his cover article to Erin and she set up the whole folder ready to upload to the web site.

She brought up the address and got the message: website not

available. Ted tried from his computer. Still blocked. He felt the sweat grow on his back and trickle down the base of his spine. They tried again and again.

'Access denied. The web site's down! We're too late, Erin!'

FIFTY THREE

'Aux armes! Aux armes citoyens!'
Oscar was pounding away on the keyboard following the sounding of the klaxon that had brought him staggering from his bedroom at 2am on Sunday morning. He'd linked the device, which sounded like a muted Second World War air raid siren, to a number of tripwires around his Internet sites. Any attack on the People's Bank firewall or his '*sevensilverbullets*' web site would set it off. Both were happening.

Similar alarms were sounding via the computer screens of his companions in arms, and one by one they were checking in. The messages began to erupt on everyone's screens.

the websites down an hour. whole ISP is out. looks like a data blizzard.   –Thor–

they'll be tracking the source. our asses are on the line
–Slick Willy–

no sweat. all they're hitting is the public stuff. originals in Tor. I've got 12 mirror sites in the dark. I'm posting links to each of you. all of you take a site and keep the replication going. no matter what, shield the dirt on GA. Ted & Erin are setting up a media blitz.   –LR–

Hi Lone Ranger. We've just come on and can't get in. –Erin –

Gonna give you new web site addresses. Hope you've downloaded the Tor browser like I told you. It's untouchable. and by the way, take a look at the latest stuff I put up. we got the GA data warehouse to put out for us like u said. nice trace of big money going from GA to interesting accounts in India. hold tight.   –LR–

fabulous! And we've got new stuff to go up too! This is killer material. We need to go public.   –Erin–

you mean missile launch????!   – LR–

There was a pause in the flickering messages. Erin turned from her screen to Ted.

'They want to know if this is it, and if they can counter-attack?'

'I can read. So they've found the pay-offs to the Indian government! Ramesh is in the clear. That settles it. What's to lose?! We've got Joey waiting out there for the go-ahead to come back and swat us, Stanstead's killed one web site and I guess from what I'm seeing, the bank's under attack again. I say go.'

'You realise what will happen? And that it could all backfire?'

'Do we have a choice?'

Erin turned back to her screen, took a deep breath and hit the keys.

nuke em, Oscar!!

They stared at the screen. Nothing happened.

'So what is going on Erin?'

'We're waiting for it to start.'

'What?'

'Cyber war.'

As she spoke messages started scrolling down her screen.

'Is there any way you can explain that to a Neanderthal?'

'Let's start with the public web site. GA has knocked out our service provider with sheer volume.'

She tracked the messages on her screen. They were being copied on everything that Oscar and his gang were saying.

'Oscar knows GA is trying to track down the site owners. Namely, Oscar and his crew. But the trail stops at Tor. GA has no way of following URLs into darknets. It's a separate slice of the dark web. A website set up as a Hidden Service is accessible only when you're connected to the Tor network. They'll waste a lot of time on the public stuff but won't have a clue about the real world.'

'But we're in the public world and Oscar was using public servers. Won't that allow Warwick's team to trace them? They could be on their way round to visit him now!'

'Relax. For one, Oscar's working on a virtual machine. His hardware is shielded. For another, he's completely anonymous inside a darknet.'

Ted's forehead creased as he tried to follow. Erin pointed at her screen.

'Look! – instructions and a new link. We're going into Onionland.'

'Where the hell is Onionland?!'

'A darknet. If you're not browsing through Tor, you can't get in. The Hidden Services pseudo-suffix – .onion – isn't resolvable by the Internet's core DNS servers, and Hidden Service URLs are a jumbled, 16-character alphanumeric mess autogenerated by a public cryptography key when the site is created.'

'I have absolutely no idea what you just said. Or even what language you said it in.'

'Doesn't matter. Tell you later.'

Erin typed in the details and the screen cleared showing their now familiar menu of evidence against Warwick Stanstead.

'Right, I'll upload the Yeardon material. Why don't you hook up to the battle? I'm sending you Oscar's link.' She fired the email across. Ted double-clicked and found his screen filled with rapidly scrolling messages.

ok we're synced. we got enough replicas to snow them for days.
– Switchblade–

yeah? don't bet. seen the code these guys are using? so bad!!!
–Thor–

sooner we go public the better. what's cooking, LR?   – SlickWilly–

Erin's shooting up the hidden web now with new stuff.   – LR–

checked the bank firewall. looking cool. I mean cool!! no flames...
yet!   – Magus–

keep your peepers on your block. I've got the centre. let's see the
view from our Delhi compadres   – LR–

Ted turned to Erin. 'How long can the bank firewalls hold out?'

'Soon see. Oscar has rebuilt them with even tougher and more advanced guardian code. The bank's systems have a tough shell all round them.' She giggled. 'Oscar described it as the mother of all condoms.'

'An illuminating image. So what's to worry about?'

'We can't shift all their systems into a darknet. GA's upping the transaction volumes. They're creating and replicating dummy transactions and firing them down separate pipes aimed at People's Bank servers. Like multiple rocket launchers. Behind the dummies will be viruses. If the firewalls go down, the bugs get through and kill the bank's systems. And there's no reason why GA can't keep up bombardment for days, or weeks until the bank goes out of business. The code Oscar and his crew have put together is super-fast, super-effective and can take the punishment – for a while anyway – and still let clean transactions through from real clients. They have to keep working, providing a service or GA wins anyway.'

'You said there were two things.'

'Right. Number two is killing the customer.'

'You mean instead of going after the bank, they go for the clients?!'

'It's easy to get hold of customer accounts. We can safely assume that GA is sitting with a directory of all the email addresses of 250 million People's Bank customers.'

285

'And…?'

'They'll forge emails which purport to be from People's Bank. The customer opens it. The virus gets in and promptly destroys his computer or a client's entire corporate network.'

'Can Oscar stop that?'

'This was one of my ideas. I suggested it to the Delhi team. A few days ago the bank should have sent out an email to all its customers warning them of possible sabotage. Attached to the email would have been self-loading anti-virus code. Oscar got hold of the best software shield around from one of his gang. Worm I think. They'd trapped a slew of bugs from GA, analysed them and rebuilt their software to sift out and kill them off. Even variants should be handled as the software is trained to recognise the 'style' of the bugs and it goes on learning and adding new virus checkers all the time.'

'There are times when I miss a drink more than others.'

She noticed he wasn't doing anything about it.

'Well maybe you'll deserve one when this over. And maybe I'll buy it.'

'What's happening now?' The screen was quieter. Only the occasional message flicked across it.

'Now, I would guess, they're getting ready to go on the offensive.'

It was 4am in New York and the line was holding – just.

here's a new one. Anyone want it? It looks like a leacher – LR-

that's up my street. Goes with the other blood-suckers. – Slick –

box em up and send them over. Same for all you guys. tracer's almost done and then we can turn it round.   – LR–

'Is this the offensive line coming in?' Ted pointed at the last few messages.

Erin turned back from her own machine and squinted over her glasses.

'Uh huh. Let me just finish this. There she goes! Right, the web site's got all the new stuff loaded. I'll tell Oscar and he can do the necessary replication. Then we have to work out who we tell. Don't we?'

She emailed Oscar then stood and stretched. Erin realised she was enjoying this. She felt good. Her stomach was miraculously quiet. Anila had given her a small jam-jar of ground leaves and bark of the neem tree. She added a spoonful to a mug of boiling water, let it stew and magic. It helped that for the first time in years she felt she was doing something worthwhile. That it was a giant act of vandalism aimed at bringing down her own corporation was a little bizarre. But this felt right. She had no doubts. She looked over Ted's shoulder at the unfolding cyber drama.

'They're stripping all the viruses out of the GA blitz and rounding them into a pen. Oscar has been cutting code that will pick up every GA attacker and unpick its source address.'

'So they know where it's come from originally?'

'Right. And he's going to build that in to the firewall so that every new virus message that comes in, automatically gets bounced back where it came from. And on the way back, Oscar adds copies of every virus they've thrown at us. Plus a few of his own specials and some variations from his very wicked gang!'

'So the firewall becomes a mirror?'

'Or a missile defence system. Eat your heart out, George Bush!'

Ted's screen dissolved and a new picture started forming.

'What's happening? Have we lost? Is this Stanstead's bugs?'

'I don't think so… Wait. What the hell…!'

There was a blare of trumpets, the screen came into focus, filled with figures. A band of muscled men in loin cloths and capes marched forward brandishing swords and shields. The camera angled back leaving the small band of warriors bunched together on the left of the screen. Facing them was an endless horde of raging men on foot or mounted on horses and elephants. Tigers and leopards wrenched at their chains in their frenzy to attack.

The dull roars from both sides were abruptly overridden by one powerful voice. The leader of the small band of semi-naked musclemen stood forward, and raised his spear. His chubby face came into close-up. Oscar. With a big black beard. Just behind him was a grinning Albert. Their borrowed bodies rippled and glowed. The camera panned to the enemy battalions and fixed on the leader riding a great chariot and surrounded by screaming henchmen with axes and spears. The leader's face showed the jutting nose and high brow of Warwick Stanstead.

King Oscar saw his nemesis and drew his arm back. He launched his great spear at Xerxes/Stanstead with a mighty shout,

'I – AM – SPARTA!'

Three hundred voices swelled behind him in chorus. The vastly outnumbered, doomed warriors broke into a sprint towards the enemy legions. A great clash of arms unfolded, with screams of pain and terror and exultation. Swords rose and fell, blood spurted, limbs flew off and severed heads rolled.

Ted burst out laughing. 'It's 300! The Spartans' battle for Thermopylae. Oscar's hijacked the movie!'

Erin was laughing with him. 'It's the computer game. He's hacked it. I bet he's hooked it up directly to the server battle.'

'What?'

'GA's virus attacks are represented by the enemy battalions. Oscar and his men are the Spartans. Look, you can see some of the gang we met in CJ's back office. There's Vikram and Shivani!' she pointed at the flushed faces of the young man and woman fighting alongside Oscar. 'And he's raided GA's computer files for mug shots of Warwick and his exec team for the faces of his enemy!

'But it's not for real?' Ted asked doubtfully.

'Real enough. Representational for sure. Oscar will have written code to translate what's actually happening in the cyber war and hacked it into the 300 video game. I bet he's linked the volumes of virus attacks to the numbers of bad guys. If the baddies are winning, the Spartans will be forced back.' Her voice lost its humour. 'If Oscar goes down, it means Ramesh's bank has been overrun. For real.'

They sat glued to the images of the bloody fighting for what seemed hours. For a long time, the Spartans were on the defensive. They were pushed back by sheer weight of numbers into the narrow defile of the pass of Thermopylae. Bodies piled up. Exhaustion lined the faces of the defenders. There came a pause, a long pause as the enemy regrouped and prepared for one final push. The sound of battle dropped. From behind the Spartans came a long trumpet blast. Tired bodies righted themselves and muscles flexed anew. King Oscar turned to his troops and beat his shield with his bloody sword.

'TO ME! TO ME! FOR SPARTA!' his voice boomed out, echoing round the walls of the rocky pass.

The Spartans hammered their shields, formed into battle order and as one, charged the enemy. Instead of the few hundred that had first lined up with Oscar, a torrent of new troops poured down the gorge and into the enemy ranks. At first it was simply a chaos of shouting and crashing of weaponry. Then slowly, inch by inch, the enemy hordes gave way. Still more Spartan muscle-men filled the scene. The rout started quickly. Soon the enemy were running from the field, only to be cut down by the avenging hordes. Like a brown sea the Spartans overwhelmed the dark forces until with a snap, the screen blinked out.

Ted and Erin sat in stunned silence gazing at the pc.

'Does that mean...?' he asked.

Erin sat still, looking suddenly tired. There was no elation on her face. She looked up at him and gave him a faint smile.

'We've just killed my bank, Ted.'

FIFTY FOUR

It was 9.15 Sunday morning in Dayton, Ohio. Dave Gruby was doing his weekly admin chores. For some people paperwork was a pain, something to be put off till the red bills came in or the tax penalty loomed. Dave kind of liked it. It gave him a sense of calm. It made things feel solid and ordered. He had a good filing system and diary on his home computer. It prompted and structured his life. He kept hard copies of all his correspondence in a neat file in his left hand desk drawer.

He was on-line, paying bills, checking emails and planning the following month's banking transactions. He had to add a new monthly payment; his daughter Sue was off to college and he'd taken on the rental payments on a small apartment she was sharing with two other girls. Dave was thinking about what his little girl would get up to away from home. The thought was making him mildly panicky as he methodically approached setting up the arrangements with his GA Internet bank service. His screen lost contact. He tried again. It was pretty unusual these days for a banking service to go down, but not unheard of. They did a lot of maintenance at weekends. Nothing. He gave up and determined to try later. He was irritated though. He didn't like stuff left undone when he was half way through.

At 2.38 in the afternoon, in an over-priced store in Covent Garden, London, England, Diana Siciliano offered her GA credit card to pay for a 'must have' sweater she'd just tried on. This was the big trip to England that she and her mother had talked of for years. Ever since her dad had gone off with Sandi Thompson, her mother's one-time best friend. The planning of it had almost been therapy enough. The reality was better.

There were just the cutest stores. The shop assistant swiped the card three times and tried to key in the details by hand before noticing the GA service itself was disconnected. Diana dug out her Amex instead. It worked and she went off into the light drizzle, puzzling over her useless GA card.

It was post-breakfast and pre-brunch just off Times Square, New York. A small crowd of tourists was gathered in lines round a set of five ATMs. Each line was disappointed. No-one had been able to get any cash since 9.30 that morning. Someone said that this was the third set they'd tried. Others painted similar stories and began digging out alternative cards to try at other banks. One of the people in the queue was Mira Lindsay, a reporter for CNN on her way in to start her shift. She tried it herself then went off with a frown on her forehead.

She got to the studios and began to make some calls. Not that she had to make too many; viewers were already calling the studio to complain and ask if CNN knew anything about GA technology problems. There was a pattern emerging. Mira had a word with her boss. There was a news round-up due shortly, and things were quiet. Maybe there was a filler here. Her boss put a call in to the emergency line that GA provided. There was nothing. Zero. No way of contact. This was starting to smell like a story.

In a vast tiled hall on a hill overlooking the San Bernardo hills in Southern California, Rick Juventus was sweating. Partly because he was the supervisor on the overnight watch in which every single bank computer had died at 6.15 am, and partly because the temperature was rising ten degrees every half hour. Whatever had knocked the computer out had taken out the computer-controlled air conditioning as well. He'd noted a whole lot of activity overnight – like there had been on three occasions over the past few months – when 50% of their servers had been pressed into action by a head office tech team. No-one would tell him what was going on. Just shut up and keep the machines running was his instruction.

Well last night had been a lulu. At peak times 98% of their server capacity had been in use. Until two hours ago. Then, literally, the lights had gone out. First the monitoring screens had disintegrated in front of his eyes, then all the hard drives had gone into action at once like they were going to take off. Then nothing. Lights out.

Rick had followed the laid-down Disaster Contingency Procedures and tried to call his boss, as well as get the back-up computers warmed up for recovery to yesterday night's position. But first the internal phones were out, so he had to use his cell. Then the standby boxes had gone crazy when they'd rebooted. He'd run out of options and was starting to shout at people, which he never did. His boss, Eduardo Castina, was none too pleased at being summoned in the middle of the night from his eight-bedroomed villa above the third fairway of the San Bernardo Country Club. Eduardo had a family christening down at La Jola beach and whatever screw-up had taken place in his absence had better be fixed by 10 am, or there would be trouble. He didn't know how much trouble.

Warwick Stanstead was alone in his office. It was 11 am Sunday. None of the computers worked. None of the landlines worked. His cell phone was permanently ringing with news of crashed systems from around the GA empire. The only thing that worked was an old fax machine and once people knew about it, there was a steady stream of confirmations that GA was no longer operational. His bank couldn't dispense money through its ATM network, no-one could administer an account over phone or Internet, and around $200 billion of the bank's money, representing its overnight position in the money markets, was inaccessible. All it would take was to be out of the market for a day and the rates to shift by a mere 50 basis points – and the bank would haemorrhage $1 billion. The money markets had been like a yo-yo recently. A bank that couldn't lend, couldn't borrow, couldn't manage its money, was no longer a bank. It was a mausoleum.

Warwick had foresworn pick-me-ups or downers this morning apart from coffee. He needed to be as clear headed as possible. But all he felt was crushing depression from the catastrophic mix of events and going cold turkey. He was doing the one thing he was good at: rallying his troops. He was shouting into his mobile phone demanding the immediate presence of every goddamn executive officer of the bank. He wanted them here, now, and manning the pumps. Hackers weren't going to stop GA!

Within minutes they were on their way. Aaron Schmidt was on a private chopper on his way from his ten-room 'cabin' in Martha's Vineyard. Marcus Nightingale was sweating behind the wheel of his new 911, careless of speed traps on the I90 on his way in from Westchester County. Abraham Kubala, just off the plane from Frankfurt, was having a cell-phone fight with his wife. She'd have to holiday on Long Island without him for the moment. Charlie Easterhouse was in a yellow cab bouncing down Madison. Charlie'd left his third wife calling her lawyer and threatening to join the ranks of his ex-wives after yet another ruined Sunday.

By mid afternoon, in a variety of off-duty clothes, most of the US based executives pitched up. As they stumbled in, one by one, Stanstead told them they'd been attacked by hackers and that they had to get their asses in gear and fight! It quickly became clear to each of them that they had nothing to fight with. This bank – like every other bank in the world – was completely and utterly dependent on its technology. GA no longer had technology, ergo it no longer was a bank. No-one could quite bring themselves to say this to Warwick. Each sat manfully in front of his dead screen and his dead phone and used his cell phone and the three tired fax machines to send useless instructions out and receive bewildered responses.

'What the fuck is happening!? What is going on?!'

Warwick had called Nick Trevino, his tech director seven times in the last three hours.

'Warwick, I told you. It's a counter-attack. Wiped us out.' He was in shock. 'They turned our stuff round and fired it back at us. And they used new viruses. We didn't have the shields for them. Some of the stuff is just unbelievable. I mean our circuits aren't just wiped clean or anything. They're melted.' There was awe in his voice.

'What do you mean they're melted?! What the fuck are you talking about?'

'They did something to the operating system that manages the hard drives. They've got lasers inside – you know, for reading the data and stuff? – well they jammed the lasers and the lasers burned holes.'

'Get new ones for Christ sakes! We have to get back up. If this bank's still out by tomorrow, then we're bust. Don't you fucking understand?!'

'Warwick, of course I damn well understand! You don't! We're dead! I'm sorry, this is going to take time, I keep telling you, there's nothing we can do. It'll take weeks.' The restraint was vanishing from Nick Trevino's voice. He'd been up all night, he'd never expected a counter-attack, and even if there had been one, they had systems that should have held out, right? He was living in a nightmare. He didn't know what had happened other than their own salvoes had looped back at them – with interest! – and took out every single item on GA's fixed asset register that had a chip in it.

'Then you're fucking fired! I'll get someone who can do something! That's what you're fucking paid for!'

'Fuck you, Stanstead!'

Trevino's line went dead. Warwick gazed at his phone. He'd been hung up on!

Pat Duschene came in, minus his buttoned-up suit. Pat was wearing Sunday clothes. Black leather skin-tight jeans, black leather tank top and three earrings. The tattoos on his bare arms were on display for the first time. Pat was past caring. He had dropped everything and come as he was, leaving a special and decidedly peeved friend to finish the intimate brunch alone. Warwick had stopped gazing at him in wonder. Pat asked, hands on hips.

'CNN are on the line. What do I tell them?'

'Tell them to go to hell! No, tell them we're undergoing a major maintenance programme and we're sorry for any inconvenience. Tell them what you like! And get the team together.'

Pat swaggered out, his leather clad rear swaying jauntily. He'd been around long enough to know when a game was over. And this one was truly at an end. Pat couldn't give a shit how he looked now. He stared down anyone who did a double-take of him in his true colours. If he was going down – and he should have been doing exactly that this afternoon, he thought ruefully – he was going down in style.

Stanstead heard them being ushered into the conference room. He walked through the adjoining door. There were four of them in a motley collection of clothes – except for Kubala who'd managed to find a suit. Typical. They were sat waiting for him to tell them what to do. Warwick didn't know. For the first time, he didn't have a plan. He'd not prepared for this. But old habits got him going.

'Let's do status. None of these work I guess?' He threw his arm round the wall at the dead video screens. Heads shook. 'Ok, so it's just us. Let's take this one at a time. I want a report on your region and your function. Now. Schmidt?'

'Canada and North America are out. Not a flicker. None of the ATMs, or systems are up. I've got guys phoning in on these,' he held up his cell phone, 'in blind panic. What do I tell them?'

He ignored him. 'Tell them it's being fixed. Kubala?'

'Same. I'm in cell-phone contact with my leads. The entire EMEA territory is gone. All back-up systems are inoperable. It's like a fucking nuclear strike.' Warwick's eyebrows rose a fraction. No-one used that language in his presence. And certainly not Mr control freak Kubala.

'Why?! Why no back-up? We spent millions of fucking dollars on self-standing back-up sites. That's what they're there for! They were completely separate from the operational systems. Surely to god some of them are running?'

'Nothing. Take our Michigan centre. Like everywhere, they took back-ups all the time. Kept 'em in secure bunkers off site. Then sent copies to our North America parallel data centre. It should have come up the moment the front-line systems went down. But whatever hit us, breezed right through the operational systems, tracked down the parallels and took them out too! We think they used the fibre links between the two systems. When the ops boys called through to the parallels, the viruses took over the lines. Maybe some of the back-up data is ok but we've got nothing to run them on. There isn't a single computer alive in the division. We're abso-fucking-lutely dead.'

'How long?! To get operational?'

Easterhouse was looking incredulous. 'To get operational?! Warwick, you're not listening! We may never get operational. Sure, we can buy new computers and maybe we can resurrect old software and data from the back up data centres, but this will take weeks, maybe months. And by then, as a bank, we're history!'

Warwick looked round the table. They all had the same expression: a mixture of shell-shock and rebellion. They'd given up hope and in doing so, there was nothing to play for and therefore nothing to worry about any more. They were looking into the abyss and had lost their fear for him. He couldn't accept this. One by one he went back round the table and one by one they came back with the same story. No-one could believe a hacker team had done this. It was beyond imagination.

Schmidt asked the burning question. 'Did any other bank get hit?'

'Only us. I've been calling around.' This was Kubala.

'You better not have been talking about what's going on here!' shouted Warwick.

'I didn't have to. They already knew. Does it matter, Warwick?'

Warwick's fist hit the table, jarring the cell phones.

'It matters to me! Now hear this. We are not dead yet! I want you all back out there and working. I want technicians in. I want systems up. I want us not playing fucking dead! You got that?! Now get back out there and fight, damn you!'

The men got up looking sullen and weary, and began their pointless mission.

FIFTY FIVE

It was midnight in New Delhi and Ted and Erin were still in front of their screens. The phone sat between them, its speaker light glowing red.

'Oscar, I'm just off the phone from the Tribune. My boss tells me the news services across the States are all saying the same thing: Global American is out of action. Dead. No-one at the bank is saying anything other than they're having maintenance problems and expect to be back up tomorrow. I'm getting the same message from the Internet news pages.'

Oscar sounded tired but content.

'That's what I see too Ted. I think you can safely say we did it. And I don't think they'll be back in action this side of Christmas, far less Monday.'

'What about our own guys?'

'No serious damage. Shivani tells me they lost about thousand or so customer units but all their central systems are holding up.'

'Unbelievable, Oscar. You and your team are just un-bloody-believable. But the news boys are also saying that a bunch of mad hackers have struck. They're speculating like crazy about the darknet stuff, and the FBI are already mounting a global search.'

'I know, I know. We've covered our traces, but once they find out how bad things are at GA they'll come after us with everything. They have guys who know their way round darknets as well as us. They'll know who's capable of a job like this. I hope you have a plan, Ted. Otherwise you and I are going to be sharing a cell in San Quentin for the rest of our naturals. Now I don't mind that a bit. You know what I think about you. But maybe your lady friend would have something to say?'

Erin laughed. 'Oscar, you're impossible. But you've got a point. You know the plan and we're ready to roll.'

Ted nodded. 'How's things at your end?'

'My end is just fine, dear. By the way, take a look at the twittersphere. #savethepeoplesbank is going viral. So do we light the touch paper?'

'No going back now. Let's ride, Lone Ranger!'

Erin reached out, caressed her mouse, aimed it at the 'send' icon and pressed. A blizzard of emails started to fan out across the Internet. At the same moment in the hot afternoon sunshine of Lower East Manhattan, Oscar unleashed a clever little set of instructions that attacked every Information Service Provider with more than a million users. Oscar wasn't intent on destruction, just on subverting, briefly, the home page of every ISP and putting his own full page advert on display.

Within seconds, nearly two thirds of the available Internet advertising space around the planet had been taken over to spell out the attractions of a certain named web site. Every Google 'search' would come back with just one result for 24 hours. To prevent either the web site going down because of too many hits or attacks from any authority, Oscar had replicated the site on all public ISPs and then carefully shared out the addresses of all the replica sites. In extremis he could copy sites from the darknet up onto the public providers.

Oscar turned his attention to the cell-phone networks. His fingers flashed out a new set of commands that hijacked their central servers. Texts started to flow across the networks until cell-phones world wide were receiving the message to check out Oscar's web site. Then he commandeered Twitter, or specifically the accounts with the highest number of followers. Suddenly Katy Perry, Justin Bieber, Lady Gaga and the President of the Unites States were urging their followers to check out #globalamericandirtytricks. He also retweeted using the #saveourpeoplesbank. Within seconds, the twittersphere was awash with frenzied comments about the behaviour of Global

American. Erin watched her screen fill with confirmations of their arrows going home.

'If this comes off, Ted, I'm going to ask Ramesh if he needs a new district manager. Alaska region. What do you think?'

'He won't know what's hit him. Let's go.'

He grabbed their cases and headed for the door. A car was waiting in front ready to take them to a different hotel. Just in case Joey put in another showing. A large number of dollars bought them anonymity – they hoped – at the front desk.

As the car swept them into the night, both were thinking the same thing. Monday was going to be an interesting day.

FIFTY SIX

On Monday morning, Ramesh Banerjee sat in the cool courtyard of his head office in Delhi preparing himself for the first day of his trial. He and his defence team had done everything they could to prepare for the event. They had waded through several inches of witness statements – all patently false but so hard to disprove – and several inches of defence documents and rebuttals. He shook his head. He knew that no matter what they did in court they would lose. This wasn't about justice or right or wrong. It was about politics, and he didn't play politics. Or rather he was no good at it.

It was 6.30 am. He had woken early as usual and decided to enjoy the fresh morning air before the heat sucked away the vitality. His lawyer Medha Sardar would not arrive until 8 o'clock. He was sipping tea and thinking fondly of his brave daughter Meera. She'd sounded strong and happy yesterday on the phone from her new district. The gamble had paid off sending the reporter and the bank woman with Meera. Even if it didn't make any difference except a kinder word in an American newspaper, Ramesh thought he'd got some of his message through. This was all he could hope for: that one man, or one woman would see the point of it all, would understand his impossible dream.

He was so proud of his daughter. So bright, so energetic and with the wonderful faith and hope of youth. He imagined he'd felt the same twenty five years ago. He could change the world then. But now he knew better. You could shift things a little, you could bend things, but finally one man couldn't change anything. Not even Buddha or the Christian prophet. Deep down inside men would always be driven by the basest of motives: power, sex, greed. Maybe they were all the same thing? He wondered how or if he was different? Was it all about power for him? Power to do good was just as potent a drug as power to do evil.

He put his glasses back on, picked up his book of poetry and began to immerse himself in the rhythms of the Sanskrit. He had deliberately avoided newspapers and radio and TV this morning to keep his mind clear.

Medha Sardar and CJ Kapoor burst in on his tranquillity at 7.30. Ramesh dragged himself back to the present, carefully placed his bookmark in the book it, shut it, and turned to see why they were so excited. CJ was waving a newspaper like a flag.

'Ramesh! Ramesh have you heard?'

Ramesh smiled at his lieutenant. It was unusual to see the calm and sober CJ Kapoor so agitated.

'I have heard the birds singing and the trees rustling in the morning breeze. Is that what you mean?'

CJ seemed impatient at his humour.

'No, no! It is in all the news. On the television. On the radio. And here in the newspaper. Look!' CJ placed the now somewhat mangled first edition of the Times of India in front of him on the table. On the front page, with banner headlines, the story was set out in sensational language. But when was it not, thought Ramesh.

Global American and World Bank in Evil Plot

The People's Bank of India has been the target of a nefarious attack by the largest bank in the Western world and the World Bank institution itself. In the hours of darkness, astounding revelations were made to a sleeping world. A series of emails and texts showered the globe with references to a web site containing incriminating evidence of double dealing and wickedness.

The Times can report that according to our legal team and technical experts the information contained on this startling web site may well be genuine. It contains mind-boggling transcripts and recordings of conversations between the Chief Executive of Global American bank and a series of high profilers, including the President of the World Bank himself. They show a catalogue of jiggery pokery and foul play over many months to bring down the People's Bank. It is clear – if the information is to be believed – that the Indian Government has been duped by a powerful cabal of Western gangsters and their henchmen.

In an amazing parallel incident, the whole of the banking system of Global American appears to have been bowled out by a gang of cyberspace hackers. Is it all coincidental on the same day that the People's Bank appears in court charged with embezzlement and corruption? The Times asks 'what is going on here?!' Stand by for more revelations of this astounding story in later editions.

'It is the same on the TV and the radio. The world has gone mad!'

CJ was sitting opposite Ramesh, jabbing his finger at the headlines. Ramesh read and re-read the column trying to make sense of it.

'Let us stay calm. Let us go inside and check this out on your screens CJ.'

'Let me tell you, Ramesh, our teams have been working round the clock to keep our systems going. It seems we have won!'

They passed clumps of bank employees chattering with excitement in the corridors, or gathered round their computer screens pointing out items to each other. Some however were slumped across their desks, exhausted beyond interest in the latest revelations. CJ led the way to his own table in a corner and began to pull up news screens.

'Look! Look! It is on every news channel. The same story.'

'I can hardly believe it!' said Ramesh to his colleagues. 'Go into one of these web sites they are talking about.'

CJ did and they clicked through Erin and Ted's simple menu, reading and listening to some of the damning material. CJ and Ramesh hardly spoke, but listened open-mouthed to the steadily mounting evidence of megalomania and corruption. The lawyer was bumping up and down in his seat in demented excitement, scribbling notes furiously and calling for hard copies to be run off.

'I almost feel sorry for him.'

'How can you, Ramesh?!'

'He was caught by the machine that drives us all along now.'

'Not us. We are different!' CJ was offended.

'Are we?'

'But it will kill this trial. It shows the Government taking bribes from this American bank. They cannot proceed now, can they?' asked CJ of the lawyer Sardar.

Sardar's arms were overflowing with bundles of print outs.

'It is wonderful! But we've still got to appear in court this morning. In one hour.'

Ramesh stood up. 'Come CJ. We will continue with our business. We must go to court. It is our duty.'

The three men gathered up their papers and walked through to the foyer. They opened the doors leading out onto the main street and were hit by a barrage of flashbulbs. The entire world's press seemed arrayed in front of them. A car was waiting for them but it was completely swamped by photographers and reporters. They fought their way through and climbed in. All round them were cries for comments amid volleys of shutter clicks.

Their car eased through the crowd and crawled forward till they reached the Chandni Chowk. They honked their way across the busy cross-roads and turned right along the Chowk. At the T junction opposite the Red Fort, they forced their way through the red-light jumpers and the whistle-blowing policemen and turned south. All they had to do was follow the Netaji Subhash Marg until it gave way to the Bahadur Shah Zafar Marg. The Supreme Court sat in on the right. It should have been a journey of 15 minutes, perhaps half an hour, if the traffic was thick.

The traffic was relatively free-moving as far as the Delhi Gate but Ramesh noticed a growing number of people on either side of the roads. They were all heading south. They had reached the intersection of the Vikas Marg and the Bahadur Shah Zafar Marg when they noticed that the streams of people were flowing together and forming a tighter and tighter crowd. Within a hundred yards the crowd had spilled across the road, and forward movement for all vehicles had stopped. Still more people poured through. Up ahead a noise was gathering like a rhythmic chanting.

Policemen were vainly floundering about, blowing whistles and trying to push the people back on to the side of the roads. Their batons flailed uselessly. All that happened was the people streamed either side of the islands of policeman leaving them stranded and ineffectual. Ramesh rolled his window down and asked a sweating officer what was happening.

'Please to stay in your car. We do not know what is happening. The court is completely surrounded. We are not coping yet with the crowd.'

'But what is the noise? What are they saying?'

'It is just a bunch of mad people. Do not pay them mind.'

'But we have to get to the court. We have a trial today.'

The policeman took a closer interest in them. He peered into the car and inspected Ramesh's face in the front seat. Then he peered at the two men in the back.

'Maybe you should be walking to the court? But I am not thinking you will get through today. I do not think the judges even will be able to get through.'

Ramesh and his men climbed out of the car and pressed forward into the crowd. Suddenly there were cries about them.

'Look! It is him! It is Ramesh Banerjee!

'Sir, Sir! We are here for you!

'Let him through! Let Ramesh through!'

A phalanx of self appointed guardians formed in front and to the side of Ramesh and his party and began to cut a swathe through the mass of people. Their shouts cleaved a path like a hot poker pushing steadily into pat of ghee. As they progressed, the crowd either side picked up the news and a steady chanting began.

'Ramesh, Ramesh, Ramesh!'

'My goodness, they are going to make you Emperor I think,' shouted CJ in wonder. He smiled at the crowd to show them he was friendly.

'Or lynch me,' shouted Ramesh back at him.

Steadily they moved on and the top cornices of the Supreme Court building could now be seen above the crowd. The chanting of the crowd immediately around them had changed to tie in with the better established chorus at the centre of the mass. Now they could make out the words.

> 'Bank for the poor!
> Bank for the poor!
> Don't let them kill
> The bank for the poor!'

FIFTY SEVEN

Round and round went the simple rhyme like a temple chant. Banners grew in size and number with the noise and the chanting. Yet there was no bad mood about the crowd. It was festive. People were wearing flowers and carrying children on their shoulders. They were rough people, poor people mainly, but here and there was a well dressed Indian and the odd Westerner. Ramesh moved forward in an increasing daze. The day was growing crazier by the hour. But something in his heart was lifting and lightening. He smiled and waved and called his thanks as they made their triumphal progress.

Without warning they found themselves pressed up against waist-high metal barriers that marked the edge of the crowd's sway. Beyond was an open space with some figures planted on the steps leading up to the court. Flustered policemen were holding tight to the barriers, keeping them from being tipped over. Ramesh worked to the front.

'I am in court this morning officer!' He had to shout. 'I must get through, please.'

'Who are you?!' shouted back the policeman,

Ramesh felt a little silly in the circumstances. 'I am Ramesh Banerjee.'

The policeman called to a sub-inspector who was directing affairs. The sub-inspector summoned a harassed inspector who demanded proof of Ramesh's identity. A barrier was pulled back and one by one the three men were let through. As they walked towards the steps and what looked like a camera crew, a shout went up like thunder behind them. The roar of support went on for long seconds and Ramesh wondered what he had let loose. A young Indian woman was running towards him. His day was complete.

'Meera! What are you doing here?!'

'Come to support my father!' She gained another roar from the crowd as she hugged him and was hugged back.

'Was this your doing, daughter? I cannot approve of mob rule you know.'

The light in his eyes belied his words.

'Not me. Your customers'. Come and meet the woman who started this.'

They moved hand in hand towards the camera. It was being held by one man and being directed by another tall westerner with a microphone in his hand. A white woman stood beside him. Alongside her was an Indian woman with the fold of her sari pulled up over her hair. Her arms were wrapped round a little girl who stood in front of her. Both had the same big serious eyes. The white people's faces came into focus, but they looked different these two.

Ted Saddler was thinner and browner and had a large plaster on his head; Erin Wishart looked ten years younger and happier. And her hair was different. Was she using henna? What had he done? What had they done? As they got within range he could hear Ted speaking into the microphone. He was wearing headphones.

'I'm now about to speak to Ramesh Banerjee the Chief Executive Officer of the People's Bank.' Ted held out his hand and shook Ramesh's.

'Mr Banerjee, are you aware of the sensational overnight revelations about the plot to close down your bank?'

'I have read some of this in the papers and seen the news.'

'And what would you like to say about it, sir?'

Ramesh gave himself a second or two to think. 'I would like to say how sorry I am for the misguided man who has been trying to close me down.'

Ted looked surprised. 'You mean Warwick Stanstead, the CEO of Global American. The man who has apparently tried every dirty trick in the book to stop you?'

'If the reports are accurate, yes. It is a great tragedy when a man is driven to such lengths. It is the curse of our age. None of us starts out wanting to be more than we are. The pressures in our society have many harmful effects, and some of us fare worse than others because of flaws in our make-up.'

'A generous interpretation sir. But what do you think these revelations mean for the trial today? Do you think the Indian government can possibly press ahead under the circumstances?'

'That is not for me to say. We are here to defend ourselves in a court of law. If these so–called revelations provide us with more evidence to defend ourselves then that is good. But forgive me, we do not want to keep the judges waiting.'

'One last question sir. Did you organise these crowds of supporters today?'

Ramesh turned round and looked at the multitude packing the roads and stretching as far as he could see. The camera swung with him to show the world. Then it cut back to a close-up of the wonder on Ramesh's face.

'No, I did not. I am astonished. I don't really know who they are.'

'I can say who they are.'

Meera stepped into the camera angle and held her father's arm.

'They are the customers of my father's bank. They are the poor people of India. The ones that my father's bank has helped. This woman,' she tugged a shy Anila into the shot, 'is the villager who started it all. She is a customer of our bank and she tweeted that she was going to Delhi to support my father and telling them they should do the same.'

'What is your name?'

Ted held the microphone out to Anila and smiled over the top of it. Erin smiled behind him and waved her arms in encouragement.

'My name is Anila Jhabvala.'

'Why did you organise this Anila?'

Meera translated to make sure she'd understood it.

Anila looked panic-stricken for a moment, but then she responded steadily and clearly.

'I did not organise this. I sent a tweet on the Internet,' she said with a mix of embarrassment and pride. 'I told everyone I was going to Delhi to show my support. I did it for this good man.'

'Why is he a good man?'

'He saved me. He saved all of us.'

The camera swung round to follow her hand and take in the crowd. Then it panned back for a close-up on Anila and her daughter.

'No-one else would help us. He gave us...' she turned to Meera and asked for the English word. 'He gave us dignity...' She smiled down on her daughter and stroked her upturned face. '...and hope.'

Her face shone with simple conviction. It was to be the definitive news shot of the day. It would end up on nearly every channel, web site, YouTube clip and newspaper across the globe. Ted knew a headline grabbing sound-bite when he heard it. He thanked her and turned the camera on himself.

'Dignity is a word you don't hear much around big corporations these days. And certainly those of you who've read or listened to the material on the world's most famous web site – since yesterday – won't associate dignity with what's been happening lately at Global American and the World Bank itself.'

He paused, looking for the words. 'I started as a sceptic about this People's Bank. A few weeks ago I was writing about them as if they were robbing the poorest of the poor. Nothing gives me greater pleasure than to say I was wrong.'

The camera lens moved closer for a full face shot.

'I've been out to a village. A dirt-poor village in the middle of a man-made desert. I met some of the people there. In particular I met one young woman – you just heard her.' He smiled to Anila off camera. 'Anila and her friends showed me a level of courage and determination that shamed me for making so little of the talents and opportunities I've had in the west.'

'I've also spent time with the managers and the staff of this bank. And I'm standing here today in front of a crowd of maybe a half a million customers of this bank. Do they look to you like people that have been robbed?'

He let the camera pan the sea of smiling faces.

'Me neither. Nor do I think that the prosecution team, in this building behind me, will find any evidence for any of their charges now.

'What we have to ask ourselves is what we can learn from this sorry story. Maybe Ramesh Banerjee, the man we just interviewed, had it about right: the curse of our age is losing our perspective. Being blinded by money or power – or the possessions they bring – so that we forget what's really important. So that the soul dries up.'

The camera held Ted's burning gaze for a long, silent three seconds, then panned back to show him against the massed and festive crowd.

'It's not too late. For any of us.' He paused. 'The Tribune will be keeping you up to date with events as they unfold here in New Delhi and in New York. This is Ted Saddler, New York Tribune, signing off.'

In his ears as the shot was cut, came the voice of Stan Coleman.

'Getting religion, Ted? Nice job. Stick with this and we've got another Pulitzer.'

Ted replied into the throat mike. 'You weren't listening Stan. That's where I went off the rails before.'

FIFTY EIGHT

Eight hours later, as dawn swept over Manhattan, Warwick Stanstead sat at his desk without a friend in the world. Technicians had worked through the night to get a rudimentary phone and computer system up and running using tablets and laptops linked by off-the-shelf WiFi packs. Warwick had been using the phone to call in favours and make appeals to a shocked board of directors and senior figures in the establishment. The President of the World Bank was not taking his calls; not taking any calls. As news of the revelations on the web site reverberated, the World Bank was effectively incommunicado.

Warwick got up and moved to the open balcony door, to watch the yellow light creep over the peaks and dip into the gulleys. The air conditioning was still out and the cool air was welcome. But neither the steadily increasing noise of the traffic heading into the city, nor the warm strokes of the sun, were getting through to him. In his mind he was running again. But this time he could see what he was running from. Having seen some of the material beforehand, Warwick was less minded to plough through it again.

His body was on fire, aching and shivering. The pain was deep in the bones. Hot metal had replaced the marrow. There was no respite, no matter how much Tylenol he swallowed. He lost count of the unproductive retching in his washroom. Hardest to take were the bouts of sneezing. It was like the worst hay fever; thirty, forty, countless sneezes that wracked his whole body and left him trembling and exhausted on the floor of his office. He kept dragging himself onto his feet, and pouring water down his throat. But nothing quenched the agony or the all consuming need for just one big hit of smack. Just one would do it. Then he could cope. He could get through this and then take the cure.

But something in him knew he had to take the punishment. If he could get through withdrawal he could get through the financial disaster. It's how he succeeded. It's who he was. Suck it up!

Between bouts of pain he rounded up and deployed his legal forces. They were rousing senior figures in the justice system to get court orders to ban the web site and sue the backside off the Tribune. That goddamn broadcast from Delhi seemed to be in a loop on all channels. He wanted to wipe the smug look off that reporter's face; him and Miss Erin fucking Wishart!

He had his PR team putting out the line that the web site lies were part of the vicious hacking attack that had brought down the bank. The web site was muck and deception, and a deliberate and vile attempt to shatter both Warwick's image and that of the bank. But the feedback was that the news services weren't buying the bank's version. Even if they did, it was still such a horrible story that the mud would never lift.

'Warwick?'

He looked up and saw Charlie Easterhouse standing in the doorway that led into the conference room. He'd come in without knocking. Charlie looked as tired as death. His fat body hung like a sack of potatoes from a frame that was bowed down with care and despondency. Behind were the others.

'Warwick, we want to meet with you.' It wasn't a request.

Easterhouse turned and shuffled back down the short corridor. Warwick noted that they didn't expect him not to comply. He gritted his teeth and forced himself erect. His whole body shook and swayed. Sweat broke on his brow and poured down his back. For a moment he thought he'd pass out. Then it passed. He was left weak. He bit his knuckle to stop himself screaming with the pain.

He began to put one foot in front of the other and shambled through to the conference room. He took up his usual seat at

313

the end of the oval table. Cool air from the balcony played over him. He studied them. Easterhouse, Schmidt, Nightingale and Kubala. The four executives looked exhausted to the point of keeling over. How must he look? They sat slumped in their chairs looking at him with something approaching surprise and curiosity. Well, he hadn't fallen over yet, and he wasn't about to let this bunch of spineless bastards see him on his knees.

'Give me an update.' He barked. The men stared at him as though they found it funny. 'I said let's go. Where have we got to? Is this bank starting up today or not?!'

The men looked at each other, then Charlie spoke. It was a tired voice but one with an edge to it.

'Warwick, this bank is fucked. There is nothing – I mean not a damned thing – that can be done to breathe life into this organisation.' He waved Warwick quiet to pre-empt an outburst. 'But that's not why we're here. We want simple answers. Have you seen this web site?'

'Yeah, it's shit! Absolute shit! This hacking crew have done a real job on us.'

'Warwick, didn't you see the report from Delhi? Erin Wishart leading the opposition?! Aaron, have we got any juice?' Aaron Schmidt was sitting with a portable computer in his lap. 'Enough.' He directed a cordless mouse at the screen on the wall. It came to life and Schmidt fingered the keyboard to bring up on the wall screen the web site itself.

'We want to talk about this.'

'Well I don't! This is all shit and I'm not going to waste my time on this or you!'

'Warwick, you'd better. You'd just fucking better waste some fucking time on this!'

Kubala's voice was a shout. It was full of an anger Warwick had never suspected from him. Warwick waved a hand and slouched in his seat. They began to pace through the menu, opening up documents and recordings. They dealt first with the attacks on the People's Bank. The chronology led from the earliest efforts of Warwick to close it down, through to conversations with Nick Trevino during the onslaughts on their rival.

'So this wasn't just any old bunch of hackers, was it Warwick? This was the People's Bank fighting back?' asked Charlie quietly.

Warwick had had enough. He was seething. The craving was devouring him alive.

'What the fuck else did you expect me to do? Don't tell me you didn't know we were going on the offensive? I told you yellow-bellied scum a year ago that this bank was eating our lunch!'

Kubala's fine black features were twisting with anger. 'Mister, if you call me a name one more time, so help me!'

'Leave it, Abe.'

Charlie leaned over to motion him down. His voice began to take on the fury that he felt. The loss of all those years defending this man. The family life he'd given up.

'Abraham's right though. We're tired of the bully-boy stuff, Warwick, so just cut it out. What we're trying to get at here is the truth, so we know what the hell we do next. And it seems that the truth is, there was no hacking crew out there. Not till you started the war! You never thought they'd hit back did you?' he asked ruminatively.

'Just like us, Warwick!' Marcus Nightingale was pointing at him, accusing, angered beyond words. His heavy face was livid and blotchy.

Schmidt moved them on to the next topic. It was the Yeardon dossier. The atmosphere had long shifted from despair and incredulity to outrage. Warwick wasn't hearing them. He had pulled himself into a ball upright in his chair and was staring into his own small hell. They were half way through the tape recordings when Kubala got up and walked over to Warwick and stuck his face an inch away from the other's.

'You little shit! You're not even listening to us! You've screwed this bank. You've ruined all of us! We're finished, and we deserve to be, for letting you get away with this. Erin Wishart's got more balls than all of us put together! I'm ashamed of myself. I'm ashamed for all of us. We're going to go down with you, Stanstead, and we deserve to.'

Warwick broke from his trance. Rage distorted his face.

'Get your greasy black face out of mine!'

He pushed Kubala back and uncurled from his chair. He stood at the end of the table, crouched like he was ready to fight them. It brought the others to their feet. He snarled at them.

'I'm not listening to any more of this spineless shit. None of you had the guts to face up to me before. And now when it gets tough you're wetting your fucking pants! Look at you! A bunch of second rate, little shits with fancy houses in the Hamptons, and fancy cars, and fancy expense accounts, and fancy kids at fancy schools. You and your fancy little wives – *white* wives – would have been nothing, nothing without me! I made you. I handed out those big fat bonuses. And now you're going to have give it all back. You'll be back to nothing. Back to being jellyfish! You make me vomit!'

Stanstead's face was contorted with contempt. The tableau stayed frozen for what seemed like a minute. Kubala straightened up, looked across at Nightingale and nodded. The two men moved forward and grabbed Stanstead by the upper arms. Behind them, the other two unfroze and stepped forward. They bent and snatched him by the knees and lower leg. They lifted, and the stunned figure of Warwick Stanstead began to wriggle.

'Put me down you motherfuckers! What the fuck is this?!'

He was kicking and tossing his body around, but the four men held him tightly. They stumbled onto the balcony. Stanstead was ranting and swearing as he realised what was happening. He threw himself even harder against the restraints, but these men were strengthened by shame and wrath.

They were near the edge of the balcony. They thrust his head out over the parapet. His shoulders wriggled on the guard rail. Suddenly Warwick's body slumped, and for a moment, taken by surprise, the men almost dropped him. Then the two front men hoisted him up and pushed his upper body out into space. Stanstead's hands gripped the rail and his eyes were staring, but not at them.

'I can't do this,' said Abraham Kubala.

'Me neither,' replied Charlie Easterhouse.

The men pulled in Stanstead's limp body and laid him gently down on the soft grass. They stepped back, staring at their fallen leader. Stanstead's eyes flickered and cleared. He took a deep shuddering breath and got to his knees. Then with all his remaining strength, and fighting the terrible gravity of his leaden limbs, he battled to his feet. He glared at them, eyes full of derision. He wiped the spittle from his mouth.

'True to the last. All of you. You didn't even have the guts to do this, did you.'

He pointed his finger at each one of their slumped chests in turn.

'It was always me, wasn't it. I had to wipe your asses. I had to take all the risks. Right?! Well this is how you do it.'

He turned, took hold of the rail and with his former athlete's skill, leapt up and balanced with a foot on either side of the rail. He raised his arms high above his head, brought his trailing foot over to the outside, and steadied himself. The men behind were glued.

He bent his knees slightly, then sprung forward in a perfectly executed swallow dive. The four men rushed to the rail and looked down. They saw his dive position change. Saw his limbs buffeted by the increasing wind of his descent. Then his body took a new shape. He began to make pumping movements with its arms and legs. In his mind, Warwick Stanstead wasn't falling, he was running.

FIFTY NINE

A week later and the small plane roared down the runway and tipped up into the air. The great sprawl of Delhi eddied below them and was gone. They banked and turned south and Ted turned to Erin and asked,

'Why didn't we travel like this before?'

'Because Meera thought it would be good for our pampered Western souls?'

They landed at Bhopal airport and with their newfound insouciance at travelling in India, batted off the beggars and touts. Outside, waving from the running board of her battered Land Rover, stood Meera. They embraced and were off down the road towards Chandapur in a buzz of excited conversation, catching up on events since the demonstration a week ago.

'How's Anila?' Erin was the first to ask. 'Did the paperwork do the trick?'

'You will soon see. Ask her yourself.' Meera smiled at her in her driver's mirror.

Ted broke in, 'But we're still worried about Oscar. We've heard nothing since the big night.'

'Isn't he just lying low? Didn't you say the FBI was going to take some persuading?' Meera asked.

'That might be it. I wouldn't blame him for steering clear till things settled down some. Joey swears on his mother's life that they hadn't found him, far less harmed him.'

'Not that we believe any of Joey's claims about having a mother,' called out Erin from the back.

'Joey?' asked Meera.

'Joey Kutzov. Stanstead's hit man.' He turned to Erin. 'But he did deliver Veronica Yeardon.'

'Only to save his lizard skin.'

This time there was no pretence about fetching water. The women squatted on their heels under the neem trees in small groups, knees tenting their saris. They were chattering excitedly. There was much to be excited about. First there had been the huge row in front of Anila's hut a week ago. That horrible mother and her lazy son had met their match in Anila's new friend from the bank. They had been left spluttering in the dust as Anila and her daughter had sailed off to Delhi in the wonderful jeep. Anila's mother had simply barricaded herself inside the hut till the pair of them were hoarse shouting at her closed front door. They'd stomped off to stay with the only friend they had in the village – a distant relative – to wait for Anila to come back.

And the next thing, there is Anila Jhabvala and her daughter on television! What was happening to the world? The whole village had shut down for the day until everyone had a chance to see the hourly news shows with Anila telling the whole country about this wonderful bank of hers. Her mother-in-law and sweaty husband had hardly known what to do. Anila's fame was burning a hole in the fat husband's soul. But Anila's importance meant that she had to have even more money than they thought. Anger and avarice wrestled for control.

Two days later everyone saw the jeep coming from miles away, and the mother and son took up position outside Anila's hut, standing and holding hands. The jeep bounced up the lane and rocked to a halt sending a last cloud of dust over the two waiting figures. Meera climbed out, holding a briefcase, and walked confidently round to meet the Jhabvalas. Anila followed, sheltering behind Meera's upright figure. Aastha sat in the car to watch. From both ends of the lane, villagers began to crowd round to see the fun.

Dilip's mother was the first to speak.

'So you have come back, have you. With your fancy car and your important friend.'

319

Dilip jabbed his finger at Anila. '– and you think you are important now too, don't you, wife of mine!'

Meera put her arm round Anila's shoulders, and replied.

'But Mr Jhabvala, Anila tells me you divorced her. You threw her and her daughter out of your home.'

'Well, that was to teach her a lesson. I did not officially divorce her. She still belongs to me.'

'I see, then you must listen to what we have to say.'

Dilip's mother raised an accusatory finger to Anila 'No, we are not listening to what you have to say. Who are you anyway, miss high and mighty. Our business is with that person there!'

Meera moved her body in front of Anila.

'I am Anila's lawyer, and I think you had better listen to what I have to say.'

That stilled them. It was of course an embellishment; her degree was in business law and she wasn't actually a practising lawyer. But it held enough of the truth for Meera to sound convincing. Looks of unease were filling their faces. Meera grabbed the initiative. From inside her briefcase she drew out a slim sheaf of papers. She separated them into two sets and gave one set to Anila. She took two steps towards the pair, causing them to flinch. She held out the papers.

'This is a legal injunction drawn up by the magistrate's court in New Delhi. It has authority here. It tells you that you must leave Anila Devi, formerly Anila Jhabvala, alone. That you must not touch her or her daughter or her mother and that you must not harass her or harangue her. That means you are not allowed to come near her or shout at her, do you understand?'

She went on before the woman exploded. Dilip was grabbing his mother's arm with both hands in his agitation.

'If you seek to harm her or even look at her in a bad way, she will call the police. Anila, show them your satellite phone.'

Anila dug into her shoulder bag and with some embarrassment, pulled out a smart cell phone and waved it at the stunned pair. Meera continued. 'You saw that I was able to get the police here before? And you saw what happened to the old money lender and his wife?' She left the threat hanging.

But the old woman wasn't finished that easily.

'This is my son's lawful wife. She must do as she is told, as his wife. What about our money? What about our dowry? He has a right to his money.'

Meera shuffled through the papers and thrust them into the woman's unwilling hands.

'You will also see here that Anila has filed for divorce. Properly this time. She has good grounds; desertion and grievous bodily harm to start with. You may of course contest this, but it will only prolong this sad business and cost you a great deal of money in lawyers' fees. My bank will pay all Anila's. If however you accept the inevitable then you will receive all the remaining dowry money that you are owed. But not until Anila's divorce has come through.'

The pair grabbed the papers and rifled through them. They looked very official with lots of red stamps on headed notepaper.

'And don't think you can just tear them up. That is an official copy. We have the originals.'

The mother and son stepped back several paces and a furious but indistinct argument broke out. Mother seemed to be gaining the upper hand. She led her sullen offspring back to stand in front of Meera and Anila. Cunning had stolen onto her old face. She waved the papers.

'We do not trust you. And we do not know if these are proper legal papers. We will find out. But if they are, there is interest due on the outstanding amount. And what about recompense to my son? He has been left without a wife or a daughter. It is only right that his wealthy wife makes some recompense for his cruel loss.'

Meera had clearly been expecting this move. 'We will pay five per cent per annum for the three years the so-called debt has been outstanding.'

'Compound!' demanded the woman.

Meera sighed, 'Compound. But there will be no recompense. Not unless you want me to go back to the courts and seek recompense for Anila. For all the years of mistreatment. It would probably mean that your son would be arrested and have to stay in prison till his trial came up. One of those nice overcrowded prisons in Bhopal. And you know how clumsy our policemen can be when they arrest someone. And they might – just might – have to arrest you too for harassment of Anila and her mother. What do you think?' she asked calmly.

The pair seemed to deflate in front of them. Meera almost felt sorry for them. Almost. The woman grabbed her wide-eyed son and hauled him past his former wife and her clever lawyer. They barged their way through the now-laughing and crowing crowd.

SIXTY

That had been four days ago, and now there was more excitement. The bank lady had returned with the beautiful Scottish woman and the big American. Both of them had been on the television with Anila. They walked in procession from her hut, Anila holding Meera's hand and Ted and Erin behind her. The boy, Ranil, had shown up and was proudly sporting the Yankees T shirt and baseball cap Ted had had FedExed to Delhi. He was holding the big American's hand and jabbering excitedly at him.

Their arrival stilled the waiting women, like the approach of a man sends silence into a tree full of birds. Anila kept telling herself that this was the same group she'd spoken to just a few weeks ago, telling them of the amazing first trip to Delhi to seek a loan. That nothing had changed. But everything had! She took up position under the tree where a space had been left for her and her companions. The big American went off and sat at the back of the group so as not to disturb the women too much. Just as well; the ones nearest him were casting eyes at him and giggling among themselves. The boy joined him.

Meera and Erin sat down leaving Anila standing in front of her. This was how they'd planned it. Anila looked round the womenfolk and caught the eye of Leena and Divya and was encouraged by their smiles. She took a deep breath and was about to began when Sandip called out.

'Look, it is the famous film star! Can we all have your autograph, Anila?'

The women broke into laughter and applause. It was just what they'd all wanted to say. Cries of well done and congratulations echoed round the little square. When they had quietened, a flushed Anila faced them again.

'Thank you. I am not here for autographs. I told you that the bank would send someone soon. To look after our loans and maybe see if they could help other women. Well as you know, the bank has kept its promise. Meera Banerjee came all the way from Delhi and helped us get our money back from that thief of a money lender.'

Meera made a steeple with her hands and bowed to the women. The applause burst out again, and more chattering and smiles. Anila looked embarrassed and thought she would never get to say what she wanted at this rate.

'Those of you who saw her on the television will know that Meera's father is the Chief of the People's Bank. But today, she is here in her own right as the bank's district manager, and she has come back to talk to you about the bank. And you can ask her questions.'

Anila felt weak, and gladly stepped into the shadow of the tree and took up the seat vacated by Meera.

'Well done Anila. That was just right,' whispered Meera as she took Anila's place in front of the women. If she was nervous it didn't show. But there was no hint of arrogance either.

'Good morning, ladies. I have come to tell you about the People's Bank and what we are going to do here for Anila and her two friends whom we gave loans to. I also want to talk to the cooperative that Anila set up. And I am very happy to talk to anyone who needs some help with money.'

'That is everyone here!' called out Sandip to much laughter.

Meera launched into a description of how her bank worked, keeping the ideas simple but not hiding anything. She told them about the principles of micro-credit and got much shaking of heads in agreement. She told them why the bank preferred to work with women and the heads shook even more vigorously with many side comments between the women. At the end of it

324

there were several questions from the crowd culminating in the key one from the irrepressible Sandip:

'This is all very fine, and sounds simply terrific. But what happens now? Are you going to stay here? Who will look after us if we want to use your bank?'

Meera smiled and turned and asked Anila something. Anila got up and stood shyly beside her. Meera continued.

'I am not going to stay here. I will be based in Sagar looking after the whole district, but I will visit here every two or three weeks. However we will leave a representative of the bank here.'

She reached out and touched Anila on the shoulder.

'I am very pleased to tell you that Anila Jhabvala – sorry, Anila Devi – has agreed to be the village representative for the bank.'

There was a roar and an outbreak of dizzying clapping. Meera and Anila explained the exciting future: a bank in the village with internet access for all. It would bring new ideas and new teaching methods and opportunities to pull themselves out of the mire of poverty.

The crowd of women tried the new ideas from every angle. There was excitement and incredulity among them as they broke up and went their way. Some of the women came up to Meera and asked if they could talk with her about loans.

Erin and Ted left them to it, and walked to the edge of the village. They stood gazing out over the dried fields and were enveloped in the thrumming of the insects.

'Why are you crying?'

'My lenses. You know what the dust's like around here.' She dabbed at her eyes.

'I'm happy too. For Anila. I don't think I've ever felt anyone so deserved to have good things happen to her.'

They were quiet for a while, each reluctant to broach the next question.

'Well that pretty well wraps things up, Ted Saddler. What are you going to do now?'

Ted had been thinking hard about just this. He wanted to tell her that he didn't care what he did next as long as it was near her. But he was scared. Like a kid. Scared she'd laugh at him and tell him he was too old and fat and useless. That the intimate outpourings on the roof and the kiss in her hotel room had been born of the moment, like a war time affair, but not so grand, and this war was over.

He looked round at the torn earth and the distant trees and wiped the sweat from his brow. He pulled up his trousers and cinched his belt another notch. He'd ducked the question already from Erin in the last few bewildering days. It had been easy to shelter behind the round of constant interviews and reports as the trial collapsed and the Indian government itself began to disintegrate.

There had also been the nagging 24 hours after finding a snivelling Joey Kutzov waiting for them in the lobby of their hotel. Joey knew when a game was up and was offering Warwick's head in exchange for his own, though by then it was a little irrelevant. The news of Stanstead's suicide was blazing across all channels. But Joey's surrender was just in time for Veronica Yeardon. The FBI had found her alive – just – in a log cabin deep in the Everglades guarded by two of Joey's goons.

Ted blew his nose. In some ways, the answer to Erin's question had become easier. She had been spending more and more time with Ramesh and his colleagues in the aftermath of the court order. It had been little surprise to hear her declare her intent to take a marketing role in the People's Bank. At Meera's prompting she'd even tried on a sari for dinner at the hotel with Ted and Ramesh. The growing line of red in her hair only added to the exotic sense of her. Ted had never seen her look better, and saw heads turn as she walked into the restaurant.

So he'd planned to save up his answer for the final fleeting moment in the departure terminal. Save it so that when he told her, there wouldn't be time enough to debate it or mull it over.

He'd just say it, check her reaction and then get on the plane. After that would depend on her. He could coat his answer in maybes and easily change his mind when he got back to New York. He didn't want to be pressed into it yet, so he was evasive.

'Well, I'm taking a trip out to Denver. Go visit the folks and my brother. Then,' he took a big breath, 'call me crazy, but I thought maybe I'd ask Stan if I could take a sabbatical, make a start on that book. I've got plenty of new material.' His hand swept the scenery and encompassed their last few weeks.

'I think you should, Ted Saddler. I think that's exactly what you should do.'

He didn't know how to take that. But it didn't sound like an offer of any sort. He let it go at that and brushed a fly from his face and tried to count his blessings.

SIXTY ONE

The light was sending a glare across the screen of his laptop, and Ted got up to pull down the blind. It was late morning and the December sun had finally snuck round and was reflecting off the snow that lay in a 200 foot carpet from the condos up to the tree-line. He was glad he'd paid the extra for an apartment with the spare room and the view up the mountain. Even though it entirely blew his half of the money from the sale of the New York apartment.

Away to the right he could see the quad-lift loaded with skiers, rising up through the bare aspens and plunging into the firs. Discipline, he told himself, discipline. Two hundred more words then he could quit and catch the gondola up to Lion's Way. He'd stick to the front runs now. The snow on Avanti was perfect; a mogul field was maturing nicely down the left hand side of the long black run. His knees still ached from the weekend, but some of the skill was coming back, if not the elasticity. The back bowls would be scored to pieces by now, but if it snowed again tonight, he'd reverse his day and catch the early morning powder in China Bowl.

He turned back and seated himself at his desk. He patted the small but growing pile of paper on his left. It wasn't bad for four months' work; more important, it was fresh. He'd walked back into his old apartment and taken one look at the yellowing mounds of verbiage on his desk and knew what he had to do. The Great American novel was ditched for the inside story of the downfall of Stanstead's bank. He reached out and fingered the well-worn spine of Ramesh's gift to him. His own opus was never going to be Passage to India, but with luck it might make a few folk think.

Stan had already fixed him up with an agent who was in the final throes of a publishers' auction. The book wasn't finished yet but Spielberg had already taken an option on the film rights. The trade was referring to it as the antidote to The Wolf of Wall Street.

All he needed was a snappy title; something better than his working label of *Cowboys and Indians*. But he'd learned not to get stalled on stuff that didn't matter.

As he settled his fingers on the keys, a glowing email prompt caught his eye. Erin sometimes emailed him. And Anila too. She loved practising her English by dropping him news of village life. He recalled with a smile her first, stuttering text, full of thanks and relief that Meera had bought off Anila's foul husband and mother-in-law. She had a new life.

He'd even heard from Veronica Yeardon. Once pal Joey learned about his boss's swallow dive, he'd been quick to plea-bargain for his own neck. Veronica's emails were very persistent about having him visit her in the Spring; check out the cherry blossom. The only one he hadn't heard from was Oscar. And he wondered how he'd deal with that in the book. He'd just have to make up an ending. Hero or villain?

He recalled a conversation with Erin as they flew down to Bhopal after a week of silence from Oscar and his gang:

'It was like putting a bunch of safe crackers inside a bank vault, with the keys,' she was saying.

'I don't believe it. Won't believe it,' he said.

Erin raised her eyebrows. Ted continued.

'They'd be found out. Wouldn't they? I mean when they get the bank up and running again?'

Erin mused. 'Depends how closely they can reconcile the positions before and after. It's almost impossible to do an audit trail if you don't have records for a huge chunk of time. The market moves, deposits come and go, deals are half way through being struck, interbank transfers are interrupted. If I were the regulators and auditors I'd be happy to get within – let's think

– 1%? – of the last known position. And let's say the bank had minimum $100 Billion in free money swilling about. That would be $1billion to play with – so to speak.'

Ted stared at her. 'Mother of God…'

He clicked on the screen prompt, and retrieved the message. He felt a familiar pang. It hurled him back five eventful months. This time he didn't hesitate to open and read it.

I've just heard from Oscar!!! Take a look at the attached and tell me what I should do!

–Diogenes –

Dearest Erin – how are my goldfish? I bet you've been wondering when this old carcass of mine would wash up and in how many pieces? Well at least I hope you've missed me! And how is that reprobate Ted? I don't see his words of wisdom in the Trib these days. Not that we get the papers much, where we are (wink, wink). Anyway darling, remember that favor you promised me? I want to call it in. It won't cost you a thing and in fact you might earn a dollar or two out of it (if you need it?). The thing is, I need some advice. Some investment advice. Why don't you email me with an address I can send an air ticket to and you could come visit us here, first class of course. It's lovely at this time of year. The flowers, the water, the boys… such a life.

– Love Oscar–

Ted threw himself back in his chair and hooted with laughter. He wondered how the North American marketing director of the People's Bank would square her sense of fiscal duty with her sense of honour. Would she feel obliged to pay her dues to Oscar?

He also recalled her saying that the Fed and the FBI couldn't afford to cause another banking crisis by suggesting the markets were at serious risk from a bunch of nerdy kids. So maybe she could take a quiet trip to whatever island in the sun Oscar was hiding on. A quick in and out, like a vacation. He leaned forward and typed, his neat fingernails clicking quickly across the keys:

Diogenes. I think we need to talk about this one. Face to face. It's too risky on email. Can we meet?   – Ted–

The screen went quiet. There was a knock on his door, the one that led to the dining room that doubled as a second study. The door opened. A mop of red curls jutted into the room.

'Before or after skiing?'

In the doorway Erin Wishart stood grinning from freckled ear to ear.

Acknowledgments

I owe a very big vote of thanks to a small army of people over the many years of gestation of this book:

First and foremost, my agent Tina Betts who saw enough in an early version of The Money Tree to sign me up and stick with me through the long, lean years. Richenda Todd, the professional editor of my *Douglas Brodie* Glasgow Quartet and the strategic editor of Money Tree.

Most of all, I want to thank my many gifted amateur editors and supporters: Robert Cardinaux, Candace Imison, Helen Ferris, David Henderson, James Hanley, Nilima Patwardhan, Kathryn Ferris, Hazel Rice, Tricia Sharpe, Ray Barker and Alan Johnson.

But above all, my wife Sarah, who's reviewed and commented upon more versions of Money Tree than Doctor Who's had reincarnations.

Appendix 1 – The real People's Bank

There is a real People's Bank and there is a real-life hero. This book is dedicated to Muhammad Yunus, founder of the Grameen Bank in Bangladesh. In 2006 the Norwegian Nobel Committee awarded the Nobel Peace Prize, divided into two equal parts, to Muhammad Yunus and Grameen Bank for their efforts to create economic and social development from below. The Committee stated that:

> *"Lasting peace cannot be achieved unless large population groups find ways in which to break out of poverty. Micro-credit is one such means. Development from below also serves to advance democracy and human rights."*

In 1983, Professor Muhammad Yunus threw away his economic text books and established the Grameen (or village) Bank to lend tiny amounts of money to the poorest of the poor in his native country of Bangladesh. The personal and compelling story of his conversion and long struggle against convention, mistrust and self-serving interest groups is set out in his 1998 autobiography.

Professor Yunus was educated in Bangladesh and the US and thus has an unusual understanding of the economic systems of East and West. Appointed head of Economics at Chittagong University in 1972, he found himself two years later preaching doctrines that had no relevance to the world outside his classroom. It was a year of famine. Each day on his way to and from work, he was faced with the mortal truth that wealth does not trickle down. Loans to governments, and their consequent centrally planned programmes only benefit the people who manage the loans and implement the programmes. The poor stay poor. And starvation comes to them first.

His answer was to start at the lowest level of society and give tiny loans to the last people on earth on any sensible banker's customer list: the utterly destitute; the ones without even rice in their bellies, far less a glowing credit history. The professor's view is, "Our clients do not have to show how large their savings are and how much wealth they have, they need to prove how poor they are…"

Against all logic, he demonstrated that the very poor are the ideal borrowers. Their desperation to get out of the pit and stay out of it, means they will do anything to repay the debt and inch their way to self-sufficiency through a series of low-cost loans.

But surely this idea of micro-credit is only applicable in the developing world, where $25 can turn round the lives of 40 people? Doubters in the developed world claim that their economic context is far too sophisticated for the destitute to flourish as entrepreneurs. The poor are feckless. They'd need expensive training, they'd squander the money on drink or drugs; they'd never pay it back. The arguments Muhammad Yunus heard in Bangladesh are the same ones espoused about the council house tenants of Glasgow's wastelands, or the welfare recipients of Arkansas. And they are just as hollow.

Throughout the developed world a number of groups promoting Grameen's ideals are active. A particularly energetic organisation is RESULTS, a grass roots lobbyist with sister groups in the UK, Canada, Germany, Australia and Japan. In the UK the most striking example is the Prince's Trust. Since its inception in 1983 by the Prince of Wales, over 80,000 disadvantaged young people have been helped to set up in business. Over 60% of these tiny businesses are still trading after 3 years, a track record that the typical bank could only dream of.

The proof is in the statistics: as at 2008 the Grameen Bank was achieving an unheard of loan recovery rate of 98%, more than any other bank in the world. Of perhaps greater significance is that 97% of the 8.5 million borrowers [as at 2011] are women. Male traditionalist in this Muslim country are enraged at this emancipation of their women-folk. This may have been a contributory factor in the Bangladeshi Government's determination to oust Muhammad Yunus from the Grameen Bank.

Bangladesh has a long history of banks and cooperatives being used as political instruments. State owned banks have regularly extended loans to elite borrowers who default at high rates as a form of patronage. The governing Awami League were determined to gain control of this upstart bank despite Grameen's extraordinary achievements. There may even have been straightforward jealousy on the part of Prime Minister Sheikh Hasina at Yunus's renown and world wide regard. Hasina made it clear that she thought the Nobel Prize should have gone to her for signing a modest peace treaty in 1997.

At any rate in 2010 the Bangladeshi Supreme Court launched an action against Muhammad Yunus claiming misuse of funds. This was disproved, but in 2011 the Government fired Professor Yunus on the spurious grounds of his violating the country's retirement laws by staying on past 60.

This has not ended Sheik Hasina's vendetta against Muhammed Yunus; in 2013 she put him on trial again, this time claiming he had received his earnings including the Nobel Prize award, without obtaining permission from her government.

In a final act of spleen, the government has effectively nationalised the Grameen Bank and it is likely to go the same criminal way of all other banks in that corruption-ridden country.

But losing his job as head of Grameen has not silenced Muhammad Yunus. His goal is quite simply the eradication of world poverty.

"Our [Grameen Bank] success is measured not by bad debt figures or repayment rates… but by whether the miserable and difficult lives of our borrowers have become less miserable, less difficult."

To that end, Muhammad Yunus has become one of the founding members of the Global Elders, serves on the board of the UN Foundation and is a Counsellor at One Young World summits since the inaugural meeting in London in 2010.

The final words are his:

"Grameen is a message of hope, a programme for putting homelessness and destitution in a museum so that one day our children will visit it and ask how we could have allowed such a terrible thing to go on for so long."

Appendix 2 – The Neem Tree:
the Village Pharmacy

The title of this book has both an allegorical and a botanical reference. The image of a spreading tree, with deep roots, bearing fruit and providing shade is a fine symbol for a 'People's Bank'. But it also describes and draws on the reality of the Neem tree.

To a villager in a country where summer temperatures frequently rise above 40 degrees, where shade is at a premium and where the nearest pharmacy is several hundred miles and a financial mountain away, the Neem tree is a god-send. The word Neem in Hindi means 'blessing'.

The Neem looks a bit like an oak, grows to 50 foot, lives for two centuries, and can survive happily on 18 inches of rain water per year. It is a botanical cousin of mahogany and bears masses of honey-scented white flowers followed by olive-like fruit. The leaves, bark and sap from the 20 million trees across India provide a ready range and supply of medicaments in daily use across the sub continent. The Neem has also been successfully planted in Burma, Central America, the Middle East and Africa. Near Mecca, for example, a Saudi philanthropist planted a forest of 50,000 Neems to shade and comfort the two million pilgrims who camp each year on the Plains of Arafat. In short, the Neem is an ideal tree for anywhere hot.

Shade against the equatorial sun is one blessing. But the Neem's greatest gift is medicinal. It has a hallowed place in Indian Ayurvedic medicine for its extraordinary range of properties. Neem compounds have been found in the 4500 year old ruins of the great Harappa civilization in North Western

India. Scientists are still grappling with understanding and proving its many applications, but villagers and farmers have no doubt about its daily use as:

Insecticide: the bark and leaves act as powerful insect repellents. Neem trees are the only green things left standing after a plague of locusts. But it is the oil extracted from the seeds which is most potent. Not only do villagers use the products in their every day life – as a mosquito repellent and salve for bites – but the tree is now cultivated and used in commercial quantities as a natural protection for major crops such as cardamom, tea, rice and vegetables in both India and other developing countries. As well as having a strong pesticidal effect the great advantage of Neem over synthetic compounds is that it is harmless to humans, animal life and the ground itself.

Medicine: Ayurvedic lore describes some 100 medical uses of Neem, most of which are still being practised today in the sub continent. Neem works against a variety of skin diseases, septic sores, and infected burns. Poultices from the leaves have proved effective against scrofula, boils, ulcers, ringworm, eczema and varieties of fungi that have proved hard to control by synthetic fungicides.

General: Neem twigs are used as toothbrushes with powerful results against gum disease. Neem oil – though smelly in its untreated state – is a ready source of lamp oil. Parasite control on domestic animals is one of the most promising applications.

Any product with such magical properties was bound to attract the attention of the money men, especially if it was sitting there unpatented (it never occurred to the Indians to patent something that grew in their own back yard and had provided such a variety of benefits – free – for thousands of years.) In 1995, the European Patent Office (EPO) granted a patent on an anti-fungal product derived from neem to the US Department of Agriculture and W. R. Grace and Company. The Indian government challenged the patent when it was granted, claiming that the process for which the patent had been granted had actually been in use in India for over 2,000 years. In 2000, the EPO ruled in India's favour but W. R. Grace appealed, claiming that prior art about the product had never been published in a scientific journal. On 8 March 2005, that appeal was lost and the EPO revoked the Neem patent.

That doesn't mean there are no commercial products available in the West. There is a small but growing range of Neem products including toothpaste, a spray against dust mites and a dog shampoo.

But the future of the Neem is surely brighter than as a poodle shampoo for pampered Western pets. More science needs to be applied to understanding its complex and extensive range of applications. In the meantime, the Neem's most obvious impact could be in the reforestation of areas hit by drought and where tree felling for firewood has led to silting, flooding and erosion. Perhaps as a counter to the ill-effects of 45,000 large dams?

THE HANGING SHED

**Douglas Brodie Book 1 –
the #1 Kindle Bestseller**

Glasgow, 1946: The war is over, but victory is anything but sweet. Ex-policeman Douglas Brodie is back in Scotland to try and save childhood friend Hugh Donovan from the gallows.

Donovan returned from war unrecognizable: mutilated, horribly burned. It's no surprise that he keeps his own company, only venturing out for heroin to deaden the pain of his wounds. When a local boy is found raped and murdered, there is only one suspect...

A mountain of evidence says Donovan is guilty, but Brodie feels compelled to help his one-time friend. Working with Donovan's advocate, Samantha Campbell, Brodie trawls the mean streets of the Gorbals and the green hills of western Scotland, confronting an unholy alliance of church, police and Glasgow's deadliest razor gang along the way.

Can Brodie save his childhood friend from the gallows? Or will Donovan meet his fate in the notorious hanging shed?

Praise for The Hanging Shed:
'The word-of-mouth hit that is leaving its fellow thrillers in its wake. Ferris is a wonderfully evocative writer'   *Observer*

BITTER WATER

Douglas Brodie Book 2

Summer in Glasgow. When the tarmac bubbles, and the tenement windows bounce back the light. When lust boils up and tempers fray. When suddenly, it's bring out your dead...

Glasgow's melting. The temperature is rising and so is the murder rate. Douglas Brodie, ex-policeman, ex-soldier and newest reporter on the Glasgow Gazette, has no shortage of material for his crime column.

But even Brodie baulks at his latest subject – a rapist who has been tarred and feathered by a balaclava-clad group. Brodie soon discovers a link between this horrific act and a series of brutal beatings.

As violence spreads and the bodies pile up, Brodie and advocate Samantha Campbell are entangled in a web of deception and savagery. Brodie is swamped with stories for the Gazette. But how long before he and Sam become the headline?

Praise for Gordon Ferris:
'Electrifies readers...a rising star of Scottish literature'
Scotsman

PILGRIM SOUL

Douglas Brodie Book 3

It's 1947 and the worst winter in memory: Glasgow is buried in snow, killers stalk the streets – and Douglas Brodie's past is engulfing him.

It starts small. The Jewish community in Glasgow asks Douglas Brodie, ex-policeman turned journalist, to solve a series of burglaries. The police don't care and Brodie needs the cash. Brodie solves the crime but the thief is found dead, butchered by the owner of the house he was robbing. When the householder in turn is murdered, the whole community is in uproar – and Brodie's simple case of theft disintegrates into chaos.

Into the mayhem strides Danny McRae – Brodie's old sparring partner from when they policed Glasgow's mean streets. Does Danny bring with him the seeds of redemption or retribution? As the murder tally mounts, Brodie discovers tainted gold and a blood-stained trail back to the concentration camps. Back to the horrors that haunt his dreams. Glasgow is overflowing with Jewish refugees. But have their persecutors pursued them? And who will be next to die?

Praise for Gordon Ferris:
'Ferris is a writer of real authority, immersing the reader in his nightmare world...everything speaks of an original voice.' *Independent*

GALLOWGLASS

Douglas Brodie Book 4

He's dead. The Glasgow Gazette announced the tragic death on 26 June 1947 of their chief crime reporter, Douglas Brodie. The obituary staunchly defended him against the unproven charge of murder – a brave stance to take, given the public outcry and the weight of evidence against him.

Just three weeks before, life was rosy. After a tumultuous winter chasing war criminals across Glasgow, Douglas Brodie was reveling in the quiet life. His relationship with Samantha Campbell was blossoming and he'd put the reins on his impulsiveness. Hope and promise filled the tranquil summer air.

A day later, Brodie is arrested for the kidnap and murder of Scotland's top banker. The case against Brodie is watertight: caught with a gun in his hand next to a man with a bullet in his head – from Brodie's own revolver. He has no alibi. No witnesses. Despite Samantha's best efforts, Brodie faces the gallows. Locked in his cell as the evidence mounts, his old demons overwhelm him. There is only one way out for a man of honour.

Is this the sordid end for a distinguished ex-copper, decorate soldier and man of parts?

Praise for Gordon Ferris:
'Compelling story telling at a dashing pace, with a superb eye for post-war Glasgow.'   *Daily Mail*

TRUTH DARE KILL

Danny McRae Book 1

The war is over. But there are no medals for Danny McRae. Just amnesia and blackouts; twin handicaps for a private investigator with an upper-class client on the hook for murder.

Danny's blackouts mean that hours, sometimes days, are a complete blank. So when news of a brutal killer stalking London's red-light district starts to stir grisly memories, Danny is terrified about what he might discover if he delves deeper into his fractured mind. Will his past catch up with him before his enemies can? And which would be worse?

A fast-paced thriller by the author of the Kindle sensation *The Hanging Shed*, the first Douglas Brodie investigation.

Praise for Gordon Ferris:
'Great feel and authenticity... terrific'   *Val McDermid*

THE UNQUIET HEART

Danny McRae Book 2

London, 1946. Danny McRae is a private detective scraping a living in ration-card London. Eve Copeland, crime reporter, is looking for new angles to save her career. It's a match made in heaven... until Eve disappears, one of McRae's contacts dies violently and an old adversary presents him with some unpalatable truths.

McRae's desperate search for his lover draws him into a web of black marketeers, double agents and assassins, and hurls him into the shattered remains of Berlin, where terrorism and espionage foreshadow the bleakness of the Cold War. And McRae begins to lose sight of the thin line between good and evil...

The thrilling sequel to Truth Dare Kill by the author of the Kindle publishing sensation, *The Hanging Shed*.

Praise for Gordon Ferris:
'Evocative, beautifully told; Ferris might just become the new Ian Rankin'   *Daily Mail*